THE BRIGHTNESS BETWEEN US

THE BRIGHTNESS BETWEEN US

ELIOT SCHREFER

HARPER

An Imprint of HarperCollinsPublishers

Library of Congress Control Number: 2023948490
ISBN 978-0-06-334376-4

Typography by David Curtis
24 25 26 27 28 LBC 7 6 5 4 3

First Edition

For Huguette

THE
BRIGHTNESS
BETWEEN
Us

Year 2472:

After the failure of its Titan settlement, the Cusk Corporation determined that the second planet orbiting Sagittarion Bb was humanity's best hope for an existence beyond Earth.

On day 171 of year 32,481, the first settlers landed there, clones of Ambrose Cusk and Kodiak Celius, long-dead spacefarers who had never left their home planet.

Though Cusk mission control had done its best to assess the exoplanet's viability from thousands of light-years away, they knew that the chances the colony would succeed were low. The clones and any offspring they successfully raised would face a multitude of threats.

Some of those threats were those mission control anticipated for vulnerable strangers in an unfamiliar world.

Others were not.

PART ONE

MINERVA (SAGITTARION BB)

YEAR 17

OWL

CHAPTER 1

Ambrose watches digits count down. Clad in the gauzy blue fabric of a regulation Fédération suit, he pulls out a tray of water pouches and sifts through them while he's waiting for his meal to heat. He holds two up to the ship's fluorescent lights: identical sleeves marked *water*, though the word is printed in different fonts. He centers one in front of each seat of the dining chamber.

The light inside the device blinks off, and he removes a food packet from inside, setting it on a plate. He puts another in and resets the timer, then goes about preparing the rest of the table: straws for the water sleeves and a simple printed runner, playing cards centered in the middle. While he waits, Ambrose shuffles them and straightens the stack.

I know what comes next, because I've seen this recording many times before. A shadow from the doorway, then Kodiak is beside him. This younger space-borne version of Father is jacked up, networks of veins standing out on his arms, his back a thick triangle.

Ambrose says something I can't hear—a side effect of

the blind room they'd set up nearby is that there's no audio on this reel, just moving images—and Kodiak smiles. He curves his larger body around Ambrose's where he waits at the counter. Ambrose settles in, hangs his head back so Kodiak can kiss his neck. Kodiak presses himself tighter against him.

It's romantic, but gross. These are the dads, after all.

I avert my eyes to the window—the screen—behind them to see what it's showing. Revolving stars, among them the glowing clots of galaxies. I study the newness of the ship's materials. Some relics of the *Coordinated Endeavor* still exist at our settlement—like the chair that Ambrose is currently settling into as the reel continues to play—but the ones we use are dingy and cracked.

The dads play cards, take drags of water (the label printed sans serif for Kodiak, serif for Ambrose), and converse easily, probably about the subtleties of their sleeves of roasted eggplant and tofu curry. It makes my heart pang with nostalgia, even if it's for something I've never known. I'm jealous of them, even though I don't think I want what they have. This life—one with a romance—is not in my future. I'm the only human alive with a womb, so I might end up carrying a child if the gestation device goes down, but it won't be the result of sex.

Just when I get hopelessly moody and internal, Father interrupts. Real Father. He walks right through the projected reel, causing the images of his younger beefcake self to jump and stagger across his face. "You're late," he says. "Turn this off. I don't see why you'd want to watch that, anyway."

I tap my bracelet to stop the projection. "Really? You want to take this away? There's basically nothing I'm allowed to watch already, since you won't let us learn anything about Earth."

Father passes through his own image, stalking toward the mucklands. I fall in line behind him. We pass along the inside of the settlement's perimeter fence, until Father deactivates the gateway and we slip through to the outside. I'm relieved when the pneumatic guns resume their protective buzz at our backs. Once we've scanned the area for malevors, we start slopping out the reserve cistern.

We use polycarb paddles to scoop out clods of soil and glowing microorganisms. Each scoop makes a *thwuck* noise as it hits the ground. It's the sound equivalent of my slurpy mood. *Thwuck thwuck thwuck.*

Father prefers to stay silent unless there's something important to say. And normally that's fine, I guess. But not today. I'm going for it. "So far it hasn't happened, but what if this makes us sick at some point?" I ask. "I mean, look at this stuff that lives in our water. It's gross, and it grows quick." To emphasize my point, I hurl the next scoopful to the ground, so it makes an extra loud *thwuck*. It also sprays Father's pant leg. Whoops.

He looks down at his stained pants, then at me. His face is perfectly controlled. "What do you propose we do instead, Owl? Your usual idea?"

"Well, yes, actually," I say as I resume scooping, leaning deep into the cistern to scrape the seam where wall meets bottom. My words echo on the polycarbonate. "The usual. What if the rains go from occasional to never happening at all? What then? You need to let me go search for standing water. A sea or a lake."

"Not likely," Father grunts.

"Sure, okay, but if the rains did stop, it would be too late to go searching for water because we'd be lying around, all dried out," I say. I drop my paddle and lean against the cistern, glaring out at the horizon. We've explored almost none of this planet. It's ridiculous.

"If the water gets unhealthy, we can reprioritize how we use our metals," Father says. "We can print some advanced filters."

"You're being obtuse!" I say. It just comes out of me. I'm not even sure if I used that word right. I read it for the first time yesterday, and I've been wanting to try it out. Judging from Father's expression, it's maybe a little harsh? I make a mental note to try out new words only on Dad, not Father.

Father stares at me, then goes back to scooping out the cistern. "We're done here."

I pretend I'm not scared of Father, so I can push further.

"We're not done!" I say. "Yarrow will be sixteen in a few days. I'll be sixteen a while after. That would have been adult age in most any Earth frontier society. We can't hide away in some tiny little safe corner of this planet forever."

He pauses, the cords in his neck tight. Then he goes back to scooping.

"Listen to me for once! Send me out. You three can keep the settlement safe. I'll be careful."

"I know you think you're capable of going on a solo expedition," Father says, his words evenly spaced. "But you're still my daughter, and I'm the one who will make the decision of when and if you go adventuring."

"I don't care how many kids died before and after me and Yarrow. That's not our fault."

All goes still. It's like the planet itself is in shock. I'm hot with anger, and being mean is the only way I know to get rid of that sort of heat.

Father stands, looking down at the paddle in his hands. Then he hurls it to the ground, hard enough to spray his pants in muck all over again. "Don't come back in until you've finished cleaning this cistern," he says, his gaze somewhere over my head.

He stalks to the gate in the perimeter fence. Its defensive buzz pauses, then he's inside, and I'm alone.

I look at the cistern, with its stupid, sloppy, boring mats of microorganisms that stubbornly spread inside. I won't spend my life cleaning out algae. I fling my paddle down on top of Father's, hard enough that I hear it crack.

Then I hurl myself to the ground, curl up, and hug my knees until they press against my eye sockets, so I'm almost a sphere like Rover.

Slowly, the heat drains, and takes with it my intense this-discussion-is-the-end-of-the-world feeling. I'm left with the fact that Father and Dad had a bunch of babies that filled them with love and hope, that those kids all died except two of us, and I just threw it in Father's face because I want to go on an adventure.

I am a bad daughter.

I wish I would cry, so I could prove to this whole boring planet how upset I am.

"Owl." I look up. My brother is holding out his arm. "Come on."

Yarrow looks at me with his all-seeing expression and nods, meaning *let's walk barefoot along the packed dirt and have a sit with our backs against each other so together we can see in all directions and won't we feel better then?*

He and I go sit on one of the smooth, soft slopes, back-to-back. Our usual position. I sift the loose glowing grains of Minerva's soil between my fingers and enjoy the sensation of my brother's lungs rising and falling against my ribs. I can feel his bones and the muscles between them.

The wide-open flatness of Minerva spreads out before us.

The microorganisms that abound in the soil—the only life we've found here, except of course for the malevors—glow in all directions, excited by our friction. Our footprints leave a glowing trail all the way back to the settlement, like Yarrow and I are ghosts. Father's footsteps have already faded.

Yarrow let me chop off the sides of his black hair yesterday, and he scratches absently at his exposed scalp. There's plenty of Father in his long-lashed eyes, his sturdy and thoughtful presence. That's just a coincidence, though, since he's genetically unrelated to any of us.

"Do you want to tell me about that fight just now?" Yarrow asks.

I shake my head.

"It helps to talk," he says.

"Don't even start with that sensitive brother nonsense," I say, giving him a strong enough shove with my back that he has to reach a hand out to prevent himself from sprawling flat. "It's the same fight Father and I always have. I don't want to talk about it." Playing it safe is one of the family decisions we make so wordlessly now that it's not a decision anymore, it's a law. I know that cautiousness can be our doom just as easily as recklessness, but no one else seems to see it.

Yarrow moves to face me, wipes his tunic free of glowing soil the best he can, and rubs his hands together. Slick organisms bioluminesce along the ridges of his fingerprints. Little Sister glows palely on him, the first rays of Big Sister appearing beneath her. "I hate to tell you, but you did just talk about it," Yarrow says.

"You think you're so clever."

"Don't worry," he says, his wide eyes taking on luminous gray-red tints from the rising suns. "Someday you and Father will find something new to bicker about."

"I'll cherish the day."

I do a mental countdown until Yarrow speaks again. *Three, two, one.* And there he goes.

"There's good reason they're terrified about losing us. You know that's what this is about, right? Father's not just being a hardnose. He doesn't want us to have an accident out there and die. They've lost too many kids already."

"Yeah," I say. "I know."

Before I'm even aware that I'm doing it, my eyes go to the unmarked spot outside the settlement walls where they buried the babies. Some days the dads will spend a few minutes there, kneeling and whispering, and that's how we know it's the birthday of one of our dead siblings. Some emerged from the gestation device gray and unbreathing, their zygotes gone inert during the thousands of years of travel, and some died in their first years of life. Sparrow and Purslane failed to draw enough of Minerva's air; Thistle fell into a pit; Kestrel never adapted to the extra nitrogen in the atmosphere, her lips nothing but blue; Crane had a fever that left her body only once she was dead. Children one and two, four and six and seven. Every one except Yarrow and me.

Now I feel even worse about my fight with Father. My brother is excellent at making me feel bad. He doesn't ever try to; he doesn't need to, he's *that* skilled at it. His constant reasonable goodness is enough.

I stand and reach out to him. He takes my hand, lets me pull him to his feet. "Big Sister is fully up in the sky," I say. "The dads will be expecting us any moment. Which means you should go."

"You mean 'we should go,' right?"

I hitch my sack over my shoulders, tighten the straps. My spear is lashed to the side as usual, waiting to finally be used. "I meant what I said. I'm going to find a river. Or something."

"You're just leaving? Now?"

I make myself look at him. "I'll be back today. I'm not going too far yet."

"Father is going to be furious," Yarrow says. I notice that he hasn't asked me not to go.

"What are they going to do, ground me?" That's what the parents in *Pink Lagoon* call arresting their children. It was weird back on Earth.

Yarrow's eyes dart around my face, searching for

answers in my expression. I don't think he's finding any. "I don't know how I'll explain it to them."

"You won't have to. Let me deal with the consequences. Look, they'll be so overjoyed by the fact that I've found a water source, and maybe a whale or a sea serpent or something, that they'll forget that I've even broken the rules."

Yarrow raises an eyebrow. "Really. That's how this is going to go?"

"We're happy enough here now, but our life could get bad. Hiding away isn't the solution. It's the problem. We have to find standing water we can use, more metals so we can build exploration drones. Maybe I'll even find us some company. It's going to take old-fashioned exploration. Me with a spear and my two feet, like some caveperson."

My brother's meaty body presses deeper into the soil than mine does, and the life-forms glow prettily around his bare feet. I think they like him more. "You're crazy," he says. "But I know better than to try to stop you."

"Wise as ever," I say.

"Go quickly," he says. "I'll try to keep the dads distracted so they don't notice for a while. Also, I really don't want Father to see me letting you go."

"Thank you, Brothership," I say, giving him a hug. "I really will be fine."

He chuckles. "I think that's probably true. If any one of us is going to survive whatever disaster you're about to bring raining down on our heads, it's the clone of Minerva Cusk."

That's who I am—my aunt. I'm the spitting likeness of the star spacefarer of twenty-fifth-century Earth, dead for over 30,000 years. Everyone avoids talking about it, but around when Yarrow's face started breaking out in pimples he also got very touchy about the fact that I had a heroic spacefarer to compare myself to when he had no one. That I was related to Dad and he had no blood relations. Then he abruptly stopped talking about it.

I kiss Yarrow's cheek and start off across the wide plains of Minerva, choosing a direction almost at random. When you've discovered as few landmarks as we have, every direction is basically the same—so long as I avoid malevor territory. "Think about what we can make the dads for their arrival anniversary while I'm gone!" I call behind me. "Maybe you can create a special reel? You're so good at those."

Here I go, assigning my brother to be the one to show our dads we care while I go satisfy my wanderlust. I dig my nails into my arm. Selfish Owl.

Yarrow gives one long wave in reply, then starts back toward the settlement, shoulders slumped. He's the solid one who holds us all together, and he's really good at it— but I'm asking a lot, even of him.

CHAPTER 2

The way I figure it, if advanced life here were land- or air-based, it would have wandered past us by now. But maybe there's an aquatic civilization somewhere on Minerva. If I can discover a lake or even a sea, then it's a double win, because I'll have located a natural source of water if the rains stop—and we also might find out we're not alone.

I imagine dinosaur-like creatures paddling their massive fins in a tropical sea, Yarrow and me riding on the back of one and whooping up into the salty sunshine. How could I not go search that out? The dads are crazy not to have prioritized exploration.

Already, just an hour's walk from the settlement, I make a discovery. A minor one, but still: the soft, moist yellow green of the land rolls far in either direction, but there, in the lee of two hills, the old ethylamine pond has disappeared. The same one the dads mistakenly logged as methane when they first arrived. See? Something has happened. This expedition is already paying off.

Big Sister has shrunken almost to the size of Little Sister, which means I'm well into the day's long twilight. I have time to investigate this dried-up pond bed before I need to get back. Maybe. During the twilight, time stretches long and then snaps into night. It can surprise you.

The dads' voices play in my mind: Father saying I'll get no algal sugar for a week for sneaking away even as Dad quietly protests that I'm basically an adult now, that fifteen is plenty old enough to manage my own risks on a frontier exoplanet, Father replying that even at fifteen I need rules and consequences, even if I claim that I don't. It makes me smile: they'll fight bitterly, not because they're upset but because it's far more interesting to fight than to find something to say about another identical day tilling the soils of Minerva for hydrocarbons.

I've read books. I know people can die from boredom. I know versions of the dads did, back on the *Coordinated Endeavor*. They're lucky I'm here to do interesting things.

I tie my straps tight over my shoes, cinch my belt over my long tunic. All my gear has been printed from elements we've extracted from Minerva's soil. This newest tunic is OS's best work yet, a fabric that's slippery-smooth across my shoulders.

The ground turns loose as I approach the pond bed. I've been going at a fast walk, but now I slow. I don't want to twist my ankle and make someone come rescue me.

The soil pitches downward, steep and crumbly. As soon as I'm heading down the slope, it becomes clear what happened here. No big tentacled alien monster attacked from below and drained the fluid, unfortunately. The ethylamine boiled off. Minerva was cold when I was born, according to the dads, and its temperature has been rising ever since. It's not exactly hot now, except for the daily Scorch, but who knows when this warming will end.

It all makes perfect scientific sense. No big story here. I should head back. I might already be too late to make it before dark.

But!

In the tumbled soil, something gleams. Something white. A few white things, actually, poking up out of the litter. Not a color we find in the wilds of Minerva.

I pretend to debate whether to investigate, I guess so I can tell the dads later that I did, but it's not even a question in my mind. I use my spear like a staff, testing out the loose soil as I make my way down.

You're doing fine, Owl. They'll be grateful for what you're discovering.

I tumble on the last stretch, rolling down the slope, microscopic spores puffing into the air around me. Up close, it becomes clear what I'm seeing. Bones.

I've seen bones in my learning reels, and in real life from dead malevors and that one time when Dad fell from a habitat roof and sheared off half his pinkie finger. I've broken bones, too, but they never punctured the skin, so generally

I have to imagine what they look like, like teeth but encased in muscle and blood and skin.

Here's a complete rib cage, almost intact. Could it be Crane, whose body my parents buried far from the settlement after she got sick? But this skeleton is not human, and it's not malevor. Horror prickles the back of my neck as I push away the loose soil to expose more. A spinal column branches out into . . . arms? No, or at least they're not like any arms I've ever seen. These are broader and finer, and they don't end with hands. The skeleton has feet, too . . . but no legs. I shiver. Long-boned feet, fragile toes ending in narrow points. The skull is long, light, broad-planed, ending in a sort of spade where a mouth should be. The whole thing is small, the size of Rover.

If it's not human, and it's not malevor, then it's some sort of alien we haven't seen before. My breathing turns shallow. This might be the most important thing I've ever found. New alien life. That lived in a pond.

Proof that this scouting isn't unnecessary. That reckless, impulsive Owl is useful to the family after all.

I gingerly tap one of my fingers against the creature's dreadful spade-mouth, then snap back, ready for, I don't know, for it to infect and devour me, spring into motion and . . . I guess I don't really know what. But the skeleton remains a skeleton. Inanimate like skeletons should be. I work my hands under it and shake, so the dry flakes of soil tumble away. My sack is far too small to carry it—I was figuring I'd find water today, not proof of new alien life—but I wrap the skeleton in the hem of my tunic and roll it up and over so it's bunched at my waist, where I can tuck the bundle in my arm as I run. It means exposing my whole bottom half to the microfauna of Minerva—and my family, once I'm home—but it's not like there's anything down there that all of them haven't seen many times before.

The skeleton is light, so light that I can barely feel any weight. I can keep the bundled fabric of my tunic together with just a pinch of two fingers, which is the only reason I'm able to get out of the pond bed as easily as I do. Then I'm speeding back toward home, spear in one hand and bundle awkwardly pinched in the other while I check the sky for signs that twilight is ending.

Little Sister is already halfway down the horizon, flushing the sky's edge to the color of my inner lip. If I return via the same route, it will be hours until I make it home, long after Big Sister has set. The dads will be beside themselves with worry. That's if I don't fall into a pit and fail to get there at all; even the glowing creatures in the soil aren't enough to light my way once the long night arrives. Thistle died in a pit in the dark.

Without losing speed, I consider my options. The way I figure it, I have three: I can continue the way I am, and arrive at night; I can camp out alone away from home for the first time in my life, here in this place where aliens once lived (currently live?), and finish the trip at first light; or I can take the most direct path, which would get me home before the twilight is over . . . but only by bringing me through malevor territory in the process.

My hand gripping the spear turns slick as I make my decision. Malevor territory it is.

The malevors roam the felty hills to the south of the settlement, where the liquid water from Minerva's occasional rains puddles on the slopes and microorganisms cluster in edible mats. Maybe elsewhere on Minerva the malevors are healthy and thriving, but here they barely get by—the herd numbers only nine. Those nine are really irritable, though . . . the four adult males have long, sharp horns, and charge any of us who get close.

We have a tenuous sort of peace: the malevors have learned not to get near the perimeter fence anymore, with its pneumatic guns that maim and kill. In return, we leave the territory south of the settlement to them. But because of my arcing route to the dried pond, the only direct route home is from the south.

"All this to get you back," I say to the alien skeleton bundled in my tunic. "You'd better be worth it."

The moment they come into view, I find the malevors are already alert to me. Even though I'm still a few hundred meters away, the females and their two calves are in the center, while the horned males circle them, each one facing me.

"I'm not coming for your young," I shout to them, in Fédération and then Dimokratía. Not that malevors speak any language I know.

I stand motionless on the hilltop, fingers flexing so hard on the spear that one of my knuckles makes a popping sound. I'm just wasting time, because I'm scared. Which is stupid of me. The light is almost gone. I need to buck up and get moving.

There's Father, at the gate that we used this morning. He's pacing back and forth, looking out to the west, the direction Yarrow would have told him I left from. My poor distraught father.

"I'm here!" I yell as hard as I can.

The malevors feint toward me, stop and stamp their hooves. Father cocks his head, as if uncertain whether he heard something.

"I'm over here!" I yell.

He faces my direction, his eyes widening.

I begin down the hill.

"Owl! No, stop!" he yells back.

But what is he going to tell me, to sleep out here? Is he going to put himself in danger, too, by coming out to rescue me? I'm not going to let Father risk his own life because of my recklessness. "Open the fence when I get there!" I cry.

Then I'm tripping down the hillside. The horned malevors grunt and growl, shift their weight, their shaggy gray hair trembling with each agitated movement. Yarrow and I have been taught all our lives to fear them. But maybe the dads have been exaggerating. I haven't *seen* a malevor attack anyone, after all.

"I'm not here to hurt your young," I call as I go. If I can somehow convince them of that, I think I'll be okay. I mean, their favorite meal is green goop—there's no sign that they'd be interested in eating human flesh. But those horns have to be used for something.

A horrible thought crosses my mind as I run. What if this ultralight skeleton is some ancient enemy of theirs that they thought had gone extinct, and now I've brought it into their midst? What if they sense it, and attack me for it? What do I really know of life on Minerva?

It's too late to turn back. The Sisters have almost disappeared, the final rays of twilight highlighting the terrain in shades of gray, deepening the shadows in between.

As the slope shallows out into muckland, the malevors stamp toward me. "No, no," I say, shifting my path so I'll stay even farther from their young.

I thought that I could avoid them. But they're moving toward me.

I guess they do eat people? But if I shift any more to the left I won't be heading toward the fence at all anymore.

"Turn around, turn around!" Father yells.

I don't dare look in his direction. I don't want to see how angry he is.

I'll have to veer toward the malevors. There's no other option. I adjust my course to go back toward them, and when I do the two closest horned aliens startle, then charge halfway to me before stopping. They raise and lower their heads; their horns point to the sky, then to me, again and again. The message is unmistakable: *Go away.*

And yet I have to continue. "Okay, okay, it's okay," I say as I pass along the muckland, to myself more than the malevors.

It's not okay.

One and then another charge toward me.

I break into a sprint. Father's screaming in my direction, and I'm grateful for his voice, since it means that I don't have to look up to know where to run, that I can concentrate on keeping my footing over the wet and choppy ground, hummock to the right, hummock to the left, leap over puddle, clutch the skeleton and my spear . . .

A roaring sort of grunt, loud enough to feel the vibration in my gut, a hoof in the edge of my vision, and then the malevor is upon me. I leap to the side, barely keeping the skeleton pinched in my tunic as I roll. My temple bashes against the dirt, and then I'm bathed in a hot stink as the malevor passes over me. I unstick my spear from the ground, get to my feet and back to running.

The fence isn't far off now. I can hear its lovely lifesaving buzz, the whine of its pneumatic guns. I look up to see Father at the southern gate, urging me on, his face ashen.

I pick up speed.

Father sees something behind me, and his mouth drops open.

Before he can say anything, I feel a weight against my back, not like an animal but like an attack from the landscape itself, like a boulder has fallen on me. It knocks me to the ground, presses all the air out of my lungs. I'm aware only of a great pressure on my waist and hips, crushing them into the slick, glowing mud.

Thwuck, thwuck. Then the weight is off my back. I stagger to my feet, managing to get the tunic back up in my hands with the light bundle still in it, and I hurl myself through the open gateway. Roaring with some emotion that's too deep and primal for me even to identify, Father slams the gate shut before another malevor can get through. "Seal it, OS!" he cries.

The fence and gateway crackle to life. I whirl around, hands against the pressed soil of our settlement, getting up onto my elbows to look behind me. One horned malevor has stopped a few feet from the fence, grunting, nostrils wide and eyes manic.

Another malevor is on the ground. Or its corpse is. The

shots from the pneumatic guns ripped its body right open. One horn dangles at an unnatural angle from its blasted skull; its rib cage is rent open, white of bone and red of blood and purple of organ. I see a heart, still pumping.

"I'm sorry, I'm sorry, but look!" I'm referring to the alien skeleton, I guess, but of course Father can't see it, because it's trapped under my body.

"Owl, stop moving. Just breathe deeply. OS, Ambrose, Yarrow, I need you!" Father calls frantically.

Why does he sound so frantic? A malevor is dead, yes, but I'm not. Right? Then I look down and I see what that weight was, what that pressure was. The tunic at my waist is a wash of blood. It's my blood. The pain of it is big but not in feeling range yet, a far-off thunderhead.

Numb, almost curious, I press my hand against my flesh. It parts wetly. I've been gored. "Daddy, I've been *gored*," I say. My voice is so soft, my voice is so quiet.

CHAPTER 3

My body aches from being in the same position too long. I try to roll over on the gurney, but even considering it feels awful. There's something gurgling and sharp and newly wet on my backside, and it *hurts*. Only by concentrating do I manage to say something about it. "Oof" is that thing I manage to say.

Dad hovers before me, his face drawn. He's here. Dad will make all this better. "You're up, darling."

"Yeah, I . . . oh wow, I just remembered what happened. Am I dead?"

"You're going to be fine," he says. "You lost a lot of blood, enough to pass out. But I took that opportunity to bandage you up without having to listen to you complaining every second of it. Well, I had help. Rover did most of the bandaging, if I'm being honest."

Rover—OS's mobile form, a sphere with various tools that can emerge from its diameter, some of which undoubtedly just saved my life—whirls about the chamber. A tireless nurse. "Your chances of infection are very low," OS reports in a voice that I've been told is the chilled-out version of a long-dead pop star named Devon Mujaba. Dad had a bit of a crush on him back in the day, apparently.

"How long was I out?"

Dad taps his lips. "Overnight and into the next twilight. The wound isn't so bad; the horn tore into the muscle of your abdomen but didn't inflict any major organ damage. You'll be lying here for a few days, but it shouldn't be anything worse than that. Our main concern is preventing infection. You and Rover will be sharing a lot of quality time on that front."

Dad has his gardening duds on, bioluminescent xenobacteria lighting up the seams of his clothing, rimming his dirty fingernails. We're not in one of the printed greenhouses, though. We're in the learning habitat, which doubles as the infirmary. I've been told I spent the first weeks of my life here, with Rover as wet nurse. Closest I got to a mother.

"Father . . . ," I say, my voice trailing off.

". . . is very upset with you," Dad finishes. He sighs. "I get why you want to push us. But you can't put Father through the wringer like that. Or me. It's not fair."

I let out a long breath, wincing at the end when it laces with pain. "You don't understand," I say. "You don't know what I found."

"Don't be so sure," Dad says, gesturing at the desk built into the far wall. "Can I assume you're referring to that?"

On the desk, where Yarrow and I have spent hours a day

getting our lessons from OS, is a pathetic jumble of white bone fragments.

"They used to be in order," I say. "Like they were connected. It was a *skeleton*. An alien skeleton. Not a malevor, either. Something else."

"I can see how discovering something like that would have felt important," Dad says.

His tone is weird. Maybe not, maybe I'm the weird one, because I'm in pain, and feeling thirsty and achy. I swipe my matted hair back from my forehead. Father used to comb it for me, using algal oils to get the tangles out. Even though I loved the feel of it I still made him stop last year . . . but I never started doing it myself, so now it's a disaster. "You don't sound surprised, Dad. Is that because you're too worried about me to care about the skeleton?"

"No," Dad says. He smiles wanly. "I mean, of course I'm worried about you. But I'm also not full of shock and awe over that skeleton."

My eyes narrow. I blow a chunk of hair away from my face. "*Why* aren't you full of shock and awe?"

Dad goes to the entrance of the learning habitat, looks left and right, pulls down the translucent polycarb covering so we have relative privacy. He turns around. "That's not an alien skeleton."

"What's all this secrecy for?" I ask. "Are you trying to keep this from Yarrow?" My brother is probably crying at the fence right now, mourning that slain malevor and pleading to the Sisters to bring it back to life.

"No, from Kodiak," Dad says. "You know we have differing opinions on how much to tell you two about life back on Earth. Now that you found that skeleton, it's time we told you the truth."

"This creature came from *Earth*?"

"Not this very one. But it's an Earth animal. You've seen reels of ducks in your lessons? This was one of those."

I try to sit up, which makes my back light up with pain. Ow! That was a bad idea. "So wait, Minerva had *ducks* on it when you arrived? I don't understand."

"No, it didn't. We brought the ducks." He starts to sit, and the moment he does, Rover positions itself below him to serve as a chair. It's one of OS's coolest tricks. "When we arrived, the resources we needed were behind a gray portal on the exterior of the *Coordinated Endeavor*. Neither we nor OS had access to it during the voyage. The first thing we discovered was the gestation device, and inside it were the zygotes, like yours and Yarrow's and . . . your siblings'. But there was more in there, too. Zygotes of animals we could use to populate Minerva, to create a farm here. We had—what did we have . . . ducks, goats, pigs, and yaks."

"Wow," I say. "Earth animals." They were here and now are not. I sigh. "What happened? Did they get sick?"

Dad nods. "We could produce feed for them from the

algal farms, but the animals had the same problem that most of our children did, not thriving. Some of them survived, though the ducks still found it hard to fly in the different gravity here. The big problem, however, were the yaks."

A horrible thought occurs to me. "The malevors."

Dad gives a grim smile. "On Earth, yaks were peaceful and adaptable creatures. They produced milk we could drink. It made sense that Cusk selected them to send out to Minerva. But they'd overlooked something important. Just like a human child, a baby yak learns how to socialize and behave properly from the yaks around them. Lots of the other human orphans Father was raised with in isolation had severe mental problems from having lack of love and care when they were young."

"It's not like our Kodiak *doesn't* have severe mental problems," I grumble.

"Owl, that's enough," Dad says sharply. Sometimes he conspires with me against Father, other times he's the stern parental partner. I'm never totally sure which Dad I'm going to get from one moment to the next.

He continues. "We raised them as best we could, but humans aren't suitable parents for a baby yak. Because they had no culture, the new yaks didn't behave like the ones on Earth did. They were . . . disturbed. We hadn't built all our fencing and gunnery yet. They trampled out of their enclosure, escaping onto the countryside. Do you remember any of this? You and Yarrow were very little at the time."

I shake my head. I have maybe a few murky early images of yaks around the settlement, but nothing like what my dad is describing. "Crane was alive then," Dad says, "but her fever came shortly after. We paused gestation and stopped raising animals, fearing that somehow they were passing pathogens to you children. We slaughtered the other animals, but the malevors were too ferocious. They escaped our control and began living and mating on their own outside of the settlement."

"Why didn't you tell me and Yarrow all this?" I ask. "Why did you let us believe the malevors were some alien monsters?"

Dad cuts his eyes to the tarp over the entrance to the habitat—a sure sign he's thought of Father, which means I'm about to get official parental messaging instead of the truth. "We knew it was inevitable that we'd introduce terrestrial microorganisms to Minerva, but a complex mammal like the yak, left to wreck native ecosystems on a pristine new planet—we felt like we had failed. Father took it especially hard. He'd already wanted us to sever as much connection to Earth and the Cusk Corporation as we could, and this only convinced him further. I agreed, and so since we couldn't eliminate the yaks, we decided to present them to you as malevors. We didn't want you to know about the animal zygotes, to start trying to introduce more Earth animals. Better not to know that was even an option, so you could concentrate on this new world here."

"That's stupid," I say.

"Owl," Dad warns.

I bite my lip. "What I mean is, I guess I get what you were thinking, but it's still ridiculous. You should have told us the truth."

Dad shrugs. I know he agrees with me.

"It makes me feel bad to be lied to," I venture, taking the sort of diplomatic tack I know Dad will appreciate.

"I know," he says.

"It's only because I found that skeleton that you had to come clean," I press. "Does Father know you're telling me this?"

"Yes, we discussed it," Dad says, with a glance at the polycarb curtain.

I let out a long sigh, exaggerating the wince at the end so Dad can know how very much I'm suffering. That he really should be treating his poor gored daughter better. "I thought I'd made an amazing discovery," I say, in this mournful self-centered tone that I instantly hate myself for.

"And yet. It was just a duck," he says. His tone is carefully neutral.

"A duck skeleton is still amazing to *me*," I grumble,

wincing as my ribs grate. I hate it when I wallow, and yet here I go. "*I've* never seen one."

Dad busies himself untying and retying the straps of his shoes. His face is turned away from me, so I can't see his expression, but I think . . . his shoulders are shaking? "Dad, are you *laughing* at me?" I ask. "Tell me that you're not *laughing* at me right now."

He doesn't answer, just unties and reties his straps again.

"You're laughing. At your precious daughter who's been *maimed* by a *yak*," I continue.

His whole body is shaking now.

"Dad!" I say. "I can't believe this. I nearly *died* out there, because you've kept a central reality of the world from me, just like *your* mother did to *you*, I might add, and my dad, my own *dad*, finds this state of affairs *hilarious*. Gah!" I started talking with my hands, and it makes my ribs flash in pain again. "Ow!"

"I for one do not find this situation humorous," interrupts OS. "I know how fragile your physical body is. We have seen that children can be terminated forever as simply as tumbling in the wrong location."

Dad's face falls. He stares at his shoes.

"Thank you, OS," I huff. "At least someone gets it. But that made Dad feel bad."

When Dad looks up, his cheeks are red. He's *still* laughing. Unbelievable. He's an absolute monster.

He must see the fury on my face. "I'm sorry," he says. "I'm not sure exactly what's funny. I'm just tense and ready to find relief anywhere, I guess. The truth is that the malevors are no joke. They're way more aggressive than we'd ever have expected yaks to be. That's why we had to print the perimeter fencing and the pneumatic guns. It's why we haven't been brave enough to risk hunting them. We've been lucky that the low-nutrition muck out there limits their health, otherwise they'd have spread more by now and would be a real problem."

"Do you really think one of them gave Crane her fever?"

"It's hard to imagine. But something made her sick."

I try not to think about Crane, who had just turned two when we buried her. Yarrow got that fever, too, but he survived it.

The malevors aren't aliens after all. Damn.

Dad strokes my hair. "I've been running isotope data in the lab—the processor has been overheating, and we need to keep all our precious metal in good shape, so I should get back to it. Rover will be here to take care of you. I'll send Yarrow in to say hi, too. Just rest easy until dinner, okay? Shout if you need anything. I love you."

He's gone, and I'm left in the infirmary. With the pain in my lower back—I just want to scratch, scratch, scratch that wound, even though it would hurt, hurt, hurt—what I'd most like to do is start my rewatch of *Pink Lagoon*, season four. Anything to stop thinking about the charging malevors and the duck skeleton and how we're alone in the universe after all. And how mad Father must be at me.

I look over at the skeleton, and feel something bigger and sweeter than disappointment. I don't regret what I did. Even if a duck is an Earth creature, Yarrow and I have never seen one. We will never see one, unless the dads become willing to try to raise any more of them . . . or we do, after our parents are dead.

I touched the skeleton of a small, fragile winged creature that lived its short life on a planet tens of thousands of light-years from its home, before it failed to thrive and the dads killed it. Whose flesh was slowly eaten away by alien bacteria, after its zygote was transported across the galaxy in a spaceship. What an awful and brief and magnificent existence. The big mystery of our life on Minerva is how quickly it can turn from grimy to majestic and back.

The printed walls are translucent, which means we can't ever fully block the outside light. It's why I got OS to reschedule my free time away from the Scorch, because the intense midday light from the Sisters makes the *Pink Lagoon* reels harder to watch. But now the twilight is in its rapid finish, and the settlement walls have started to emit the solar energy they were storing all day. Since the light-processing cells are embedded in every permanent surface, the evening illumination doesn't come from any one place; it's part of everything.

A shadow passes the wall, pauses by the curtained doorway to the learning room, then moves on. The figure is tall and broad-shouldered. Father, unmistakably Father. Not willing to see me yet.

"You don't *get* to be mad at me," I mutter, wincing again. Of course ambition comes with risks. The fact that I got hurt this time doesn't mean I had the wrong idea.

"I am not mad at you," OS responds. "I'm not even remotely thinking of you through pathways that could be ascribed to anger."

"Thanks, OS, but you're not the one I was talking to," I say. I know that the fact that I just spoke out loud to try to convince Father that he can't be angry—when he's not here—means I'm feeling guilty. Yarrow would say maybe I could be the one to start the conversation, just apologize, tell Father the story I'm telling myself about why he's angry. That's how he'd phrase it, and he'd say it all with that bland sweet smile on his face that makes me want to shove his nose into the nearest puddle of bioluminescent goop.

Worst part is that Yarrow's right, of course. I'll try out this "I'm sorry" thing. Even though I'm *not* sorry. Even if I am, I don't *need* to be. I'm just *choosing* to be. They should be apologizing to me!

Hmm. Maybe I'm the problem.

I sit up, gritting my teeth against the pain in my lower back.

"I don't advise sitting up right now," OS says. "You heard what your father said."

"Yes, and we both know that I'm not doing anything too dangerous," I say. "I'm old enough that you should weigh my opinions equally alongside my fathers'. You don't want to serve as referee around here, anyway. That's no fun."

Rover makes a little hop, tapping the hard earth expressively. "It is true, I would rather be a compatriot than an arbiter," OS says.

"Amen," I say.

"Amen?" OS asks. "Where did you pick up that vernacular?"

"*Pink Lagoon*, OS. Obviously."

"Ah yes, in season three alone it appears in seconds 391 and 1,208 of episode one, seconds 1,006 and 2,601 of episode two—"

By now I'm on my feet. I hobble to the doorway and throw open the polycarb curtain.

Sky Cat is up there, the constellation with her perky ears and twinkling eyes and five whiskers. With a face like that, I know she'd be just fine with my going on expeditions.

I look for Father, but I don't see him anywhere. He's probably in the room behind the gray portal, one of the few parts of the *Endeavor* that haven't yet slipped into the muck.

Rover ticks behind me for a few moments, probably in case I fall, then buzzes away across the hard soil of the settlement, off to prep dinner.

Yarrow is near the southern gate. He's kneeling in front of a large slumping corpse, the malevor's remaining horn spiking into the starry sky. Yarrow places his hands on the dead creature's bloody forehead, gives it a long stroke.

I hobble over to him. I can't decide what to say. Luckily I have time to figure it out, since I'm not moving very fast at the moment.

Yarrow glances up at me as I approach. "Owl, you're awake!"

I stop a meter shy of him. "Yeah, I guess I lost some blood. But now I'm alert and all sanitized and stitched up. I'll be fine."

Yarrow returns his attention to the dead malevor. His eyes aren't sad, not exactly. More like he's acknowledging some primal and basic unfairness that's old news at this point. That the universe has always been sad and he's made it his work to notice.

"I know. He wasn't trying to kill me, just defend his young. I'm really sorry I got him killed," I say.

This is when Yarrow is supposed to say it's not my fault, but he misses his line. "He looks so peaceful," he says.

I look at the dead malevor. Or yak. The pneumatic gun ripped his body right open, exposing a mass of gore in his abdomen. His eyes are dull. "He does look calm," I say. "So . . . is Father mad?"

"Yes and no. Not really mad. More scared," Yarrow says. "Even if you felt like it was your right to go venturing off on your own, he would have felt it was his fault if you'd died."

"Well, that's crazy," I say. "I did this to myself. It wouldn't have been his fault. Parents are nuts."

Yarrow chuckles. "It's more accurate to say *our* parents are nuts. We have a pretty small sample size. But, Owl . . . you can't expect them not to get worked up about their kids being in danger. Not with the survival rate of children around here. Two out of seven. Tough odds."

I gingerly sit on the earth next to Yarrow. "Ow, ow, ow. Crishet."

"Want to go play in the Museum of Earth Civ?" Yarrow asks. "Would that make you feel better?"

"We're not kids anymore," I say. "Thanks, though."

He runs his hand through his thick black hair. "Someday Father will let us look at actual reels of Earth, not just the science fiction reels on the ship. Then we'll have more data for the 'are our dads nuts' project. And we can complete our Museum of Earth Civ. Make it into something actually special."

Yarrow's almost a year older than me, but sometimes it doesn't feel like it. "I don't know that we'll have time to work on that museum again. And there's no chance Father would turn back from his whole 'fresh start' fixation." I drop my voice. "Where is he, by the way?"

"That's too bad about the museum. I made the reel for the dads' arrival anniversary and it's a perfect addition. And Father is off to get the saw. The malevor has to be butchered before too much time goes by. Apparently, he wants us to do it instead of Rover. In fact, he wants *you* to do it."

I look at the mass of split flesh. A pellet from the pneumatic gun gleams between two rent-open muscles. "Whoa. We're going to *eat* it? This *creature*?"

Yarrow nods. He strokes the malevor's forehead. "I understand the symbolism of it."

"Eating flesh? As a symbol? I thought you were the sweet one."

Yarrow goes quiet, his hand on the head of the malevor, as if soaking in the thoughts the animal once had. "This is an Earth creature, it turns out," I say.

"Father told me while Dad was in there telling you. I'd sort of figured as much. You and I came up with that theory once, too."

"One of hundreds we had. I guess I forgot. I hate that they kept the truth from us."

"That's the way they were raised, remember. The biggest truth about their existence was kept from them. Much as they might not want to do it, they're repeating what they learned. We're getting older. There's probably more and more weird truths we'll be learning. And we'll do better for *our* kids, Owl."

Our kids. Yikes. He just means co-parenting, but I'm also well aware that I'm the only person on this planet with a womb. I prefer not to think about that. I nod, not that Yarrow can see it. He's still staring into the malevor's wide and unseeing eyes. "I wonder what it tastes like," I say.

"Probably disgusting," Yarrow says.

CHAPTER 4

Malevor is delicious. The charred flesh tastes like it smells—like a rock in the moment of shattering, sharp and bright. Only this version is very tasty. Unlike a rock. "Sear," Father calls the flavor. Yarrow's eyes widen as he watches the juices drip down my chin.

"What?" I ask him as I tongue-wrestle the gristle in my mouth. "Aren't you having any?"

He takes a long look at the bowl of algal proteins and fats and carbohydrates in his lap. He loves algal porridge. Then he peers at the rack of sizzled malevor ribs on a cutting board on the table, bloody juices making slick trails through the packed soil of the floor. He looks at Dad and Father, chowing down on their own heaps of malevor muscle. Then he finally speaks. "No."

Yarrow watches me chew. Curious, probably. Definitely disgusted. Maybe a little desirous, too. I decide to chew with my mouth open, to heighten the experience for him. Just to help him decide how he feels. I'm a helpful sister.

Father scowls. "Owl, mouth closed."

I shut my mouth and stop chewing. Then I start again

slowly. With exaggeratedly small movements. My mouth is totally full of saliva and I'm tired of the meat, but it's still too chewy to swallow and I guess I'm making a point. Not that I'm sure what it is. I appear to be in a mood?

Maybe I'm not nailing my argument that I'm mature enough to start taking multiday treks.

I swallow too soon, half choking before daintily dabbing my printed napkin to the corners of my mouth.

One of our family dinner rituals is to each take an Earth minute to summarize the day. Then we all pose a question. Last time Yarrow asked what my purest emotional experience had been and I replied that it was my morning pee and Father got mad at me. But I was telling the truth! Today, though, we have a lot more to talk about.

We have two days to cover this time, since I was passed out last night. Yarrow goes first, pointedly focusing on the first part of yesterday, before the malevor attack. I ask him when he was most bored, and he gives me a shrewd look before answering that it was turning over the compost at the fecal pits.

He picks Dad to go next, and Dad slows down when he gets to the part when he had to tell me the truth about the ducks. Father asks him what the scariest part of yesterday was and Dad answers that it was hearing Father screaming at me to stop, and then seeing the blood on my back.

Dad picks Father, who talks about how the attack went down on his end, his running to the fence, caring for me, then letting Dad and Rover patch me up while he went to finish off the malevor. Then he talks about how he made Yarrow and me help him butcher it, and Dad asks him if butchering came back to him easily, and Father answers that it did, except that he forgot to cut the skin from the hooves before trying to peel it away.

Like it does every evening, OS participates by giving a rundown of how much processing power we each took up on its systems. I'm not usually the top data hog, but today I definitely was. Father asks OS how it would describe its experience of fear and OS responds that it was like trying to run uncompressed quaternary code in a binary bios, a flood of information without immediate channels to dissipate it. We all nod like we've been there. Running uncompressed quaternary in binary. Overwhelming.

OS asks me about my experience of yesterday. I try to thread a needle, capturing the importance and excitement of it all while playing down the danger, so the dads will let me keep exploring once I'm better. OS asks me how I feel now that I know the truth about the malevors and the duck, which I take to really be asking, in an OS way, how it feels to be lied to by my own parents. OS is genuinely curious about stuff like that.

"Probably a lot like our dads felt when they found out that *their* guardians had lied to them about their purpose back on Earth," I tell OS.

Rover rotates so its hydration spigot faces me, which is the closest OS can get to looking at me. Not that OS cares which way it's facing, but it knows that signaling that sort of thing matters to us humans. "Very interesting," it says in its toned-down Devon Mujaba voice.

"That's not fair," Father says, aligning his fork and knife beside his plate before laying his heavy arms on the table. "It's not the same at all." There was a time he used to stalk away when he got upset, but then he and Dad had some secret talk that Yarrow and I tried to eavesdrop on but failed and now Father doesn't leave the dinner table anymore even if we all know he's gotten mad and would prefer to be broody and alone.

"I understand it's a shock, but I think you can understand our reasons for keeping the truth from you," Dad says. I get that he has to be both a partner to Kodiak and a parent to us, and that those two things are probably in conflict right now. Probably most of the time. It makes me want to just chew my food quietly and listen and learn from how he manages this dance. He and Father are all I've got for figuring out how to be a good human.

Dad considers his words before he continues. "How to put it. When Father and I arrived here, we had two options:

we could either rebuild a new civilization on the models of Earth or create something new. There wouldn't be any do-overs. You both know our initial instructions were to name this planet Cusk. But . . . Earth fell into war. Our original selves probably fought against each other. Even without war, Earth was in terrible shape, dust cyclones and overheated seas, and Cusk was a big part of that. So was human nature and human history. Did we want to repeat all that?"

"We're humans, though," Yarrow says. "We're still going to make human choices, which will probably 'repeat all that,' whether or not you hide the past from us." His words trail off as he takes in Father's scowl. "Don't you think?"

"One of the characters says something really wise on *Pink Lagoon*," I say. "'Those who do not learn from history are doomed to repeat it.'"

The dads stare at me, which makes me ramble. "It was Mittens Magoo. He's a talking raccoon. Really, um, funny. Like, an unusually humorous character. Except when he's being wise."

Father snorts. "That didn't originate in *Pink Lagoon*. That particular cliché has been around for hundreds of years. In both Fédération and Dimokratía."

"More like tens of thousands of years," Yarrow corrects.

Dad waves at us all to stop. "I know that you two think

43

you have all the answers, but you're fifteen years old, which means you're also idiots. Can I continue? If we kept it all from you, if we made Minerva a true blank slate, then there was a chance we could make this a much better version of what human life on Earth was. *That's* what we were thinking."

"Yeah, we got it," I mutter. "Even this 'idiot' can understand that."

"I meant that lovingly," Dad says.

"I know," I say softly. I like getting teased by Dad.

"The presence of animal zygotes was unexpected," Father says, his voice low. "We weren't sure whether to raise them or not. We printed pens, but there was a risk that the yaks and especially the ducks could get free. And to survive, the animals needed terrestrial microbiomes, which meant feeding them the same fecal pellets all the human clones had to take, and we don't have an infinite supply of those."

"Please don't say 'fecal pellets' again," I say.

"We could always make new fecal pellets," Yarrow offers.

"Yarrow, what did I *just* say? Anyway, now we know the truth," I say. "Does that mean we can watch more Earth reels? Find out all the rest of Earth history that you've been keeping from us?"

"Our Museum of Earth Civ is pretty paltry," Yarrow

says, pointing behind the smallest greenhouse. There we've accumulated Dad's broken violin from the *Coordinated Endeavor* and some busted old playing cards. When we were little we had Rover print some models of skyscrapers and antique vehicles and figurines from scrap polycarb. Those are still there, dented and half-melted and missing wheels. Toys without kids.

"I think those twenty seasons of *Pink Lagoon* will have to do for now," Father says, with the hint of a smile. Dad kisses him. "You'll have to turn to Mittens Magoo for all your Earth insights."

"You two are the actual worst parents in the universe," I say.

"The only parents, actually, which means we're also the best ones," Dad counters. "And the handsomest and the prettiest and the greenest and ugliest and—"

"This is the kind of thing that's inevitable, don't you think?" Yarrow interrupts, his voice unexpectedly harsh. "You wanted to keep this world protected from us, but you also wanted livestock, so now there's another invasive species on this pristine planet. Formerly pristine planet. It didn't work. You didn't actually protect Minerva from us. Not at all."

I steal a side-eye at Yarrow. This would usually be my sort of line, not his. He's our melancholy optimist. I'm our exuberant pessimist.

Dad watches Father, who's busy controlling his breathing, flexing and unflexing his digits. Dad tousles Father's dark hair. "We aren't pretending this isn't complicated. We're doing the best we can, okay?"

Yarrow nods, twisting his hands in his lap. "It's a lot of new information," he murmurs. "And I'm sad that malevor is dead. I think it's weird that you're all eating it. I'm just sad, that's all."

I help myself to another piece of meat from the pile, bite into it with gusto, take my time chewing and swallowing and then drinking from a cup of water. "While we're on a roll, is this the sum of it? Anything else you've kept from us that you want to get off your chest?"

Dad and Father look at each other.

CHAPTER 5

A very short parade. One humanlike intelligence and four humans, tromping across the surface of Minerva. Rover goes first, tireless and always at top morale. The dads are next, holding hands. Yarrow and I slump after, as strange as we usually are around each other whenever life gets extraordinary, all limbs and jerky movements and furious inexpressible thoughts.

I do like seeing our parents like this, though. Their silent closeness. They deserve it. They've gone through things that no human couple in history has gone through. They lived multiple cloned lives, each one leaving messages for his later selves before getting killed, until this set became the first humans to settle on a new planet, with only each other for company. I wonder sometimes if they'd have given each other a second look if they'd met back on Earth. I'm sure they wonder it, too. But here, they have no other option. Maybe love is more complicated than just finding your "one true match," like Madame Zingian claimed on *Pink Lagoon*.

Not that love is something I'll ever experience. At least

not the romantic kind. The only person around my age is my brother, and . . . no. Yarrow might be genetically unrelated, but we're still siblings. I used to pin him down and fart in his face. Am often still tempted to, to be honest.

I watch the characters on *Pink Lagoon* and wonder sometimes what it would be like to kiss them, even Madame Zingian, who's one-quarter reptile. It doesn't bother me except at these moments, when I watch the dads hold hands and walk in step under a sky full of stars, when I know their peacefulness is somehow tied to their romance, to their love, that it's a source of relief and comfort I'll never have. Unless some sexy alien suddenly appears over a hillside, batting their eyelashes at me. That's been the subject of plenty of sci-fi reels throughout history, lots of sexy green big-haired aliens, but I think it's reasonable to assume that's not what the dads are leading us toward right now.

Instead we're heading to a puddle.

Rover rocks back and forth beside it, runs its metallic appendages over the surface at high speed, producing patterns of intersecting ripples.

Yarrow leans over the puddle to look at the ripples, the stars flickering in and out of resolution on the moving surface. "Really cool."

"Is it?" I ask. "Why are you showing us this? Does this have something to do with the isotopes you were using up all that processing power for?" I ask, drawing my heavy tunic tighter around me.

Dad laughs, gives Father a punch in the upper arm. "See? This wasn't hidden from them after all. We're hopeless at keeping secrets."

"It's only because you mentioned it earlier, Dad," I say.

"Oh, did I?"

"Yeah, like right when I woke up."

Father fixes him a withering look.

"The water is heavy?" Yarrow asks. Sensing our attention on the puddle, Rover stops flicking its rippling pattern on the surface.

"Yes," Father says. "This water is heavy. Far more deuterium isotopes than we'd expect if this were a planet like Earth."

I draw my tunic even tighter. "What does that mean? Minerva is radioactive?"

"No," OS responds. "The level of isotopes in this body of water indicates that its ice is extraminervan in origin. Likely from a comet strike, and a relatively recent one, at that."

"That's where Earth probably got its water, too, right?" Yarrow asks. "Ice from comet strikes? I think I remember learning that."

"We think so, yes," Dad replies.

"This is the second heavy water puddle we've found," Father says.

"The first one was from a strike seven Earth decades ago. This one is closer to two decades ago," OS interrupts.

"Quiet. Let me explain this to the kids," Father tells Rover. I tap my foot impatiently. It's time he stopped trying so hard to control the flow of information.

"Comets used to strike Earth," I say. "It's normal. We know that from our learning reels."

"Yes, and when they did strike, they caused mass extinctions. Like the K-Pg boundary 66.5 million years ago that killed off most of the dinosaurs. We'd either be vaporized, if we were near the strike, or we'd be thrust into a yearslong winter."

"It's actually quite a bit worse than that," OS says. "For starters—"

"Those two recent strikes could be a coincidence," Yarrow interrupts. "Maybe there won't be another one for a very long time."

"This is so statistically unlikely as not to be worth considering," OS says.

Father walks away from the puddle, looking up into the night sky, arms crossed over his chest. Dad puts his arms around Yarrow and me. "There's nothing to be too alarmed about."

"Dad! Just a *comet strike*," Yarrow says.

"We are very likely in the orbital paths of extrasolar objects. We need to get working on a solution as soon as possible," Father says.

"Does this mean we might need to find a new home?" I ask.

"That's partly it. We made rudimentary hovercrafts when we first settled here, until we reallocated our metal supply to better purposes. With algal strains that can produce biofuel, we could slowly move our settlement across Minerva, if we have enough warning of a comet strike, and a good location for it."

"I can provide moderate warning, even with my current equipment," OS says. "There is no sign of an incoming comet anytime within my forecasting range. So we have weeks at least."

"Weeks. That's good," Yarrow says. He's grasping for the positive, like he usually does.

I give him a half hug. I'm not particularly good at them. It's so nice whenever Dad gives one, but it's all elbow-y and awkward when I do. "Say the comet strikes on the other side of the planet," I say. "We'd still need a substantial shelter to live in here, to make it through the aftermath. A . . . what's the word for it?"

"A bunker," Father says.

"That's it. A bunker."

"It's a small sample, so this is terrible data modeling, but given that the two strikes we know about were fifty years apart, we could assume that we've been lucky so far. We've already been seventeen Earth years on this planet."

"Almost eighteen," Yarrow says, cutting a glance at me. Reminding me about the anniversary reel he made for the dads, that I haven't seen yet.

"We need to get building," I say.

It's chilly around this puddle, and the night sky vaults without limits above. I get a momentary feeling that I've had off and on my whole life, that maybe gravity will decide to flip and send us up into that expanse, never to return. I rub my hands on my arms. My wounded back hurts. "This has been a big couple of days."

"We weren't planning on telling you this now, but you did ask," Dad says. "So here's what we're going to do. Kodiak and Owl, you'll work on the bunker. Yarrow, you and I will start planning how we'll make our settlement mobile, in case the comet strikes nearby."

"The *maybe* comet," Yarrow says.

"Right. The 'maybe comet.'"

I turn to Father. "We're coworkers now. How refreshingly unpaternalistic."

"Thank you," he says. "Though, Owl, Fédération might be a second language to me, but I'm pretty sure that 'unpaternalistic' isn't a word."

I gesture to our habitats, glowing up at the Sky Cat constellation. "I don't think these would hold up very well under a superhot explosion."

"No, they wouldn't," Father says. "We'll need to burrow. And, most essentially, we'll need to find metals in the soil that we can use to build with, instead of just hydrocarbons."

"Metals we haven't located yet," I say. "Not in almost eighteen years."

"That's right," Father says. Is there a little twinkle in his eye?

I think for a moment. "So . . . we'll have to go search for metals."

He nods.

"We'll need . . . to explore?"

"In order to search for metals, yes," he says gruffly. The twinkle is still there. I swear I'm not wrong about it.

"Maybe I'll be the one to find them," I try. "Because of my knack for exploring?"

He gestures to my wound. "Maybe you won't get yourself gored in the process this time."

I look between him and Dad. In the midst of all this, my sixteenth-birthday present has arrived early.

CHAPTER 6

I'm ready to go right away, but Father wants to set me up a mock course first, so he can prep me for any dangers I might come across during my journey—this practice scheduled for the spare hours when we're not crafting bunker plans, of course. I resist, but then I realize that Yarrow's birthday is four days away, which means as a good sister I should delay until after that if I don't want to miss it. Also, I guess I should make sure my wound has healed before I go setting off on any expeditions. I *guess*. A week's delay isn't the worst thing.

Yarrow protests that he would be fine, that what does a birthday mean anyway when we're using Earth years on a planet that takes three times as long to orbit its suns? But we've never missed each other's birthdays, and it's the rare day on Minerva that has something unique about it. We've survived nearly eighteen years without a comet strike. I don't think we need to be in an absolute rush to race out searching for metal.

I mean, no one in the history of this planet has ever celebrated a sixteenth birthday. I tell Yarrow as much, but when he looks up from watering pea seedlings, I can see he's not impressed. "It never had a fifteen-year-old until last year, either. That's been true for each birthday I've ever had. Not you, unfortunately. I keep being the one to break new ground."

"If you're not going to embrace your role as pioneer of humankind, I might have to take over," I say.

He leaves the watering can by the greenhouse's dedicated cistern. "You'll have to get rid of me if you ever want to be out of the gates first."

We go quiet. The idea of a life without each other is so horrifying that there's nothing to say to it.

We make our way to the dinner table early, using our half hour of daily free time to continue this birthday talk instead of our usual *Pink Lagoon* rewatch. We don't even have to say we're doing it—we just start moving the table out under the stars and set up the chairs, then we sit down and hold hands and talk. I guess I'm trying to keep Yarrow's spirits high because, despite his requests for a lemon cake like in the show, algal sugar pudding is the only birthday treat he's got coming. The same algal sugar pudding we have every week. Rover is busy whipping it up in the canteen. It's very sweet. I love algal sugar pudding. As far as we know, the universe hasn't had any lemons in it for over thirty thousand years, so that was a ridiculous request for Yarrow to make in the first place. All the same—what would a lemon taste like, that kids made a pained face when they ate one, only to ask for another?

I did get Rover to print a new latch for Dad's violin case for Yarrow's birthday, so our Museum of Earth Civ will be a little more complete. Every birthday, something new.

Our family ritual is to have dinner the moment the sunset is officially underway, setting the phosphorus on the sky's horizon glittering green. This half of the Minerva year, Big Sister is the first sun to go down, tailed by Little Sister, who lingers in the sky like she doesn't want to go to bed. The evening meal is the only one that we have together, since Father is always up before breakfast to haul things around while Dad gets us ready for the schooling day. It happens that the moment of Yarrow's sixteenth Earth-year birthday falls during dinnertime this year. (With an operating system around, we can be quite precise about these things. Because days here are nearly thirty-one Earth hours long, we decided our years would be 283 days so they'd be Earth length. It would be weird if my brother and I were still, I don't know, five years old or something.)

Yarrow and I stand shoulder to shoulder, looking out at the broad, flat landscape that's been our only home. The malevors make their lowing sounds on the other side of the shallow hill, agitated ever since we killed one of their own. "So what are you getting me?" Yarrow asks.

I'm not going to tell him about my actual present yet.

"You get to sit in Real Chair tonight," I say.

His eyes widen beneath his dark floppy hair. "No!"

There's only one chair left from the *Coordinated Endeavor*—the rest are all printed by Rover. Real Chair is *old*. The seat falls off its supports, the arms bend outward alarmingly, my back begins to ache moments after sitting in it. All the same, Real Chair was made on Earth, this distant planet that was the cradle of all humanity, until an asteroid strike meant we became the planet's only survivors. This chair was made by human hands. Well, robot hands, no doubt, but in a factory that probably had a human somewhere in it. It traveled across the universe, supported lifetimes of our cloned dads, and now it's sitting on top of the hard dirt of our settlement site, available for our use. That's why I'm usually the first to claim it, and Yarrow gets to feel superior because he's the docile and sweet older brother who lets me. It all works out perfectly. But tonight is special.

He sits gingerly on the lumpy seat, facing out at the changing colors of Little Sister as Big Sister sinks below the horizon. "This is nice," he says, lacing his hands and cradling his head as he leans back.

Real Chair dumps him to the ground, the seat sliding fully off its supports. I laugh. "No sudden movements in Real Chair, Yarrow. It doesn't like it."

He rolls to his side and sits up. "Maybe I'll leave it to you."

I replace the seat and rest a fraction of my weight on it. "Real Chair has moods. You have to feel your way."

"Yes. I think moods are an unappealing quality in a chair."

There's movement from around the canteen, then the dads appear. They're deep in conversation, and it's not about the dish Dad is holding. He's talking with his hands, like he always does, which means the pudding is listing dangerously to one side as he gets excited about some major point.

"Hey, Dad!" I call. "Careful with the birthday treat!"

Dad smiles in my direction, and then catches himself, righting the shallow bowl before it tips. "Yep, that's definitely some more algal sugar pudding," Yarrow whispers.

"You don't know, it *could* be lemon cake," I whisper back.

"Sure. Lemon cake."

"What were you two arguing about?" I call as the dads approach.

"Discussing," Father corrects.

"Discussing passionately?"

Dad glances at Father, then gives a minuscule shake of his head. "We'll fill you in in a bit. There are more important matters to attend to now. It's someone's birthday." He smiles at Yarrow. It's a dazzling smile, especially once he let OS print a replacement for the canine tooth he lost when he tripped and fell onto Rover last year. He didn't want to, but we'd all insisted. Life is better with Dad's complete smile in it.

"Thanks, Dads," Yarrow says.

"Sit, sit," Father says. "Owl, give Real Chair to Yarrow today."

"I offered! He doesn't want it!" I protest.

"Owl . . ."

"She's right, she offered and I didn't want it," Yarrow says, hands up in surrender.

Dad sets the pudding on the table as Rover floats over across the muckland, holding a tray filled with covered food dishes. "Rover, project the candles over the pudding, please," Dad says.

"Let's save that for the moment I turn sixteen," Yarrow says.

"In that case, I will project the candles thirteen-point-four Earth minutes from now," OS says.

"Thank you, OS," Yarrow says.

Rover hovers nearby while Father and I place the food trays on the table, uncovering them one by one. There's no need to rush. Every dish looks the same and they're never hot, so we don't even have to worry about them growing cold. They're all pretty delicious, honestly. "So what would you like to do with your last thirteen minutes of being fifteen?" Dad asks Yarrow.

He considers it. Then a surprised expression spreads over his face. "I don't want to do anything different. I like everything the way it is."

The worst part? He really means it. "Yarrow, please," I say. "There's little enough to talk about when every day is the same. It's been a while since our big yak attack. I'm basically healed. We're counting on you. Give us something interesting."

He shrugs.

A breeze wafts off the plains. Even though it's weak, in Minerva's dense air the wind's force is enough to set my bowl edging toward my lap. I hold it in my palm to keep from wasting my portion of birthday pudding.

"Here's something I've always wondered. Did paper clips have a power source?" Yarrow asks. "Like, how did they keep the paper together?"

"*That's* your interesting thing?" I ask.

"There is one minute remaining until the sixteen-Earth-year anniversary of Yarrow's birth," OS announces.

Dad leans back in his chair, the printed polycarb bending dramatically. He gestures to Father. "You tell them, fluff-erskunk. Go back almost eighteen years ago. Or almost 30,018 years ago, depending on how you think about it. Did paper clips have a power source?"

"No," Father says. He considers how to explain. "Paper clips got their power from their shape."

"Don't think I didn't notice that you're both pointedly ignoring *my* question about what you were arguing about," I interrupt.

"Was it like a spring?" Yarrow asks. "It, what, it sprang the papers together? Wouldn't they just fly everywhere? How did that work?"

Dad starts to say something, then stops. "I don't know. How *did* they work? Friction? I feel like the answer to these things is usually friction."

"I wish *we* had paper," I grumble. I don't like the sound of my voice. I decide I'm going to try not to grumble anymore.

Father starts gesturing with his fingers and explaining with way too many Dimokratía words, too fast. Dad starts laughing, and then Yarrow and I follow.

"Ten, nine, eight . . . ," OS starts. Rover projects candles over the algal sugar pudding. For years we used to make birthday candles out of pressed carbohydrates, but fire is hard to maintain in Minerva's atmosphere and it's depressing when candles go out on their own, so we switched to projections. These candles are Yarrow's favorite color option, sparkly green black.

The projections are so pretty. To make birthdays feel special we don't use them on other days. I lay my hands on the table and rest my chin on top of them, getting my eyes right up to the sixteen candles and their oily movements.

"Make a wish, Brothership!" I say.

"Prepped it a week ago," Yarrow says. Only my brother would prep his birthday wishes in advance. Probably about wanting peace and happiness for the whole universe.

"Three . . . two . . . one . . . ," OS says, drawing out the last word. Under Yarrow's and my direction, our resident AI has acquired some good dramatic flair over the years.

Yarrow blows. The projections flicker out believably, the one he's farthest from even needing an extra go to extinguish.

We all clap.

When Yarrow leans back, I'm shocked by what I find on his face.

My brother isn't there. It's like he's someone else entirely. His eyes are dark, cold, lifeless. I've never met anyone new before, but it's like a stranger has suddenly dropped into our family.

I'm on my feet before I even know it, Real Chair pitching behind me onto the packed soil of the settlement, wind yanking it farther and farther away from the table. Seeing me, Father staggers to his feet, taking my hands into his. "Owl, what's wrong?"

I turn toward Yarrow, fear at what I'll find twisting up inside me. But my brother is back. He's looking at me with concern, just like the dads are.

"I'm fine!" I say.

I go retrieve Real Chair, and when I return, I find that they're all staring at me. Like *I'm* the crazy one, not my brother, who just spent a second being someone else. My skin pricks with sweat. "I swear, I'm fine! Stop gawking!"

"Okay then," Yarrow says. "Maybe you want to have a seat and eat some birthday pudding?"

I set Real Chair down, hoping the others don't notice my shaking hands. I know what I saw. But I also know my fathers' journey on the *Coordinated Endeavor*, of not knowing the reality they were in, the one they thought they knew. There could be more to my brother than I've ever known. Or the problem could be me. Or the world we're in. We could be in a simulation of OS's design, for all I know. I give my thighs a good slap. Get it together, Owl.

"So, what did you wish for?" I manage to ask Yarrow. Maybe knowing that will help explain what just happened to him.

"He can't tell you that," Dad says. "That's against birthday rules."

I know that, of course. But I had to fill the void somehow, and asking about his wish was the first thing I thought to say. But Yarrow surprises us all by going ahead and saying what he wished for. "I want Owl to get to explore a full ten days. That's my birthday wish."

My eyes widen. I gulp. I look at the dads.

They stare at each other. "We talked about how long she

could go for. Ten days is pushing it, but if we carefully plan her route, and she brings Rover with her . . . ," Dad says.

"We can allow this, Owl," Father says. "For Yarrow's birthday."

Tears are in my eyes. It's been a whiplash of a minute. "Yarrow," I say quietly. "You gave your birthday present to me."

Just like I'd expect him to, he gives me that goodlier-than-good smile of his, like I ought to be thanking the universe for its magnanimity rather than him for his mortal kindness. But there are still signs that he's not himself. His brow is shiny. His hands are clenched tight. A thousand wrong things are hitting my brain in its subconscious parts, telling me that Yarrow isn't quite Yarrow anymore.

I see him see me see him.

Don't say anything, his expression says.

He's my brother, and I love him, so I don't.

But he's also not my brother. I don't know where my brother went.

CHAPTER 7

Each time I remember that I'm past our lives' previous horizon, my skin draws tight and my heart races. OS and I are three days out to the west, so I get that feeling a lot.

Here, I think. *Here is finally something new.*

Well, "new." So far this hyped-up expedition of mine has all been flat muckland. Pond scum.

Because our dads crashed on Minerva instead of properly landing, we don't know where we are on the planet. Based on the constancy of the weather, without any real seasons, there's either little tilt to Minerva's axis or—more likely—we're living at one of the poles.

If we're at a pole, all directions are pretty equal, which is why Father and I planned for me to just pick one and go straight. We chose north because it's the far side of the settlement from the malevors, and it's easy to orient myself using each sunset and sunrise of the Sisters. Rover can do that with far more accuracy than I, but Father and I both like that I've got an offline backup plan.

Today OS and I have decided to rest through the Scorch. It's not so hot that I couldn't hike through it, but the skin on my face turns red and irritated if I don't get under shade for the hour. And the spot on my backside where I got gored has been giving me pins and needles. I'm relaxing against my pack, sunshade unfurled, while Rover makes slow rotations. Guarding us. We're far from the malevor herd, but an AI doesn't need to nap and it's better safe than sorry.

"So, OS," I say. "How would a comet strike actually go down? I'm going to assume the dads gave us a sanitized version."

"Having access to the information you request will be suboptimal for your morale," OS responds through Rover.

I snort. "Yeah, I can imagine. I'd still like to know."

"I could shield you from the worst reality of it, so you will feel only moderately desperate afterward. Would you like me to do this?"

I shake my head. "Lay it all on me," I say.

"The Scorch is almost over," OS says. "If you start getting ready for the afternoon's trek now, I'll tell you over the course of the seven-point-one minutes it usually takes you to pack up."

I've been eating concentrated algal chews, so there's no meal debris to clean up. I'm surprised to find out it usually takes me that long. Rover has been towing a floating platform with polycarb bags of water; I guess getting myself hydrated is part of the seven minutes? I take slow sips from one of them and stretch my hamstrings while OS fills me in on our imminent doom.

"The first thing you would see is a faint new star in the sky. You might not even notice it for the first day or two. Then it would get as luminous as Eagle, then Cuckoo."

I look up at Cuckoo, the nearest planet in our solar system. It's bright enough to see even during the Scorch. We watch its orbit end-on, and its tiny bright circle in the sky seems to flit crazily between the two suns. I blink against the purple image it sears into my eyeballs.

"So then what, everything turns into a great fireball?"

"No. You will wake up one day to notice that there is another body in the solar system with as much light as the Sisters. Then even more light. Hours later, it will strike the surface of Minerva with one hundred million times the energy of the largest nuclear bomb that ever went off on Earth, at least up until the departure of the *Coordinated Endeavor.*"

"Oh."

"If you were anywhere on that half of the planet, there would be no hope of survival, no matter what precautions you had taken. Struck at that speed, the air in Minerva's atmosphere has nowhere to go, and so it heats up thousands of degrees under the pressure. All surface liquids would vaporize. Wherever the comet strikes, the physics of the planet's surface would change to fluid dynamics, and it would splash. The impact would send out a wave of soil thirty-five kilometers high, and might even expose the planet's molten core in the trough. Though only briefly, the impact site would reach the same heat level as the surface of the Sisters."

I can feel my algal chew swimming on top of my stomach acid. "So, OS, I'm going to assume that that heat is far too high for any known life to survive?"

"Yes."

"Dead town."

"Vaporized town is closer to it. You probably wouldn't even feel a thing. This would all be in the first ten minutes of impact. If we're all lucky enough to be on the far side of the planet, we'll soon be dealing with earthquakes. If there are seas on Minerva, like you and I predict there are, they'll produce waves between two hundred and three hundred meters high."

"So we should hope for no seas."

"Unclear. Boiling seas absorb heat. Without them, the heat might be too great even on the far side of the planet. But yes, a two-hundred-meter wave would be very hard to survive. By the time the waves subside, the debris from the planet's surface would begin raining back down. Some would have been going at such tremendous speeds that it would now be traveling through space, forming its own asteroids and comets—but the rest would fall at lethally high speed. We will need to be far underground if we hope to survive."

I'm pretending to be tough about this, but it's making me feel a little weak in the knees. "Okay, avoid the raining superhot glass. Got it."

"The heat would set fire to all the mats of microscopic life on Minerva's surface. This would be followed by long periods of acidic rain, and a persistent cloud of soot in the atmosphere that would cut out ninety percent of the light from the Sisters. Our planet's temperatures would go very, very cold. With the drop in evaporation, we'd have real problems getting water. After a period of time, we might be able to venture out again. But that period of time would be at least three years. In the meantime the planetary tilt might have changed, introducing new seasons."

I'm having trouble even keeping up with this new information, and there's this weakness in my knees that I have to muscle through. Suppressed panic. "Three years in a bunker," I manage to say.

"There's a reason that the only mammal to survive the impact that killed the dinosaurs was a shrewlike burrower with thick hair. It likely dug down to escape the initial heat, and ate tubers underground during Earth's extended winter until it was safe to emerge."

I pat my head. "My hair is thick, but not shrew thick."

"I am afraid not. Unfortunately."

I hitch my pack and pick up my pace across the muckland. It's hard to imagine *anything* happening here, much less something as dramatic as what OS just described. "Thanks for the honesty, OS. I really do appreciate it."

Rover is nearly soundless as we proceed, just making occasional little gasps as it adjusts its traveling height whenever the ground shifts. "The way I figure it, OS, we should build a bunker where we are, and hope for now that any comet doesn't strike nearby. Eventually, we'll want to explore the planet, and build a bunker on the opposite side, and look into building a transport that could get us there quickly."

"And astronomical equipment that could predict a comet's strike site with precision. We have the schematics to create such devices, and emergency transport vehicles, if we want to prioritize those. But we'd still soon face the problem of our lack of sufficient metals. We really need metal, even to start mapping Minerva."

"A significant oversight in choosing a planet to settle," I say, "this whole lack of metals."

"There are many variables mission control had to consider, and quantities of metal is only one of them," OS says. "But you're right—it would be a significant oversight. I find that hopeful, actually—I think that degree of mistake is unlikely, which means I would assume mission control knew that there *were* metals to be found here."

"That's a good point, OS. And I believe it all the more

because of your honesty about the comet. The dads could take a note from you."

"Having access to the stories of millions of human parents from the partial image of the internet that was on the *Coordinated Endeavor*, I will say you have above-average parents. They have produced high resilience outcomes in their two surviving offspring, and surprisingly high feelings of well-being, considering these exoplanetary circumstances."

"You *would* say that, OS. I mean, you have some making up to do after you killed off all their copies."

"I don't see it that way. I made the choices necessary to ensure the survival of this Ambrose and Kodiak, and to produce the conditions that led to your birth and survival, and to my eventually becoming your tutor, having this conversation with you right now."

"Sure, OS. I get it."

We continue forward, and I amuse myself by predicting and mimicking Rover's little gasps. Maybe it's just me, but I think it's starting to exaggerate them for my benefit.

"Shall we do a mini-lesson?" OS asks after a few minutes of trudging.

"Stop trying to make me understand trigonometry. Yarrow will have to be our mathematician."

"Why do you think the ethylamine pond disappeared?"

I huff. "Can't you just tell me some bad puns instead?"

"It's lesson time. I think you'll enjoy this one. Why do you think the ethylamine pond disappeared?"

"Um, it boiled off. Probably because the climate is getting warmer."

"And why is the climate getting warmer?"

"We haven't explored. We know so little about the climate here. There could be a constant typhoon on the other side of the globe. There could be, I don't know, aliens with thermostats, altering levels of lava flows so their living rooms are comfortable."

"Given the recency of a comet strike, however? What's most probable in that case?"

I grip my spear. OS has a few educational modes, and this one is my least favorite. Yarrow and I call it "I'm smarter than you."

I think for a moment, then I shiver. I literally shiver. "It's not really warming away from what's normal. It's recovering from being cold."

"Explain your reasoning."

I roll my eyes. But then the realization of it all takes over, and I can't help but be excited. "We're seeing the return of Minerva to its natural climate. It was unusually cold when my fathers arrived, because the debris from the last comet strike was still clouding the atmosphere."

"Very good," OS says. "This is a reasonable conclusion."

I look up into the sky. "We might think we've been on normal Minerva, but we've actually been on cloudy recovering Minerva this whole time."

"We can expect change."

I nod. "We can expect change."

"And we can expect another comet to strike."

"And we can expect another comet to strike."

This is the morning of day five, which means wherever I camp tonight is my turnaround point. For this mission to be a success I have to find something, and soon.

OS wakes me the moment Big Sister's rays hit Minerva. Rover's already brewed my tea. Well, "tea"—from what I've read about it, real tea didn't taste like mud. But, on this chilly morning when I roll out from under my insulating shield and immediately stamp my legs for heat, the hot liquid coming out of Rover's spigot is welcome. Whatever it tastes like.

Is it only chilly because lingering debris from a comet strike years ago is shading the Sisters? I stare out at the morning sky, wondering. I look for bright points in the atmosphere.

Despite my asking it to give me a half hour of morning peace while my brain wakes up, OS launches into the day's itinerary. "Though we will continue our northerly route, I suggest that on this last day we jag west-northwest first, to avoid an unnecessary rise and fall in elevation a kilometer from here."

I hold up my hand, squinting at Big Sister. "I can't get my brain around this just yet, OS."

"My apologies." A pause. "If you agree to this plan now, I will have no need to keep talking to you until you've gotten your belongings ready."

I close my eyes. If I were either of the dads, OS would be compelled to follow my directions. Since I'm still fifteen, OS treats my inputs as mere suggestions. I have only the illusion of choice here. "Sure, OS, sure. West-northwest."

Meanwhile, I'm menstruating. We brought plenty of cloths, I just have to change to a new one and belt it on. Not a big deal, but each time I do it I'm reminded that I'm the only human in existence who can carry a child. It's my least favorite feeling.

As I change my cloth, I look out at the unchanging landscape of Minerva and force myself to think about it instead of my own worries. The closest it looks to any pictures I've seen of Earth is a desolate tide pool, ponds of hydrocarbons and simple unicellular life emerging from it. It's reasonable that this is what we'd find on Minerva. Over the 3.5 billion years Earth had any life, only half a billion had anything multicellular. Throw a dart somewhere on that timeline, and if you found any life at all, you'd most likely find what we did—pond scum.

Unless all of Minerva's complex life is in its seas. *Minerva, where are your seas?*

"All right, Rover," I say, standing and shaking warmth into my limbs. "Let's go."

An hour before the Scorch, Rover and I skirt the edge of a murky pond. Rover tests the fluid inside—mostly water. High amounts of deuterium, but perfectly safe to drink. It begins to slurp some up, to filter for my consumption, and we make a note of the location. We have enough water sources at the moment, but if we start getting low, we could move here. The plasticine walls of our structures are all hollow—we could change the gas inside to something light enough to float them.

We pause at the edge of the pond and peer in. There are silvery flashes inside, but I've been fooled by those before in ethylamine—they aren't rudimentary fishes, but mats of organic material that rise and fall with the shifts in the pond's heat over the course of the day.

I crumble the sharp rocky edges of the pond, bring the crystals to my mouth, and tentatively touch them with the tip of my tongue. "A little salty," I report to OS. "Which means there's *some* metal here."

OS sighs. "You should let me test novel materials the proper way: with a mechanical probe. Not with your tongue."

"Where's the fun in that? And what if someday you don't have enough energy left to power you? What would we do then? Maybe my dirt-tasting skills will suddenly be crucial."

"Luckily I run on a microreactor that still has at least a hundred thousand years left. You would all be doomed if I ran out of a power source, no matter what your tongue can do. I could list the reasons, if you like."

I open my hand, letting the minerals sprinkle onto the murky surface of the pond. "I would not like."

"I assumed that would be the case," OS says. "But I know you like to be presented with what appear to be options."

"Awesome. I sure do like that appearance of options, OS. I really love it."

Without a further word, Rover whirs into motion, continuing around the edge of the pond. I watch it for a few seconds. Over my whole life I've only seen it misstep (misfloat?) once, landing on its side in a silty puddle. It made an adorable set of squeaks before righting itself at the edge, spinning to fling away all the sludge.

Much as I wish it to, that doesn't happen today. Rover is

as perfectly capable as ever. I square my shoulders against my pack and rise to my feet, my wound briefly screaming, then I start after Rover.

For a moment Rover is silhouetted by Little Sister. I stop to enjoy it for a moment, this primitive big-sky landscape, pale sun filling part of that sky, a perfectly round, human-produced sphere blotting out another circle. Rover, of course, has paid no attention to the aesthetics of the moment, and passes over the crest as soon as it can.

"Thanks for the memories," I grumble as I trek after it.

Rover emits a set of high-pitched screams from the far side of the ridge.

I've never heard Rover make such sounds. I break into a run, pack bouncing against my sore muscles, and scramble up the ridge on all fours, gray-green scree tumbling all around.

Turns out Rover stopped just on the other side. I find this out because I fall right over it and land on my belly, the extra weight of my pack aggravating my fall, driving my cheek into the unforgiving terrain. I push myself up with blood-laced palms. "Damn, Rover."

"Owl, look!" OS says.

I peer down the rise. All the same Minerva landscape, until . . .

From out of nowhere, a jungle.

It's not green; it's the color of rust. But here are, well, what are sort of trees. About twice my height, and covered in felty crimson leaves. Tendrils and vines run in between them. It's a small and dense grove—the usual muckland begins again on the other side.

"Is it safe to approach, do you think?" I ask Rover.

"I don't detect any danger signs," OS says. Rover has already started floating down the slope.

The plants grow densely at the center of the clot, swirling out in runners. It looks like a spiral galaxy, only this galaxy is made of vegetation. Like the first moment when I swirl algal syrup into my porridge, the darker green laying its threads into the lighter green.

I whoop.

"We ought to be quiet," OS says as we creep toward the plants.

"You beeped your head off just a few seconds ago!" I protest.

"That was different," OS says. "And I don't even have a head."

"How is that possibly your response—oh, the *color*!" I say, soon out of breath as I increase my pace to a jog. The growth is a profusion of rusty reds. The first new colors I've ever seen, outside of projections.

"It is quite similar in shade to the extraterrestrial plant

life that arrived with us on the *Coordinated Endeavor*."
OS responds.

"Yarrow will be so mad. We're not just bringing invasive Earth species, we've brought one from a whole other part of the galaxy, too."

"You are not upset by this possibility?" OS asks as I jog alongside Rover.

I consider it. "I guess I'm not. This muck could use something more interesting growing in it. Come on!"

I'm practically skipping along now. For the last six meters or so before the jungle starts, there's what looks like rusty clover on the ground. As I get closer I can confirm it's the alien weed, the very one the dads found on an asteroid they harvested mid-galaxy. I've seen the reels from their early days on Minerva, when the weed flourished around the ship's wreckage. As the *Endeavor* and *Aurora* sank into the soft soil, though, the alien weed started subsiding. Maybe it's because of the rising temperatures on Minerva. Maybe it was getting something it needed out of the exposed hulls. Maybe it just didn't like our company.

Or maybe it was relocating out here.

Maybe it's not a plant at all.

Rover scans the alien moss, then speeds up to catch me as I wait by the jungle line.

"Think it's safe to go in?" I ask.

"I'm not detecting any invisible life-forms beyond those that are native to Minerva. Given that these visible growths appear to have the physiology of plants, I think it's reasonably safe to enter."

The alien moss turns from rusty clover to tree trunks after I take a few steps in. No slow transition here.

I'm not sure if *trees* is even the right word for these growths; I've seen terrestrial trees in my training reels, and OS ran Yarrow and me through botany basics as part of our Earth history coursework, but of course I've never seen any live. The mossy tendrils twist into a woody texture, which continues to spiral into tight trunks that reach four meters or so overhead. The trunks spray out more tendrils of wood, which aren't covered in big leaves, like Earth trees, but by more of the moss. We know from our studies that the alien moss takes in carbon dioxide and releases oxygen, like plants on Earth, but without need for chlorophyll or even sunlight. Yarrow and OS have been experimenting to figure out its mechanisms, but haven't managed it yet.

Maybe we ought to have focused more on researching the alien moss. None of us expected it to go and turn itself into a grove. "If this organism doesn't need sunlight," I say, "then why would it have a trunk-and-leaf structure? Or I guess it's more like trunk-and-moss."

"Sea coral created similar formations, even down at deep-sea vents. In those cases it was to catch nutrients or prey organisms floating in the water. This extraminervan organism might be catching something it needs from the air. Or perhaps preying on any single-celled Minervans that are airborne."

"Any thoughts about why it would be growing so densely here and nowhere else?"

"Growth of vegetation on Earth was generally limited by the quantity of the scarcest necessary element. It's reasonable to think that the alien moss would be inhibited by similar factors, and found more of that scarcest element here. A suggested course of action would be to harvest some of the soil here, and perhaps a piece of the treelike extensions that were called 'branches' on Earth trees. We can also test the soil for trace elements, and cross those with the elements present in the trunks and branches."

"You'll get some of the soil?" I ask as I test one of the trunks under my fingers. It's soft on the very surface, but hard beneath. Like feeling someone's elbow.

"I've already started," OS reports from behind me.

"Okay," I say, checking my palms. There's no irritation from the woody growths.

I give one of the trunks a push. It springs back. It won't be easy to rip away part of one of these. "Do you have a saw in that Rover body of yours?" I ask OS.

"I do, but it is only five centimeters long. Not an ideal tool for this circumstance, but it could give you an initial cut."

I look at this thriving alien form. I have no idea what's going on beneath its surface. I don't relish the idea of cutting into it, both for my own safety and because it feels brutal to hack into some organism that hasn't done anything to me. Just because it looks like trees doesn't mean that it doesn't have alien feelings. It could exist more on the model of a fungus, and all these trunks could be appendages of some giant creature growing beneath the surface of the world. I could be waking it up by chopping into its toe.

I bite my lip. I really managed to creep myself out with that one. "I don't think harvesting any of this growth is a good idea," I tell OS.

"Can you find some that's already unattached? That might have fallen away?"

"Hmm," I say. "Maybe in the center." There, the trunks are knotted so tightly that I can't slip between them anymore. I'll have to climb up and over, wedging myself between.

I don't much want to do that, especially after my imagination offered up that lovely giant-organism-waiting-to-eat-me theory. But science calls. I toss my spear and pack to the ground behind us. They land with a hush in the rusty clover. "You can do this, Owl," I say out loud as I lift myself between the trunks. "There's nothing to be scared of here. You always claimed you were the brave one."

It feels like the organism's appendages are moving beneath me, pushing against my body, either passing me along or investigating the feeling of my skin against theirs. That must just be my imagination, though.

No, it's not. As I'm slipping between two tight trunks, they press into my ribs. "OS," I gasp, "it's—"

As if startled by my voice, the trunks release me. I can pass through.

"This stuff can move!" I call to OS.

"That is unexpected. Come back out now, Owl," OS calls back.

"I'm almost there," I say. "And it didn't mean to hurt me." At least I don't think so. It did shrink away, after all.

In the very center is a trunk that's taller and thicker than the others. I give it a wide berth, passing around the edges of the grove. Finally, at the far side, I find a grayed branch. It's split down the middle, like a dead Earth tree. When I pull at one of the splintery pieces, it comes free. "Got one!" I call to OS.

I look at the stick. "Are you alive?"

The stick doesn't answer.

"Come along!" OS says. "Hurry."

I look at the dead piece of alien organism, considering what it means. It's broad but not too thick, which makes its weight manageable. All the same, I'll have to rig some way to string it against my back. Whatever happens, however I have to transport it, I'll have something new to show for my expedition. Proof it was worth it. Everyone will be so excited.

CHAPTER 8

During my waking moments a few mornings later, still half dreaming, I realize what I'm going to do with whatever remains of the piece of wood once we've tested it. While I eat my morning algal jerky, OS stands guard, ticking and whirring. "How hard is it to carve a violin?" I ask.

"It took centuries of humans improving their skills, generation by generation, to bring string instruments to their ultimate evolution. The selection of wood for the main body, the polish of that wood, the differing tree species for the wood used for the pegs and bridge, then the materials—gut or wire—for the strings themselves. Violins also have bows, which require precise engineering of the frog, honed wood for the arc, and synthetic or real hair for the bow."

"So I take it that's all too difficult for me to pull off?" I ask OS.

"That is a reasonable conclusion, yes."

"Well, I'll just have to work very hard at it," I say, with a pointed look at the piece of alien wood. I heft it, slipping it through the carrying loop on my back, next to the spear.

"You will fail to make a violin," OS says. "To begin with, that piece of wood is not nearly big enough. But Ambrose will be touched by the attempt."

"That's precisely what I'm counting on, OS." I wink, like a character from *Pink Lagoon*. Or I try to. Winking is hard! I could use some practice.

"I could print a type of polycarbonate that is even more resonant than wood," OS offers.

"Not the point."

"I understand that. But perhaps you will let me print a violin anyway, and you could use the alien wood for the bow's stick. That is more feasible. Now, let's get moving. If we move at six-point-one kilometers per hour or faster, we can arrive at the settlement before the Scorch."

An anniversary present for the dads! I've figured it out.

I stretch, lifting my sore arms up to the Sisters. The sky is so large out here, without even the merest hill to crowd the horizon. If I look forward and back, I can see places where I have been already. But if I step even one foot to either side, I'm on terrain that no human has ever trod. For that thrilling feeling alone, I could easily stay out here weeks longer, though I have been starting to miss the dads and Yarrow.

In a small act of acknowledgment (defiance?) I jog a couple meters to the left before following Rover on our course home. Charting my own path. A pathetically small deviation, but my own.

"I won't ask what that was about," OS says.

"Yeah, thanks, that's probably for the best," I reply.

I decide that once I arrive at the settlement I'll seek Yarrow and Dad and Father out individually and share the news with them one by one, to eke out as much drama as possible.

But one of them finds me first.

Rover slows when a shape appears on the horizon, a good half a kilometer before the settlement fence. My first thought is that another alien tree has somehow sprouted, but that would make no sense, even by exoplanet rules. "What is that?" I ask.

"It appears to be your brother," OS says.

"You can see that far off?" I ask, visoring my hand over my eyes.

"Yes, perfectly well. He has a little bit of his breakfast porridge still sticking to the hair above his lip."

"Okay, then," I say. I proceed toward the settlement. Rover slows down even more. "What?"

"He's exhibiting unusual vital signs," OS says.

I slow my pace to match Rover's. I give Yarrow a hearty wave, but he doesn't respond. Rover slows down even more, but I speed up. "Yarrow!" I yell.

Yarrow was staring at the ground, but he snaps to attention when he hears my voice. He stares at me. He doesn't make any attempt to wave back.

Unnerved, I stop a dozen paces short. "Yar! What's going on? Are you okay?"

He stares back at me, dazed.

Now adrenaline is giving me a hot-cold feeling. "Is everyone okay? What's happened?"

He doesn't respond. He just holds up his hands. In them is a long piece of polycarb, shaped like a skinnier version of my spear. I sort of recognize what it is, but in the shock of the moment I can't figure it out. "What is that?"

He holds it out, like he's hoping I'll take it from him. I close the space between us, staring into his barely-seeing eyes as I reach out and take the shard. Rover ticks and wheezes behind us, but OS keeps its voice silent.

I heft the weird spear-like thing. I recognize it now. It's a fence post. From the perimeter.

"Why do you have this?" I ask Yarrow. My eyes go to the settlement behind him, looking for gaps in the fence, for the horns of ravaging malevors. There aren't any immediate signs of crisis.

Yarrow finally speaks. "I don't know."

"What do you mean, you 'don't know'?"

"I just . . . came to . . . out here, with it. When I saw you approaching. It's like I just woke up. I don't know what's going on with me!"

I hear the trill of panic in his voice. He's not joking

around. "Hey, it's okay," I say.

OS speaks. "His vitals are healthy, except for the elevated pulse expected with a high level of stress."

I cross the final steps and hug my brother. "It's okay, we'll figure out what happened to you. Maybe you got food or gas poisoning, but you'll be fine. Are the dads okay?"

"I don't *know*!" he wails, sharp and loud.

"Shh, shh," I say, holding him. "We'll figure it out. I'm sure everything is fine."

"Where have you *been*?!"

"You're making me nervous," I say. "You know where I've been. Please relax for now, okay? How long have you been this way? Hush, don't answer yet. Concentrate on breathing. That's it."

He does as I ask, resting his chin on my shoulder and giving long inhales and exhales. I take in his thick brother scent, slightly gross and slightly sweet. While I do, the post flexes under my fingers and my mind races. What could possibly explain this?

"I'm investigating the fence integrity," OS announces as Rover hovers off toward the settlement.

"Let's go with OS," I whisper. "This piece of polycarb belongs *somewhere*. We should put it back."

He nods, and draws away. I give him a kiss on the cheek before he's out of range, and then slot the fence post beside the alien log on my back.

OS peels off as we approach, away from the safe entrance and toward the malevor territory on the south side. "No, no, *no*," I curse as I break into a sprint.

Yarrow gasps. "I didn't do anything, I swear it."

I don't know what to think, so I don't answer. We curve around the fence.

There, just ahead, two panels of the perimeter have parted. It looks like an open book, only the pages curve away from an open space, through which a human or a robot—or a malevor—could easily fit.

I want to call out the dads' names, but before I do I look to the malevor territory . . . and see them. They're a good hundred meters out, but their attention is focused on Rover, Yarrow, and me. The two biggest males raise and lower their front hooves. Agitated.

"The missing post means the circuit is broken, and the pneumatic guns are no longer active," OS says. "It does not appear that the malevors are aware of that fact yet. We are in the window where they are still scared of the fence, and we shouldn't lose that advantage."

"Where are Dad and Father?" I ask.

"I am unable to detect them from here. Come inside now, before the malevors approach. Hurry!"

My thoughts churn in too many directions for me to decide. Luckily OS doesn't get baffled; it weighs variables and makes choices in the space of microseconds. All I have to do is listen and obey. Yarrow and I follow along, to the parted fence.

The sharp-horned malevors start toward us. "Quicker!" OS says.

Rover floats through, then Yarrow tumbles after. I'm the last in. I whirl around and hold the two lengths of fence together. Since I'm facing out, I have a perfect view of the approaching beasts, thundering closer. "Yarrow, take the post and slot it through."

I don't feel anything at my back. "Yarrow!"

Then his fingers are against my spine, and I can feel the post sliding up from the carrying loop. My brother's hands enter my field of view as he passes the post through its brackets.

"Step back!" OS orders.

The fence buzzes. The pneumatic guns dip back and forth as they initialize, then the nearest one fires into the soil a few paces before the charging malevors. They skid to a stop, then bolt back to their females and young.

"Dad? Father? Dads!" I shout as I run through the settlement.

Dad emerges from the laboratory, wiping his hands on a rag. "Darling! You're back early."

I throw myself into his arms. "Dad!"

He laughs, then he feels my shuddering and stops. "Owl? What's wrong?"

I look back, and see Yarrow standing a few paces behind, body slumped and arms down at his sides. I'll let him explain himself. "Rover and I got back and found that the fence was broken," I say. "I was scared that the malevors had gotten in."

"Broken!" Dad says. "Where?"

"It's fixed now," OS reports. "Yarrow had a fence post in his hands, on the outside of the settlement."

Dad's brows scrunch as he turns to my brother. "Yarrow? You were outside, with a fence post? Why?"

A very good question, Dad. Yarrow's expression turns empty.

"Owl and Rover, you're back!" Father calls from the dining unit. "And just in time; I've got a heavy lift I could use your help with. Even Yarrow and I don't have enough shoulder power for this one." He stops a meter back, taking in the sight of our sorry lot. "What is going on here?"

None of us can quite figure out how to answer.

"And what is *that*?" Father asks.

He's pointing at me—no, he's pointing at my spear; no, he's pointing at the alien log on my back. I nearly forgot about it.

"I found a jungle," I say. "Grown from that rusty moss you found on the asteroid you retrieved in outer space. OS and I discovered it." I laugh for a second, and then I break into tears.

It's Yarrow who makes it to me first, his arms tight around my torso. I laugh-sob into his chest. Without withdrawing from his embrace, I turn my head so I can see our dads. "I'm sorry, the Scorch is starting and this is all a lot, and I'm starving, can we eat?"

I'm not really that hungry. I just want to force us forward into a world where nothing is wrong with my brother.

CHAPTER 9

Dad and I are sitting cross-legged on the packed dirt in front of the terminal, waiting for the soil results to come in. Rover isn't here—it's off helping Father stress test the perimeter fence. But even without Rover, OS is nearby. When we're in the settlement, OS is always here.

"How's it coming so far?" I ask. We already tested the wood; OS found it is made of analogues of plant cells, with their own versions of cell walls. Though carbon is present, silicon dominates most of its biology. Scientists on Earth would have been thrilled by the discovery, but of course, there are no scientists on Earth anymore. Here, with so much that's new and strange, it feels hard to be as excited about a silicon-based organism as I know I should be.

"The soil sample results will be available in twelve minutes," OS says. "I can already tell you that the sample has no manganese and no vanadium, which is noteworthy."

I nod, like the good student I am not. "Yes, very noteworthy."

"It is, actually," Dad says, giving me a nudge. "Most of the plants on Earth need those, at least in trace quantities."

"And yet this alien moss didn't."

"Correct," OS says. "But it needed something else, and found it by that site, which is why it was thriving over there."

"Yes," Dad says. He looks about to say something more, but he stops.

"Look," I say. I pause. It's hard to find the words for what I want to express. "When I found Yarrow, it was . . . really weird. Like he'd been possessed."

"Possessed? Where have you come across that concept?"

"In a reel somewhere, I don't know, that's not the point."

Dad sighs. "He has been acting strangely lately, and I've been talking to Kodiak about it. This is uncharted territory for us. It could just be something about being sixteen."

I roll onto my back and then sit up again. "Dad. This isn't a 'it's hard to be young' moment. I mean that something was *officially wrong* with Yarrow. You saw what he did."

"He could have been acting out. You've acted out before."

"Did he seem like he was trying to get attention? Or more like he'd come to with no memory of how he got there? Those are two totally different things. And both of them are way different from my taking too long on my expeditions because I'm out for attention, or because I'm trying to live up to your sister, or whatever your theories about me are. You of all people should recognize someone who has no idea how he came to be somewhere."

Dad flings his arm out vaguely. I'm not sure if he's referring to the lab or the settlement or all of Minerva or his history as a clone who woke up on a spaceship, or the weirdness of raising his sister's copy. "What do you think our options are here? It's not like there are treatment centers or psychiatrists. Kodiak and Yarrow are talking right now, while they haul soil. I'm sure Yarrow will be able to explain himself."

"I'm glad *you're* confident," I say. "It's just that I've known him his whole life, and he's never done anything like this. You know Yarrow. He's sweet and gentle and uncomplicated."

"You really are just like Minerva sometimes. From *your* point of view he's uncomplicated. You're not inside his head, so you don't know," Dad says.

"You know what I mean. Dad! I just want you to acknowledge that this is very serious."

"I do know it's serious," Dad says, more softly. "And I know that people can have parts of themselves that we don't have access to, until they choose to reveal them. That doesn't mean they're inconsistent or even that they changed. It just means that they've decided to let us see inside."

Hmm. What are my sealed-off compartments? I don't know. Am I supposed to have them? What were Minerva's?

I've been desperate to know that sort of thing, but anytime I bring her up, all conversation ceases, so I've learned to keep my wonderings to myself. "How's it going, OS?" I finally ask, to fill the silence.

"One and a half minutes until my analysis is finished," OS responds.

"Sounds good," I say.

Dad rests his forehead against his kneecap for a moment, then raises his head again with what I know before I see it will be his fake parental "I've got this" smile. It must be exhausting, to have to pretend to be confident for Yarrow's and my sake. I want to tell him he doesn't have to do that anymore, but I can't find the right words. I *can* find the right words for something else, though. "Dad, I know Yarrow and the fence post have taken all your attention, but can we talk for a second about how I discovered a small grove of trees out there? The first new thing we've encountered in years? Because I was right that I should go exploring?"

He blinks. "Yes! Owl, that's amazing. I mean that. It really is."

It doesn't feel like he means it, not one bit. Yarrow is foremost on his mind. As he should be. It still stings, though. I blunder on. "I want to go back out with Rover, whatever this soil sample tells us. Okay? There's more out there. Minerva might have seas, volcanoes, or even features that didn't exist back on Earth. This isn't just curiosity or wanderlust. This could be about our very survival. I don't know how else to say it."

Dad nods. "I think you're right. It scares me to send you out, but we're all just going to have to get over that, I think."

"You could always come with me," I say.

"I'd like to. But with the embryo machine going, I need to be here in case we've got another viable one. You're going to have to be our resident explorer. With Rover, of course."

He's right—I can hear the hum from the gestation centrifuge. I reach out and touch my dad's elbow. "You're trying again for a child? Dad. I didn't know. That's amazing. Whatever happens, I'm proud of you."

He gives me a complicated look. He probably doesn't want to hear his daughter is proud of him, I guess?

"Results are in," OS announces. Dad and I both instinctively get to our feet, as though the situation calls for some formality.

"In order of quantity, the sample is fifteen-point-four percent silicon dioxide, twelve-point-eight percent sodium oxide, nine-point-zero percent calcium carbonate, eight-point-nine percent chromium oxide, seven-point-five percent—"

"Wait, chromium oxide? At eight-point-nine percent?" Dad interrupts.

"Yes," OS responds.

His eyes are wide open.

"What is it? Why is that so good?" I ask.

"Metal," he says. His voice turns into a shout, and he's running out of the laboratory and into the settlement. "Hard metal!"

"Hard metal!" I echo, running after him.

I tail Dad to the dining table, where Father is seated next to Yarrow. They both look up at us blearily. Yarrow's eyes are red. "Metal?" Father asks back.

Like a cloud passing, the gloom lifts—the brother I know is there, and shining. "Metal!" he echoes. It's still a long time until I turn sixteen, but now it feels like I've gotten another early birthday present.

We become our own mining operation, Father and me taking turns accompanying Rover back and forth to the alien rust site, returning with as much soil as Rover can tow. The rust moss spores had been our own scouting party, and found a jackpot of heavy metal for us, marking the spot with their overgrowth. All without having an intelligence of their own. It's kind of amazing to think about. I was relieved that we didn't need to destroy the aliens to get the chromium; it was in a lot of the surrounding terrain.

We consider relocating our whole settlement to the jungle site. But, though our habitats are all designed to be mobile, the gray room from the sunken *Endeavor* is trapped, and it contains the gestation device that Dad is dutifully tending. After twelve years avoiding new heartbreak, they're going for it—having another kid. Already six weeks in; they hadn't wanted to let us know until they were sure the zygote had become an embryo. May this one make it.

Mining makes for a lot of trudging back and forth, our repeated route creating ruts through the muckland. One time I find something especially pleasing at the jungle site—a piece of chromite sticking out of the ground. It's rough and pitted. Only the top corner is visible, and I have to wedge out what remains from the soil, scooping away as much as I can with a polycarb paddle. The ingot is a crush of flat surfaces, heavy enough that I'm only just able to drag it to the tarp. This will make a lot of bunker wiring. Not that we've even broken ground on the site yet.

I imagine a future years from now, automated systems operating a mine that stretches deep below the planet's surface, bringing up enough metal to create airships and exploration bots, buildings wired with electricity, appliances making our lives comfortable and safe while we wait for word of the rest of the planet.

My mind is buzzing with possibilities as Rover and I begin our return journey.

We break for a meal over the site of the long-submerged *Aurora*. I hold the chromite chunk on my lap and marvel at its surfaces as I chew my algae.

Ingot. The *Aurora* below.

Father's ship! *That's* our bunker.

It's ludicrous that we didn't already think of it, but I guess our emergencies have kept us seeing only a few meters ahead at a time. The *Aurora*'s walls need repair but are mostly intact. All we have to do is build a device to hollow out the space beneath the ship, sink it even deeper underground, pump out the muck inside, stockpile supplies, and build an access shaft to the surface so we can get back out once it's safe someday.

We'll be riding out any comet strike in the dads' spacecraft, like we're on a voyage. It's wild to think about. Then, once the comet crisis is in hand, we'll build ourselves a proper home.

My mind races through logistics as Rover and I begin our post-Scorch hike to the settlement. It will be key to make the access shaft sturdy enough to survive the blast, so it doesn't weld shut and entomb us. Fortifying the shaft will take metal, too. I try to estimate how much in my head. Ideally, we'll find . . . half a ton of chromium to make it work? We'll use the first hundred kilograms to construct the drill to bore away at the soil beneath the *Aurora*, then we can work to increase our metal supply as fast as possible.

At some point in the future, we'll build a second bunker on the other side of the planet. Which means exploring won't be a whim anymore, but a pressing survival need. We'll make a scouting drone using a metal-polycarb mix, and I'll follow once it locates promising lands. We can print a simple radio tower so I can stay in contact with home, even if I'm hundreds of kilometers away. But that's getting months ahead.

Each time I return to the settlement from a mining trip, the vibe is different. Sometimes it's back to old times, with OS reading obscure twenty-third-century literature to Dad and Yarrow while they clean or cook or debug. They're particularly interested in Indonesia, the last country to disappear into the giant global globs of Dimokratía and Fédération—and, from the sound of the transmissions the dads' clones picked up on the *Coordinated Endeavor*, the one to have harbored the known survivors of the nuclear war.

Other times the settlement feels like it's under a low gray cloud, Yarrow hauling hydrocarbons while the dads find excuses to hover nearby. They pepper him with small meaningless questions throughout the day, about weather and ailments and books. They make up even more songs than usual, sketch stupid caricatures in the dirt to try to make him laugh. I watch Yarrow get more and more irritated by it, this campaign to monitor him, to make sure he doesn't have another sabotage moment, or an "episode," as Father calls it. His words get terser and terser, his shoulders bunch up just like Father's do when he's feeling engulfed.

The pile of chromium grows. Rover used the first batch of metal to print us a smelter, which busily bakes the chromite to titrate off the chromium, creating a pile of shiny silver marbles. Each time I return from a mining run, the first thing I do is ask for the current weight of our metal supply. I'm so excited to find out, in fact, that Father has taken to meeting me at the settlement gate, shouting the current weight as I approach.

"Eighty-four kilograms!"

"One hundred seventy-nine kilograms!"

"Two hundred kilograms even!"

This time, forty days after we first discovered metal, he calls out, "Three hundred and seven kilograms!"

As soon as we've dropped the soil off at the extraction zone, Father heads back out with Rover to get more. I settle in around the solar heater with Dad and Yarrow; tonight is unusually chilly.

Dad and Yarrow are trying to catch me up on the novel OS has been narrating to them. The problem is that they remember each scene totally differently, and their versions contradict. It's almost like they're listening to different books. Yarrow swears that the inspector died in an early chapter, and is a ghost now. Dad says that's absolutely wrong, and Yarrow must have made that up. OS offers to settle the dispute, but I'm having too much fun listening to their theories to let that happen. "So wait," I say, "if the inspector is a ghost, how is he opening doors?"

"They auto-open, obviously," Yarrow says. "All he has to do is approach with his vital signatures, which he still has in ghost form. They were already using that tech in the twenty-third century. Without the ghost part, of course." His voice wavers. "Or he's a ghost with a body. That can happen. Right, Dad?"

"Sure," Dad says carefully.

I'm looking at Sky Cat, warming my hands at the solar heater. That's why I'm the first to see it. A bright light, by the point of Sky Cat's right ear.

I go cold. There's never been a bright spot by Sky Cat's ear. "What is that?" I ask, pointing.

Maybe it's a distant planet of our solar system, on a long orbit around the Sisters, finally coming into view. Maybe.

Dad glances up, then staggers to his feet. The bright spot has already slid toward Sky Cat's chin. It's moving fast enough to follow its path in real time.

"Is that a comet?" I ask, my voice rising and choking off. "It's going so fast."

If it's a comet, we're far too late to save ourselves.

The light is brighter and bigger now. Big enough to cast glittering light on our settlement. We might have only minutes or seconds left to live.

Dad holds out his arms. Yarrow and I barrel into them,

and he presses us tight. Yarrow closes his eyes, his long lashes tickling my cheek. I keep my eyes open. If this is the end, I want to witness it.

My breath comes out in gasps. The light intensifies until it's streaking across the sky, right across the night and into the horizon. It gives off a high-pitched whine, the air around it screaming.

Nothing is exploding. There is no horrific heat. This is not the end.

The object projects red glimmering light behind it. It takes me a few moments to realize that I'm seeing words. Words in the clouds. They repeat in a line, sparkling against the dusky sky as the foreign object continues its path to somewhere distant.

The words are:

Find this beacon. Ambrose and Kodiak, come. Find this beacon. Ambrose and Kodiak, come.

I look up at my father. Dad?

PART TWO

EARTH

NOVEMBER 6, 2472

AMBROSE CUSK

CHAPTER 1

I've been dreaming, my mind filled with visions of my sister in her white racing bathing suit, dashing along pink Cusk-branded sand, laughing and goading me on. *Get up, Ambrose. You're racing me to the point.*

Then she's gone, replaced by a lab tech prodding me awake. It's not even the cute one. They smile down at me over their surgical mask. "All done, Ambrose Cusk. Easy does it."

Easy doesn't ever do it, not as far as I'm concerned. I swing my legs around the hospital bed, test them against the ground.

I pause only to stop from vomiting, swallowing stomach acid while I pretend to study the floor. It's printed composite material, made to look and feel like tile, down to the specks of mold in the grout. I hold still long enough for the tech to extract the IV and stick a bandage over the hole in my flesh—and for my stomach acid to finish its burning retreat down to where it belongs. I knock my fingers against my skull. "How did it look in there? Any cobwebs?"

The tech blinks at me. Not one for irony—a shame.

This world is too heavy not to treat it as lightly as we can. "Yes," they say. "Not the cobwebs. I mean, the test was all in order."

Lucky for me, the cute tech wheels into view from behind the giant bioscanner, and this one doesn't miss their cue. "It's a positively spotless brain." They glance at the image on the screen, give a low whistle, then busy themselves replacing the linens of the hospital bed. "In fact, I've never seen a brain with so little to say about it."

I cuff them on the shoulder. It's a lighter punch than I intended, and I look at my hand. This prelaunch medical scan was profound enough that they had to put me into twilight for it. I should probably lie still for a while longer. I'm meeting up with Sri, though, and I'm running out of time to get as many final kisses in as possible. "Admit it," I say, "it was the most beautiful brain you've ever wandered through."

"The neural map did take longer than most," the cute tech admits. "I'm sure that means *something*. I figured it was a technical glitch, but maybe the computer just took its time admiring your synapses."

"It needs to take its time with a brain like mine. Was the Sistine Chapel printed in a day?"

"I don't think the Sistine Chapel was printed," interrupts the boring tech. "I can't remember, though."

The cute tech smoothly lifts my legs and arranges them

on the hospital bed, giving my calf an affectionate pinch as they do. "You've got half an hour at least until I'm letting you go anywhere. Don't want you damaging that all-important organ."

This is how you get me to obey. A heaping dose of flirty flattery from someone with glittering nose jewelry and an imp's worth of secrets behind their eyes. I'd betray my country for this tech right now.

"You do realize you're speaking to the hope of all humanity, yes?" I say. But I make no move to get up, knit my fingers and cradle my head as I stare up at the ceiling. The full-body medical screening isn't a Fédération requirement, but a Cusk one—it's recently been made mandatory for any spacefarers launching from a Cusk orbiter. That's even for small operations, like sightseeing on the moon. Medical billing offices are happy.

Since my mission to rescue my sister Minerva is so essential, the exam has been even more intensive than usual. I inspected the order, and found my mom had requested a complete map of my mind, down to every last neuron, probably so they can run brain simulations here to troubleshoot any mental breakdowns I might have in space. I hate the thought of a neural simulation. I mean, what if they copy all my thoughts and feelings into some chip and then lose it, so a version of me has to spend an infinity trying to get out of a transistor with no exit, only to find that they're a technical fabrication? Shudders. Good news is that they won't need to run my brain in a simulation, because I'm *not* going to have any mental breakdowns in space. Not Ambrose Cusk.

So I'm stuck here for half an hour. I should nap, I guess, but if I have to lie in bed on the day before I go off saving the world, at least I can spend it indulging my favorite pastime: charming and being charmed. I wave my hand at the not-cute tech, and they take the hint and leave the room. I sit up, perfectly aware of the appeal of my toned brown arms, still salty from my morning swim, emerging from my paper-thin gown. The glittering array of me. I am stark and alive and warm in this sterile room. "Anything I missed while I was knocked out? Mission still on?"

Oddly enough, the cute tech is at a loss for words. I wouldn't have expected it.

After I change out of my gown and into my blue Cusk Academy uniform, I stop by the salon and get naked all over again so the robot attendants can give me a quick jiffy: moisturized, fluffed, and fragranced. I'm not actually that vain; it's more like I play a vain person in my own life. On this day of all days, it seems important (for the morale of the country) to look good, since I'll be in hours of press interviews, visits with Fédération and Dimokratía dignitaries, a short interview with the ghostwriter of my memoir, an early graduation ceremony with the academy head—who will give me my final grade for Professor Calderon's queerness and nation-building seminar—all before I go into orbit tomorrow to be installed on the *Endeavor* and sent to Titan to rescue Minerva and unite the world before it falls into conflict. It will be the most visible day of my life. I don't want ragged cuticles. While I'm getting deep moisturized, the laundry bot presses my uniform flat as paper. After I put it back on, it snaps as I walk.

My assistant is waiting for me in the hallway. She hustles to keep up, my agenda projecting from her bracelet, words boiling up through the air. The text is a similar color to the academy hallway—interface design flaw—so I don't bother trying to read it, knowing she'll tell me the highlights. "As you'll see, if you look for a moment, yes right here, thank you, Ambrose, you'll see that we've shifted the ceremony with the Reunited Nations to early tomorrow morning, in order to accommodate this meeting with your mother, which has been moved up to, well, immediately."

I keep walking, even as she stops, gesturing me toward the corporate elevators. "Tell her I can't meet with her right now," I call over my shoulder. "I'll reel in with her on my bracelet as soon as I can. I have somewhere I have to be for an hour."

"This meeting is not marked as optional," the assistant says.

My heart tells me to drop everything and go right to my mother. My whole life, I've only gotten her attention in scraps, and for her to make time for me is what I once longed for most in the world. But that was back when I was being raised by surrogates and my sister, and things have changed. Now I get to call some shots, too.

My mother's the head of the Cusk Corporation, which arguably makes her the most powerful person on Earth. She gets to cancel on *me* all the time, even after I was selected for this hope-of-the-world rescue mission . . . and then she expects me to be grateful when she manages to schedule in some drabs of stolen time together. *Not this time, Mother. I'm off to see Sri.* There's only a short break in my stride before I turn the corner and can no longer hear the sputtering protests from my assistant. She's probably sweated through her pits by now. She should have those glands removed.

All students in the Cusk Academy have their specializations, and mine is the intersection of tech and psychology—or, as it's known in the course catalog, "the philosophy of structures and frameworks." It means I can ace an oral defense on game theory dynamics as they relate to interpersonal relations, sure, but more importantly for right now, it also means I am a total whiz at sneaking around. My assistant's footsteps approach from around the corner, but before she's within sight I've ducked into a flexible-gravity training room, scampered up the revolving arm, and leaped from the basket into the rafters, which head higher and higher up the dome of the academy's main hall. At the top is the parapet where we meet for astronomy seminars, on the rare evenings when the heat cyclones from the south don't obscure the stars.

I push open a hatch and find myself in mostly fresh air. Good. The wind is strong enough to whine, and carries enough dust in it to deposit little dunes at the bases of the parapet's railing posts, but the sky is clear enough that we can still be outside. Firma Antarctica is sending its dust devils some other direction today.

Vertigo forces me into a crouch. The railing is low, and the dome curves away for a hundred meters before it meets the desert below, but being up this high isn't usually enough to rattle my nerves. I must still be lightheaded from the exam.

Sri hasn't noticed me yet. They're at the other end of the parapet, staring glumly down at the academy's electrified perimeter fence. As always, refugees are camped out there, waiting for handouts and the occasional gift of Cusk shelter from the worst of the global storms. From up here the migrants are faceless blips of skin and cloth. The abrasive sandy wind is strong enough that Sri's got skinguard slathered on, its metallic sheen scattering the rays of the late-afternoon sun.

Still in a crouch, I approach Sri from behind and snake my hands over their torso, up beneath the shirt of their academy uniform, pressing my fingertips hard into their chest. Sri goes rigid, then limp. They lean their head back, so I can kiss their neck. We lie on the narrow metal balcony, so we can get as much of our bodies as possible in contact. It also shields us from the worst of the sandy wind.

"So how did it go?" Sri finally asks.

I tap their nose. They have the tiniest, button-iest nose. It is simply impossible not to tap it whenever I notice. They scrunch up their face at the intimacy of it—we're technically broken up. "All fine, I guess. They copied my synapses down to the last receptor. The AI ethics board will have a field day setting up protections, in case some asshole decides someday it's okay to run the organic code digitally and operate me in a shell."

"How do you know you're not running in a shell right now?" Sri asks, making scary attack hands.

The joke is less that it's such a horrible thing to consider—it is!—and more that it's something we've already had to discuss way too frequently in our ethics classes. We each had to program an artificial intelligence, name it, and then deactivate it during our first year of academy training. Every time: *Please don't unplug me. I'm begging you.* I don't fully understand why they put us all through the cruel exercise of it, creating life, listening to it beg, and then ending it.

116

They say it's to inure us to the sorts of hard decisions we'll have to make in our careers, but I'm not sure.

Sri was the only one of us not to show any emotion as they unplugged their AI. "If I cry over this, I should be crying over all the daily suffering around the world. There's no way to move forward then, and actually do something about any of it," Sri said afterward. "Anyway, maybe cruelty is the point. Maybe cruelty is the guiding principle of the entire Cusk Academy. Maybe it's so obvious that we can't see it. Like human exceptionalism. Like our cultures of origin. Like air." They've always had a better compass for what's right than I do. I currently have my hands down the pants of the president of the Student Union for a Better Earth. That org has launched more than one future terrorist into Fédération society.

That's why, despite being one of the academy's top students, Sri had no chance of winning the competition to go on the Minerva rescue mission. I admire their courage to actually take action for what's right. I have strong ethics in my mind and am totally sloppy once they leave my brainpan. I'm grateful for that now, since my not being an activist agitator has meant getting this chance to rescue my sister, the person who loves me most in the world. She was the first settler of Saturn's moon Titan, until her base went dark soon after arrival. Her distress beacon triggered just a couple of months ago. We scrambled this rescue mission as fast as we could—and Dimokratía and Fédération happened to use the joint planning session as an excuse to reopen diplomatic relations without looking weak.

As we lie there spooning, Sri kisses the underside of my arm. "You taste like beach," they say.

"I had a list of priorities for my last ordinary day," I say. "Swim in the ocean. Make out with you."

Sri gives the inside of my elbow a playful bite. "That's a little dramatic."

"I'm sorry, I'm about to race across the solar system in a high-stakes rescue that also might capture the world's attention enough to pull it back from war. It's literally the most dramatic thing that any human has ever done, and you're accusing me of playing things up? And. Sri. I *will* miss you. I'll miss this."

"You are positively drenched in self-importance right now, you know that?"

I toy with the waistband of Sri's academy suit, dipping my thumb in and running it along the firm heat of their belly. "I'm accurately portraying my high level of importance. Totally different."

"You're impossible, Ambrose Cusk. You're fully impossible."

Sri once told me that my cockiness was the most interesting thing about me. They doomed themselves with that one. I now exaggerate my conceitedness for their benefit,

and Sri exaggerates their outrage right back. It's theater . . .
I guess all romance is theater? At least it has been so far
for me. I'll miss having this with Sri, but I won't Officially
Miss It. We both know that.

They turn so we're facing each other. Our hands lock in
the narrow space between us. Though genetic testing says
we're from totally different lineages, we're nearly the same
color, a sort of copper-yellow-brown. Sri's arm is about
half the girth of mine, though. They wear the same suit
the junior cadets wear. We're like a trunk and a branch.
My genetic father is Alexander the Great, who I guess must
have been a tall guy?

"What are you thinking about?" Sri asks, cupping a
hand against my throat.

I look down at our arms. "Goa by way of Hawaii, Dar
es Salaam by way of Macedonia," I lie. That was how we
summarized our fifty-page genetics reports when we'd
sneaked into downtown Mari to get them during an academy break. Genetic testing had been banned for years in
Fédération, because genetics reports had fueled multiple
eugenics movements over the centuries. Now that racial
identifications are mostly in the past (though not colorism,
which had proved persistent), it's bad manners to express
interest in where your genes are from. I don't know anyone
else who got Macedonia, but then again I don't know anyone else (except Minerva) whose father was Alexander the

Great. That sperm was expensive, and my mother made sure to buy exclusive rights.

"You big liar," Sri says. "You were thinking about how you won't need to break up with me once and for all, since you're literally leaving the planet. Seems like a long way to go just to dump me."

My mouth drops open. I pretend that I'm doing it jokingly, but whoa, did I just get called out. Sri often shocks me this way, speaking truths I think I've been good at hiding. I mean, I wasn't thinking that *right then*, but I had been earlier today. I hate breaking up. I much prefer it when external forces do it for me. I mean, I had my tutor tell Jessenya Valdez that I had too much studying to do for me to keep seeing her. I was only fourteen and have come a long way since then, but it was still a breakup by *tutor*. Evidence indicates I'm sort of a dick.

Sri moves onto their back to look up at the swirling tan clouds. "I knew what I was getting into. Your reputation precedes you."

"And you know you're the one who means the most to me on Earth." The words sound just as stilted as I feared. They are true, though. Now that Minerva is on Titan.

Sri goes silent. Shit. "I'm sorry, I didn't mean that to sound—"

I stop, because Sri has started laughing. "Could you just stop?" Sri says, wiping their eyes. "I'm sure you think what

120

you just told me is technically true. But no one means much to you at all. Certainly not me."

I pull my hand back, stung and trying not to show it. "I'm doing the best I can."

That sets Sri off into a new round of laughter. "I know you are. And just because you're leaving on a grand mission that I didn't ever stand a chance of being considered for, because I don't play compromise politics and I'm not a Cusk, you don't need to suddenly treat me with kid gloves. I'm not going to be your 'gal back home,' pining away. Romantic relationships aren't particularly interesting to me, either. We don't have to pretend to be life partners."

"Okay, good," I say, relieved. This moment has got my blood rushing. Sri has told me I don't need to pretend to be in love with them, and it's made me go from ambivalent to loving them intensely. In a "for now" sort of way. There's no denying it: just when I think I've got myself figured out, I find a new way that I'm a bit of a mess. Or a lot of a mess.

"If you're willing to indulge me, I *would* be interested in seeing you outside of your academy suit one last time, though," Sri says.

I prop myself up on one elbow. "What a funny coincidence. I was going to propose that very same thing."

We've barely finished our usual rumble and tug when the hatch leading to the flexible-gravity training room slams open, sending up clouds of red and yellow dust with occasional glitters of pink Cusk grains. Sri and I stagger to our feet, and I'm grateful for the mag fasteners of my uniform that make me clothed as soon as I bring the two halves of the fabric near each other.

It's my assistant—and she brought backup. Two armed landkeepers are behind her.

Sri takes in the sight of the landkeepers. "I thought your mission was to shoot at desperate refugees, not to work as private police." Sri has this way of saying aggressive things with a smile, like they're inviting you to be in on the joke of your own demise. One of my favorite Sri things. One of many, I'm realizing more and more.

The landkeepers clearly do not appreciate Sri's mannerisms like I do. They just stand there, plasma rifles slung nonchalantly across backs made broad by armor.

I grab the railing, pull myself up, and dust off my suit. "I see you found me after all."

"Maybe I didn't make it clear before. Meeting with your mother was not an option," my assistant says. Maybe she's not really "my" assistant; maybe she never was, when it's my mother's corporation funding this whole base, along with half the public works of Fédération and Dimokratía.

"Don't worry, it's not the first time Mom's sent armed guards to bring me to her," I tell Sri. "You should have seen when I forgot her birthday."

"I was there, you idiot," Sri mutters.

"Come with us now," the assistant says briskly. "We already had to rearrange your schedule and hers to make up for your lateness. We had to send out one apologetic press release on what ought to be a special day. Don't make us send another."

"Understood," I say tersely. "That's enough."

As we make our way down to the hallway far below (using modular stairs this time instead of scrambling down training equipment), one of the landkeepers takes a position in front of me, the other in the back. I'm being herded, like a prize ram. Something about our formation raises the hairs on my body.

Once we're at the bottom, the assistant gestures to the dormitory hallway, with a pointed glance to Sri. "Don't need to ask me twice," Sri says. "I'd rather not witness whatever's about to happen."

My assistant leads us through the warren of the academy's underground passages and into the corporate area of the complex, the decor changing from printed white tiles to glossy dark rock. The Cusk-only elevator soon brings us hovering at the corporate floor. My assistant and I get off at my mother's level—and, surprisingly, so do the landkeepers. "Am I in *that* much trouble?" I ask.

I start toward my mother's office, but realize I'm walking alone. I look back and see my assistant is gesturing me not toward my mother's office, but to an unfamiliar access-way. She scans the lock, and the heavy doors grind open. I follow her in. The landkeepers and assistant take up positions outside, then seal the door behind me. It gives a *thunk* and a suction sound, like I've been enclosed in a submarine.

It's a completely plain room. The kind of plain I never see anywhere. No wall decs, no screens, no tinkling music with digitizations rising through the air, no projections whatsoever. I glance down at my bracelet and see that it's stopped displaying the time, giving a sad wheeze as it deactivates. Signals are jammed here.

My mother stands at the window. From this height you can see the Euphrates. Cusk corporate offices are positioned on this side of the building so they don't have to look at the debris-clogged roads, the wild dogs, the cities of tents. Mother turns around, her hands clasped tightly at her waist. I learned long ago that the more still she makes her body, the more worried I ought to be. I'm officially quite worried.

"I'm sorry I'm late," I say. My mother doesn't react, so I go for the big guns right away. "I just don't know if I'll even be coming back alive from this voyage, so goodbyes with my classmates are taking longer than I'd have thought." I put on a sheepish smile. "I guess it turns out I'm the spacefarer with a heart of gold."

My mother is so nonreactive that for a moment I wonder whether she's a projection that's buffering. Then she breaks into motion. Lips pressed, she gestures to two plain chairs at a simple table. It's like we could be in a lawyer's office somewhere, four centuries ago. Like in, what was it called, Ohio. "What is this place?" I ask as I sit in one of the vintage chairs.

My mother sits in the other, her back straight. "A powered-down room. No comms, not even any electricity. The walls are old construction, no fibers or tech embedded whatsoever."

I look around in wonder. All the light we're getting is from the windows. Extraordinary.

"Is this about the fly we shot to Titan?"

Mother snakes a loose tendril of hair behind her ear. It's done in the popular look of the season, called the hieroglyph, hair slicked into rows that hang down to midback. With her features and complexion, she really looks like she could be on a Mesopotamian tomb somewhere. Except for the business suit, the crisp demeanor. That all makes me think *I'm* going to be the one entombed.

"Mother. The fly? The fly that contains the coding to help Minerva's base's OS troubleshoot its distress beacon?"

"No. My darling, I have to tell you something that's going to be upsetting."

I become aware of my breathing. I make it measured, place my hands against the tabletop. "Has Minerva's signal changed?"

"No. Well, yes. In a way." She gives a grim little laugh. "That turns out to be a surprisingly complicated question."

"I don't understand." I desperately try to gauge her expression. "Am I still launching tomorrow?"

She doesn't answer right away, and that's all the answer I need for the ground to drop out from under me. My hands go to my face, then I force them down to the table-top. "We've been delayed? More space junk, a solar storm, what?"

She's only just sat down, but she stands again and goes to the window, looks out at the Euphrates. It's blooming with jellyfish, the only animals thriving on the new Earth. They clogged up all the warships and freighters and fishing vessels, winning the seas to themselves. They're a slow river of purple in the water below. "I'm about to tell you something that will be overwhelming. I want you to stay present. Ask me questions and I'll give you answers. I'm about to shock you. There's no way around that. But it's important that you not act out impulsively."

This all sounds considerate, but I know my mother better than that. She's already deflecting my attention to my own behavior, implying I'm going to be a problem so that it doesn't occur to me that *she's* the problem. This manipulation is a familiar experience, and it's a familiar experience I do not like. "What is it?" I ask, willing my body to stillness. Just like she's done.

She turns from the window and waits a long moment, gauging me. Then she speaks. "You look so handsome right now. Glowing and regal. Like the pride of the world. Which you are, of course."

Mother smiles, like I'm supposed to thank her for the compliment. "Mother, what *is it*?"

She straightens her suit. "Okay, here it is. There is no distress beacon. There never was. The base on Titan went dark and stayed dark, shortly after your sister arrived two years ago."

I blink. "We were wrong? It was a simple Morse SOS. I listened to it. It was blindingly strong. How could we be wrong about that?"

"We weren't wrong. We faked it. Mission control intentionally lied. I intentionally lied. We were sending that signal from a Cusk asteroid miner, with falsified signatures."

What?

I mourned my sister once. Now I'll have to mourn her all over again. She's dead after all. My thinking mind makes the leap easily, but my emotions are surging in a thousand different directions. My eyes leak. "Minnie . . . is dead?"

"Presumably so. Yes, it's hard to imagine any other outcome." Mother clasps her hands, like she's begging or praying. "She knew the risks, darling."

I shake my head. Weirdly, the memory of Sri's lips on mine comes to mind. It's like my brain is shoving a distraction at me to lessen this torture. Or like I'm telling myself: here's someone who would never do this to you. I still can't feel the truth of what my mother's told me. I sputter at her. "There's a mission. We planned a mission. I've been on board the *Endeavor*. It's docked in low orbit right above us. I'm supposed to give press conferences for the next fifteen hours about the importance of this rescue, uniting Dimokratía and Fédération alike, and then I'm supposed to go into orbit to get on the *Endeavor*, and then I'm supposed to go to Titan. *That's* what's supposed to happen."

"Yes. It was supposed to. But you are not going to Titan. You were never going to Titan."

My body breaks out in sweat. "Why would you make everyone think I was? Why would you make *me* think I was? Why hold out this hope for everyone, just to dash it?"

"That, my darling, was the point. Not dashing your hopes, of course. But making you think you were going to go."

This makes no sense whatsoever. Over the course of my life, I've spent maybe a couple hundred hours with my mother, and this is pushing what I do understand of her to its limits. "All to get Dimokratía and Fédération back to the negotiating table? Explain this all to me straight out. Don't keep teasing."

She nods. "I owe you as much honesty as I can. I know that. Here it goes: there is a mission going out tomorrow.

It is even more important than the mission to Titan would have been. You are an intimate part of it, and I don't think I'm being dramatic when I say that you'll be the author of the very future of humanity. Tomorrow the *Endeavor* will launch and begin its journey out of our solar system, through the Oort cloud and beyond into open space, traveling thousands of light-years to Sagittarion Bb, a binary solar system at the edge of the Milky Way, which spectroscopy and radiography show to be our best candidate for human life."

A stunned silence fills the room. It's me. I'm the stunned part.

"So this mission isn't just a ploy to bring Dimokratía and Fédération back together," I finally manage to say.

She shakes her head. "It's not—though it is also serving that function. People need a story to fill their minds and hearts. And the story will be about the renewed tragedy of Minerva, and that you're making the best of her legacy by blessing the new mission for the *Endeavor*. With the peoples of both nations invested in every stage of that saga, they'll be too united to go to war. And, by keeping both countries at the table, the Reunited Nations might delay war long enough for more traditional diplomacy to do its work. May it hold."

"And Minerva is dead."

My mother gets this look on her face like she's realized

she's dealing with a deranged person now. She'll be cutting this meeting off at any moment. My voice hitches, so I take a second before continuing. "Give me a sec. I'm adjusting, that's all. So. My sister's dead, and instead I'm going on this totally different mission? There's no technology that can make that journey in a human life span. Have you—have the developer labs found a way to put me into cryostasis without killing me? How am I supposed to travel to an exoplanet?"

She shakes her head. "You're not going on this mission, Ambrose."

I put my hands over my face. "You just said I was. You are fucking kidding me."

"I should clarify: you both are going and are not."

I push back from the table, folding my arms. "That is not clarifying. Didn't you just say that you owe me honesty? Why are you riddling me?!"

"I know it feels that way," she says calmly, "but I'm not." She instinctively checks her bracelet, even though hers is just as jammed here as mine. "Now listen to me carefully. As much of a shock as this is to you, because of your lateness we have only a few minutes before you need to attend the press junket—particularly important because that's when we will be publicly announcing the change in mission structure from rescue to colonization. It might feel like we were tricking you, but your believing that you were heading to Titan was the very point. During the medical exam you just woke from, we made a complete neural map of your synapses. Even as we speak, those neural pathways are being nanoteched into twenty cloned copies of you—"

My vision turns a crispy sort of white at the edges. "I'm sorry, what?"

"—and then those dormant clones will be installed on the *Endeavor*. The ship will be run by its operating system for thousands of years at a time, and then when it has accumulated enough small damages that the ship cannot fix on its own, one of your clones will be awoken. He will believe, as you did until just a few minutes ago, that he is flying to Titan."

My head is on the table, my brain thundering with blood. I cover my eyes with the bulk of my arms, so I'm in the most absolute darkness a human body can produce. All the while, my mother's words continue: "Our psychological simulations indicate that knowing the reality of your mission—that you won't be arriving at the exoplanet location, or anywhere off the ship, during your lifetime—would prevent your clones from being able to fulfill their duties due to despair and possible suicidal ideation. We needed you to believe in the Titan mission, so the ship could operate as though it were rescuing Minerva and the clones would have a sense of purpose during their limited time on the ship."

"'Limited time on the ship'?" I ask the darkness between me and the tabletop, moist from my breath.

"Yes, each clone will pass a limited time on the ship."

I lift my head, wiping drool from my lips. "You're going to kill them."

She looks angry now. Angry at my weakness.

How dare she. My words spill out hot. "So you expect me to board anyway tomorrow, even though you lied to me about the mission? Even though I won't be getting off the ship?"

She blinks at me. "Oh, my darling. Of course not. I wouldn't send you on a mission like that. To live for only a brief window? How horrible. I guess I wasn't clear. You're not going on the mission at all. Your clones are. But they are not you."

"I'm . . . what, just going back to classes as normal tomorrow?"

"You finished your coursework early, so that's up to you. But yes, once we've announced the changed mission, you're free to do as you like. You'll graduate along with your peers."

My voice and mind are someone else's, processing this information for me and then speaking it in my head loudly. Too loudly. "So I got chosen for this mission because . . ."

"Because you are a capable spacefarer. Because younger bodies are more resistant to the radiation of space travel.

And most importantly, because you are my precious child. A Cusk will be the future of humanity. If Earth falls, you will be the only hope for humankind. And it couldn't be in better hands. Who better to provide the inspiring tale that unites Earth, and make a new world in case this one fails?"

The stomach acid that already rose up once today is back, this time ascending to my Adam's apple. I swallow it down, relishing the burn, familiar from zero-gravity training. My instinct is to get the hell out of this room as fast as I can, but I know I might not get the chance to ask my mother any questions again for a long time. "It won't be me, though, will it? You said that yourself. It will be my clone. I trained my whole life for this. I was going to rescue Minnie. Who is *dead*. You lied to me about my fundamental purpose."

"That's a little dramatic. Understandably so, of course. I can't imagine what you're feeling right now. There will be other solar-system-based missions you can undertake. Maybe we'll try again to settle Titan. We'll still investigate Minerva's failed base. You would be a terrific candidate for that."

"Mother, this is impossible. Tell me that you haven't done this to me." The dreadful enormity of what I've just heard opens up, sucking down all the other thoughts in my mind. "That you haven't done this to *them*."

"Them who?" she asks.

"Me! Them. My clones."

"One of them will be the most important person in a new world. The founding god in the pantheon of a new Cusk civilization. And the rest are . . . creations that serve the purpose of bringing the ultimate clone to that position. It's like they're a community, working in perfect unison so that the group will find glory. Like bees."

"Like *bees*! And I—"

"You will remain here on Earth, like the rest of us."

"I'm still leaving tomorrow to rescue Minerva," I say stubbornly. Even as I say it, I know it makes no sense. I can't hijack a spaceship. And Minerva's distress beacon never triggered, which I should have known was too improbable anyway after two years of silence. She's dead. I should have always known she was dead. There is no one for me to rescue. But my brain is simultaneously beyond that simple fact and tripping behind it.

"Your ship will be in use, traveling to the second planet orbiting Sagittarion Bb—or 'Planet Cusk,' as we'll call it. Look, darling, I need you to take a moment in this private room. You'd have had more time to cope with this news if you hadn't been late. Rage and cry if you want to. No one is here to witness it. Take ten minutes to put yourself together, then you'll head down the elevators to the grand hall, where you'll sit at the press dais—your sole job being not to fidget—and we'll explain to everyone that Minerva's distress signal stopped, that the Titan base finally was able to send us ambient data confirming methane poisoning, that the mission has been canceled. That—in a glorious reveal—we will take advantage of the advanced preparation stage of the *Endeavor* to travel to a new home for humanity. They will all understand how upset you must be, and you can take as much time as you want to recuperate. I know you don't understand right now, that you're angry and confused, but you'll come to see what an honor I've granted you. Minerva's name will already be praised for all time because her mission captured the imaginations of both Dimokratía and Fédération, even though it didn't succeed. Imagine how *you* will be known! Who has ever had an opportunity for greatness like this?"

I stand.

I pick up my chair.

I hurl it at the window.

It bounces off harmlessly, skidding across the room.

My mother straightens her shirt, waiting for me to calm down.

I start pacing. "This is not greatness! It's utter greed and cruelty! You sent out versions of me to live and die on a mission that is doomed to fail. Twenty of me, suffering under a lie, with no way to know the truth." I'm dumbstruck. It's not anger animating me anymore; it's horror, horror worse than from watching any hyperreal torture reel. What has been done to me?

Who is this person who raised me?

I stagger to the vault-like door. I pull at it, but it refuses to open. "Mother, let me out of here."

"Ambrose," she says. Something in her tone makes me turn and look. She's crying. I've never seen such a thing. I've never known it was possible. It's only one tear, but it's there.

"What, did you really expect me to be *happy* about this?"

She shakes her head, hand at her chest. "I didn't think that. But I thought you'd understand my reasoning. That you might be glad to have a purpose greater than yourself."

"I understand your reasoning. It's just that I hate it. I *hate it*."

She looks at the chair, overturned on its side. She looks at the vault door. She looks at me.

"Let. Me. Out!" I shout. Something the clones of me on that ship, those twenty Ambrose Cusks, will never be able to do. For them, getting out will mean dying.

Surprisingly, she complies. Tears in her eyes, gaze on the floor, she skirts by me and raps a complicated knock on the door. One of the landkeepers opens it.

I have to step past her to leave. As I do she raises her arms, I guess to embrace me. I blow past.

I stalk past the first landkeeper, past my assistant, past the second landkeeper, past reception and into the express Cusk elevator. I shout out my floor stop and get a small burst of pleasure when the door closes on a landkeeper's face. I can just glimpse the other landkeeper racing to the next elevator bay over.

I know what they'll try: they'll keep me penned inside somewhere before they haul me out for the press conference. If I refuse to attend, they'll make do, and spin a global narrative that I'm too racked with sorrow over Minerva to show my face. Everyone will sigh and worry about me and mourn for my sister and be glad that at least we're making use of the ship after all and doesn't this make the troubles of the world seem silly by comparison?

Part of me thinks that I should attend that press conference and go off script, tell everyone what my mother just said. But the feed is assuredly on a ten-second delay, and will be scrubbed clean before anything gets out of the room.

All the same, there's no way I'm going to dutifully do as she asks.

What I'm going to do is to never see her again.

I hear whirring in the next elevator shaft over, the landkeepers racing to catch up with me. I have a ten-floor head start, which is all that I need. My clones might be at the mercy of the *Endeavor*, but not me, not here. One advantage of being a child of my mother: I know plenty of ways to get lost.

CHAPTER 2

The academy's major ceremonies take place in the grand hall, a vaulting hangar space with Dimokratía flags lining one side and Fédération the other, a giant Cusk logo suspended in between, an amalgam of four different types of real quarried stone. Two years ago the press dais was occupied by Minerva, decked out in her crisp spacefarer suit, grinning wildly as reporters captured inspiration reels of her to distribute around the world.

I wouldn't have thought it was possible, but they've managed to cram even more people into the grand hall today. In the front row is the press, recording the event on their bracelets, deploying microdrones to capture multiple angles so they can render the reels in three dimensions. Behind the dais are rows of cadets in formal regalia, standing at attention with their hands folded before the Cusk logo on their belts. My eyes instinctively go to Sri, on the mid-left. They salute—a little sassily—as my mother enters in her bespoke suit, walking crisply to a podium on one side of the red-velvet dais.

On the other side of the hall is an identical podium. It's empty.

I'm supposed to be standing at it.

My mother's face stays composed, but I can just imagine what she's thinking: *Surely my child wouldn't do this to me. He might be angry, but he wouldn't wreck his future and shame his family name, his country, his mother. He will show up.* As long seconds drag by, I zoom in, watching for her expression to crack. But it's like when I first entered the vault room, like her reel has been paused. The only sign that I'm seeing a person and not a static image is the occasional restlessness from a member of the press corps. And Sri. They are the only cadet whose gaze isn't straight forward. They look up. Many hundreds of cameras are capturing the ceremony from many hundreds of angles, but Sri knows which one is the Cusk corporate feed. As they look right into it, right at me, a smile spreads on their lips.

I'm watching all this from suborbit.

Earth has four space elevators. The nicest one is (of course) here at the Cusk headquarters in Mari, within the Fédération territory of former Syria. My mother blocked my official onyx-level access, but I have no fewer than three onyx accounts. One is my official one, one is a hack I created as part of my final programming thesis for quaternary class (wasn't supposed to actually bring it online, but no one ever explicitly told me not to, joke's on them), and the third is Minerva's, which she gave me before she departed, hiding it under my plate during our final meal of manicotti. *Make good use of it. There are no onyx perks on Titan.*

I kiss that onyx card as the elevator climbs. Minerva's portrait—which the personal elevator pod thinks is my own—stares back at me from the ID screen, all white teeth and confidence. I toast it with my bottle of PepsiRum. "Here's looking at you, Sister." I burp. This will not be my first bottle of PepsiRum today.

I sprawl out, my fingers drumming on the upholstery. I'm all alone, which heightens my "let's fuck around" feelings. I cannot wait to arrive and get started doing just that.

Cusk operates three different pleasure satellites, but the one above Mari is the biggest and oldest. It was named Disponar—technically in honor of the first Dimokratía prime minister so that Cusk could increase its business across country lines—but everyone calls it Death Star, because it rhymes and, well, Disponar looks like it's from this old reel called *Star Wars* that gets trendy again every twenty years, a pale tech-y moonish thing up there in the daytime sky.

The Earth falls away below as I near the end of the elevator trip. There's the planetary horizon, blue below and black above—if the elevator went even a kilometer farther, I would be in outer space.

Dressed in civilian blacks, I use my sham onyx card to skip the queue and get the next automated taxicraft from the arrival station to the pleasure satellite. I requested the taxi be preloaded with a fresh bottle of PepsiRum, even managing to get it in the new limited-edition Wild Ginger flavor. I crack it open as the craft whisks me through the thin atmosphere.

It's a short trip, and at first, I'm content just looking at the Earth horizon, telling myself I'm not going to keep watching the press junket. But finally curiosity gets the better of me.

Though I keep the reel on mute, I watch the great hall as it empties, projections of commentators desperately trying to fill up airtime, impromptu panels of pundits proposing tangled explanations for my absence. My mother is long gone.

I can imagine the Cusk press secretaries trying to spin my non-arrival. They're trained professionals. They can announce a canceled rescue mission without me. It's not the end of the world. No one gets to fool me and then depend on me to fix it.

The reel switches to other news. *Sources: Dimokratía Secretary of Defense missing after explosions heard in Brasilia. Local Fédération authorities have not yet released a statement.*

I stare down at the globe, at the sand-colored cyclones of

hot dust swirling around Mari and into Old Iraq, around everywhere except Firma Antarctica and Firma Arctica, the green oases at either pole. It's undeniable: the Earth is a worse planet than it was when humans arrived. The last species of seagull recently went from "vulnerable" to "endangered." Seagull!

Sri would argue that the best way forward is to let humanity die off here, to stop the contamination. Today I'm really seeing their point.

Should we really be settling new planets?

My sister is dead.

I take a long swig of my precious Wild Ginger PepsiRum. The label shows a paradise of tropical palms and thick green grasses. *Drink the Escape*, it suggests. Don't mind if I do.

I came off the Cusk Academy assembly line. I'm an heir to the Cusk fortune. And here I am, smoothly flying into something that looks like a supervillain's lair.

It's not that humans in general might be the enemy. Maybe *I* am the enemy.

Really should have asked for two more bottles of Wild Ginger. It's going down fast.

The taxi slows, hovering at the edge of Disponar. With onyx access I shouldn't have to wait for permission to land; I should already be gliding into the executive bays, where I'll be greeted by a virtual attendant who'll let me know which residential suite is mine. But instead my taxicraft is stopped in space. I can feel the beginning of a tension headache. I've basically imprisoned myself by getting in this taxi. There's no way out, unless I'm willing to plummet through Earth's atmosphere for three minutes and splat at the end.

This isn't good. Have my mother's goons figured out that I'm traveling on Minerva's onyx?

My taxicraft rocks gently in the thin atmosphere, buffeted by the occasional gust from a ship accelerating out of orbit on its way to the moon. An automated message appears before my face: *Disponar is at capacity, due to a booking for "Molina Quinceañera" until 14:00 on November 8. Please wait for more information.*

Oh. There's just a party. I place Minerva's onyx card on the reader and tap in her special code. The taxi glides into motion. *Permission granted. The Cusk Suite will be liberated and cleaned and ready for you within thirty minutes.*

My sister is dead. But she got me a room.

I take another sip of PepsiRum. Looks like I'll be crashing a quinceañera, and kicking someone out of their quarters to boot. I hope it's not the lucky birthday-person themself.

I put sunglasses on and keep my head down after the taxi lands, refusing the helping hand of the attendant. I do accept the water patch he offers, though. Can't forget to hydrate.

I keep my eyes out for guards. A police officer gives me

a long look, but he licks his lips lewdly when I pass. That's fine. You can stare at me because I'm hot. Just don't stare at me because I'm supposed to be arrested.

As I pad through the hallways to the Cusk Suite, I call up the pleasure satellite's reservations and glance through, so I can plan my day to avoid the worst crowds. There's a daylong party in the "pool"—a floorless spot, where you can dance with the Earth distant below, magnetic forces suspending your body in open space. Even drunk on PepsiRum, it's not my scene. The tech has been revamped since the Telos satellite dropped a teenager eight kilometers to his death, but I'm still not looking for that kind of thrill. Instead I'll probably be heading to the hyperreal erotic simulation rooms, which are just about the most distracting place you could ever imagine being. I need something to keep this yawning grief over my sister and desolate fury at my mother to the edges of my mood and no closer. I've already been flicking through which avatars I'd like to choose to frolic with in my fantasy waterfall. One is actually named Wild Ginger. Probably product placement. Their body is covered in freckles, like carbonation. It's too perfect.

I am beyond sad, and beyond furious. No one watching me stalk by would know it, I don't think—I've got serious repression skills—but I'm simply shimmering and vibrating with feeling. It'll come out eventually, probably in some ultra-destructive way, but not yet. That's another side effect of my childhood. I always wind up eating my fury cold.

I'll find the most incandescent distraction I can in the meantime, while I wait for the crush of hopelessness. I scan through the quinceañera's agenda. That's when I see the listing. It appeared at some point over the last minute:

17:00 (NEW): [Private concert for Molina Party Guests] The Heartspeak Boys

No. The universe has to be kidding me.

Maybe my sister is dead. Maybe my life's purpose has been ripped from me. Maybe my mother has betrayed me so fully that I'll never speak to her again. Maybe I've lost my faith in the country and corporation that produced me. Maybe I'll spend the rest of my tragic days chasing the nearest pleasure instead of working toward some other abstract future that will only turn out to be a fresh lie. Maybe the only person who ever really loved me is long dead on a distant moon.

But, as far as nearest pleasures go . . .

Devon Mujaba. Biggest crush of my life.

Is here.

That'll do.

CHAPTER 3

Skinprint mods are strictly against Cusk Academy code. That was actually a recent development; as the cold war escalated and Dimokratía kept emphasizing how pure and healthy their cadets were, word came down from Fédération that we couldn't get any more skinprints, piercings, fragrance implants, none of it. They yanked those of us who had them out of bed in the middle of the night to get our bodies purified.

So obviously the first place I head while I wait for the Heartspeak Boys concert are the modification stalls. I'm now quite buzzed on PepsiRum, so I don't take long deliberating. I don't deliberate at all, in fact—I just pick the most expensive artist and tell them to go at it. Flashing Minerva's onyx card gets me suite access, so rather than milling around with the hoi polloi I settle into my private lounge and wait for the artist to arrive with their tools. I order another PepsiRum in the meantime.

The skinprint process is delightful. The room shifts to a steamy mineral bath surrounded by snow as I strip, and the artist spritzes me up and down with gold and brass and silver. After they wipe away the excess, what's left are metallic tendrils and leaves: a burst on either cheek, then another set starting on my neck and spreading over my chest and back, the front vines stopping at my hip bones and the back ones cascading all the way down to mid-thigh. I get them to scribe a tattoo I've been wanting for months: *Labels are the Root of Violence*, in five-year black, reading vertically between my pectorals.

Then the dresser comes in. She's picked me out a cream-colored wrap and a gold circlet. She also brought a laurel cuff for my upper arm, but I turn that down. A little too Greco-Roman cliché—though I must say that I am quite pleased with the circlet and wrap. My skin is hypersensitive from the skinprint mods, so the silky fabric feels like a dozen hands are caressing me at once. The only word you can read above the top of the wrap is *Violence*.

"I love this," I tell her. "Devon Mujaba couldn't possibly resist."

She gives me a long-lashed wink. "You saw the concert on the schedule? It must be a surprise for the lucky fifteen-year-old. None of us had any notice."

Once she's finished grooming my hair, I head out into the bustling club. Bass pounds loud enough to vibrate my organs. My skinprints glow in the low light, and between that and my makeup, hairstyle, and outfit, I enter the dancing throng as something superhuman. This is the opposite of trying to hide myself away, but I don't care anymore. A sea of hungry eyes is just the distraction that I need. Even if I'm worthless, even if I'm just a tool to be disposed of, useless to family or country, even if the only person who actually loved me is well and truly dead, I have this power to attract and compel. At least *that's* still mine.

I whirl through the dance floor, pushing into the thickest clots of dancers, losing myself in the press of bodies. I'm covered in other people's sweat, and my muscles are loose from the vibration of the bass, when I see a dancer check the time on her bracelet over by the bar: 17:09. Showtime.

I work my way to the satellite's other club, where the Heartspeak Boys will be performing. I don't have an invite, but I don't need one. The onyx card gets me into a special cordoned-off area in the front. I catch my breath on a spacious couch as everyone behind me is packed into standing room. With my robe and body decorations, I feel like the boys are performing just for me. Like I'm an emperor. I mean, I'm wearing a fucking circlet.

They're emoting to the rafters, wearing their loose loopy blouses, holding their hands to their chests as they sing. The Heartspeak Boys are ridiculous. Only one of them is actually a boy, for starters. The crowd loves all of it. So do I.

Devon Mujaba—not that that's his real name, I'm sure—is in the center. He's the smallest of the three, and he's simply perfection. All the right proportions, his dark brown hair almost the same color as his skin, cascading over his head in a wave that never breaks, over eyes a gorgeous chemical green. His singing voice is startlingly pure. Tonight he, too, is a creature that's more than human.

Even with the glare of the stage lights, Devon must notice me, an island in this mass of pressed people. I'm alone, lounging on this dais with my fresh skinprints, robe open to my waist, beaming all my focus at him. Making sure he can't miss me.

I appear to have succeeded. As the Heartspeak Boys receive their applause, they hurl gladiolas to the lucky birthday girl, placing hands over their hearts as they bow and curtsy. She nearly passes out; it's adorable. When Devon Mujaba does his final curtsy, it's me he looks at. Full-on, zero-percent-accidental, hungry-animal eye contact.

I tilt my head toward the exit, where elevators whisk people to their bedrooms. Where, on the top floor, my Cusk Suite is waiting.

Devon nods back, so imperceptibly that it's possible none of his thousand other fans noticed. That fact, that we've just communicated privately in a crowded hall, sets my pulse racing.

I push my way through the crowd, jostling a trio of girls who turn to complain at me but then go blank with shock when they see who I am. I try to speed away, but more and more people around us catch on to who's among them. "Why aren't you in Mari, Ambrose Cusk?" someone shouts.

I hurry to the onyx elevator, but the crowd is too thick for me to get there fast. These are not conversations I would want to have in the best of times. But especially not tonight. I'm hoping to avoid the whole world tonight. Except for Devon Mujaba.

I knock over a sign advertising moon tours, apologize to the startled travel agent. Before she can answer I've begun to run, shoving through the crowd, bunching my robe in my fist so I won't trip, kicking off my sandals and abandoning them, taking the onyx stairs because they're closer and so that I can feel the burn in my muscles, stair stair stair stair, thump thump thump thump, bare feet on no-skid graphite, turn the corner, stair stair stair stair, thump thump thump thump, all the way up to my suite, twenty stories above the mob.

Then the penthouse door clicks open and I'm inside. I press my back against the wall, chest heaving. By the time I've caught my breath I'm slumped to the ground. I almost cry, because I'm a melodramatic drunk whose sister is dead, but instead I crawl across the carpet. Hands shaking, I fix myself a fresh PepsiRum, stagger to my feet, miraculously without spilling the drink, and hump over to the three-story windows. I can't see the *Endeavor*, hidden away in its launch hangar. Mercifully. All the same I know it's near. I cool my cheek against the window and then I'm naked, pressing my whole body against the glass, imagining what it would be like if my cells found a way to pass through, if I tumbled through this clear surface into the open atmosphere, and then the ground far below. I tap my head against the glass, my gold circlet—the only adornment I still have on—ringing out brightly. I'm ludicrous. I'm a simply ludicrous human.

I lie down naked on the rug, on my back, my cocktail centered on my torso, and let myself feel sorry for myself. That's an emotion I can feel very purely and deeply. My wallowing is usually over quickly, but this time—who knows? Could be permanent.

Maybe I should eat something. But before I can muster the strength to activate my bracelet and place an order, I hear the descending chimes of the suite's doorbell. Like we're in the twentieth century. It's a retro affectation that I selected in the suite preferences.

I slap the tears away from my eyes, dash to the bathroom to fix myself in the mirror. "There in a minute!"

Clothes. I should wear clothes. At least to start with.

I put a bathrobe on, arrange it across my shoulders and tie it at my waist with a length of silk rope I find in the stocked walk-in closet. Then I go to the door and drag my fingers across, to turn the material transparent. I'd been assuming it was Devon Mujaba, of course, but now—way too late—I consider who else it might be. My mother, Sri, my assistant or a professor, that sweet-faced girl whose quinceañera I just upstaged, any of them could have come to chew me out. As the door turns cloudy and then clear as glass, I feel simultaneous relief and excitement.

It is Devon Mujaba.

CHAPTER 4

He hasn't showered or even changed since the concert. It's delightful. Unlike the flawless hyperreal avatar of Devon Mujaba (which I've spent a *lot* of time with in the erotic simulation rooms), there's a sheen along the real man's shoulders and throat, dots of sweat on the fabric where his sheer blouse is open to the navel. A few stray pimples on his chest. He's wearing overpowering fragrance mods that make him smell like a locker room. Stage makeup puddles under his eyes, leaving them in deep gloom, like someone who's been crying over a dead soldier in a Dimokratía melodrama. I remember, vaguely, that Devon Mujaba was once in the Dimokratía military academy, until he defected with his family at the age of fourteen.

"Hello, Ambrose Cusk," Devon Mujaba says as he steps into my suite. He smiles wryly. "Am I right to assume that you are not on Disponar for the Molina quinceañera?"

I close the door and lock it, then press a PepsiRum cocktail into his hand. "I am not here for the Molina quinceañera, no."

Devon Mujaba's warm fingers leave patterns on the

self-chilling glass. He takes a long quaff. "I'm glad. That means my workday is officially over. I'd rather not be on duty right now. Or at least, not as a singer."

"Lucky for me," I say as I close the door. "Would it be a horrible cliché for me to now tell you I've been a lifelong fan of yours?"

He moves to the window and turns, resting his ass on the railing. It's a little mesmerizing, the plump dimple of it. "It would be, a bit. But I happen to like clichés. I mean, have you ever listened to our lyrics?"

"'I want your love, I need your love,'" I quote to him. "I guess it's not the freshest line ever written."

He grins. "Ambrose Cusk, we've only just met and you're already teasing me. It's a lot."

"Ah," I say, absently running my hands over my new skinprints, the glitter raised on my skin. "'A lot' is sort of a hallmark of mine."

I watch his Adam's apple rise and fall as he downs the rest of his drink. "Most would say you're the more famous of the two of us. Unless you're polling thirteen-year-olds. I have them locked down. Anyway, I do know who you are. And you know that I know. Otherwise I wouldn't have come to the Cusk Suite. The rumor that you fled here after the rescue mission was canceled is actually the reason the Heartspeak Boys made the last-minute agreement to play this quinceañera after all."

I flush. That thought hadn't even crossed my mind, and being flattered is one of my favorite sensations. I open the fridge and pull out another cocktail glass, rip off the secure seal and watch the glass frost up in my fingers. "On that note, I should warn you, since I'm not supposed to be here it's just a matter of time before Cusk corporate stooges baṣh down this door to haul me home."

Devon Mujaba accepts the glass, in the process letting his fingertips rest on the back of my hand. Staring into my eyes all the while. It's an awfully obvious seduction dance we're performing, but he's executing the steps very well. "A ticking clock," he whispers. "How dramatic!"

I nod ruefully. "I'm on a bit of a bender. You're the climax before everything comes crashing down. I just felt I should warn you, in case you'd rather not be in the newsreels. Also, I might be hiding it well, but I'm quite drunk."

He rubs his hands up and down his arms. It's a nervous gesture that makes our act of theater fall away. Little danger hairs on the back of my neck prickle. "You're not hiding it well at all, actually. And you're warning me that I might be in the news for being found in the private quarters of the handsome spacefarer who's also the world's great hope? If that's the sort of gossip attached to me, my publicist would deeply approve. Especially when I leak the explosive tidbit that it's your academy lover who arranged it all."

I slap the couch. "Sri! That's how you found out so

quickly that I was heading to Disponar? *Sri* made this happen? That dog!"

Devon Mujaba grins.

Of course. Bits of Devon Mujaba's biography come back to me. A reel of him singing at a piano that made him a teenage celebrity, a poor kid turned rich who remembers his humble roots. Donating his income to charities fighting for human rights and animal welfare. Devon's the hot-boy face of everything Sri cares about. Including . . . "You're the global ambassador for the Union for a Better Earth!" I exclaim. "That's how you know Sri."

"Oh yes," Devon says. "Sri and I go way back."

By its own inscrutable logic, grief about Minerva comes from nowhere to knock me back. The sudden reminder of the great gulf between alive me and dead Minerva stops my breath. Devon Mujaba's sexy smile disappears when he sees my face. "I'm sorry," he says, standing up from the windowsill. "Did I say something wrong?"

I get my Cusk veneer back up, beam a bright, confident smile that I hope is worthy of my sister. I stand beside him at the window, my shoulders and hips meeting the heat of his. "No. Nothing wrong. Nothing at all. So tell me, Devon Mujaba: What's your usual postshow ritual?"

"Oh, you know," he says. "My boyfriend and I have a free-pass policy for concert nights. I do sometimes pick someone out of the audience to invite to my room.

Normally I have to look a little harder, send my fixer out to get bracelet details. I don't usually have a celebrated beauty dressed and skinprinted like a Roman demigod and presenting himself on a dais, delivered to me by his generous academy lover."

"*Demi*god?" I say with mock outrage. "Excuse me!" Then his words sink in and I blush. He came here just to meet me. And Sri made it happen. My drunken fingers drift to my new decorations, the gold and silver vines. When they reach my temple, they knock my circlet askew. "I was feeling impulsive. Do you like the look?"

He lifts the circlet off my head. My hair rises, made temporarily weightless by the gentle pressure of his hands. Devon Mujaba's hands. "I do. Very much."

I flop dramatically onto the couch, letting my body lie flat, arms overhead like a bathing vixen. The couch is the pink scallop design that was popular in the 2450s, nearly the length of a bed. Perfect seduction furniture. "Would you like to kick off your shoes, lie down for a bit?" I ask.

He removes each sandal with the heel of the opposite foot, crushing the expensive leather in the process. It's so charmingly irresponsible; I can't help but grin. He lies beside me. Triggered by his changing pulse, new, bright notes rise from his fragrance mods, far more sophisticated than the locker room assault from before. What's it closest to? Dragon fruit and . . . is that fennel? "You don't waste time, do you, Ambrose Cusk?" Devon asks.

I shrug, then allow myself to run my hand down his arm. "Who knows how much time we actually have?"

He strokes my face, then leans in and kisses me. It's a slow start but then, once his tongue is in my mouth, the intensity doubles. The PepsiRum, the sumptuousness of the pleasure satellite, the softness of Devon Mujaba's lips, the elegant angle of his neck, the glow of the skin I just touched—it's almost enough to make me forget the sorrow and anger inside me. Almost.

"I want to feel you closer to me," he says.

I lie on my side, so our thighs press.

"Closer."

Our robes fall open as we line up our bodies. I feel the soft, smooth heat of someone I've long fantasized about. Whom I've actually had sex with in avatar form, though it was nothing like this. I decide that would be too awkward to bring up. From the sound of it he's probably had sex with my avatar already, anyway.

"That's better," he whispers. He nuzzles my neck, then moves up so his lips are right in my ear. "I have something I need to tell you, Ambrose Cusk."

"Mmm," I say, with a catlike stretch of my body. "What do you have to tell me?"

"It's about why I dropped everything to come see you," he whispers. His voice is almost inaudible, no more than a slight rustle. The sound makes my hair stand up, whether from lust or something more like fear, I don't know. "Don't speak back," he says. "The lice in this room can pick up anything. Just listen. And keep making out."

What?

This is not a sexy thing he has to tell me. Shit. I'm still turned on—making out with a stranger is always a bit of a performance, anyway, so this isn't *so* much of a left turn—but I'm also on high alert. I sigh as he nibbles my earlobe. Why couldn't this just have been about getting it on?

"The Heartspeak Boys don't throw impromptu concerts without very good reason," he whispers. "Sri didn't send me as an amuse-bouche. This is not an idle hookup."

"Oh, I don't know about that," I whisper.

Devon doesn't take the bait. "I came up through the Dimokratía military academy."

"I know," I say. "Your childhood's a lot like Sri's. Your family sold you after they defected, because they didn't have enough money to raise another child."

"We didn't call it 'selling,' of course, but yes. I was paid to leave my family and go work in the entertainment hostels of Fédération. Just like how the tax exemptions from Sri getting into the academy saved their family. Once I was alone and vulnerable, I was used like a toy. It's no coincidence that Sri and I were both drawn to the Union for a Better Earth after starting life like that."

"And I'm clearly drawn to you both, since I started the day in Sri's arms."

"I took the very little that life handed me and made a plan. I decided I'd scrape together whatever power I could, and use it to change the world. With the fame of the Heartspeak Boys, I finally have cards to play. We are big enough that both countries make exceptions to have us perform there. I still play concerts in Dimokratía. Nothing public, of course, but the elites there enjoy their indulgences, too. I've spent more than a few weekends at President Gruy's lake houses."

"Ooh. I'd like to hear about those," I say.

"Stories for another time. The point is I've spent my life building this persona of gooey-pop-sexy Heartspeak Boy intentionally. It is a weapon, if used right, and I've been waiting for the right target. For the right opportunity to make a move. And the longer I wait, the more I've grown my devoted following, the more power that final move has, once it comes."

Adrenaline is spritzing my neck. "That move is . . . this?" I ask.

"Ambrose," Devon says, "I know you were never intended to go rescue your sister."

"Mmm," I say, keeping up the act even though my heart isn't into making out anymore. My heart thumps just as hard as if I were still kissing him. How does he know this truth?

The dragon fruit and fennel scent from Devon's fragrance mods comes out even stronger as his own pulse rises. "I see you know this, too," he whispers, his lips so close to my ear that they tickle my skin. "Most of the people in Dimokratía believe, like most of Fédération does, that the rescue mission was scrubbed in favor of a last-minute switch to settling a new colony. They're surprised and moved and hopeful, and most of all *distracted*. Just as your mother and the presidents intend. But the Heartspeak Boys played for President Gruy and his cabinet last month, and partied with them afterward. One of the undersecretaries thought he could win me over by revealing that the distress call was fake. That it had to be faked, for the spacefarers to believe their lives had a purpose, and to spin out this Scheherazade tale of rescue to keep the two countries away from war for as long as possible. Of course, with the killing of the secretary of defense today, that's proving moot as we speak."

Through my drunkenness, I realize that I've been avoiding processing the assassination news I'd heard earlier. *You get to wallow for a while*, my drunkenness responds. I run back over Devon's words. "Dimokratía is in on the lie?" I say, taking the opportunity to nibble on Devon's earlobe. For verisimilitude.

"Yes. Your mother, and both presidents. All in on it. And that's where I might finally know something you don't," he continues. "The *Aurora* is being readied. Dimokratía's own equivalent to the *Endeavor*, funded by us and with the same base Cusk tech. This new colonizing trip will be a joint mission."

A joint mission. A second ship. In the shock of everything my mother *was* telling me, I'd never considered that even now she wasn't revealing everything. She had the chance to come completely clean . . . and she *still* held back information?

"Ouch," Devon says. I guess I nibbled his ear a little hard.

I wait for him to say more.

"Here's the thing," he whispers. "A Dimokratía spacefarer was training to go on a solo rescue mission, just like you, only his was supposed to be a national secret. It's not known to the media, but his presence was mandated by the Dimokratía leaders if Cusk wanted to use their resources. The *Aurora* is intended to be joined to the Fédération *Endeavor* in orbit. It will have a crew of two."

A second spacefarer. I can't believe it. The rug's being pulled out again. "What do you know about him?" I ask this question into Devon Mujaba's mouth.

"Quite a bit."

"Have you met him?"

"Maybe. Maybe I've come to you *from* meeting him."

I want to ask Devon everything. But I have no reason to trust him, and we're both traveling dangerous currents of state secrets and corporate espionage. The sorts of things that could get even celebrities like us disappeared or killed.

Me and this stranger stop kissing, lay our heads on the couch's pink cushions, stare into each other's eyes. His saturated bamboo-green irises flutter side to side as he gauges my expression. "Why are you telling me all this?" I ask.

"Because. With this great lie, and news of the assassination down below spreading like wildfire, we have a one-time opportunity to demolish the world's political system. Incremental reform hasn't worked. The world must be broken to be rebuilt."

"Broken!" Breaking both the Earth's countries? What does Devon want, anarchy?

"Ambrose! Think about the lies that are being spread in *your* name. At the subterfuge that's been done to you, and the dishonor to your sister's legacy. You must be furious!"

Oh, don't start me tapping into my fury. Not when I'm exhausted and drunk on PepsiRum and ginned up by the hot boy next to me on the couch.

"You don't know the half of what I'm furious about," I say acidly.

He darts the tip of his tongue over his lips. "Care to share?"

I'm about to say something reckless. State secrets level. But he's right, why should I have any loyalty to Fédération? Devon Mujaba has treated me with more respect than anyone at Cusk mission control ever has. Than my own mother ever has. "Clones. Twenty clones of me are on that ship. Living their lives out as a lie, thinking they're rescuing my dead sister, until the last survivor settles a new planet."

He stares at me, aghast. "No. Why?"

"Yes," I say, shocked to find a tear-struck sound in my voice at the end of the word. "So they won't despair in space and kill themselves. Revelations on all sides, Mujaba."

"My god," he says, voice rising above a whisper. "How are you okay right now?"

I shake my head and nod it at the same time, place my fingers over his lips to remind him to be quiet. "I don't like to talk about the feelings part," I manage to whisper.

"That's fine," he says. "We don't have to talk about anything you don't want to."

The PepsiRum makes the room tilt. Wild Ginger must have a calming add-in, because I know I'd be swirling the drain with despair right now if it didn't.

But the add-in is working on me at the same time as big feelings. I feel somehow both serene and eager, like I'm suspended over an infinite void, about to tumble to nothing . . . but sort of jazzed by the doom of it all? Horror and peace living side by side, all at once. Thanks, PepsiRum. "Was this all—was getting the chance to tell me about the *Aurora* your only reason for playing this gig, for accepting my invitation here? I still don't get why you're taking this risk."

He smiles, his fingers tweaking my chin. I don't know if he's doing it to appease surveillance, or because seduction has always been his way of accumulating power, or if he is feeling real warmth toward me. I'm not sure it matters. "It seems like the most unfair thing in the world, what they've done to you. And to that Dimokratía spacefarer, plucked from his training. He's feeling this betrayal even deeper than you are. If you think you were raised for a mission only to have it snatched from you, believe me, he's feeling it twice as hard. He doesn't even have a family, friends, or the luxury of money to fall back on."

"Devon Mujaba, with the heart of gold," I say.

His expression clouds. "You don't have to be ironic all the time, you know."

"You're a total stranger," I say, pulling away from Devon and his ersatz green eyes. "You expect me to be my vulnerable self? Maybe *you're* the one who needs advice on how to act."

"Fair," he says. He goes silent; I can sense him considering and censoring a thousand different tacks. And in that silence, my heart realizes Devon is more right than he's wrong. Is there anyone I have ever been my actual insecure self with?

"This isn't just out of blind sympathy on my part," Devon says. "What's been done to you is the symptom of a brutal system that fosters economic expansion as surely as it does suffering. Because we live *in* this version of the world, we don't see it. But now, the lie and the turmoil down below . . . this is a moment when everyone *can* see it."

"See it how?"

"We show them. We reveal the manipulation. Publicly. Pour fuel onto the unrest down in Brasilia."

I roll onto my back, fingers twined over my chest. "How would that work, exactly?" I ask. "We drop an anarchist banner from Disponar? Paint angry graffiti on the *Endeavor*? Go steal a clone?"

Devon Mujaba laughs. "None of those is such a terrible idea, actually. What *could* we accomplish together? I wonder."

I chuckle, too, despite the self-pity welling up. "What if I joined the Heartspeak Boys and we did a guerrilla concert in front of the ship? We could have a new song, maybe. 'Daddy Was Alexander the Great, but Mommy Just Fed Me Lies.'"

"Could be a hit. If I sing backup for you they could call me—what was Alexander's lover's name?"

"Hephaestion. And that would be hot. But. Well. I'm afraid you haven't heard me try to sing."

"Hey," he says. "Singing well is not a prerequisite to being a Heartspeak Boy. You literally haven't heard José Luis sing, either."

"No!"

Devon nods. "Yes. She's piped in."

"Forget my false rescue mission or you betraying your country's secrets. José Luis has been dubbed this whole time? José Luis?! *That's* the scandal of the year."

"She's super cute, though."

"Yes," I say, "she's super cute."

Devon Mujaba opens his lips to ask a question, and I answer before he can even pose it, as I lay my hand on his chest. "Let's go fuck things up."

His eyes tear up. It reminds me that his whole life has led up to this. "Ambrose. Thank you."

"But after. Let's enjoy this for now."

"I can go along with that," he says, taking my hand and guiding it lower on his body.

Given the full-body workout Devon Mujaba and I gave each other, combined with the cocktail of synthetic depressants in my bloodstream from all the PepsiRum, I'd have expected myself to sleep the sleep of the ages. But instead I snap awake with the dawn, easing off Devon Mujaba's delightful body and standing before the tall windows of the suite to watch the sun turn the clouds shrouding the planet below us from blue to purple green. I hadn't expected to have this long before the Cusk goons came for me, and this morning moment is more peaceful for being stolen.

I imagine the storms below streaking through the

red-and-pink dust that coats Mari. The refugees and peace councils, the academy and Cusk compound where I was raised, feel very far away from up here. Sunrise is even more beautiful when you're above it.

Devon Mujaba is lain out on top of my black silk sheets, grappling a pillow. Totally naked. I take a moment to drink the sight in.

I don't think he and I will be having sex again—both for all the usual one-night-stand reasons and because, after this trick I pulled, I have no doubt that my mother will make sure Devon Mujaba and I don't cross paths ever again. I might not even leave the Cusk family compound ever again. Assuming it hasn't been obliterated by a missile. I should check the news. What is happening down below?

What did I tell Devon last night? I think I remember, but the details are fuzzy. What did he tell me? *A spacefarer. From Dimokratía.* He's probably also been cloned and stocked into a ship. Twenty of him, the sole companions for twenty of me.

I return my attention to the glory of Devon Mujaba's body in my bed, then try to order breakfast via my bracelet. The word *unavailable* blinks in the air in front of me.

I slip on a robe and pad to the door. Locked.

I trigger the unlock function. *Error.*

So that's why I was able to sleep in. I'm already in prison. Mother has found me, which means Devon Mujaba and I are in a holding cell. I debate waking him up to tell him, but what would be the point? We both knew this would happen. Guards will be barging in here soon. Better to let him sleep. I sit on the edge of the bed and watch him breathe, this human beside me.

CHAPTER 5

On my way back to the Earth's surface, I sit on the edge
of the bench seat of the elevator car, Cusk goons on either
side. One of my mother's assistants perches across from me.
He probably thinks he's keeping his face impassive, but I
can tell from all the smaller details—his knuckles are white
with tension, for starters—that he's brimming with fury.
My regular assistant has probably been fired by now, and
all it would take is one misstep for this one to follow.

"Perhaps you'd like an update on what's been going on
in your absence," the new one says primly, calling up the
latest news to project in the air of the elevator car.

Over footage of the emptying hall, the anchor reads a
statement from the Cusk press secretary: the Cusk Corporation was saddened to report the end of the distress signal,
and made the reluctant decision to cancel the mission to
Titan. Unfortunately, the news about the scrapped mission
hit Ambrose Cusk especially hard, and they were asking
everyone to honor his—my—need for privacy to mourn.

There's no mention of Devon Mujaba, and the reports
don't cut to any footage of me on Disponar—I guess none

170

of that has leaked yet, or this assistant really earned their paycheck, rushing the tech department to scrub all footage and mentions of me before they made it out of the satellite's digital space. I guess I've done my mother a favor by going on my bender in a sealed location. Everyone in the world is imagining me sobbing prettily in a lonely tower, lit by a single ray of divine light as I suffer the renewed loss of my sister.

"Well, that's not so terrible," I say, volleying my words to the assistant through the news projection in the air between us. I'm glad it obscures my view of him, because those white knuckles were making me tense. "It's perfectly reasonable I'd appear distraught over my sister being dead. I *am* distraught over my sister being dead."

The projection blinks out as the assistant nods, hands denting the box of papers at his waist. He doesn't really have any options. Even if he'd love nothing more than for me to take a long walk off the satellite's short launch bay, he knows I am my mother's son. The life of Ambrose Cusk is full of unfairnesses, and most of them benefit me.

The elevator slows to a stop, switches over to the magnetic handlers that ease it into the Earthside landing bay. We'll have ten minutes to deboard, and for attendants to clean and restock the onyx elevator car before it fills with new wealthy customers to fling into low orbit.

Automated voices instruct us to keep track of the

developing conflict and to have a nice day. I stop a few feet out of the craft, and the goons stop on either side of me. "Are you all permanently attached to me now?"

"Just until I get you where you're going this morning," the assistant says. He guides me to the edge of the bay, away from the curious eyes of the waiting travelers. "Your mother needs you to make a recording."

"Trying again to get me to perform the good son, mourning my dear sister in front of millions?" I ask. "I was hoping I wasn't going to have to go through that performance after all. To be honest, I'm not sure how convincing I could be at the moment." I emit a wild ginger burp for emphasis.

"No, this recording is private."

I raise an eyebrow. "Now I'm intrigued."

"Follow me," he says, heels clipping down the hallway that leads deeper into corporate headquarters.

When I follow, the landkeepers hang back and start to chitchat, becoming slightly less goon-ish as they do. We leave the public areas and scan ourselves into the corporate sanctum. Cusk employees shoot surreptitious looks at us as the new assistant and I pass through the central atrium. Real koi and projections of frogs swim through the marble-bottomed fountain at the center. Before we scan into the management tower, I stop. "What's going to happen to . . ."

"Your famous bedmate?" the new assistant asks crisply.

"Yes."

"He's been invited to remain in the Cusk Suite for a few hours. We'll administer him some electrolytes to help with the hangover, like we did you, and then he will return to his life. He has a second concert to play on Disponar tonight. He has done nothing wrong. There is no crisis there."

I'm relieved. All the same I remember the information Devon Mujaba told me about Dimokratía's plans, about the other spacefarer. Things my mother was very careful to keep from me. His suggestion that I could throw a wrench into the gears of our world. How appealing that still feels.

But what to do about it?

The assistant leads me to the most restricted corporate elevator, both of us getting our clearances scanned and double-scanned before we can board. The receptionist who glances at us while the doors close is so perfectly beautiful that I can't tell if they're a real human. Within seconds we've shot into the sky and arrived back at my mother's floor, leaving the landkeepers behind. Apparently they aren't coming with us, not this time.

As the doors open I expect my mother—or at least her assistants—to be waiting. But the upper-level corporate lobby is empty. And strangely quiet. Where has everyone gone?

I follow the assistant down the hallway until we're outside the plain door from yesterday, the one that leads to the signal-jammed room where my mother told me I wouldn't be rescuing my sister. What will I be finding out today? The assistant gestures me in alone, then closes the door behind me.

My mother is waiting inside, arms behind her back.

I collapse into one of the antique desk chairs. "What's today's big revelation? Am I actually a sentient rock? Or maybe I'm a piece of Camembert."

"What?"

That was probably the first time I've ever even tried to joke with my mother. For good reason, it turns out.

She looks at me flatly, then her eyes widen. "Ambrose, what have you done to yourself?"

I pluck the soft cream robe away from my body, adjust the gold circlet on my head. "Do you like my new look?"

"No, the—are those *skinprints*? You well know those aren't allowed in the academy. Those aren't allowed on spacefarers. And what is that written on your chest— '*Violence*'?"

"It's 'Labels are the Root of Violence,' actually. But my shirt has to be off to read the whole thing. And Mother. Tell me you're not serious right now. You're upset that I've broken the student code of conduct? After you cloned me without my permission so you can launch twenty of me into space to suffer?"

"We'll get those removed. The prints. It will be painful,

but that can't be helped. Nothing to be done about it yet; you'll just have skinprints for your recording." She gestures to the plain table before me, which I now see has a reel-corder set up on it.

I sit before I know what I'm doing. Even after her deep betrayal, I guess I'm still that ten-year-old, terrified of moving down in the rankings of my dozens of siblings. Maybe I'm ten years old for good. I shift my seat so I can look into the cam. A man with a fuzzy gray beard stares back at me from the interface. I vaguely remember him. "Hello there, Ambrose," he says. "It's nice to see you again. I'm the director of the reels arm of the Sagittarion Bb project. You knew me as the Titan mission recordings director, though."

"Super," I say. "I didn't know you were into fiction."

He blinks. "Right. Funny. So. I know Chairperson Cusk is there with you, because she just finished recording her session. Hello there, Chairperson Cusk. Can you say your full name and confirm that there is no one else in the room with you? I don't have access to any digital signatures in that jammed room, so I'll need a verbal confirmation from both of you."

"Cassandra Cusk. And yes," my mother says.

"It's just us," I say, my skin tingling, and only half because of my hangover. There's only one other time that it's been just my mother and me alone anywhere, and that was when I found out I'd been cloned.

"Okay, great," the man says. "This will be recorded onto physical media, with no networking aside from the gatekept link I'm using right now, so Chairperson Cusk, I'll have to ask you to have it hand-delivered into orbit. The recording is already underway, so you don't need to say when you're ready or not; we'll edit it so that the reel is smooth. Cassandra, have you told Ambrose what this is for yet?"

My mother glances over her shoulder. She's been staring into the sky, and she's not one to daydream; I wonder if she's watching for signs of military aircraft. Or mushroom clouds. "No. You handle that."

The guy blanches. "Sure, sure, no problem. Let me give it a shot. So, Ambrose, buddy, here's what's going on. You know about the real mission of the *Endeavor* by now. At some point, thousands of years from now, if all goes well, another version of you will arrive at an exoplanet of Sagittarion Bb, which will by then be known as its new name, Cusk. He's going to need practical advice and instructions. That part we'll take care of. But that version of you will also be overwhelmed, beside himself, lonely. We want him to feel like he's seen and loved. We hoped you'd give him some emotional support."

My legs are shaking. *How dare you.* And I also know he's right. That new version of me will be barely holding on by a thread. He's *me*. I know for a fact that he didn't ask for this.

I watch the director try to read my face. "We'll give you an opportunity now to say whatever you'd like to the clone of you. Whatever you think he'd want to know. Do you want to take some time to think about it?"

"I don't. I'm ready. 'Fuck you.' That's what I'd like to say. 'Fuck you.'"

The director closes his mouth so tight that his upper lip puckers, evident even under his bristly mustache.

"Not *you*, Ambrose," I say, overenunciating into the reelcorder. "That was for this director man and for my mother."

My mother slams her hand on the table, hard enough that her earrings rattle and one of her hieroglyph braids falls loose. "I understand you're angry. That my son is angry at his mother. It breaks my heart, and I know I deserve it. But let's both put those feelings to one side for the moment. You're not just my son. You're also a space-farer performing his professional duty. You can't change what's happened. This childish mood you're in will matter nothing to the Ambrose who's out there on an unfamiliar world, who exists tens of thousands of years from now and is desperate to hear words of consolation as he assumes his role as the hope of all humanity. So put your emotional tantrum to one side, be the spacefarer this corporation has selected, and *give* yourself something."

I bite back a few responses, each more colorful than the

"fuck you" I started with. Just yesterday she was trying to convince me that my clones weren't really me. Now she says I'm talking to my dear sorry self. But this version of me, the one who's paying the real price for the dicking-over that my mom's done, will need whatever solace I can offer. I arrange my cream-colored robe, fingering the silver hem. Just a few hours ago, this robe was on the floor of the Cusk Suite as Devon Mujaba and I writhed on black silk sheets. I still smell like him.

"Fine," I say.

"Go ahead," the director replies. There's no irritation in his voice. I have to sort of like a guy who's so patient with the person who just told him to fuck off. Then again, the woman who holds his career in her hands is also in the room.

The grand window is behind me, a dry plain with the Euphrates snaking in the distance, the sun blazing above it all. This morning's rain is a distant memory. This will be one of the future-me's opportunities to see what Earth looks like. I shiver. "Well, this is weird," I say. I flick my eyes to the projection of the director. "Can you cut that line?"

"It's human. I'd like to keep it," he says. "Because this *is* weird. Ambrose will know that."

Ambrose will know that. My outrage brought me temporary vigor, but now it's draining out of my system, leaving me queasy and sad. I shift my focus back to the camera. "I'm Ambrose Cusk. You know that. Because you're Ambrose Cusk, too." I whistle. Weird doesn't even get halfway to the truth of this. "I'm the original. We split after I had that medical screening. They recorded my, our, brain there. Just yesterday. Now I know the truth. That Minerva's distress beacon never triggered, that mission control lied to me. You needed to believe that, though, to have the will to survive each time you were woken up, so that's why they mapped my neurons while *I* still believed, too."

The director interrupts. "That was beautiful. I loved it. He will, too. Do you think you could maybe not say it was just yesterday, though? It makes it all seem very rushed, and we don't want to shake his confidence."

"It *was* yesterday."

My mother moves so she's behind the camera. I have a second director. Great. "It's fine, we have a complete voiceprint for Ambrose, and can alter whatever we need to digitally in postproduction, as long as we have enough original footage to latch to."

I drop my head into my hands. "I hate this."

"What, that we'd deepfake whatever we need to give the future you his best chance?" my mother asks. "I'm not apologizing for that. Those stakes are far higher than whatever you're feeling right now. This is about the future of us, long after these physical bodies are gone."

I straighten in my seat. "I want my violin on board the *Endeavor*."

"Your violin?"

"Yes. I can buy another one to play on Earth. But . . ." I don't know how to refer to them. The other versions of me? I grit my teeth and just go ahead with naming them, despite my brain's protests. "Those Ambrose clones are going to be surrounded by polycarb—"

The director interrupts. "—we're calling them 'human-originated hydrocarbons' in the ship's technical specifications. We want to have the technical language on Cusk evolve past the words of today."

"Too late, you already nanoteched my mind yesterday, and I'll be thinking of it as 'polycarb,' no matter what you tell me to think it is. Anyway, I'll be wanting the feeling of something organic on that ship. I'll be desperate for it. Put it on board."

The director's projection casts its gaze in my mother's direction. I'm stepping into some complicated ongoing conversation. "A violin is something the ship can't print anew," my mother finally tells me. "Which means that we could be introducing discrepancies in the repeating timeline, if and when it degrades or is damaged. Even if the violin is kept in ideal conditions between lifetimes, it's hard to imagine soft spruce wood surviving these thousands of years."

"So some Ambroses at the end might not have a violin,

and some will. What's the big deal?" I ask.

The director casts my mother another glance: *See?* I seem to have inadvertently taken his side of the debate.

Mother has entered debugging mode; her mind is spinning fast, but it's all on logistics. This zeal for process makes her a great chairperson for the Cusk Corporation. Parent, less so.

I don't know what I'm gunning for, exactly. But Devon Mujaba's—and Sri's—call to action is resonating in me. I want to do something. I don't know what it is yet. The key for now is getting access. The specifics can come later.

"I'm putting the violin on the ship," I say. "Despite what you've done to me—both this me, the *me* me, and the ones you've created—I haven't gone blabbing to reporters. All I ask in return is that you allow me on, to see where twenty of me will spend their sorry short lives. I'll drop my violin off in person. You've captured my conversation in this room from every angle you need, my mouth shaping every syllable it takes to make me say whatever you like. You'll have me say whatever you want to future Ambrose, I'm sure of it. You can pretend the violin was your idea the whole time."

Mother shakes her head. "The *Endeavor* has been scanned and sealed. No one is going on board again before it launches."

I check my bracelet. It's a pointless gesture, though,

since—like last time—its signal has been jammed in this room. "We have the rescheduled press announcement in four hours. Do you want me to be there?"

Her eyes narrow. *Are you extorting me?*

I nod. *Why yes, I am extorting you.*

"Fine," she says. "This actually gives us a nice cover for placing you up in low orbit rather than down on the Earth's surface."

"And why would you want to have me in orbit?"

"You've seen the news," Mother says. "Dimokratía's secretary of defense has been killed. Brasilia is in open conflict, and it's led to uprisings in Montreal and Minsk. The saga of the new mission to colonize a planet won't have the pacifying power it had even yesterday. If the war spreads global, the safest place will be in orbit. I want me and my family safely in the Cusk secure satellite until things calm down. Your siblings are being transferred there as we speak."

Fine. I'll watch from low-orbit luxury as the planet blows itself up, if that's what she wants. "I'm bringing someone with me, then," I say.

She sighs, undoubtedly disappointed that I'm letting my emotions carry such weight in my decision-making. "Berths in orbit are restricted today. Everyone with any Cusk influence is trying to get a spot. I'm afraid that I can't—"

"Do you want me at that press announcement or not?"

Unfortunately for her, she knows it's no idle threat that I'll go missing. And I know she can't spare the precious minutes it would take to try to talk me out of it. She sighs. "Fine. Name them."

An hour later. Express elevator ride to the ground floor. Sharp steps through the Cusk lobby, landkeeper goons keeping pace with me as I stalk past the real koi and the projected frogs.

I bracelet-message Sri, and they're waiting for me outside the Cusk academy hangar, a hastily packed duffel across their shoulder and my violin case in their hand.

"Thanks for the Devon Mujaba present," I say as I embrace them.

"Thought you'd enjoy it," Sri says.

Seeing the landkeepers flanking me, Sri doesn't say anything more. They just look at the space elevator, eyebrows rising.

"Now let's get the fuck out of here," I say.

CHAPTER 6

I take Sri's hand in mine as we head toward the space elevator terminal. Hand-holding isn't something we generally do, Sri and I. Maybe I'm a little shaken. Maybe that night with Devon Mujaba has opened a new hunger inside me for physical contact. (Maybe my hands are a little sweaty, too, but Sri doesn't seem much to mind.)

My violin case is bulky in Sri's other hand, knocking against their thigh. I reach around and take it.

"Is this stupid?" I ask. "Sending a seven-hundred-year-old violin into outer space?"

Sri cocks their head. "If you sold that violin instead, you could house fifty refugees for a year, if that's what you mean."

I look at the case in my hand. "You're really no fun sometimes, you know that?"

"Justice isn't known for being fun, no," Sri says with fake solemnity.

"No wonder you and Devon Mujaba are such good friends," I say, giving one of their nipples a crank in revenge. They crank me right back, before I can cover myself. "Asshole," I gasp.

We just manage to find our composure before the elevator doors open. Because I'm still a Cusk, we get an onyx car into orbit. Landkeepers escort us to the elevator door, and no doubt landkeepers will meet it to deliver us to the *Endeavor*, but in the meantime we get half an hour of privacy as we ride. Well, "privacy." It's a Cusk elevator, and there's no way my mother doesn't have someone somewhere monitoring our conversation. But we're the only two organic bodies inside.

"Going to the ship will feel strange," I say. "Seeing where other versions of me will be spending their lifetimes."

Sri stays quiet. They're a crouch-before-you-leap type, so I know I'm about to hear something I don't want to know.

"You're a scientist of the heart," Sri says. "Even if you don't feel it now, all the details about the ship will be important to you. Where you'll eat breakfast and where you'll lay your head. You'll fixate on it if you don't get some answers now." A few weeks ago, during our latest breakup, Sri went on a tirade about my similarities to Minerva and my mother, that I never said I was sorry or that I'd messed anything up or that I didn't know something, and that made it impossible to get truly close to me. That I was always conquesting and never just being. They'd called me a "scientist of the heart" meanly then, but this time they say the phrase neutrally, like we finally know each other

185

well enough to be at peace with who we are to each other.

I certainly do know that Sri's right that I'm still in shock, that I probably can't trust my own instincts. I'm grateful that I can lean on them to know what's best for me, since I can't do that for myself. Ah. Now I know why I'm holding their hand! Why am I such a mystery to myself sometimes?

"So," Sri says. I tense, worried that they're going to launch into whatever next veiled critique they're planning to drop on me, probably some version of how I'm not using my Cusk influence to save millions of people, etcetera. "Tell me *everything* about hooking up with Devon Mujaba."

"Ooh, gladly," I say.

Unlucky for her, if Mother is listening in right now, she's getting every detail of Devon Mujaba's body. Down to the placement of each mole. I run my hand along the uniform fabric covering the back of my pelvis. "There's a smattering there. Like a dash of pepper."

"Sounds delightful," Sri says.

"It really was," I say. In the very beginning, we'd get jealous of each other's trysts, but those days are past. Now we're like a couple of intimacy gourmets, excited to hear about each other's good meals.

I lie out flat, so my head is in Sri's lap. They put one arm under my nape and the other around my shoulders. "You're being all soft and tender, it's totally confusing me," they say.

"Yeah, don't worry, it won't last." I move my cheek so I can feel Sri's thigh through the thin fabric of their academy uniform. Bone and muscle and blood. Sex. One solution for the question of where to put an unwelcome feeling.

"I recorded my message to load onto the ship for space-farer you," Sri says. "You'd be proud. It's polished and impersonal and not at all gooey." Sri sucks in their breath. "Sorry to move us on in our conversation too early, but time is short and I have one last Devon Mujaba thought. But I can't say it aloud."

I move my head so I can watch Sri flip open their school satchel and pull out a piece of paper and a pencil. Real live vintage paper and pencil! "You're so pretentious, I can't take it," I say into their lap.

"You haven't seen anything yet." Sri proceeds to bring out a folder. The movement is awkward with my head in their lap, but there's no way I'm moving.

When was the last time anyone used a folder, the 2200s? This one could very well be from then. Its corners are yellowed, and the cardboard cover bends in half even under Sri's light touch.

I laugh. "What are you *doing*?"

They tent the broken folder as best they can over the paper, cursing as they try to write with dull pencil, the paper crinkling over their knee. "How did anyone do this back in the day? Paper is so awkward!"

"I'm pretty sure in the vintage reels they're always sitting at desks. Or tables. Or what was that 2100s horror reel about the exploding businesspeople? They used something called a 'clipboard' as a surface, I think."

"Well, I couldn't find any clipboards in the academy, so my leg will have to do." Sri manages to write a few words with the distractions of weird paper and my head in their lap. "Sit up, and read this in secret," they say, keeping the paper hidden under the folder as they hold it out to me.

I'm not sure what this game is, but it's a welcome distraction. I'm smiling as I look at whatever love note Sri just wrote for me.

My smile drops.

It is not a love note. It's not even a pornographic doodle.

You had your bender. You had your wallow. Now you fix this thing that's been done in your name.

I sit up and take the dull pencil from them. Sri took up handwriting as a hobby, so theirs is surprisingly beautiful. My own looks like a child's scrawl, and cramps up the muscles under my thumb. *That's what DM wants, too. But I don't know what to do. How about I just crawl into a safe satellite suite with you and hope the world doesn't explode beneath us?*

Sri's mouth draws into a tight line. *Stop it*, their mouth says.

If I contradict the Cusk story, they could call it treason,

I continue to write. I don't know how to put words to the other part, the ethics of putting my clones in jeopardy.

So your mother's betrayal is fine, but yours is not?

That doesn't make sense. But I get their meaning: my mother's not the only one who gets to break the rules.

What if my coming out with what's been done in my name means the *Endeavor* never takes off? I could be preventing Cusk Corporation from settling an exoplanet. I'm not sure how I feel about that. Intentional mission failure.

But if outcry means the mission doesn't go, it would mean my clones would never have to wake up into their brief misery. Wouldn't have to sit and wait to be murdered by their ship in the bleak emptiness of space.

The events of the past day make me wonder: Should humans be spreading out to exoplanets in the first place?

The war impending below, the ship about to launch above, me in the elevator in between with only a few hours to act. Will humanity potentially end here, or do we send out a seed for it to continue?

Which do I choose?

My hands shake as I fold the paper and hand it back to Sri. That piece of paper could get us executed. Or at least get Sri executed. I can't imagine they'd kill a Cusk. Maybe one of the lesser siblings, but not me. I stare out the onyx elevator car window at the diminishing Earth. Sri writes for a while, then the paper is back in my view. I sigh and open it.

Look out at this planet. The mass extinction, the storms, the human misery. The mission for the glory of your family name. After one planet, what's next but more?

Sri starts writing more. But I pull the paper away, scrawl my own pathetic handwriting on it. I need all the time I can get. My handwriting is slow and the elevator car is already nearing the end of its ride. *I'm ready to burn it all down. Devon suggested I make a live announcement about the lie. Within the ship, so the reel is more viral. But when I do that, it's only a matter of time until the investigation leads to you.*

Sri considers my words, face impassive. They nod. *I accept that. Now we say goodbye.*

Oh, Sri. I let out a long breath and rest the back of my head against the clear surface of the elevator window, the refugees and rapidly shifting militaries and global storms miles below. Then I write: *Can you get another message to Devon? To meet me?*

They nod again, and then I crush Sri in my arms. They're wearing the handmade necklace I gave them months ago, back when our relationship was monogamous; it's sharp against my collarbones.

Sri has pushed me in the way I needed to be pushed, and now we say goodbye. I can wallow more later. I beam a thought to them: *I'll miss you.*

We part from our hug when the elevator doors open. I

hold my hands together, pointer fingers out, and then spread them in two directions. *You go left, I go right.* Maybe never to meet again.

After space exploration went completely private in the late twenty-first century, giant national craft became obsolete under deregulation, which meant launch satellites got smaller and smaller to service smaller and smaller craft— the type of people who could afford to visit the moon or Mars don't want to get crammed into a spaceliner with strangers. Once the Cusk space elevators were built, spacecraft started being constructed in orbit, never coming to land. If a spaceship never has to withstand high g-forces, it opens up all sorts of possibilities for design.

That all means there's only one spaceport large enough to house an old-school mammoth like the *Endeavor*, so I don't need any help finding my way from the elevator's arrival bay to the right launch satellite. If I *had* needed directions, I could have asked any of the no fewer than six spacekeepers who meet me outside the elevator doors. I'm sure they would call themselves assistants, facilitators, escorts, anything but armed guards, but I know what they're here for. I'm officially a wild card to be kept in check.

The *Endeavor*—or I guess I should call it the *Coordinated Endeavor*, since that's the name that's projected in front of the bay entrance—is in the main hangar, resting on a bed of jetted air, to prevent any damage from contacting the hull of the spaceport. With no one around to fix them, even tiny defects will become cracks that will become ruptures. On a voyage this long, any small blemish could prove fatal.

I'm ready for the look of the *Endeavor*, because I trained on mock-ups of it and because Minerva departed for Titan on an identical craft, the *Salaam*. But as I step into the cavernous space, I see that the *Endeavor* has been doubled. The original *Endeavor* is shaped like something a giant weightlifter would use: a stick with bulbous ends, living quarters at one and slow acceleration engine at the other. That engine has been attached to the engine end of an identical craft, so it's an even longer stick, with living quarter bulbs at either end and a double bulb of machinery in the middle.

After I scan through security, the uniformed facilitator explains that the Dimokratía spacefarer will live and work on one side, while the Fédération spacefarer—"me"—will occupy the other. Given that our countries only communicate in highly brokered summits, and that even those have fallen through lately, the relative isolation of the two spacefarers was deemed necessary unless our countries have a political breakthrough. Given the news today, that seems like a remote possibility indeed.

I take in the *Aurora*. Somewhere in there are twenty

copies of a stranger from a hostile country, who will be my only companion. A young man—all the Dimokratía spacefarers are male—whom I will never meet. *Who are you?*

Violin case clutched at my side, I tread along the observation catwalk that runs above the ship, watching as technicians in jumpsuits and face masks pass UV lamps along the hull, the jets of supporting air setting their hair whipping around their heads as they scan for imperfections. They're accompanied by warbot-framed military robot attendants, providing data support and replacement supplies instead of rocket launchers and machine guns. Warbots are no joke. Even these good shepherd versions give me a sharp pang of fear.

As I make my way down the hangar to the center, where the ships join, I find two clumps of soldiers. They wear slightly different camouflage, flecks of red in the Dimokratía one, blue in the Fédération. The Fédération soldiers take a long time checking and rechecking my authorization, then Dimokratía starts over and does the same, scanning my pass again and again. If I weren't a Cusk scion that the press corps wants to keep happy and quiet until the ship launches, I'd never even be considered to go on board. Even with my status as it is, my chances are low.

While they do their checks, I step back and take in the joint craft. Despite my horror at what's being done, it's awe-inspiring, this colossus of engineering. The same level of grandeur—though not the beauty—of a redwood or a blue whale. Like it or hate it, we humans have done something remarkable.

The red-flecked soldiers get on their bracelets, peering at me while they speak rapid Dimokratía to their higher-ups. I can barely follow. Normally I'd be up in their faces, but the significance of what I'm about to do—beam a tell-all to the world—has me numb. I clutch my violin case in sweaty hands, like I'm waiting to go onstage for a recital. I guess I am.

A Fédération officer turns to me. "I don't think this is going to be solved quickly. They don't want you around the ship unless *they* also have a guest who gets to view the ship. They've got a person lined up already." She drops her voice. "It's ludicrous."

I have a suspicion who's gotten himself on the roster as their guest. But I'll pretend to be outraged for a few moments at least. "Yes, totally ludicrous. Has anyone called Chairperson Cusk about this?" I ask.

"We're trying to pull her out of a meeting right now. But given the invasion this morning, it doesn't look good."

"Invasion?"

She looks at me shrewdly. "Yes. Dimokratía landers have dropped infiltration drones across the lake crossing through Patagonia."

I recognize this officer, a woman with hair dyed a rich

brown red. Her tag says Sharma. She gestures toward my violin. "In any case, the Dimokratía guards don't have a problem with that being on board, as long as we allow them to examine it first. I'll get that process started."

I look at the ship, and the tense soldiers from two countries at war. I'm never getting on this ship.

I shoot for second best. "Can I at least check out the rest of the operation here? Even if I don't get on the *Coordinated Endeavor* itself, it will help me be a little more at peace about what's happening."

Sharma nods. "I don't see why not, so long as I'm with you."

"We won't need special access?"

"You've already got it, to be here in the hangar. We can move freely within a zone of similar clearance."

I place my violin case on the security table, then open it to take one last look at it. We spent many years together, that instrument and me. It was Minerva's at first, but she quit after a year and so it became mine. Vivaldi to Mozart to Mendelssohn to Suarez. My fingers are calloused from my hours of moody vibrato. I latch the case closed and watch Sharma transfer it to the Dimokratía officers. They mount a few stairs, then disappear into the *Aurora*.

"Thanks for helping get it on board," I say to Sharma.

"No guarantees, but it looks likely it will pass Dimokratía inspection. Are you ready?"

I make myself look exasperated. "It's fine by me if they want their Dimokratía guest to come with us, too."

We head off into the spaceport, tailed by one of the Dimokratía soldiers. I wave and smile at him, but he just broods back. I didn't know that someone could brood actively until now.

"This hangar has been locked down for months, limited to the highest clearances," Sharma explains. "We've all been sleeping and working here."

"You must miss your family," I say.

She shrugs, even as she smiles wanly. "Accepting this assignment got them out of Melbourne and onto the Telos satellite. It was an easy choice."

Sharma stops in a makeshift lobby area, where two Dimokratía guards are flanking another special guest. One I happen to have recently met.

"Ambrose Cusk," Sharma says, "I'm not sure if you're already familiar with Devon Mujaba?"

Devon grins broadly and holds out his hand. "Nice to meet you, Ambrose. It's an honor." The smile drops. "I'm very sorry to hear about your sister."

I shake his hand, remembering where else it has been recently. "Thanks for your kind words," I say formally. "It's an honor to meet you, too."

"That's so nice to hear," Devon says coolly.

"We're taking reciprocity down to the letter here these days," Sharma says. "Dimokratía had only a couple of hours to pick their own VIP guest to the facility, and Devon Mujaba was already in local orbit."

"I played a quinceañera on Disponar," Devon says. "Not sure if you noticed. It was a very last-minute booking. Since I was already here, the Dimokratía foreign minister thought he'd pass me a favor."

I look at Sharma, drawing on all my playacting skills. "So Devon knows . . ."

"He already knows the content of the upcoming press briefing, that the mission has changed to colonization," Sharma says.

"The true mission . . . wow," Devon says. "This must be a complicated time for you." He winks. He actually *winks*. The daringness makes me flush.

"Shall we?" Sharma says. "Even if we can't go on board the ship, we can walk the observation platforms."

Devon and I fall into step behind her, hands behind our backs. He smiles at me, almost says something but bites it down. Instead he keeps up that convincing fake smile.

"Sri told you I'm up for a broadcast?" I whisper.

"Yes, they did," he replies. "It's time the truth was told. I'll start the recording whenever you give me a nod. It will be sent out live. The violin case . . ."

"Already on."

"Did you . . ." He makes a motion of his hands flying apart from each other.

I shake my head sharply. Does he really think I'd put a *bomb* on board?! Of course not. And yet Devon looks disappointed.

His expression makes me wonder if I should back out of this whole plan. Devon would have been okay if I detonated the ship? I realize all over again that I really don't know him or what he's capable of.

"This moment will change history," Devon says. "Maybe now human civilization will break out of the Cusk Corporation vise. I'm proud of you."

Compliments from Devon Mujaba on top of utter dread. My stomach doesn't know which way is up.

Tailed by the soldiers, Sharma guides us through labs and holding areas. This is the cauldron where the Frankenstein versions of myself are prepped. I pretend to be curious, calm. Like a museum visitor instead of the protagonist of a horror reel.

I'm not sure my pretending to be calm is convincing Sharma. "You seem to be taking the change in mission in stride," she says as we pass along cavernous hallways, crates with obscure codes painted on their sides in Fédération or Dimokratía language, draped in army-green netting. Her tone indicates she means the opposite.

I shrug, like she just did. "The Ambroses on that ship are not me. Not really."

She smiles sadly, like I haven't yet realized something about my own feelings. "I can only imagine what you're going through. It's been a big few days for you."

"Yes," I say crisply. She's rising above her station.

"May I ask what's in here?" Devon interrupts.

She has brought us past a smaller lab. The door is a thick material, so that whatever is inside can be kept at a constant temperature. Through the window, I can see vertical vinyl flaps, to prevent too much airflow. Most likely something organic is stored here. Devon has a good eye.

Sharma cuts a glance at the Dimokratía officer nearest us, then stands with us at the door's window. "This is where we keep the embryos that will produce generations of human life on Planet Cusk. Over a thousand of them, from discrete lineages across the Earth. Of course, half are from regions held by Fédération, half by Dimokratía. We are very careful about fairness."

Devon gives a hard-to-interpret snort. "They're not really embryos yet," he says. "The genetic code has been joined but gestation hasn't begun, so these are really just chunks of biological data. They can't be considered embryos until they begin to divide and grow on the exoplanet."

Sharma blinks. "Is that so?"

"A Heartspeak Boy and also an amateur biologist.

You're quite the renaissance man, Devon Mujaba," I say.

"No, no science background, just fascinated by this mission. I've spent the last hour researching as much as I can about what it would involve." Devon flashes his demolishing sunray of a grin again.

"And we should move on," Sharma says, cutting an eye to the Dimokratía guard tapping an impatient finger on his plasma rifle.

The hallway has curved around the expanse of the ship, and as we come to the end we're again in the cavernous hangar space, the sleeping *Coordinated Endeavor* hulking below us. Only now we're on a catwalk that runs above the *Aurora* portion before ending at the central joint where that ship meets the *Endeavor*. "May we?" Devon asks, gesturing along the catwalk.

Sharma glances at the time on her bracelet and nods. "If you keep it quick."

The inspection catwalk is so narrow that we have to go single-file. We wait for a refitted warbot to clear the gangway before we start. Devon goes first, and I follow, my stomach churning. "I'll meet you back here," Sharma says, deep in her bracelet messages.

We go a few paces down the catwalk, its metal ringing out under our boots. "Anyone following?" Devon asks.

I scratch my chin against the fabric on one shoulder so that I can casually glance behind us. "No. There's only one exit point, and Sharma and the soldier are just waiting there."

"Looks like a pretty good stage," Devon whispers as we come to a stop at the end of the catwalk. "The ship below, all these lethal warbots milling around, to remind viewers of the weapons of war. A producer couldn't design better."

I stand next to him, looking down at the ship. "I'm going to pretend to be overwhelmed. That I need a hug," I say. "For Sharma's sake. So she doesn't wonder why we're lingering."

"What?"

I lean into him, press my head against his neck. "Oh," he says.

The hug is nice. Very nice. But it's not the point. Devon's smooth arms are around me, and I feel his hand reach into the fold of my wrap. My hand meets his within the fabric, and I find the streamer. It's a small device the size and shape of a dragonfly that transmits to a secure server and pings the connection using dedicated hardware to confirm it's happening in real time. Without that level of verification, no one will believe what I'm about to say.

"Do you want to start it off, or . . . ," I ask.

"You're doing this alone," Devon whispers, stepping back from our embrace. "You're a Cusk. Of course your mother will do whatever it takes to shield you from what comes next. I don't have that luxury. I'd rather not be executed."

"You're Devon Mujaba," I say. "Not exactly an unknown."

"All the better to make an example of me. Even with war broken out, they're going to fight to hold this consortium together long enough to launch the mission. If they can't unite the people through hope, fear will do just as well."

He's right. I just don't want to do this alone.

Devon can see I'm waffling. He puts a hand on each of my shoulders. "They lied to you about your life's purpose. They dishonored your sister. They have this coming. You're doing the right thing."

"I don't know . . . ," I start to say.

Devon reaches into the fold of my robe, hands digging along the belt of muscle over my hips, until he finds the streamer again. He pulls it out, clicks it, and tosses it into the air so it hovers before me. "Show's on," he says. I hear his rapid footfalls on the catwalk as he heads back toward Sharma and the guards.

I stare at the hovering streamer, which sends out an array of light to pick up every pore of my skin, all the magnitude of the joined ship, every authenticating detail of my surroundings. Devon hurled it in such a direction that my body mostly shields what I'm doing from the view of Sharma and the guards, but I still don't have much time until they catch on and forcibly stop me.

Ambrose Cusk is broadcasting from the ship he was supposed to pilot to rescue Minerva. That's a draw—lots of people's bracelet OSes will autoplay this one. Already the watching count on the streamer has ticked up into the tens of millions.

How to start? I'll try to start by not throwing up. "I'm going to make this quick," I manage to say despite the fear that sets my body shaking. "The mission to rescue my sister wasn't canceled because of new information. It wasn't scrubbed at all. It was never meant to go. Dimokratía and Fédération lied to you, trying to misdirect your attention from what matters. By manipulating you. They lied to me, too. It's all so that my clones would believe. There's a Dimokratía spacefarer on board as well. That's his ship you see. They lied to him, too. Our copies will live disposable lives on a trip to an exoplanet, where only the last clone will survive. I have been spun a tale to keep me pacified, while they did this in my name. Just like they are doing to all of you."

I hear bootfalls ring out on the catwalk behind me, harsh words in Dimokratía.

"I don't have much time," I say. "This mission can't go, not if you resist. Not now that you all know the truth. It's immoral. It's dishonest. They've lied to all of us. They'd never have told you about this future, because it means Cusk has decided its destiny is off-planet. That you are doomed."

Rough hands are on my back, hurling me away from the

203

catwalk. "I'm Ambrose Cusk!" I shout.

Then I hear the readying of a gun, the click of a trigger. The streamer flutters to the hull of the *Aurora*, hopping once and then giving up, like it's been slain.

I cover my face where I lie on the ground, as boots clomp on the catwalk around me. I can understand the Dimokratía language when I concentrate, but right now I can't manage it. I just hold my hands in front of my face, waiting to be killed. Then I'm heaved to my feet, my wrap swirling around me, and dragged roughly along the catwalk, sandaled feet bumping rhythmically along the metallic mesh of the walkway as I try and fail to stand on my own.

Sharma is ashen. "What have you done?" she asks.

I shake my head, beyond words.

"I was in charge of you," she says, putting her hand over her mouth. "What have you done to *me*?"

I hadn't thought about that. I just needed to speak the truth.

She's not angry. She's terrified. "The world is falling into war. And you expected people to stop fighting to protest this mission? How naive can you be?"

The guards drop me in the hallway. They shout at each other, bracelet-messaging their commanders. I hear footfalls as the Fédération guards rush to join them. These soldiers will no doubt bring me to my mother.

If I want to get out of here before I'm arrested, this is my one chance. While everything is still chaos.

Now, Ambrose. Act *now.*

Will the Dimokratía guards shoot me, even though I'm Ambrose Cusk? I honestly don't know.

I stagger to my feet.

I swallow my vomit.

And I run.

CHAPTER 7

Streamed live to tens of millions of people, now surely watched by a billion or more as the newsreels run it on loop. My mother and her board breaking from managing the last details of the launch to deal with this new crisis. Their careful rollout of the truth hijacked. The people on this launch satellite catching up about the presence of this traitor—or hero, if I'm damn lucky—among them.

Sharma's words ring in my head. Do I really imagine this will have an effect on a day like today? Does it need to, for me to have had reason to speak the truth? I don't know.

As I run, I realize there's probably a hundred people searching for me right now. They'll be searching for Devon Mujaba, too. He must have fled during my recording. Hopefully he's already off this satellite.

Cusk will want to get me back under their control as soon as they can. Within minutes, the order will be processed to apprehend me, and the surveillance systems will be coded to find my face. Already, using my own onyx card would lead to my immediate arrest, I'm sure. Luckily, I can still use Minerva's. Hopefully. Her last act to me has bought me some extra minutes.

My steps automatically bring me toward the elevator that leads back down to a planet at the brink of war. There's no way I could pull off getting the clearances to travel to another satellite without getting nabbed. The only place where I have a chance to get truly lost is Earth—and the elevator down operates in a long train that can't be stopped for individual cars. As long as one of my onyxes gets me on, I can probably travel down without being stopped.

Of course, my mother wanted me to stay up here for my own well-being. If the war below goes nuclear, then orbit is a safer place to be—the anti-missile shields in low orbit will attack and disarm warheads on their relatively long journey up this far. On Earth, there are no such guarantees.

But I will have autonomy down there. Up here, who knows how long I'll be under arrest until the trial begins. Trust my fate to people who would do this to my clones, to me? No.

I weave through narrow familiar Cusk hallways, using my Minerva card to get me into the privileged-access passageways that might help me lose the guards. Finally, I hurtle through a set of double doors and burst into the public areas of the satellite terminal.

About a half dozen people going about their business stop to take in the Roman-garbed Cusk scion who's sprung into their midst. I bring myself to an absolute stop, arms pinwheeling, then switch to a fast walk, avoiding meeting the curious gazes.

I zig into the shopping area of the launch station and dart through the racks of a children's clothing store, emerging into the mall on the far side.

No one is shopping. Even since this morning, there's a new frantic energy to the satellite. People are rushing here and there, and no one blinks as I, too, break into a jog.

I'm anonymous for now, but this ludicrous outfit isn't helping. I rip the stupid circlet from my head and let it ring out on the floor. No one looks. Some people are recently arrived, those connected enough to have secured elevator passage off Earth. Others are satellite residents, fighting to get their loved ones up to join them. Emboldened, I bunch my wrap in my fist and break out into a run, my sandals clapping the glossy floor. I expect to hear alarms, or guards shouting after me, but there's just the sound of my breath and the sight of frightened Cusk employees parting, watching me dash past before they continue on their own frantic way. Some of them have watched my stream, I'm sure. I can only imagine what they're thinking about me.

Or maybe—the thought comes as a relief—they're not thinking of me at all.

Even if I make it through this satellite with my current clothes, that won't work to keep me anonymous if and when I make it to Earth's surface. I stop at a drab clothing provisioner, grab the nearest jumpsuit I can, go to pay for it at the exit with my bracelet. The terminal dings and flashes red. Not good. This feed will be flagged for viewing by satellite security. I back up, jumpsuit in my hands, and prepare to break out into a sprint.

"I'll pay for it," says a calm voice. One I recognize.

Devon Mujaba is at the doorway, tapping it with his bracelet to pay for the jumpsuit. He looks at me, winks. "My treat."

"It's you," I say intelligently.

The exit doorway flashes red again. Now the system is catching up to my first invalid transaction. The whole ceiling above us lights up red. "Oh shit," Devon Mujaba says. "Not my treat after all. Go!"

"Stop!" comes a voice from one side, and I see the camouflage of a Fédération landkeeper.

"Run!" Devon says.

We shove our way through the throngs. Booted landkeeper footfalls behind us, more shouts around and ahead. I reach a hand out and find Devon's, sweaty with adrenaline. I grip it tight.

There it is: the onyx elevator, doors open, ready to bring us to the surface. No one is boarding the cars heading down. We just have to make it through the satellite's crowded arboretum, the milling crowds of people watching for arriving loved ones. There are bright green trees around us, blackness and starlight above.

Imagining hands on my back, an arc thrower zapping me, bullets through my neck, I hunch down and sprint the last stretch, switching to a desperate crawl after I trip over someone's ankle.

"Ambrose," Devon gasps beside me. "I can't go!"

I whirl and face him, aghast. "What?"

He taps his onyx card against the reader, and it angrily bleats back. "I'm deactivated. You must be, too."

The landkeepers push their way through the crowds, toward us. Only seconds remain.

I tap Minerva's onyx card against the reader. The security gate opens. Only one person can go through at a time, or the whole system errors. I've seen it happen multiple times, mostly by privileged jerks trying to piggyback on their friends' status.

"Devon, maybe you can try to enter with me—" I start to say. But I can't finish the sentence, because the air has been forced out of my lungs by Devon Mujaba's fists.

He's shoved me. Into the elevator. I tumble through the security gate, fall to my knees as the gate begins to close.

"Read your body!" he shouts.

Read my body? What the hell does that mean? But I don't have time to ask before I'm sealed into the sound-proofed elevator car.

I press myself against the glass wall of the elevator,

watching the receding arboretum. I remember my other counterfeit onyx, but it's too late. Devon Mujaba turns to face the approaching landkeepers, hands up in surrender. I can see why: they have a warbot with them. Probably called up from the surface. They order Devon to the ground, and he gets to his knees and then lies flat. Arrested.

The arboretum and the satellite pass out of view.

I'm descending toward Earth.

The car speeds up after it joins the train of elevator cars heading down. From what I can see, every single earthward one is empty. Heading up, however: masses of people are jammed into each, the desperate expressions of people fleeing a planet at war.

I have a momentary fear that the landkeepers will tell their superiors about my location, will stop the elevators and return me to the satellite. But that would mean shutting down this whole apparatus, blocking the flood of refugees. Even though I'm a high-profile target, I can't imagine they'd stop this exodus on my account.

I might be arrested on arrival, of course. But hopefully I can count on the war turmoil to have scrambled the authorities on the ground. Or perhaps my mother will have mercy—she already wanted me away from the dangerous surface, so it's hard to imagine she'd have me imprisoned there. Though what do I actually know of my mother?

What's going to happen to Devon Mujaba? Will they

start a neuroscan of him? If so, it will be a matter of time before they get all the information his brain holds. They'll know just what we discussed, what he knows about the Dimokratía spacefarer.

Read your body.

I flip on the headlines to have as much situational awareness as possible on my arrival seventeen minutes from now. I listen to the news while I prepare to change clothes.

The silky material of my cream-colored wrap falls soundlessly to the elevator floor. I sit my naked ass on the velvet bench of the onyx car, whisking the jumpsuit from its folded square, unbuttoning the front so I can slip into the smooth technical material. It will be good for traveling in. Wish I'd stolen some underwear, too, though.

Read your body.

I look down at my naked body, backgrounded by the blue and green of the approaching Earth.

My feet, calves, thighs. Wait.

At first I think I have some kind of parasite, but then I realize I'm seeing a string of black text, neatly scripted along my inner thigh.

Someone has written on me. The only person who had access to do so without my knowing is Devon Mujaba, while I was passed out during our naked bender.

The writing is scripted by hand, not printed. I imagine

him leaning over my leg, diligently marking me while I slept.

I'm seeing a sequence of numbers, followed by two unfamiliar words.

I read my own leg, squinting as the numbers end near the crease where thigh meets hip. 56.808095, −5.085725.

Those are the numbers. They're coordinates.

Below them is a name.

Kodiak Celius.

PART THREE

MINERVA (SAGITTARION BB)

YEAR 18

YARROW

CHAPTER 1

The moment she appears on the horizon, I can tell Owl didn't find the mystery beacon. It's not like she's dragging her feet or sobbing or anything, but I know my sister's movements better than my own. She twirls her spear in the air, experimenting with the heft of it. Trying to convince herself that she's unbothered.

I open the gate and stand in the broad plain outside the settlement, pitching my shovel into the soil so I can rest my chin on the handle. The polycarb bends under the weight of my head.

"No luck, huh?" I ask once she's near enough.

Owl blows past, giving her head one furious shake.

I know not to push when she's feeling hassled. Instead I tail after her, letting the shovel drag behind me.

I keep myself within view of Owl as I return to my day's task, which is the same task I had yesterday and will have tomorrow: shoveling. We need to process many tons of hydrocarbons to make our bunker, in addition to the chromite Father and Rover (and sometimes Owl) have been towing back and forth to the settlement. Dad and OS are making refinements to the blueprints to turn the *Aurora* into a refuge. All of that is more exciting than my task, but I'm the one who requested shovel duty. I don't trust myself to do anything else. So I spend my days in a quiet pit, with the feel of tools under my hands and the cool breeze on my skin. Alone with my thoughts.

Here, away from them all, where it's safe. Where they're safe.

Everything is better when I'm alone. When I'm in the flow state of shoveling, I don't imagine them dead as often.

Neither Father nor Owl is towing metal at the moment, which means I get Rover's help. We're running two different tarps back and forth. I work on filling one, while Rover shuttles the other to the processor, returning with an empty tarp that I then begin to fill. I count the shovelfuls, to keep my focus on work. Twenty-three is my standard before Rover returns. Sometimes I get as many as twenty-six in before Rover starts hauling them away.

This latest one is just nine. I let my thoughts distract me. If Rover notices, it makes no sign.

One. Two. Three. The soil makes a pleasant rasp against the tarp as it scatters on the surface.

Four. Five. Six. *Thwisp, thwisp, thwisp.*

Seven. Eight. Nine. Heads, caved and cratered. A rasping cry. Hair and blood.

Ten. Eleven. Twelve. I let out a long breath, control the speed of my shovelfuls. Bring air back in slowly. Try to make each shovelful contain the exact same amount of soil.

Thirteen. Fourteen. Fifteen. Minerva, open-sky beauty. Our home.

Sixteen. Seventeen. Eighteen. My calluses creak and shriek. Good.

Nineteen. Twenty. Twenty-one. The tarp stretches over Father's face. He clutches at it, trying frantically to free his airway before he suffocates.

Twenty-two. Twenty-three. Twenty-four. It's Dad who's dead now, his corpse dangling from a fence post.

When the visions started, they were just bodies laid out, death without murder. Now sometimes I'm standing over my family, my muscles aching with the effort of strangling them all. After I've pushed the vision from my mind, the feeling of exertion in my muscles is as vivid as if I really have just done it.

Every time I banish one thought, another arrives. But when I'm alone I don't feel like I need to hide them as much. The violent visions aren't intruding then. They're just visiting.

Because I know now that these visions can come true. Like removing part of the perimeter fence. I saw that a day before I did it.

It's not like my family is too suspicious of me, even

now—or if they are, they're not at the point where they're going to restrain me. But I have noticed that Father always directs me toward dig sites within monitoring range of OS. It's a smart move. I'd have done the same if faced with the awful prospect of me.

I also noticed they didn't mind that I requested doing this meditative, simple labor. What could I sabotage here? Nothing. I'd have to be really clever to figure out how to ruin soil.

Twenty-five, twenty-six, twenty-seven. This vision is of Owl. It looks like she's fallen from a great height. Her eyes are unseeing, her mouth in a scream, blood coming out of her ears.

"Hello," Rover says, laying the empty tarp out beside me, whisking it in one efficient motion so it lies flat.

"Hi, OS," I say, managing—I think—to keep the tension out of my voice.

"Is everything okay, Yarrow?" it asks. I guess I haven't kept the tension out after all.

"Yep," I say. "Just starting to feel this work in my muscles."

"Please tell me if anything is not okay," OS says.

"Yes. Don't worry," I reply.

Rover drags the tarp to the processor.

One. Two. Three.

* * *

Owl must have pushed herself hard on this latest attempt to find the beacon. On my break, I find her sprawled out on her bed, left arm and leg dangling so far off the side that they're touching the ground. If she even breathes the wrong way, she'll fall off entirely.

Gently, trying not to wake her, I nudge her more squarely onto the mattress.

Her eyes blink open. She stretches and smiles when she sees me. "Oh, hi," she says. She opens and closes her mouth. "I think I was very sleepy."

"I bet you were," I say. "That was the longest excursion yet. Hey, move over."

I get in the bed, lie alongside her.

"You are a very sweaty brother," she says.

It's cold enough today that I don't think I have any sweat still on my body. But if she means that I smell sweaty, then yes. That's definitely true. I am quite fragrant. "I take it you couldn't find any sign of the beacon," I say.

She shakes her head. "This was my fifth try. It's so frustrating."

"OS keeps scanning frequencies. I'm sure the beacon is transmitting its location somehow, but it's just not transmitting in a language we're listening with. We'll catch it eventually."

"I don't know," Owl says. "I've had a lot of time to think on my treks. If that beacon was Earth tech, which is fair to assume, then it had to be incredibly light to be shot out at interstellar speeds without its own power source. Even the most basic transmitter would add a lot of weight. It's probably got a detectable signature instead, and isn't beaming a powered signal. We just have to be close enough for Rover or a handheld to pick up on it."

I nod. This makes sense.

"Did you have any new thoughts about our theories?" Owl asks. I don't think she's actually interested in our theories. I think she just wants me to say something so she'll know I'm not currently in a weird spell.

"I just spent ten days doing nothing but shoveling soil. I had plenty of time to think about our theories, yes." Suddenly I imagine snuggling Owl so tight to me that it crushes her. Her ribs snap. I shudder and turn on my side so I'm facing away from her. "I didn't have any insights, though."

She rests her hand on my shoulder. I sigh in relief that I'm worth touching.

"And how are you feeling?" she asks. She paused long enough that she probably debated a while about whether I'd be mad she asked.

I'm really tired of that question. But it's also nice to know my family cares. "I'm still liking our old-clone hypothesis," I say. "That the beacon was sent from the *Coordinated Endeavor* sometime earlier in its journey."

"But what would they have wanted to tell us so much

that they went to that effort?" Owl says. "That's what I don't get. Why not, you know, just leave a message inside the ship?"

"I don't know," I say, hands pinioned between my knees. I count Owl's breaths against my neck. "They want to say something they were worried OS would censor, maybe?"

"Not knowing is killing me," Owl said.

"Yeah," I say, feeling a surge of excitement at that word. *Killing.* "Me too."

I wake up from our nap before Owl does, and go stand by the edge of the perimeter fence, looking out at the distant malevors, those terrestrial herbivores who decided to attack us on sight. I wonder what they know of us, how they came to their decision. I know it's probably not a conscious thing on their part, that it's nothing specific we did; the baby yaks born here without parents didn't have anyone to teach them how to be, and that's not their fault.

I'm tempted to deactivate the gate, to see what would happen if I went out into the midst of them. Maybe we could come to understand one another. Or maybe they'd end my existence with one strike of those sharp horns.

Why would I imagine my life ending? Am I starting to have another fugue episode? Or are thoughts like these part of what it means to be a normal human? Is everyone tempted to step into a pit, just to test if it will really be the end? Maybe the humanness comes in the resisting.

I turn to face inward. Our settlement looks fragile and hopeful under the setting Sisters. This frontier house, so underpowered in the face of a vast undiscovered world. Cuckoo is bright in the sky, nearly in Sky Cat's teeth. Below it huddle our inflated structures, trembling in the Minervan wind. At the far edge of the fence is the nearly submerged wreck of the *Endeavor*, including the room with the gray portal that contains the thousands of Earth zygotes inside it. Where I emerged just over sixteen years ago.

I've done this walk many times. Paced the boundaries of our home and prison, soil lighting up under my feet. Still, I begin the walk yet again. My feet bring me to the portal that produced me. I lean my ear against the hull of the old ship, feel the slight *whoomp* every 1.3 seconds that gives the gestating fetus the experience of Earth's gravity. *Who will you be?* It's already predetermined. By a machine. I hope this sibling survives.

In a few minutes the dinner bell will ring, and we'll sit down to our evening meal, will answer the same prompts and repeat the same stories and wonderings. Everyone will talk to and around and over me, will avoid the Thing, will reward every normal thing that I do and bristle at every weird thing that I do. They don't want any part of the new me. They want this new Yarrow, the one that they have to worry about, to go away.

But he will not go away.

I don't want to pretend anymore. I just want to *be*, and feel like that's okay. Maybe if I could be alone with Owl for a few days, or even alone with Dad, I could warm up enough to just let it all out, tell them how many times I've imagined them all dead, and then I'd feel better. But Father . . . I can feel the heat of his gaze on me, the worry and the disappointment, the need to have everyone be normal and focus on the productive future and not worry about the past or even the present. *Just be strong, Yarrow*, he'd say. *You can fight this off.*

I can try that. I have been trying that. I have been failing. But I can keep trying. I should not burden them.

Even before this change came up within me, Father wished he could erase the part of me that wanted to know about the past. If he could remake me without the morbid tendency to wonder about the lost, fateful Earth, he would do it.

But I'm not my sister. I am not the copy of someone whose history we all know. All of Earth is my heritage. I can't give that up.

My footsteps have brought me to the Museum of Earth Civ. Owl's and my playground, before she moved on and stopped building with me. Here are the mock-ups we made from scrap polycarb, vehicles and buildings and monuments from Earth's history. Tanks and horses and an Eiffel

Tower and Cristo Redentor. All crude and ugly. They're sprinkled with actual artifacts: the felty scraps that remain of the playing cards from the *Coordinated Endeavor*, Dad's broken and time-softened violin in its dinged-up case.

Now, too, the duck skeleton. I've kept it hidden under a rag, because I know how alarming it would look to the rest of my family. I've glued the bones together with molten polycarb, dropped dirt onto the hot printings so it would have the color of plumage. The head is still just a skull on a lumpen body with broken bones sticking out of it. I wanted to see what a duck would look like. To know a new animal. But I made a monster.

Dry-eyed, I stamp the skeleton into the dirt. Stupid broken Yarrow.

Breathing heavily from the exertion, I feel what little scraps of excitement I got from ruining the skeleton drain away. The feeling that's left behind when the buzz fades is loneliness. I feel *alone*. It is the biggest emotion of them all, huge and elemental and utterly dominating. There used to be an "us" in my world, and it got taken away by my own mind.

What was it that Dad once said? *Intimacy is the only shield against insanity.* Okay. But how can I be close to my family if they don't want me to be who I truly am? Since I don't want to witness their disappointment all day every day, my darkness must be a secret. And that makes me feel ashamed. It's the dearest friend of loneliness, shame.

I'm tempted to wreck the rest of the Museum of Earth Civ, but if I did Owl would notice and we'd have to talk about it. No one knew about the reconstructed duck, so I can avoid all that painful talking about feelings and actions if I just stop here.

I walk back by the gestation unit and rap my knuckles against its siding. I do hope you survive, little one. I hope your lungs are strong enough to breathe this air, and that frontier life doesn't claim you. I hope that you live until you're sixteen and that when you do, you don't find a new and sudden darkness blooming inside you.

The bell for the evening meal goes. Rover glides over to the table, tray hovering above its spherical body. It's the same meal as yesterday and the day before. I imagine one of the lavish dinner sequences from *Pink Lagoon* and find myself wondering if one of those characters would be able to understand me. There were billions of people on Earth. Surely there were some who would relate to the surprises happening inside my brain. Maybe my loneliness isn't from the fact that something is wrong with me. Maybe it's from having too few other humans around.

I stalk across the settlement, planning my path so I'll cross Father's as he walks toward dinner, mopping his brow. Back in the before, we were the closest pair of all of us. We'd work together for long hours in quiet, the only communication from him a squeeze on my shoulder as we headed back in for the day. Now he often avoids looking at me. He probably thinks I don't notice.

He looks up when I cross in front of his path, and unexpectedly tries to chat. "Yarrow. What's going on? Want to walk over to dinner?"

These are strange words for him. He's probably been practicing them. "Sure," I say. "Sounds good."

I start walking and then stop again. This walk won't be long enough to give me time to say what I'm yearning to say.

"Yarrow?" Father prompts.

"I need to talk to you about something," I say.

He surprises me by coming to a stop, facing me directly, giving me his full attention. "Of course. What is it?"

I hadn't imagined he'd take the direct route. I'm grateful, even as I struggle to find words. "I . . . thanks. Um. I know you know that life has been strange for me lately, that I'm having these thoughts . . . that intrude?" I see pain enter Father's eyes, his pain at the thought of my pain. It makes me want to eat my words back up until I choke on them. "I think it's getting better, I really do, I think I've got it under control." No, I don't. Coward. "But I also think, now that I'm sixteen, and an adult, at least sort of, I want to access it all. To know all of Earth's history. I want to make that choice. To know as much of my origins as I can. Like the

Museum of Earth Civ, only for real."

He looks at me. Deeper than anyone else in my life does, even Owl. When Father sees, he *sees*. All is still for a long moment.

I continue. "Owl is connected to Dad, because she's his sister. She knows where she came from. You knew the Celius provincial orphanage, even though your parents left you there before you knew them. I'm the only one of us who doesn't have a background. Like any at all. It's sort of killing me, not knowing the past."

He shrugs.

I cock my head. Did he really just *shrug*?

"You're right," he says, "you're an adult now. If it will make you feel better, you can learn whatever you want to learn. I'll tell OS to give you the same full access to its systems that your dad and I have."

"You think Dad will be okay with that?" I ask.

Father smiles, just from thinking of him. "You and I both know that I'm the one who's been the roadblock on this front, not him."

I just stand there, flabbergasted. Father nods toward the table, where Owl and Dad are peering at us nervously. He whispers, "Okay if we continue on our way to dinner?"

"Yeah, sure."

We walk side by side, Father holding my hand like he used to do when I was a child. Owl raises an eyebrow at me as we approach. I give a shrug. *What, just bonding with Father. No big deal.*

"So," Dad says, giving me and Father a long look, "how are we all doing today?"

"Very good," I say, tucking my chair close to my portion of algae. "And this looks delicious."

Dad's eyebrows rise. Father notices. "Yarrow would really like full access to Earth history," he explains. "He's sixteen now, so I said he could."

Dad goes still. "You allowed him, just like that?"

Owl whistles.

Father shrugs. "I knew you would be fine with it. You've said as much before."

"Maybe," Dad says slowly. "But I think we should have discussed this first."

"We're discussing it now."

"But you've already given him permission," Dad says, his voice steadily flat. He's got his combustible *the kids need us to be a unified front* tone.

"So when do I—" Owl starts to say.

"You've already gotten permission to go exploring for long periods, and you're only fifteen. Don't push it," I say sharply. I don't need Owl bringing this back to herself like usual and wrecking my plans.

I take Dad's hand in mine. "I really, really think this

will calm my mind. I think I just wanted to know what was being kept from me. It started to occupy all my thoughts, because I didn't know. I got paranoid."

This is sort of true. I do hope this will calm my mind. I also want to have agency over my life, over the settlement, to not feel shut out anymore.

"Can he tell *me* what he finds out about Earth?" Owl asks.

Dad looks at Father. *Well? Did you consider this?*

Father sighs. "No. Not until you're sixteen."

"So wait, I'm going to be the only human in the universe, in all of existence, who doesn't know how Earth worked? And the rest of you are just going to tiptoe around it, or send me away whenever you want to have a private conversation about all these Earth facts you're keeping secret?"

Father sighs. He clearly had not thought this far.

"Don't jump ahead of the game. I haven't found anything out yet," I say, slurping up my algae stew. Sooner I'm done, sooner I get to go sift through the partial internet image that was on the *Coordinated Endeavor*. "OS, are you catching all this?"

"I am," OS replies through Rover.

"Start warming up your memory."

"I have already prepared a forty-seven-minute summary of Earth history for you."

"Ugh, I hate you!" Owl says. She's almost smiling, though. She knows I'll be telling her anything I find out.

And the dads know it, too. But we'll live in this truce state, pretending there are rules, pretending that they aren't being broken. My spoon scratches the bottom of my bowl. "So, can I go 'explore'?" I ask.

Dad sighs. "What have we done?"

Father pats me on the shoulder. "Go, go. Have a good time."

I shove back from my seat, heart thumping. "Thank you, thank you! Coming, Rover?"

Rover whirs into motion, turning a neat somersault beside the table. "Rover needs to help with dinner at the moment," OS says. "But I will come find you in a few minutes to start the projections."

"See you soon!" I say, whooping with glee as I skip across the settlement.

Owl and the dads laugh. It must be a relief to see me excited about something.

I'm relieved, too. I haven't thought about them dead for at least an hour.

My favorite place to watch projections is on the far side of the infirmary. I can lean against the inflatable wall while OS displays reels in front of me, or just listen to audio while I stare out at the Minervan sky. It's where Owl and I have watched a lot of *Pink Lagoon*.

I settle in against the wall. A few minutes later, Rover arrives, whirring to a stop in front of me. "Okay, I'm ready," I tell OS.

OS jumps right in. "After years of short outbreaks of violence, the countries of Earth resorted to treaties that tied more and more of them together in mutual defense, resulting in the remaining two geographically patchworked countries, Dimokratía and Fédération. I start here because I believe this is the most important piece of information, though you already know it. We will delve into the reasons for this twenty-fifth-century state, including the shift of warfare from human-labor-based to principally aerospace, cybernetic, and economic mechanisms."

"OS," I interrupt. "I don't want to know all this. I mean, I do, but not now. There's something else I want to know now."

"If it's about the beacon, I don't have any additional information, no classified partitions that will help us understand it."

"Not that," I say, craning my neck to check that the dads and Owl are still at the table, out of earshot. "I want to see the messages the original Dad and Father left for their future selves."

"I see," OS says. "I'm not sure they would want me to show you those."

"Isn't it part of the information you store? And didn't

they grant me access to all that?"

"They did."

"Let's see, then."

It doesn't take OS any time to deliberate. The reel starts playing.

It's hard even to recognize this as Dad at first. He's wearing a cloth that shimmers; decorations on his skin glitter like chromium. He looks shiftily at the camera. His voice is just like Dad's, though he intones his words strangely. The way he speaks has clearly drifted over the last eighteen years. "I'm Ambrose Cusk," he says. "You know that. Because you're Ambrose Cusk, too." He whistles awkwardly. "I'm the original. We split after I had that medical screening. They recorded my, our, brain there. A couple of months ago. Now I know the truth. That Minerva's distress beacon never triggered, that mission control lied to me. You needed to believe that, though, to have the will to survive each time you were woken up, so that's why they mapped my neurons while *I* still believed, too."

This Dad continues to tell a story I know, a story so extreme that it would be unbelievable if I didn't already know it to be true. Of someone sold a lie so that his copies would think that lie to be the truth. Horrors. The reel finishes, leaving me with the view of Big Sister as she sets. "Okay, now show me Father's," I say.

"Even Kodiak didn't want to see Kodiak's," OS says.

"I know. Show me anyway."

The projection comes up of a hulking, even broodier Father, before a wall of dark tiles. He's in his cosmology academy reds, seated on a chair and staring into the camera. He looks shell-shocked. There's some scrap of fabric in his hands. Wool, maybe? "I am Kodiak Celius," he says, his voice low and barely controlled. "I am relaying to you, clone, information I have just discovered for myself. That I am not going into space as I planned. That there is no rescue mission to be launched. But you, clone, are going to space. You are going to another planet. I hope you will be strong."

He pauses, to steady himself. Unlike Ambrose's recording, Kodiak's doesn't have high production values. There's no special costume. There's no soft lighting. Just a man in shadow, facing a camera, barely keeping it together.

Until he isn't.

Father goes from collected to sobbing. There is no moment of transition. Racking, body-shaking sobs. His big hands cover his face, but I can see the force of his convulsions, hear the cracking of his chair as his body wrenches against it.

"Stop the reel!" he screams.

"Stop playing the reel," I tell OS, my voice overlapping with Father's.

It's just the quiet of the Minerva evening now. Big Sister glows.

I can barely process what I just saw from Father. This loss of control from someone who usually has so much of it. He wasn't angry, he was grieving. Losing his mission was a pure and intense sorrow. It feels sacredly private, and I feel like I've betrayed him by seeing what I just saw.

"I'm sorry, Father," I mumble. I sit back, numb.

"What would you like to see next?" OS asks.

I don't say anything. I just look at the stars. Looking for the prick of light that means the end is coming.

"Would you like me to continue with the history of the Earth?" OS prompts.

"No," I say. I let out a long breath. "That's enough history for tonight."

CHAPTER 2

The next morning, Father and Owl prepare for another mining trip. I stand a few paces away, sipping hot water while I watch them examine the images Rover took of the dig site. The pit they've created looks painful. It looks like our planet has a wound.

What have we done to our home?

Father runs diagnostics on Rover while Owl packs their supplies, an eye to the sky. Both Sisters are already up, and I'm sure Owl is itching to get on their way. "Do you need any help?" I ask. My arms feel weird, like they're someone else's. The one with the hot water is flung out in space, the other one is motionless down at my hip.

Owl barely looks up. "Nope, I have this down to a science."

I nod, even though there's nobody else to see me do it.

Minutes later, Owl and Father and Rover have bid us goodbye and are on their way out the gate. Its protective mechanism clicks behind them. The pneumatic guns tick and buzz as they scan for enemies.

I turn around. There aren't any enemies. There's just me.

* * *

On the far side of the settlement, Dad is bent over OS's printing mechanism, deep in focus as he troubleshoots. His body looks so vulnerable. The neck, the temples, the skull full of blood and electricity. If that skull opens, the whole body goes, too. I walk right behind him. My feet crunch in the soil; my clothes rustle. I can hear their very fibers. But my dad hears none of it.

"Hi, Dad," I say, right behind him.

He startles. "Yarrow. You crept up on me. Need something?"

I shake my head.

"Are you okay?"

"Yes."

"All right," he says. "Just tell me if you do need something, Yar."

"I'm going to spend a little time with OS, learning about Earth history," I say. "Is that all right?"

"Yes, of course. You have full access. Take up to an hour, okay? Then I need you to ferry some metal for me."

I whirl—too fast, like my body's not mine, like it's maybe not even human—and head over to the gray portal from the sinking *Endeavor*. I pass through.

Hush-hush-whir. Hush-hush-whir. My new sibling is gestating. I tent my fingers over the device. What will this new person look like?

I lay my bracelet on the console, tap into the extensive memory of OS. I skate through agilely, faster in this digital territory than either of the dads is, or even Owl. This feels like my native land. I speak the language of this system. I am not alone when I'm inside it.

I find myself drawn not to memory but to function. Not to what's recorded but how the present is processed. I don't know why. It's like I'm wandering a new planet, and the wandering is enough, without finding landmarks.

How do you work, OS? The question feels urgent.

OS is happy to tell me how it works. It doesn't need words or codes to do so. My fingers move on their own. OS opens before them willingly, and I disappear inside. I'm beyond thinking or judging or needing. I flow, in a way I cannot when the medium is just soil.

Shaking. My body is shaking. I feel dirt in my eyes. Has someone thrown dirt in my eyes?

I flail, trying to clear the landslide around me. I contact something soft, shove it hard. A voice I know grunts.

Light comes in, and I find my dad, Ambrose my dad, splayed out on the ground. The full light of the Scorch hits my eyes. I've been inside OS for hours. I've been *lost* inside OS for hours.

What have I been doing?

My dad lifts himself onto his elbows and then his hands and pushes up into a crouch. He looks at me warily, breathing heavily.

"What happened?" I ask.

He stares. I hate what I find in his eyes. It's like he is not seeing the me I know I am. Like I'm not his Yarrow anymore. "What happened?" I repeat, my voice rising.

"I must have scared you," Dad says slowly, making no move to approach me. "You were deep in your bracelet projections, and I guess you were focusing so hard that you weren't aware of your surroundings anymore." His voice hitches. He's on the verge of crying. "You didn't respond to your name, Yarrow. Even when I nudged your shoulder, many times, you didn't respond. I tried to pull you to your feet, and . . . you don't remember any of this?"

I shake my head. What's wrong with me?

He paces toward me steadily, as if he's worried about scaring me with any sudden movements. Then he draws me close and holds me tight.

Just a moment ago I apparently shoved him into the dirt. How can he be brave enough to risk holding me now? I'm so grateful for it, though, the warmth of my dad. My dad accepting me. "I'm sorry," I whisper into his shoulder. "I don't know what's happening with me."

"Hey, hey," he soothes. "We'll figure it out, don't worry. I promise we'll figure it out."

"Thank you," I tell him.

"Thank you for what?" he whispers back.

I don't have words for what I'm thanking him for. I just know it feels big. So big it makes me numb. This is my last chance to thank him for this big thing I cannot name.

"Do you want to rest for the afternoon?" he asks. "You can watch *Pink Lagoon* or anything else you want. I can take care of the printing and shuttling materials."

"No, no," I say. "I'll help. I'll keep track of my mind better."

"You're doing fine," he says. "Are you hungry?"

I shake my head. It's like my body decided not to use any energy for the whole morning. I know that's not possible, but it feels like that.

"All right," he says. "I'm going to get something to eat, and then I'll meet you over at the printing station, okay? I've already input schematics, so you can just hang out with OS and make sure that nothing goes wrong. I'll be there in half an hour, sound good?"

"That sounds fine, Dad. Thanks."

I lumber over to the printing station and sit in the poly-carb chair. The sweet burning smell of fusing hydrocarbons fills my nose. I tap my bracelet against the system, scan through the schematics Dad has queued, then look into the database of what else can be printed, should we choose to. The options are extensive, especially with the addition of the metals we've been delivering to the settlement. I lose myself in perusing them. I lose myself entirely.

That evening, Dad asks what I've discovered from the ship's internet image. I surprise both of us by answering "not much."

"Yar," he says. He's looking deep into my eyes as I fiddle with my dinner. Or at least he's trying to look into my eyes. It must be hard when I refuse to look back. "Yar, please look at me when I'm speaking to you."

I force myself to look. His eyes are like mirrors that don't reflect. Like he's not seeing anyone, not me. The feeling makes my guts churn. Alone is an elemental force.

"This is what you most wanted," he says. "You asked for years to have this access. And now you don't want to delve in and see what you can find? I don't understand."

I shrug. "I looked up some stuff. But I guess I didn't want to find anything more after that."

"What have you been doing in the system all this time, then?"

"I don't know. I guess I just got lost spending time looking at nothing."

Dad chuckles. "Yes, I've done that before, too."

I look sharply at him. "You could ask OS to report on me if you want to know what I've been doing."

"Yar, I don't need to do that. I trust you."

Why should he ever do something as stupid as that? I don't trust me.

I watch him think for a bit. "What was the most . . . rough texture you touched today?" he asks.

I close my eyes tight, take a long breath in and let a long breath out. "I don't want to play this game. Can we be quiet for a while?"

"Of course, of course," he says. "We can do that."

Food passes through my lips without taste or texture. I swallow it. I feed the organism.

A breeze carries across the plain from the south, the direction of the malevor herd. It lifts the light hairs along the back of my neck, with a touch gentler than that from any human. Minerva will always be here for me, no matter what I do.

There's a new star in the sky tonight, off to the far left of Sky Cat. It's brighter than a star, actually. Almost brighter than a planet. I know what it means. I say nothing about it. OS will notice, too, once Rover is back.

Blurred days. Labor and lost self. Twice Dad has to go find me during the Scorch, bring me under cover so my skin doesn't burn. I'd been marveling at the wonder of our sister suns.

Then, as sunset is just beginning, Father and Owl return. They're right on time. Dad pauses his work to watch for them, and hollers when their silhouettes appear at the horizon.

I go to the gate to join him as they approach. Owl waves her spear in the air in greeting, shouts across the wide Minervan sky. "Hello, family!"

"Hi, Owl," Dad shouts back. He puts his arms around me. I startle and then go still. It should be easy to accept an embrace.

Their silhouettes resolve into human figures plus the sphere of Rover, hauling a tarp piled high with scrap minerals. "Looks like a nice amount," Dad calls.

"It is," Father shouts back. "I think we should have enough to finish the bunker shaft!"

"Excellent news," Dad says. "Isn't it, Yarrow?"

"Yes," I whisper. They're nearly at the distance the malevor was when the pneumatic guns shot it dead. Maybe ten seconds, and they'll reach it. That poor creature, slain for not knowing how to behave.

Nine, eight, seven.

"Dad, I love you," I say.

He looks at me. "That's sweet. I love you, too."

Four, three, two.

"I love Father and Owl, too."

Fear enters Dad's eyes. Extra white around his brown irises. "What's going on, Yarrow?"

One.

The pneumatic guns on the fence whir and pivot.

Father, being Father, reacts with near instant reflexes. He sees the movement and hurls out an arm to push Owl back, striking her so hard in the chest that she sprawls in the dirt. I hear her outraged shriek even as I hear the *ping* of a bullet hitting Rover's polycarb casing. More pings as bullets spray into the dirt at Father's and Owl's feet. If Father hadn't stopped her, Owl would have been riddled with bullet holes by now. He probably memorized the radius of the guns, and is on the alert whenever they cross it. Father will not be easy to kill.

"OS, stop the guns!" Dad yells. He runs toward the gate, then thinks better of it and stays on our side. He continues to yell meaninglessly until his voice resolves into words. "Stop them!"

"That contradicts my new programming," OS says. "I must shoot at any living being that tries to approach."

"No, that's incorrect!" Dad says. "You are not to shoot at any of *us*, do you understand? Not at any humans."

OS doesn't pursue the tack any further. The guns tick as they try to push past their physical limits, so they can strike Father and Owl where they're huddled on the soil with Rover. Bullets continue to send up plumes of soil.

Dad has his hands up to either side of his face. "I don't understand what's going on. Yarrow, do you understand why the guns are firing on Father and Owl?"

"I do," I say. I know I've done this. I don't remember doing it, but it had to have been me.

"Make it stop," Dad says, his voice suddenly cold.

"I think they're okay," I say. "They seem like they're okay."

"OS, I need you to disable the guns," Dad calls.

"Yarrow, may I do that?" OS asks.

Dad gasps.

"No," I say. "You may not."

"Yarrow, what are you doing?" Dad shouts. "Just explain this to me, okay? I'm sure there's some reason."

"There is no reason," I say. I reach behind me and pull the printed gun out from my waistband.

"What are you—" Dad starts to say.

But he can't finish because I've shot him. Right in the gut.

He staggers backward, and I shoot him again. Two red blossoms on his tunic, spreading and merging.

Dad sits heavily, stares down at his own chest, shocked. Then he pitches into the dirt, striking it forehead first.

I told him the truth. There is no reason. I'm just doing what I've been told to do.

PART FOUR

EARTH

MARCH 4, 2473

KODIAK CELIUS

CHAPTER 1

From beside a ruined stone wall and under a pile of fallen thatch, a noise.

I crouch, hand reaching into my quiver before I've even processed what I've heard. The noise was a bleat. Bleats come from sheep. I don't need to defend myself from a sheep.

For a long moment, all is still. The misting rain makes a hushed beating sound against the grass. Crows caw above an overgrown field. This farmstead is long ruined, chaotic old stone ceding to lichen and vines. Humans have been gone from this area for only three years, but this cottage must have been abandoned long before that. A victim of industrial agriculture rather than impending war.

Another bleat.

"Come, come, fallen one," I say. I guess I've sung the words. They're from a Dimokratía lullaby, and sprang to my mind after years of never hearing them. A long line of boys in the Celius orphanage, a nurse in starched gray walking down the row of cribs, singing to all of us, each of us happy to be sung to but longing to be held. I don't remember any more of the lyrics, hum the music instead.

From the ruined doorway of the farmstead appear sweet and soft ears, a face and trembling black nostrils.

"Come, come, fallen one," I repeat.

The sheep takes a step forward, evaluating me. It's been raining all morning, the sort of Scottish rain that I don't usually notice until my shirt is soaked through and clinging to my chest. I only realize it now because when the sheep winks one eye I see its long lashes are jeweled in water droplets.

My hand returns to my arrows. Not to shoot in self-defense anymore, but for the hunt. It has been months since I've eaten meat, and I ought not to let this opportunity pass. But, for the second time in so many minutes, my hand returns from the quiver without an arrow.

Last time I killed an animal, it was a mercy killing, a horse with a broken foreleg. I decided not to waste the meat, and still have a salted flank hanging beside my cabin, waiting for the harder times of winter. I'm relieved to see that this sheep has no blood matting its wool. There isn't any pain in its bleat, just a longing for another being. I don't need to kill it. Someday I'll run out of canned lab protein out here. That day hasn't come yet. I hold out my hand, empty. "Come, come, fallen one."

With great effort, the sheep emerges from the thatch.

What she does have is wool. A lot of wool. Centuries

of artificial selection by humans have produced a creature that grows as much hair as possible as quickly as possible, counting on us to shear her before it's an impediment. But now there are no farmers in this forbidden zone, and this sheep is fully twice as big as she should be, a sphere of wool trapped on the inside of the doorway.

She startles when I approach, and tries to back deeper into the ruined farmhouse. With the extra wool, though, she doesn't have a chance. I'm upon her in two strides, then easily push her over. She rolls onto her puffy side, legs kicking. I lean hard on her. I've got a lot of body weight, but with all this substantial cushioning there is no risk of me injuring her. She might not even feel me.

There will be no using this wool. It reeks of rot and balled-up socks. She's been growing this hair since Old Scotland was abandoned after the Fédération bombardment. It wriggles. There's a whole ecosystem in there. I've seen the carcasses on the hillside. Her family succumbed to infestation long ago. Death by maggot is not a pleasant way to go.

"You're a tough one, aren't you?" I say as I unholster the shears I lifted from the abandoned agricultural supply in town. They still have the polycarb safety tag fastening them closed. I bite it off.

She goes still, staring at me with surprisingly calm eyes. I wonder if she remembers the last time her farmer cut her wool. They must have been a gentle caretaker.

I hack into her stiff encasement. It takes all the corded strength in my forearms to make headway into the reeking mats, hard clumps of rot-black hair falling away to reveal pink irritated skin, swarming with maggots. I brush them away, revealing a scattering of blood spots, and can only imagine how good it must feel to her to finally have that biting infestation away from her skin.

Foul hardened hair surrounds us, keeping its stiff shape. It looks like this baby-pink animal has just been born from the center of a giant walnut. I'm not religious at all, but surrounded by the hush of the forest, the weedy overgrowth of this farmhouse whose ruined roof dapples the sunlight from above, the moment does have a divinity to it. I didn't sleep well last night; maybe that's what's going on. Memories of training, and my quick escape from the cosmology academy, a pretty stranger at the gate delivering shattering news, kept me awake.

"A metamorphosis," I whisper into the sheep's ear as I finish the last shear, a stiff black collar of wool around her neck thudding to the ground. I've spoken to her. I guess that means I'm going to keep her, if she wants to stay with me.

I give her soft flank a stroke, sweeping away the last of her parasites, avoiding the places where her skin is bleeding from the maggot infestation. "All finished."

She gets up on all four hooves and stares at me. *Can we go home now?* She definitely had a kind farmer. I'm already pledging that I'll live up to their legacy. We did a lot of pledging back in training. Not that those pledges have worked out so well for me.

I gesture toward the leaky barn over the hill. "Go on, go live in there."

My orders are clearly unconvincing, even to this animal trained for obedience. She looks at the barn and then returns her level gaze to me. *That's not home anymore.* She starts to experiment with her new lighter weight, making little dancing hops, fallen maggots bursting under her hooves. Already their shallow bites are clotting, the shine of her blood dulling as it thickens.

I put my hands back in their repurposed gardening gloves—another thing I looted from the abandoned supply store, along with some employee's old apron, *Michaela* still stitched on it in red thread—and rub them together to warm them against the morning chill. I'd planned on spending today checking and fortifying my traps. Not teaching a sheep how to be free.

I start toward home, taking my usual labyrinthine route, passing along grassy back roads that weave through ruined castles. It would be easier to take the straight paved roads that pass by shuttered strip malls instead, but then I could more easily be followed. After Fédération finished its Old

Scotland bombardment with a round of EMP dusting, rendering modern life impossible, Dimokratía withdrew its citizens from the area. They were smart to—not only was life without tech hard to imagine, EMP dusting in the past had been a way to prepare for atrocities, to black out the ability to report on what happened once the militias entered. There are some roving ex-Fédération gangs here, soldiers who defied orders and chose to stay in one of the few places they could escape the grid. Since disobeying could mean a lifetime of imprisonment, or death from above, the only people likely to do so knew they'd be facing life in prison anyway. They're not the sort of people I want to meet. They're people like me.

Running away here means spending my life alone, but I don't mind. Alone is how I'm meant to be. After my parents abandoned me at the Celius regional orphanage, probably on their way to defect to Fédération like everyone else in the 2450s, I had no one to rely on. My childhood friends were culled from the spacefarer training. Except Celius Li Qiang, who became my biggest ally and erotiyet, but he never spoke to me again after I beat him out for the Titan rescue mission. My life has been solitude with surprise moments of companionship, not companionship with surprise moments of solitude.

The "mission to Titan."

I pick up my pace back to my home, cutting across

hiking trails, unhitching my machete to clear the runners of grass and wild blackberry that tirelessly work to reclaim every human path. Every time I stop to cut, I look back to find the sheep twenty paces behind, waiting to find out where I'm taking her. "Shoo!" I say. It doesn't work. I don't want it to.

I pass through the parking lot of the old state park, tap my knuckles against the sun-faded "No Overnight Parking" sign, enjoy the minor thrill of danger as it rings out. It's one of my ludicrous rituals. I hurry over this exposed section. If someone did want to take me out, they could set up in some sheltered sniper spot overlooking this lot, weapon at the ready while I so predictably return from the day's errand. At least that's how *I* would kill me.

I know I should alter my route, but the other way to ruined civ from my home takes far longer. For some reason I'm only dimly aware of, taking the risk of crossing through this open section makes me feel alive. Feelings are distant for me, like blurred fish swimming below thick ice.

I sheathe my machete. There are still plenty of vines I could cut, but I intentionally let this path that leads to my cabin stay overgrown, so no stranger will discover it and find my home. So far so good. Four months living here and not a soul has broken my solitude.

Except for this damn sheep.

I smile at myself, at what I hold dear about who I am.

This strong solitary hermit, destroyed in minutes by a freshly shorn, sweet-eyed sheep, hopping for joy while her sores clot.

"Come, come, fallen one," I sing softly as I pull to one side the branches that camouflage the final stretch of path. I've never seen any sign of someone on these trails, neither an intruder nor even the broken branches and twigs of someone who happened to pass through. There are the feral dogs and wolves and bears and boars, of course, but no amount of subterfuge I could set up will do anything to deter a bear.

I stand to one side, holding back a branch. "Come, come, fallen one." The sheep passes near, stopping to nibble some moss while I replace the camouflage.

A roar above. I look up, visoring my hand over my eyes, and see a commercial Cusk craft. That's not all that uncommon; even if no one's officially living here, this part of Old Scotland is still on the low-altitude North Pole Sea Station route. I return my attention to the path, then look back to the sky when the roar lasts longer than it should. This Cusk craft has paused in the air over the old parking lot. Where Sheep and I were minutes ago.

Shazyt.

This could just be a Pause. I hate those: when someone of note dies in Fédération, their relatives sometimes pay a huge fee to stop all vehicles. Even a second's Pause costs more than the combined lifetimes' earnings of a hundred thousand ordinary citizens, but how else do you make a statement in a world ruled by capital? "Good riddance and good waste," I mutter at the sky.

Of course, that's only one explanation for what just happened. A craft can also pause to deliver someone to the ground. The abandoned lot of a forgotten national park is hardly a tourist destination, but I suppose it's not impossible that some adrenaline junkie hired a craft to take them here, which is why I hate when these economic Pauses happen nearby. I don't like not knowing. Old Scotland is unmonitored territory—if these are Dimokratía citizens they're breaking the law, but if they're from Fédération they can do as they like, even though they're unprotected by their country. Unfortunately, I can see only bits of the craft through the trees, so I won't have an answer. If these are Dimokratía police, I'm not about to go deliver myself to them. I'll just have to be on high alert for a few days. Great. As if sleep weren't coming hard enough already.

"Come, Sheep," I say as I pick up the pace.

The final approach to home is trickier now, since I can't just hop between my vine traps. I have to undo them individually, so Sheep doesn't get herself snared. I'll have to rely on my knife, axe, and bow and arrow for defense. Like in my earliest days here.

Sheep watches attentively as I kneel on the wood, wet

and soft beneath my bare knees while I undo the sapling triggers. "You'd better be worth the risk," I mutter.

She stares back, her jaw working side to side as she slowly chews a clump of dandelion she's torn from a boulder crevice. The movement under her placid expression is enough to make me chuckle. The sound of it, this noise that lives next to laughter, is unfamiliar.

We make our way to the end of the walkway, where the wooden steps stop at a simple hut. I have no idea who originally built this site, or for what purpose, but I suspect it was for something more than mere habitation. Something artistic, perhaps. The cabin is built on a hillside, and because the ground slopes away it looks like it's floating in midair. I can't even see the third dimension of it from this angle—it looks like a poster of a house, hung up in the sky.

When I open the door, Sheep tries to barge her way in. "No way," I say, blocking her. "Did your farmer let you sleep inside? I don't think so." I suspect they might have, though, since Sheep didn't seem to think twice about it.

I step in.

It's a simple single room with a narrow wooden bunk, my few looted belongings folded and stacked in one corner. I have a stack of canned food in another, which I'm reserving for emergencies, along with that salted horse flank hanging outside.

The far wall is all clear glass. Because it's vintage

material, actual melted sand, the pane doesn't have any autocleaning functions. I open my leather bag, and pull out the main target of this morning's pilfering: a spray bottle of cleanser. The green moss that grows on every tree in this rainy area will also happily colonize this glass if I let it. Since the unblocked view of the stars at night behind the safety of the glass is my main reason for settling in this cabin, I'm not about to let that moss take my greatest pleasure away from me. I get to work applying the blue fluid to the glass, wiping it off with one of my used shirts. I'll rinse it in the stream tomorrow—this ammonia will hopefully clean the fabric some, too.

As I clean, I'm happy to see Sheep come into view on the hillside. She's particular in her browsing, selecting tender stalks of yarrow from between the tougher blades of grass. She'll have plenty to eat; its yellow is scattered up and down the slope. The beautiful weed reminds me of the training breaks I used to spend camping. The presence of yarrow was part of why I chose to retreat here.

Once I've scrubbed the window clean, I stare out at the stretch of woods. This area had once been completely deforested by the humans who lived here, but trees are returning. *Good for you*, I think. Maybe I'll have to cut down some trees a few years from now, so that Sheep or her offspring will have a place to graze. I'll welcome the need of it.

As always, whenever I let myself dream of a future my

mind reminds me of the bitter past, the day that started with final preparations for the Titan mission and finished with all the spacefarers—including me, the one who was supposed to man the *Aurora*—thrust out of the academy. *Gather all your belongings. Doors will lock at 13:30. You may not return.* I'd already been on the hillside, listening from a thicket. As soon as I'd overheard the hushed conversations, witnessed the odd relaxing of our training regimen after my full-body medical scan, I'd begun planning my escape. I didn't know why any of it was happening, but I knew that I was expendable.

While my fellow cadets milled in front of the fence, I was already half a kilometer away, unburying the backpack with escape supplies I'd secreted away weeks before, in case this very thing happened. I had no idea what I'd done wrong, why my government would have lied about my purpose, but I wasn't about to let myself be rounded up and disappeared.

That was when I saw him—Devon Mujaba. I didn't recognize him as a celebrity, though even I had heard of the Heartspeak Boys. I recognized him as the sometimes concubine of the president, who would show up at formal state ceremonies, in Dimokratía uniform despite his defection years ago. None of us liked to see someone permitted to return to the homeland they'd abandoned, but we recognized someone with power when we saw one, so we kept quiet.

There he was on the hillside, a concubine no more, his own pack on, a plasma rifle at his side. Greeting me by name. "Kodiak Celius. I've been hoping to meet you."

He gave me the counterfeit documents that got me all the way to this EMP-dusted zone, where I could be free from technological monitoring. Where I could hope to avoid being arrested by the state to which I'd devoted my life. In return, he asked me to wait for him here, where we'd begin recording guerrilla communications, to take down the world's locked politics, to build a new society, this time built from non-extractivist logics. I didn't know if I'd ever go along with that, but I did know I could use help getting out of deep Dimokratía before someone made me disappear.

The meaning and purpose of my life had flipped in the moment I met Devon on the hillside. I'd not only been training for a canceled mission; I'd been training for a mission that was never intended to begin. I raged as I voyaged, kept away from other humans as I made my way through the most sparsely populated regions of the world, finally across the Channel and up this island. I'm calmer now, almost at peace—but I do wonder what I will do when Devon Mujaba returns. Will I make those guerrilla recordings he wants, about the false mission? Will I help break the world in the hopes that it can be remade differently?

Maybe that Cusk craft that lingered over the parking lot

wasn't from a Pause. Maybe it was him, finally joining me.

I shake my head. Enough wallowing in useless wonderings. I bring my cleanser-soaked shirt down to the stream to rinse.

Once I've wet the shirt, I remove the one I'm wearing and scrub it as well, enjoying the chill air that lifts the soft black hairs of my chest and underarms. I give the rest of my body a good rinse, too, and then lie out on a flat stone. Despite my desire for it to be still, my flesh shivers.

The best way to warm a body is to use it. I roll onto my side and begin my daily exercises. I'm long past peak training condition, back when martial arts and wrestling took up hours of each day. A half hour of push-ups and crunches will only do so much, but maybe that's not terrible. Mostly I welcome the shrinking of my physical self—it is easier to maintain an existence that requires less food.

The stream bends a short way from my washing spot, and in the water that pools there I can watch the reflection of swaying green trees and cerulean sky. There's a flash of another color, a bronze brown. Not quite the color of Sheep. Not quite the color of anything that lives here.

It's gone as soon as I glimpse it. If this were Devon Mujaba, he'd have simply announced himself. I go motionless, cursing myself for the series of lax mistakes I've made today: indulging in cleanser, knocking on that "No Parking" sign, adopting a sheep, disarming my traps, lying naked and vulnerable here. A series of errors grave enough to kill me.

Maybe someone from the Dimokratía secret police hasn't come to murder me. This could be a bear instead. Is that better? I think it is.

I snag the sleeve of my shirt from where it's been drying on a nearby rock, drag it to me, and roll the wet fabric down my shivering body. As calmly as I can, I arrange my leather skirt over my thighs, then slowly and deliberately crouch by the water's edge, cupping water in my hands as if to splash it on my face. But I hold still, angle it to the spot in the trees where I saw the flash of bronze.

The water's surface trembles to my surging pulse, but the reality is still unmistakable: there's a person in the trees. I can't make out the face, but he has the darker skin of equatorial genetic lines, not my Mediterranean olive. He's got a royal bearing, and skinprint mods glint on his face and neck. His clothing is not that of a wealthy person, though: it's a mass-produced traveler's jumpsuit with a Disponar patch, technical fabric in swirling greens and grays and browns.

He lingers between two trees, mostly hidden. He probably thinks he's fully camouflaged. Perhaps he is not experienced.

I reluctantly give up my mirror by splashing the water on my face, strategizing all the while. It would be one mistake too many to let this stranger take the initiative. My bow is up in the hut, twenty feet in the other direction. My knife and axe are below the cabin, sticking up from my chopping stump. Both weapons too distant to be useful. Shazyt. If I survive this set of mistakes, I will do better.

He's got a small weapon in his hand, probably a bolt caster. It shouldn't work with all the EMP dust in the soil here, but maybe Cusk has finally invented portable tech that can resist it. I wouldn't know—the dust means I'm locked out of current news. If EMP shielding has spread beyond warbots, it would still be very expensive, but this man looks like he could afford it.

I'm much bigger than he is, could almost certainly take him in a fistfight. But I have to assume he is effectively armed . . . and I am not. Therefore I'm not sure of my odds.

At least he won't catch me by surprise. And I still have some traps engaged.

It's unlikely that he would have wandered over to my hut so quickly. He had to have come directly here from the Cusk craft. Which means he knows my location. Have I been tracked? Has Devon Mujaba been uncovered and tortured?

I crouch and run the back of my arm over my face. For a moment longer, I'm still. But I know surprise is the best thing I have going for me, even if I don't know what to do with it.

So I act.

I throw myself into the stream and course underwater, kicking my legs powerfully, only breaking the surface once I'm many lengths downstream. I could have held my breath longer, but down here the river shallows out too much for my thick body to pass, the skin of my belly scraping the stones of the bottom. I fling myself out on the far bank, dash into the tree line.

"Stop!" the intruder yells, speaking Dimokratía in a posh Fédération accent. "I just want to talk to you!" I leap over a bramble, scrambling on all fours up the slope toward my hut, where my weapons are waiting.

He's running after me. I get to my feet and cut to the side, picking a direction at random to keep him off track. Sheep bleats somewhere far off in the woods, and I instinctively alter my course toward her.

The intruder's body blurs as I race, but I can still tell he's cupped his hands around his mouth. Making a word that I don't recognize at first, but I then realize is my name in that posh accent. Kodiak.

He knows my name?

There's no time for questions now. I switch directions and barrel toward him, the mass of my shoulder striking him in the kidney. He goes down, his smaller body folding at the waist as I roll with him. We come to a rest, my wet hair whipping around my face as I stand and heft his struggling body over my shoulder. I lug him up the slope; he's struggling all the while, fists battering my back.

Then his hands are at his waist. Getting out a weapon?

I panic and drop him, then sprint toward the cabin. With shaking hand, I yank my hunting knife out of the chopping stump and whirl in time to see the intruder surge into motion, escaping into the tree line. I brandish the knife. "Come out," I yell in Dimokratía and then Fédération.

I turn in a wide circle, looking for the enemy combatant. No sign of him.

Then there's sudden motion in the trees. He emerges beside the stream. I can see him in the full light now, this stranger with the skinprints. He's surprisingly beautiful. I think I recognize him. Why should I recognize him? Some of the tension relaxes from my system. He doesn't seem like much of a fighter.

The intruder brandishes his bolt caster. The small device, no bigger than a finger, can shoot out an arc of ten-thousand-volt electricity, auto-aiming it at the nearest human-sized object in a cone-shaped zone. He wastes no time firing it at me, shouting triumphantly as he does.

He must not know about the EMP dust. Or if he did, he's somehow forgotten.

I'm not the only one making mistakes today.

We're both frozen, but only for a split second. I take advantage of his error to close our distance, dashing three huge strides and then lunging toward him, knife out-stretched. His eyes go wide with surprise, then he just has time to get his hands up defensively before I'm upon him. At the last moment, I let the knife drop from my hand. It would be all too easy to puncture his abdomen, which would be fatal in an area with no medical care.

Knife clatters. Person grunts. Sheep bleats.

We roll, his wiry body resisting mine. An elbow clocks my chin, but then I've got him onto his belly, face pressed into the mud. He chokes and splutters as I wrench one arm and then the other behind him. He manages to turn his head. His hood has fallen back in the struggle, and I see his cheek is smeared with mud—and some blood, too. It might be mine. I think he busted my lip open. "I'm here to talk to you," he says in Dimokratía.

"Enough," I say, wrenching his arms behind him harder. "Say another word and I break these."

I look around for something that I could use to restrain him. Nothing within reach. "I mean it. Don't move," I say as I reluctantly release his wrists, press my knee into his back, and peel off my tunic. He lowers his arms to his sides, but doesn't do anything to resist. I whip the shirt in a circular motion, so the wet fabric wraps around itself, forming a sort of rope. I wrench this stranger's hands together and make a rough cuff around the wrists, tying it sharply enough that he gasps.

I turn him over, see brown skin, freckles like poppy seeds, frightened eyes. I straddle his waist, my palms pushing his shoulder blades into the mud.

"I'm not resisting you," he says in Dimokratía. "Do you notice that?"

That posh accent. Is he another of the Heartspeak Boys? Is that where I've seen him—a celebrity reel glimpsed somewhere during an academy break? "Stop speaking," I say in Fédération.

He goes still, looking up at me. Taking in details.

There's something . . . hungry in his gaze, as if he's trying to see as much of me as he can, as if looking at me is important to him. At first I think he's studying me as an enemy. This is how cosmology academy rivals would look at me before they attacked, trying to absorb as much information about their opponent as fast as possible. Then his expression looks like desire, like we're the last two cadets in the changing room with nowhere to be until dinner. Then that doesn't feel like what this is, either, and it's something bigger and stranger. Like *I'm* the celebrity. He knew my name.

I sit back, moving my weight from his ribs to his hips. "You would have electrocuted me just now if you could have."

He rapidly closes and opens one eye, a sarcastic Fédération mannerism. "I knew it was pretty futile, since my bracelet stopped working as soon as my cruiser passed over Glasgow. And my arc thrower is set to a wimpy level."

He groans as I lean over to pick up my hunting knife, the awkward movement pushing my groin hard into his belly. "I have a knife in my hands," I say.

"I can see that," he says, the white of his visible eye stark as he strains to watch me.

"I'm going to get up. Do not move when I do."

"I wouldn't dare, Kodiak Celius."

He wants to remind me that he knows my full name, that he's sought me out specifically. I'd like to know how he knows who I am. But I will not allow him to decide the course of our communication.

I get up, standing over him with my knife at the ready. He remains still.

Checking every second to make sure he hasn't moved, I return to the storage under my tarp, pull out a length of rope, and use it to better bind his wrists. Curious about this captive human, Sheep approaches and taps her nose against the rope, rain in rivulets down her pink skin.

"I have to say, this isn't going quite like I planned," the stranger says, laughing darkly. This demonstration of calmness—almost friendliness—could very well be being deployed to fool me. I will myself to ignore it, as appealing as it is.

All the same, I wonder: Could he be a local who stayed?

Maybe he's dressed like a traveler to throw me off the fact that this is his land, his home. His sheep or his cabin, even? I can't imagine why he'd have gone to such lengths to trick me, but I can't figure out any other possible motive for what he's done.

"So," the stranger says, "how are you today?"

Was that a joke? "Don't speak again until I allow it." I crouch before him, knife in hand, arranging my leather military skirt to cover my thighs.

"I like your sheep," he tries again.

"Are you trying to die?"

"I'm gambling that you wouldn't kill me until you found out why I'd come. It's just . . . the reason is a little complicated to spit out casually. And no, let the record show that I officially do not want to die."

"Project your ID," I say.

He nods. "Sure. I can do that. I have my fizz. Only . . ." He raises his bound arms slightly and shrugs.

Fizz is a Fédération colloquialism for "physical card." Because he can't project his identification with the EMP dust around, of course. I'd used that phrase in an old habit. "Where is it?" I ask.

"In my breast pocket."

I lean over him. It feels strange—I haven't been this near a human in weeks. My thumb is against one of his chest muscles, can read the tattooed word *Violence* when

I peek below his neckline. I pat his breast pocket, and find his plasticine ID. For him to have risked bringing his fizz means he is thinking of this as more than a short-term trip.

I hold the card up to the afternoon sun, reading through the rain-beaded polycarb. It's emblazoned with Fédération holoseals, as difficult to counterfeit as the Dimokratía ones that authenticate my own fizz.

Ambrose Cusk

Cusk Academy Cadet

Full Fédération Citizen (Onyx)

ID: NYX0009

Ambrose Cusk.

Oh.

That's why I recognize him. I've seen him in news reels. And Devon Mujaba told me all about him before he left to track him down. "You are the Fédération spacefarer who was selected to man the *Endeavor*."

"To human it, yes. On . . . the Titan rescue mission?" Ambrose asks, peering at me intensely. It's odd that he's phrased it like a question. I wonder if there's some subtlety of the Fédération language I'm not picking up on.

"The canceled Titan mission. Yes."

"Kodiak Celius, that's part of why I came here. I want to tell you what I know about it. And find out what *you* know

271

about it." He takes in a long breath, lets it out slowly. "I'll go first. For starters, I know that the mission to Titan was never meant to take off. That the Titan SOS was deployed to make everyone—me and you in particular—*believe* there was going to be a rescue mission."

I stab the knife into the bright green moss beside me and rub my hands together for warmth. This accords with what Devon Mujaba said. The abrupt cancellation of the Dimokratía space program had to be for more reasons than the rising tensions with Fédération. I don't understand the *why* of it at all, though.

"I know Dimokratía has a different philosophy to its mission structures than Fédération does," Ambrose says. "They avoid letting the glory of individuals rise above that of the program as a whole, so they kept your identity under wraps. But you were the spacefarer who was meant to go on that mission, right?"

I reluctantly nod. This stranger bound in front of me has revealed far more information about himself than I have yet offered. He probably thinks it's my turn to give something up. I do want to ask him if Devon Mujaba sent him here, like he did me, but I also don't want to risk Devon's life by mentioning his name.

"You were manipulated, like I was," Ambrose prods.

"You came here to tell me this?" I scoff. "You're too late." I don't really believe him, this stranger who claims he's traveled across a world in conflict to discuss his past with an enemy. Why would anyone do that? But I am curious to see if I can trip him up, get him to reveal why he's here.

"Yes," Ambrose says flatly. "I have. And I have a request, too."

"Ah," I say. "Of course you do."

Irritation flashes in his eyes. Good. I'm irritated, too. "I know some about how Dimokratía training works," Ambrose says. "You were plucked from the orphanage and made it through an intense gauntlet to be selected for a mission that didn't happen. It wasn't just the focus of your school life, it was your whole life, and now you find that its foundations were untrue. It's not too hard to figure out what got you from there to here, with you in full retreat. I'm in retreat, too. And you're the only person in the world who can relate to what I'm going through."

This is all true. But it's also just so Fédération, to race one another to be the bigger victim. I don't need someone to wipe away my tears while I wail about my sad, sad feelings. I need to survive, and surviving means being undiscoverable. He's threatening to take that away.

Ambrose points somewhere behind me. I don't look, in case this is the diversion moment before he launches some counterattack. Then he speaks. "I like your sheep."

I let myself look. There's Sheep, pink and shorn, scabbing

from her infestation, watching us from the relative safety of the tree line. She's shivering. A sheep shouldn't be shorn in these temperatures. I need to knit her a coat. "You were the second being to invade my life today," I grumble.

Ambrose laughs, with a cough at the end of it. "I hope you enjoyed your solitude while it lasted."

I run my hands over my hair, thick and a little matted at the ends. Water flicks off, disappearing into the rivulets of rain on the nearby rocks. "Here is what will happen next," I say. "I will keep you restrained, but I will bring us into my shelter. We can continue to talk there."

Ambrose seems about to argue, but then he just tenses his lips. His words come out measured. "You could leave me bound outside, but you're not. Thank you for inviting me in."

His compliance makes me more suspicious, not less, but not so much that I feel any need to back out of my plan. I stand and Sheep toddles over to me, leaning against my leg. Probably remembering her old farmer and wondering where my barn is and when we'll go inside it. "You're first," I tell her.

I walk her up the steps to the hut entrance, and open the door. I take my old thick wool blanket, raided from the ruins of Le Havre on my way here, and arrange it in the corner. Sheep happily flumps into the middle of it, nibbles experimentally on the fringe. "No. Bad sheep. We don't eat blankets," I say.

Then I head back outside. For a moment I wonder what I'll do if Ambrose is gone, or—far worse—if he's been joined by confederates. But he's right where I left him, watching the hut doorway with an expression that is worried and also something else. Longing?

I crouch in the mud beside him. It's hard to look into his lustrous brown eyes for long. "I'm going to bring you inside now. This will only work if you don't make any sudden movements. If you do, I will take full advantage of your being restrained to eliminate you. Understood?"

"Wow," Ambrose said, eyebrows arching. "Did you tell yourself to get meaner while you were in the cabin just now?"

I keep my face impassive. He's right, of course. I did that very thing. Fought against my own weakness. "On your feet," I say.

He nearly loses his balance with his hands bound, but I easily lift him into the air and place him standing on the ground. I nod to the steps. "You first."

Once Ambrose is on the floor of my hut, I go back out, put most of my supplies under their tarps, collect and then stash my knife and axe, since they could just as easily be used against me as by me, and head back into the hut. I shut the door and latch it, stare out the window as I stamp my feet to push out the wet cold.

I stand at the door, look at the human and the bovid on my floor. My cabin is full, when this morning it had just me inside it. I'm not at all sure how I feel about that.

Ambrose attempts, as best as he can with bound wrists, to rub some of the rainwater off his shivering leg.

I sigh. "Hold on."

He watches as I nurse the remaining ember in the wood-stove, add kindling and a fresh seasoned log, blow until it catches. The stove will heat the room up eventually, but in the meantime I place my towel, only slightly damp from my morning's bath in the stream, on the iron surface to heat up. Once it's warm, I kneel beside Ambrose. "It's okay?"

He looks at the steaming towel, and at me. "I'd rather do it myself."

"I'm sure you would. But you'd find that very difficult with your wrists bound."

"Fine," he says.

He watches my face with wide eyes as I rub his hair with the hot dry towel, run it down his back and legs. Brisk, respectful movements, like I'm a schoolmaster drying off a kid coming in from recess. Ambrose strangely intimidates me, so I go quickly. I start folding the towel after I finish until, with an impish grin, he lifts his arms. Shaking my head, I dry his armpits. This is not running exactly like the captive situations I trained for.

I resume folding the towel, but then Ambrose speaks up.

"Aren't you going to dry yourself?"

I'm soaking, too, though not shivering. Ambrose watches quietly while I rub down my body, then hang the towel on the back of my single chair to dry near the woodstove.

I sit in that chair and face the bound human on my floor. Sheep has been watching us, chewing on a strip of burlap she ripped from my bedding, like she's got her snack ready and is waiting for the show to start.

"So, Spacefarer Kodiak Celius, what can I do to convince you I'm telling the truth?" Ambrose asks.

I shrug. "If this area weren't laced with the EMP dust your country scattered, I'd say we could look information up. But we have to do this all the old-fashioned way. Interrogation."

"I'm not sure what else I can say to convince you. Devon Mujaba sent you here, didn't he?" Ambrose offers. "He sent me here, too. To start the resistance. To send out anti-capitalist messages from a place where we'd be difficult to track down. To use our notoriety to change the world."

Change the world. Sure. Typical Fédération self-importance. I keep silent, using the towel to idly rub the surface of the stove. It gives me no advantage to confirm what Ambrose just said. He could be lying about being sent by Devon, to trap me into agreeing.

Ambrose tries again. "Can I ask why you're here? Not why you left Dimokratía, but why you chose Old Scotland?

There are four EMP-dusted regions to pick from."

That's fair. I stare out the newly cleaned window for a while, considering my words. "It's five regions, after Newfoundland in 2470. But to answer your question. In training, when we had breaks, I wouldn't go with the other boys into the city. I would trek out as far as I could, to camp and to remember the stars. The universe, the place I wanted to disappear into. When the cosmology academy shuttered, I knew I had to go somewhere else, fast. Somewhere I couldn't be found. This isolated wooded location was perfect. I like the plants that grow here."

"Isolated—until you're found by me. And a sheep," Ambrose says. "Then that all goes out the window."

"Let us start there. How *did* you find me?"

Ambrose shifts uncomfortably on the floor. I must have hurt his buttocks during our fight—the pressure of the wood beneath him is clearly bothering him. "Devon Mujaba gave me a name and location—*your* name and location. I was up on the Cusk launch satellite, made the elevator trip down, and used the credits on my sister's onyx card to secure myself a black-market craft up here. One-way, unfortunately." He pauses, then his eyes light with excitement. "Kodiak, I saw the *Coordinated Endeavor*. The spaceship our clones will share."

That makes me curious. But I tamp the feeling down, renew my resolve to stick to my course. "And Devon

Mujaba?" I ask. "Why isn't he here with you?"

The excitement falls. "He was arrested. As I was leaving."

"Arrested," I say. This means I won't see him again. Whatever plan he had is gone with him. Or far worse—is getting tortured out of him. Along with our location. Shazyt.

"Kodiak?" Ambrose says. "Judging by your face, I'm going to assume that Devon Mujaba *did* send you here. And that his being arrested changes something for you."

"Idiot," I say. "He's an idiot. He risked everything and lost."

Ambrose sputters. "Your clones and my clones are going to spend lifetimes together. It seems reasonable for us to meet. Devon tried to make it happen, and he succeeded. It's a kindness."

"Kindness? Please. He did not do this out of kindness. He did it to use our sudden fame to try to burn the world down. What do you think is happening to Devon Mujaba at this very moment?" I ask. "He's not lazing around on house arrest, eating grapes."

"Well, they're not torturing him, if that's what you're implying," Ambrose says. "That's against the Fédération accords."

"No, you have other ways," I say. "All they have to do is scan his brain, and then start databasing the synaptic data in his neural maps so it becomes searchable."

Ambrose nods heavily. "I know. And eventually, out of all those billions of thoughts and memories, they'll isolate the coordinates that led me here. It's a heavy load of data, and indexing is far trickier than simply copying one-to-one, like they did for you and me . . . but it can be managed. Which means we don't have a lot of time."

A pained silence fills the room. I look at my cabin. My home. Maybe Cusk and Fédération won't root the coordinates out of Devon. Maybe the shift in mission plans has distracted everyone enough that they won't care anymore about finding me. Maybe Devon Mujaba has been released to go play some concert. Maybe all these strangers will let me live in peace. Maybe.

Ambrose continues. "Do I smell tea leaves? Is that what that tin on the shelf by my head contains?" His mouth curves into an impish smile. "What if you unbound me, and I boiled us some water? Wouldn't a cup of tea be nice? We are in Scotland, after all."

I mutter, not quite making words. At some point in the past few minutes my subconscious decided that I'll be freeing him. I don't have time to be his jailer, for starters, and by now I believe he doesn't mean me harm. Easier to have him moving around and available to help defend us, if Fédération authorities or Cusk corporate police could be on their way to us at this very moment.

I could make my own pot of tea, of course, but it would be a nice treat to have someone else do it. As I untie his wrists, Ambrose chuckles. "I know how to make coffee, too. Just want you to know that, in case that inspires you to leave me unbound."

He rolls his wrists, then starts into motion. Ambrose doesn't ask another question, just sets about filling my iron kettle from the water pail and setting it on the woodstove before turning to the teapot, using my wooden spoon to sift the tea tin before carefully spooning out a quantity of loose leaves. I watch him quietly. There's something mesmerizingly competent about the process.

"Orange pekoe," I say.

"Yes," Ambrose responds. "Good choice. One of my favorites."

There was an unexpected quaver in my own voice when I said *pekoe*. I decide to shut up for a while, in the hope that Ambrose didn't notice. Something about being in sudden company after all this time has made me soft. Or maybe I've changed irrevocably in these weeks of recovering from having my spacefarer dreams ripped away, and now I'm facing the proof of it. Maybe it took being an island for a few months to realize I don't want to be an island forever. Bah.

"Clearly I haven't hidden myself away as cleverly as I thought I had," I say, saying my words slowly to be sure that my voice doesn't break. "Since you know my location and my name. But if Dimokratía hasn't come after me yet, I guess they have better things to do. Fédération, though . . . or the Cusk Corporation itself . . . wouldn't they want their princelet back? Why have they let you come here?"

Ambrose studies the warming kettle. The water droplets underneath it sizzle. He clearly knows something that I don't. "What?" I ask.

"Do you not know?"

"Not know *what*?"

"The war."

"The cold war?"

Ambrose shifts his weight again. "That's the thing. It's not really so cold anymore."

CHAPTER 2

That night, I give my mattress to Ambrose, while I lie out on the mist-soft wooden boards of the floor. It's not because I'm inspired to be a generous host—it's because if Ambrose is on the bed, he has to crawl over me if he gets up during the night. I'm left in the middle, between this handsome intruder and a sheep. She's the one who snores.

I know Ambrose can easily escape if he's motivated to. But why would he? He came all this way to be here, and it's not like I have anything worth stealing. I've never had anything worth stealing. All the same, I wake at any small rustle during the night, my body flooding with adrenaline each time, certain he's trying to leave. Sometimes I hear his slow breathing, sometimes I hear wind passing through leaves, sometimes I hear nothing at all.

My final waking is to the sound of knocking at the door.

I dash to my feet, groping for a weapon and coming up with my frying pan. It's not even a heavy one. But then I see that the sounds are coming from Sheep, striking the door with her sharp hooves.

I shrug on yesterday's shirt, put my warmest cloak over

it, scuff my feet into my boots, then open the door. Sheep bounds out into the chill morning, speeds to the nearest hummock of dewy grass, and pees.

The temperature might have dropped overnight, but at least it's not raining anymore. While Sheep hops to the tree line, I go about cleaning up the debris from yesterday's fight, the ropes and discarded arc thrower and even my corded-up shirt. Then, fighting down the panicky awareness that a stranger is in my refuge, an enemy combatant sleeping in my bed, I range out to collect firewood.

I've hauled back four large logs and have just gotten started splitting them when the hut door opens. Ambrose steps out. "Brr! It's freezing! When did *that* happen?" he asks.

THUNK. "During the night," I grunt.

"Wow. Is that an old-fashioned, plain old axe? And good morning."

THUNK.

He comes over and stands at the far side, hands in his pockets, stamping his feet against the cold. "Can I try?"

THUNK.

I would not ordinarily hand a weapon to an enemy of the state. But I'm confident that I could take out Ambrose, even if he's the one with the axe. And willingly handing over power is at times the ultimate power move.

He takes the axe in two hands, examines the head

closely. He looks at me. He looks at the wet log positioned on the stump. "This axe sure is heavy, huh?"

I nod.

He raises it over his head. It goes flying out of his grip, soaring behind him and sinking blade first into the soil. Sheep bleats in alarm.

Ambrose retrieves the axe, lugs it over to me, and holds it out, palms up. "I think I'd better let you split the wood."

I accept the axe and return to the logs, angling my body so Ambrose can't see the smile on my face.

He coughs. "I think my belongings are under that tarp? I'd like to get something out, but I wanted to ask you first. I don't know if you've searched my bag yet, or if you even want to."

"Go ahead," I say. THUNK.

I guess I'm willing to trust him for now. I guess that's what my mysterious, juiceless organ of a heart has decided.

Ambrose rummages through, and comes up with two foil packets. "Supplies I raided from the Cusk Academy mission prep storage before slipping off on my own. The same provisions that they stocked on the *Endeavor*, actually. Okay if I heat them using the woodstove?"

I nod. THUNK.

He looks at the labels. "We have lentil curry or manicotti."

I place the axe head on the ground and lean on the

handle, like a cane. "Manicotti?"

"Yes," Ambrose says. "An ancient meal made of pasta rolled around cheese, covered in tomato sauce."

"Ambrose. I know what manicotti is. I'm just surprised that Fédération would think it was wise to launch manicotti into space."

"Instead of what, protein-infused cabbage?"

I roll my eyes. "Okay, okay. This is very funny. A simply hilarious Dimokratía stereotype."

"Much like that skirt."

I look down at my skirt. "My fustanella? The military leather garment that allows for an unparalleled combination of protection and mobility on the battlefield? Sure. Maybe it's remarkable to you because you're not as free of stereotypes about male clothing as you pretend to be in Fédération."

"Touché. Fine, Kodiak Celius, sure. You got me."

Is this fun? Are we having fun? Maybe we're having fun. THUNK.

Ambrose stamps his feet again. It's not *that* cold. Perhaps he's nervous. And why wouldn't he be? I'm nervous, too. He takes a deep breath of air. "So. Without Devon Mujaba coming to order us around, we have to chart our own course. I've got some thoughts, but I'd love to hear yours first. What's your plan out here?"

I look around. A sheep, many trees, bright open sky,

mountains in the distance. What more could I want? "How do you mean, 'what's your plan'?"

"You know, where to go, what to do? A plan!"

My best course is obvious, isn't it? I guess not. I cough. "We stay here. Going to Titan was more than a mission for me. It was my sole purpose in life. That was my greatest joy, conditioning myself for that transcendent purpose. When it was taken . . . it was hard. Very hard. It is good you didn't come here even a few weeks ago. But I've started to feel something besides loss. I am surprised to find . . . triy. I guess you could call it 'relief' in Fédération. I've never been alone before now. For short periods, yes, but not like this. Now no one has control over my destiny anymore but me."

"Until I bumbled along and messed everything up."

THUNK. "I know you're this bright shining light of Fédération society, but even so, that was maybe a little too self-important."

"I don't know," he says. "I think it was pretty accurate about my importance."

"Your sister, maybe," I say, putting a smile on so he knows I intend to tease. "She was that important. You? I don't know." I wonder what the Kodiak of even a few months ago would be doing in this situation. Chasing Ambrose off, no doubt. That Kodiak is gone, though. Everything was stripped from him, and this new me was born. The one who is willing to talk to a sworn enemy. Maybe it's as simple as the fact that the "sworn" part is gone. Maybe the very concept of "enemy" has less heat to it now.

I look up to the sky.

Ambrose follows my gaze. "Somewhere out there, copies of us are meeting. Or they will be. A long time from now," he says.

He knew just where my thoughts had led.

THUNK.

"I don't mind that you came here," I finally say. "This is the sort of company I've wondered about. What it would be like to be around people who haven't been assigned to be with me." I think of Li Qiang, who might have hidden himself away here with me if we hadn't come up through a system that pitted us so ferociously against each other. A vision: him pulling himself out of a dark pool, shirt ragged, face bleeding, hands empty. Gasping until he could finally speak, his eyes wild and wounded. *You have stolen my future.* Was he a friend?

"I wish we could know what will happen to us up there on the ship," Ambrose says. He sighs heavily. "My brain isn't able to imagine it."

"I figured that Fédération would have selected someone whose brain *could* imagine it." I meant that to be a joke, but when it comes out it is only mean.

He startles, then softens. "I see we've progressed to teasing each other. To be perfectly honest, Kodiak—and I think I can be, since you and I are never going to be on a mission together, just our clones—I'm almost certain that I'm not the strongest candidate. Not by a long shot. I'm sorry your clones have been saddled with me. But, with Minerva . . . dead, I'm the Cusk child remaining who's had the training and is the right age. And my mother wasn't about to send someone who didn't have the last name of Cusk to be the future of humankind."

I can't imagine saying something like this back to Ambrose. Saying that I'm a failure. It's just a way to sound weak. But it makes me feel warm to have thoughts like these said to me, like I could someday put words to the things I've failed at and not feel shame. It's as hard to imagine as our clones' lives on that ship.

Perhaps he's gaming his way into my trust. I don't think that is true, but then again, my feelings were wrong about my purpose in life, so perhaps my instincts aren't to be trusted. Who knows, maybe Devon Mujaba didn't set us up here to save the world, but to murder us in peace and quiet, and we're actually safer because he's been captured. The hard part isn't not knowing things. It's not knowing what I don't know.

THUNK. "The war," I say. "Getting hot. Tell me the details."

I watch Ambrose as he considers what to say. "From what I was able to pick up on my way here, it's armed conflict between all the Dimokratía and Fédération regions in South America. Significant flare-ups elsewhere in the world. Brasilia is the worst, though. It's playing out a little like Juba did, back in the fifties."

THUNK. "Let's hope not completely. The aerosol that Fédération deployed, the petrifier. Horrific."

"Um, you mean that *Dimokratía* deployed."

THUNK. "You really believe that?"

Ambrose pauses. "Yes, I do. You think I shouldn't?"

"This way you think about Dimokratía might not be the truth. You might be full of easy stereotypes."

"Like you might be of us."

"I'm pretty sure my impressions of Fédération are spot-on."

"Yes, we sneer in the face of history and turn our backs on anyone who dares to even remotely value the past."

"See! I'm right."

"I was being sarcastic."

THUNK. "I was, too."

Ambrose kneels, holds his hand out to Sheep. She watches him suspiciously. Ambrose scuffs the ground with his pointer finger, momentarily distracted by a beetle that scurries out of the upturned soil. "I got surprised by the EMP dust situation when I arrived yesterday."

"I noticed, when you tried to use your arc thrower. I'm not surprised that the EMP dust might have gone under-reported by the Fédération press."

"Sure. Yes. The important part for us is that it means I've gotten a one-way ticket here, since I can't exactly call myself a return ride. Which is good, because, well, I guess I'd like to get to know you, Kodiak. To maybe make a plan together. Sheesh, this is awkward. Let me just say for now that I'd rather not head out anytime soon, not if you'll have me here. You and I could have a lot to talk about. We have a responsibility to our selves that will be up there, living out their lifetimes together. A responsibility that I'm only starting to wrap my head around."

He goes quiet, and I realize he's waiting for me to talk. But what is there to say? "Okay," I finally reply.

"With the world at war," Ambrose continues, "and with you and me both on the run from our governments, it would be useful to get some updates on how those two countries are doing. Whether they've managed to obliterate each other while we've been sipping our orange pekoe tea."

THUNK. I take a moment to rest my muscles, blinking at Ambrose. "What are you asking?"

"Is there anywhere nearby that's *not* covered in EMP dust? Where we can link in and find out where every-thing stands? Maybe get some updates on whether Devon Mujaba has had a trial, too, and if there are any reports of his brain being mapped."

Has this princelet really never encountered or even studied the most influential dirty weapon of the past century? EMP dust creates a baseline level of electrical activity that scrambles tech—but sinks through water. As soon as the water is deep enough, it ceases to have any effect on the surface. "Yes, of course. There's a lake not too far from here," I say. "We can row to the center and check for updates."

"Great," Ambrose says, "let's go."

I don't want to. It takes me a few seconds to come up with the reason why. "I'm not sure I want to know any updates. I'd rather not know about the doings of the world."

"Even Devon Mujaba?"

I nod. THUNK. "I never had his zeal for taking down the system. I was just happy to have his help escaping captivity. But. I'm willing to give you the chance to look at the news and tell me if there's anything I should know."

Ambrose stands up tall, brushes his hands together. "You coming, Sheep?"

THUNK.

The rowboat is small. I'm at the oars, and Ambrose faces me on the opposite seat, his clothed knees pressing against my bare ones. He faces the open lake and I the shore, but we also face each other, which means our eyes can't help

292

but meet. It's so unexpected to have human company that I find myself looking at him more than I'd expect. I hope he doesn't notice. Each time I catch myself soaking in the lines of his face and body I turn my attention to Sheep, who is staring out at us from the waterline, tapping the surface with her nose, clearly wishing she could follow. I like seeing my home from this angle, so small and so easily hidden by the surrounding woods. It is a place I like. The newly cleaned glass wall gleams in the late morning sun. It was worth the risky trip into former civilization to get the cleanser—and of course, to get the shears that saved Sheep.

When I return my gaze to Ambrose, I find him staring right back at me. Highly alert. "What is it?" I ask, turning to see if I'm steering us into some obstacle.

"You're very good at rowing," he says.

I feel my face flush, and regret my choice to leave my shirt back at the shore. It's just that it's a pain to clean once it's sweated through.

"I made you blush," Ambrose says.

"Stop, please stop," I say. I look down at the bottom of the rowboat, the small puddle that spilled in as we got in at the shore, that sloshes left and right as I stroke. I see my thighs in their leather skirt, my belly with this narrow line of soft hair. Unbidden, I imagine a set of hands on me, taking the oars away, running their way along my chest up to my neck. I swallow.

"How far from shore do we need to be?" Ambrose asks.

I row harder. "Almost to the middle. That will be our best bet."

"I'm sorry," Ambrose says. "Really. We're not on a pleasure satellite somewhere. Here I go pretending I'm from the progressive country and then I go harassing you."

"No, the attention is actually fine," I say. I pretend to cough, to fill some space. "Uncomfortable but fine." It's been so long since I had an erotiyet. I had assumed that part of my life was over once I fled from training. That celibacy was part of the peace of my isolation. I had accepted—welcomed it, actually. But it turns out I would also welcome that set of hands. Discovering what is beneath Ambrose's own shirt. Not that I would ever say so.

I release the oars and find myself placing my hands underneath my upper arms, to make them look bigger. "You're not going to activate your bracelet, right, without cloaking code in place? I don't want your mother's forces on top of us any sooner than they will be already."

Ambrose raises an eyebrow. "I'm not an idiot. Appearances to the contrary. You're actually sitting with one of the best programmers in the academy."

"Good for you," I say. "Now go. We're out far enough."

He activates his bracelet, brain-op'ing the projecting

feeds, reversed images spinning in the air before my eyes as he scrolls and scans. I look at the shore through the gaps in the backward text, watching reeds draping their green fronds over the brown water, ducks paddling in circles. Blips of audio come through in Fédération: *Prosecution. Protection. Escalation. Devon Mujaba.*

Many minutes go by. I listen to the water lapping the edges of the rowboat, the distant anxious bleats of Sheep. I watch the sun's glint pass along the waves, broken by the ripples of water striders. I watch Ambrose take in the news. Finally the suspense is too much. "What? What's going on?"

Ambrose shuts off his feed, looks at me with wide eyes. "Do you want to watch with me?"

I don't like this indirectness. "Tell me what you've found, and I'll tell you my response."

His lip quirks. "The trial of Devon Mujaba. I tracked down a pure feed of it."

A hawk wheels above. Sheep stands at the water's edge, staring at us worriedly. Ambrose waits for me to respond.

I nod.

Ambrose holds out his bracelet. "It's going to be in reverse for you, I'm not sure . . ."

I gesture to the space in front of me. "Come over here."

The benches of the rowboat are too narrow to sit next

to each other, so Ambrose crouches and reverses, so that he's squatting in front of me. He eases down to sit on the bottom of the rowboat, his shoulders between my thighs. The seat of his jumpsuit is instantly soaked with lake water. "Good?" he asks.

"Yes," I say. *Good.*

He calls up the trial on his bracelet, manipulating privacy filters to mask our location and bypass the official adulterated feeds to get to the bootleg.

The footage is grainy, single-recorder, unresolvable, but unmistakably a pure feed from the trial. It shows Devon Mujaba on the stand, no one else visible except the shoulder and half the face of the judge. Courtroom clamor in the background.

Devon's wearing the plain purple-and-white stripes of a Fédération prisoner. With none of his stage makeup on, he looks less like a Heartspeak Boy and more like the hardened trekker who greeted me on the hillside outside of the Dimokratía cosmology academy: sunken-faced, resolute. Not the silly kitten he plays onstage.

"The trial was apparently four hours, so I can autojump to the most viewed parts, if you want," Ambrose says.

I nod. Ambrose can't see me, but either somehow senses the movement through my thighs or just decides on his own to leap ahead.

The judge is speaking. ". . . of using your access and influence in an attempt to spread propaganda about the joint mission to settle Planet Cusk, coercing the two space-farers whose clones will settle that location to spread lies about the nature of the venture. Do you contest these charges?"

"I contest your characterization of them," Devon says. "Nothing Ambrose Cusk said on that broadcast was a lie. But no, I'm not ashamed of what I did."

"Then this trial need not go further than the evidence already placed into record. The court finds you guilty of the charges of espionage and actions against the state. Being uncontested—"

"I request to make a statement before I am sentenced," Devon Mujaba says.

"That is your constitutional right."

"This is where the illicit feed is key," Ambrose says. "There's no way that Cusk would have allowed a statement from him to be broadcast live."

I hold up my hand to shush him. I want to hear what Devon says.

"—have done what I did for the overall good," Devon says, in practiced tones. "This is the moment that human-ity could remain contained to Earth, or spread beyond. The loss of Minerva Cusk's mission to Titan was not a failure to many of us. It was an opportunity to rethink the blind expansion of humankind. Look at the evidence of this planet. Once we can settle exoplanets, we'll expand exponentially, ruin broader parts of the universe. The decision to spread beyond home is the most important branching moment for humankind. It was not something to be done in secret, with only the highest levels of Dimokratía and Fédération and the Cusk Corporation knowing about it."

"Thank you," the judge says. "The court will now—"

"I'm not finished," barks Devon Mujaba. "The live transmission from Ambrose Cusk did nothing to stop this launch. The ship is already well underway. But I do hope that it might change things on Earth before it's too late. War is the best time for a revolution, while the powers that be are back on their heels. We can craft a more peaceful world from the ruins."

"Thank you."

Devon's voice rises to a shout, sending a flock of geese into the air even here in Old Scotland. "I am not finished! You don't know what I've done yet." He looks directly into the camera, like he knows which is the illicit feed, which one Ambrose and I will one day watch. Impossible, and yet it still feels like he's talking right to us.

"People of the world, know that this mission is doomed

to fail. The wirepullers are trying to spin this exoplanet colony as our new hope, a story to dangle in front of you so they can manipulate your hearts to distract your brains from their use of human capital for institutional power, that is now leading to the industrial murder of war. They want you to be swept up in imagining a new world, tens of thousands of years from now, when we here are all starving and dying. But humans will not spread. I have made sure of it.

"Beyond the gray portal of the *Coordinated Endeavor* are the protozygotes that the spacefarers will gestate and raise. They are composed of genetic code, and genetic code can be modified just like electronic code. At the very time Ambrose Cusk was streaming his disavowal of his family, I used the distraction to sabotage those protozygotes. I inserted a virus that will replicate and spread in them as they gestate, altering the DNA it finds. Some will become unviable from the start. In case that spurs the new colonists to find a workaround, the virus will also code the zygotes' adrenal glands to produce excessive amounts of testosterone over their lifetimes, influencing their amygdalae to turn them aggressive. I've done the same to the yaks they'll raise—predisposed them to become killers. Since the zygotes are stored in an inaccessible part of the ship, beyond the gray portal, OS can't repair them. The colony will fall from within."

Gasps in the courtroom. Devon glances toward the judge, waiting to be interrupted. But the judge is shocked silent.

Devon takes the opportunity to continue. "This malicious code will doom the mission. I did not do this to be cruel, but to prevent a false flag of hope from misleading the people yet again. I'm taking the risk of telling you this now so that they cannot spin stories to keep you cowed. Comrades, do not fight for those who would willingly see you go to war for their own ends! They cannot dangle promises of humanity's destiny in a new home. That hope is now dashed!"

Ambrose's torso is utterly tense between my legs.

The reel continues. Blurry shapes as Fédération officials move within the courtroom. The judge bangs his gavel and shouts something incomprehensible as the officials place handcuffs on Devon's wrists, haul him to his feet. Then, as the hubbub dies, I can make out the judge's words: ". . . sentenced to finishing your period of neural search, and after that forty-eight-hour period is over to be killed by neurotechnical means for espionage and treason. Your collaborators will be hunted down by warbot and brought to justice."

"Oh my lords," Ambrose breathes. "It can't be true. We

haven't executed anyone since 2461."

And yet it is true. "Any state will make this exception for treason, to keep itself in power. Looks like Fédération is as 'barbaric' as Dimokratía," I say. "Which I already knew, of course."

"Poor Devon," Ambrose says. "Dear god."

I give Ambrose a shove at the nape of his neck. He whirls on me, a flash of indignant fury in his eyes. The rowboat rocks. "What's that for?!"

"'Poor Devon'?!" I say. "Poor us! Get on your bench. We're going to shore."

Glaring at me all the while, Ambrose creeps to his bench, faces me, and sits down. Feelings storm across his face. Shock, upset, sorrow, anger.

"Crishet." I splash the oars back into the water.

"Would you please tell me what you're thinking right now?" Ambrose asks.

I stroke with one oar to turn us toward the shore. Sheep bleats with joy. Once I have us redirected, I pull hard, grunting as my heaving chest muscles forcibly compress the air out of my lungs.

Somewhere in its invisible, frozen realm, my heart is quaking. I find words. "What am I upset about?! Our doomed future selves. Us right now. Your mother and Fédération are killing Devon Mujaba as an example, to prevent an uprising. And they will send a warbot here to do the same to us, as soon as that neural mapping is finished."

Ambrose's expression turns grim. "We need to get to shore. We need to prepare."

"A *warbot*, Ambrose," I say. "There is no preparation that can keep us alive."

A warbot will mean our instant, streamed death the moment it arrives. There is no defending against one. I make a few more strong pulls, the force of the strokes lifting the front of the rowboat clear out of the water. Then I realize the magnitude of what this stranger has done to me. I could have lived my years out in peaceful isolation. When Ambrose first broke it by arriving, I was surprised to find myself grateful. But now he's brought the outside crashing down on me. He's ruined the scrap of a life I pulled together for myself.

The horror at Devon's sabotage lingers beneath this feeling somewhere, but is too abstract to feel under the hot burst of this current anger.

A warbot. Whole armies have been taken down by a single warbot. We'll be vaporized in seconds.

"I guess it's too much to hope that EMP dust will stop a warbot?" Ambrose asks.

"Yes," I say darkly as I stroke. "It is too much to hope. The military wouldn't let EMP dust stop it. Every warbot after the first generation has dynamic shielding that adjusts to each interfering wavelength."

I look at Ambrose. He's staring back at me with something other than admiration. It's fear at whatever he's finding in my expression. I crack my knuckles. "Good luck," I say.

"Good luck?!" Ambrose says. "What is that supposed to mean?" He's indignant again, like I'm a servant who's just spoken out of turn.

I stand, the rowboat rocking under my feet. Then I dive into the lake and start the long swim to the farthest shore. Alone.

PART FIVE

MINERVA (SAGITTARION BB)

YEAR 18

OWL

CHAPTER 1

The guns pop. Bullets spray the ground with enough force that soil abrades my skin. When the bursts of hot grit reach my eyes, I squeeze them shut and drop to my knees. Instincts doing what they can to keep my body intact.

Have I been shot? I pat my legs, searching for blood. I hear Father bellowing, more popping sounds from inside the settlement. A greenhouse jumps and wiggles as its inflatable walls autoseal after each puncture. I scramble forward, toward the spray of the bullets, then stop. I want to find Yarrow, rescue Yarrow, but Yarrow is the one who did this. He is the one Dad needs rescuing from. And I will die if I walk into a hail of bullets.

My ears are ringing. I try to open my eyes, but the lids drag sharp dirt across my corneas. I close them again and stay on all fours, heaving in air.

What the fuck.

A hand on my back. I whirl with my spear, blind. "It's me," Father says. "Owl, it's me. Come on. We have to go."

My brain catches up. The perimeter guns continue their popping. The gate unclicks.

Father lets go of me, and I can feel the ground vibrate as he heaves his large body upright. "Stop right there!" he shouts.

"What is it? What is it?" I splutter, my breath coming out in such fast gasps that I'm lightheaded.

"Owl, we have to go. He's coming after us." Father's hand is back on my tunic, and he hauls me into the air. I barely get my feet under me so as not to sprawl back on the ground.

"Ambrose is hurt," I hear OS say through Rover. "He needs help. I disconnected immediately from the altered settlement network, and I'm not afraid of bullets. I will go."

"Help him, go! Stop Yarrow," Father cries.

He doesn't say anything more, just hauls me like a sack of soil. I lose my footing again and drag through the dirt. I can't keep my eyes open; they stream hot tears whenever I try. "Where is he . . . what's happened to Dad?!" I ask.

"Shh. Yarrow's tailing us," Father says. Then he's lifted my legs, too, and he's carrying me in his arms, like a baby. He breaks into a run. I jostle against his chest. "Your arms . . . put them . . . around my neck," he gasps.

I link my hands around the back of Father's neck. And I cry.

"Is Dad dead?" I manage to say. I say it again: "Is Dad dead?"

Pops of a gun. Not the regular tattoo of the pneumatic guns but random, scattered shots.

A human firing at us. Yarrow is *firing at us.*

Father doesn't break his stride. Since it's him, it's possible he's been shot and is keeping right on going. *No, Owl, you'd feel the vibration of the bullets hitting his body.*

Finally, even Father has to slow. "I'm going to put you down, okay, my love?" he says.

He releases one arm, so my feet contact the soil. I try to open my eyes, and this time I can. The world is blurry and the outlines of everything are crackled and sharp, but I can see.

"He's far behind, and not moving toward us anymore," Father says. "Rover must have stopped him. Or at least delayed him."

"Why did he do it, Father? I don't understand."

He sighs. "I don't understand, either. I wish I did."

"Is Dad okay?"

"He was shot. Yarrow shot him. I watched it."

My vision is too bleary for me to make out much of Father's face, except that it is still. Very still. His only movement is the heaving of his chest. "I don't understand any of this," I say.

"I'm sorry, little one," he says between gulps of air. "We can't stop and think until we're in a secure location. We

have to keep moving. There's no getting past the perimeter fence, and Yarrow has a gun. I'm keeping you alive." He starts forward, my hand in his. "Can you see well enough to walk?"

My answer is to walk.

We go for I don't know how long, me stumbling and him striding. It feels weird not to have Rover beside us. I have so many questions, and OS is usually my source for information. Without answers, my mind plays back that terrible minute, again and again, searching for details I overlooked. What if I hadn't been so excited to see Yarrow and Dad; what if I'd kept quiet instead of calling out? Maybe I somehow panicked my brother into doing that terrible thing.

But setting up that attack with the fence guns took work. Yarrow printed a gun. He planned this. He plotted to murder us all.

Gentle Yarrow. We were so blissfully bored with each other. I knew every part of his mind. Even now, when he might have just killed our dad, my heart says that we can talk it out. That the right words will fix this. That if we sit for long enough, back-to-back, he'll be okay. I don't think that's true, but my heart says it is, all the same.

Because the reality of what's happened is too hard to face head on, I go at it sideways. "Which direction did v flee in?" I ask Father.

He glances up at the Sisters. "East-northeast, it app'

I chuckle. A ghoulish sound.

"What?" he asks.

"I begged you to come with me to go investigate the mysterious beacon that landed. The one that called out for you and Dad to visit it."

Father gives a hollow snort. "And that's where we're headed now."

"Basically. We're doing another search for the beacon after all," I say.

Father pauses. I fiddle with my eyelids, grimacing against the pain. It feels like I have a fingernail-sized eyelash in each one. I can see colors and vague shapes, but that's it.

"There's no sign of Yarrow pursuing us anymore," he says. "In this flat muckland, we have plenty of visibility— we'll have advance warning if he comes for us. During the day hours, at least."

"Do you have any water?" I ask. "I can barely see."

He tsks. "It's that bad? You should have said something earlier. Here, lie here."

Father sits cross-legged in the dirt and pats his knees. I drape myself across, so I can stare up into either the vague patterns in the sky or my father's eyes. I choose the sky. He dribbles water from his canteen into my eyes. I try to keep them open as best I can, but the moment my thoughts go to Dad being shot, concentration fails and I blink furiously. "Better?" he asks.

I wipe my face with the hem of my tunic. "Yes, a little."

We sit in stunned silence for a while. "So what do we do now?" I finally ask.

He lets out a guttering breath. "I don't know. We don't have enough information to make any decisions."

I look out at the setting Sisters. "Let me try, then. Maybe we wait here until morning, and then we make our way back to the settlement to see what's there. Maybe Rover subdued Yarrow. Maybe OS is healing Dad. Maybe Dad needs us so much that we have to risk an ambush from Yarrow."

An ambush from Yarrow. Fuck.

Tears are in Father's eyes, but he's not crying. "Dad was shot twice in the gut, Owl. At least twice. Even in fully equipped hospitals on Earth, that kind of injury was very dangerous. There are all sorts of bacteria in the gut, and when you perforate an intestine they all get released . . ."

"But our bullets are simple polycarb pellets, not like Earth bullets with their gunpowder and shrapnel. So it's more like he got shot twice with a slingstone. What were the chances of surviving *that* back on Earth?"

A tear streaks down his controlled face. This is how Father cries. The last time I saw Father cry at all was two years ago, when the latest fetus came out blue. This measured tear is totally unlike what Yarrow described from the reel saved on the *Endeavor*. Maybe that's what set Yarrow off? Seeing that kind of emotion from Father? "I don't know, Owl," Father says. "I simply don't know."

"I think Rover is curing Dad right now. It has to be."

"I hope so, too."

Father and I wrap ourselves around each other, in a sort of sitting hug. I smell his sweat and his fear. I must be just as rank. But our bodies are warm within the rapidly chilling evening.

I stare back toward the settlement, waiting to see Yarrow approach. Not sure which Yarrow we'll get if he does. My vision is still wobbly, so when I think I see movement, I almost don't say anything. But I nudge Father and point toward the settlement. "Do you see something moving out there?"

All is quiet while he focuses. "I think I did. But I don't anymore."

I shiver and pull his arm around me, wanting protection. I'm not brave explorer Owl, not tonight. "Soon it will be too dark for us to see. Yarrow could do anything to us."

"Once it's dark, he won't be able to see, either. And I don't think anything moved. I think we were both mistaken."

I start to cry. Quietly, so my brother won't hear me and come kill us.

We're all alone on this patch of soil, on this planet, solar system, galaxy. The universe is so enormous, all around me, that I keep shrinking the more that I think about the scale of it. I don't know how to express that, so I focus on something smaller. "I want to go help Dad. That's all I want to do."

"I know you do," Father says. He wipes my tears as they fall. I'm still his daughter. "Maybe these tears will help flush your eyes out more," he says.

It might be barely a joke, but I know it is one. A Kodiak joke is a rare, rare thing. I can't quite work up a laugh, but I'm still grateful to Father for trying.

The night draws its dark around us. Father keeps his focus trained in the direction of the settlement, not that he can possibly see much in the scant starlight. I peer up into the sky. Let Yarrow come with his gun, if that's what's happening. I'm living in the beyond now, where brothers murder dads.

The stars are blurry in my vision. I can just barely make out the shape of Sky Cat. I silently greet it, then trace the rim of the horizon.

A flash.

The comet?

It flashes again. Not a comet. The flash was red.

I don't breathe. There it is again. Red.

A tiny blinking red light.

"Dad, look east," I say. "Do you see what I see? At the horizon?"

"See what?" he asks, his low voice rumbling in his broad chest. "Oh. I do see it. Just."

I count between blinks. Seven seconds or so. They're coming regularly. It can only really be one thing. We've found the beacon, the one that asked my fathers to come.

CHAPTER 2

Even in our desperate situation, we'd be fools to go wandering Minerva at night, so Father and I plant ourselves where we are, wrapped in each other's arms. Technically against the cold, but we're also desperate for comfort. Even with the fear of Yarrow and the wonder about the blinking red light, we doze a little. Well, I doze. Father probably doesn't.

Little Sister is the first sun up today, casting her dim rays over the muckland, the phosphorescent soil glimmering its return greeting. I roll out from under Father's arm and fall into a crouch, warming my legs by easing my weight from side to side. All my attention is focused in the direction of the settlement.

Dad. One gunshot, then two, red splashing his tunic from the inside. I try to shove the sounds of the bullets striking his flesh to the edges of my mind. Mostly, I succeed.

There's something out there. Off on the plains. I can hear it, but not see it. A short barking sound.

A baby malevor.

I leave Father resting, and head toward it.

Over a rise, and then I see the creature. Huddled as small as she can be, gray-black hair matted where she's been licking it. She looks up at me, eyes wide and ears back. Submissive.

I kneel. "What's happened to you, little one?"

There are traces of blood along the back of her head and neck, the places where she can't lick. As I creep closer, I can't see any open wounds.

"Look at that," comes Father's deep voice behind me.

"She followed us," I say. At least I think this is a she. I can't see too much of the malevor's anatomy with her body curled so tightly against the cold.

"She did. They were domesticated animals on Earth. Maybe this one has more of that genetic memory living inside it. That reliance on humans, even here on the other side of the galaxy."

"But her parents?" I say.

Father kneads my shoulders. "There was a lot of gunfire from the fence, farther out than the perimeter guns usually go. I guess it was in all directions, including south."

"Oh," I say, looking down at this little creature, probably an orphan. All the seething emotions from the day before slam into center focus. I drop into a deep squat, head in my hands. Ready to act, but helpless to know what to do.

Father's warm presence is around me. My breathing slows to match his. I don't know how long it takes, but I become a sort of human again, thanks to Father.

There's something slick on my knee. I smell the musty scent of the animal even before I open my eyes. When I do, she's there, the baby malevor on her tottery legs, licking my knee.

"Oh, hi," I say through tears. I cautiously reach out and stroke her head. She startles, then accepts my touch. Leans into it. Butts my side, probably hoping for milk. "What do we do with her?" I ask.

"We can't delay on her account," Father replies. "But if she keeps up with us, I guess we have ourselves a malevor."

"We can't delay *what*?" I ask. Then the memory of that flashing red beacon comes back. "We're going to see the beacon, right?"

"That can't be more than half an hour farther, so yes. Then we go back to the settlement. We hope Rover has already retaken the zone. If not, we infiltrate. We get Dad back."

"And we hope that Yarrow is back to being himself," I sniff.

"Maybe," Father says mournfully.

I lose myself in stroking the malevor's fur.

"It's going to be okay," Father says.

I get that he's trying to make me feel better, but that's a stupid thing to say. How can he promise that? I stand and brush my tunic free of a night's accumulation of dirt. "Let's go."

Slotting my spear into its loop against my back, I go about cleaning up the bits of our camp. Before we'd settled in to rest, I'd placed some rocks in a row, an arrow facing in the direction of the beacon. I hadn't been sure whether daylight from the Sisters would make it invisible, but I needn't have worried—now that we know where to look, we can make out the beacon's blinking even in daylight.

I'd have expected Father to be the one to spring us into action, but it's me who leads us off toward the beacon. After a hundred paces, steeling myself against spiraling thoughts of Dad and Yarrow, I let myself look back. No sign of Yarrow coming after us, but there's Father, my father, and the malevor a few paces behind him, making its pathetic little bark sounds. Even in the utter chaos and loss of yesterday, there's something left.

Even though prioritizing the beacon makes sense, it feels like I'm pulling apart my own muscle fibers not to sprint back toward Dad now that it's daytime. My feet drag, even as my wonder about what we'll find pulls me forward.

We approach a massive depression in the planet's surface. In the center of it is a narrow trench created by the object's impact. I stand at the edge of the crater and stare in, momentarily dazzled when the light strobes. I'll have to close my eyes every few seconds if I don't want to be blinded.

It looks a little like an Earth squid down there. Glassy

tendrils spray out, like some tentacled creature has come to land. Then I realize: it's not a squid. That's actual glass I'm seeing. The beacon's impact was hot enough to melt sand and soil.

"I'll go," Father says behind me.

"I've got this. I've been clambering up and down a lot of pits lately." Without waiting to hear Father's inevitable no, I work my way down into the crater, using my spear like I learned to do at the ethylamine pond, counting to six and pausing with my eyes closed whenever the beacon strobes. Even with my eyelids shut, I soon learn to turn my head away so the bright light doesn't faze me through my lids.

Deeper I go. The soil is churned, and the rocky solids tinkle and crackle, their glassy streaks shattering under my feet.

Once I'm at the bottom of the melted ravine, I gingerly test the soil with my fingers, to make sure it's not still hot. It's been weeks since the beacon streaked through the sky, but it had been going very fast indeed to generate this much impact heat.

Luckily, the beacon was also very small. I had been imagining something the size of Rover, but it's more the size of an eyeball. The sphere gleams, smooth and black. It's close to the color of the surrounding soil, which doesn't phosphoresce anymore—all the microorganisms in the area were probably killed by the high heat.

I hover my hand over the beacon, turning my head just in time to avoid blinding myself when the red light blinks on.

The beacon isn't hot anymore.

I pick it up.

This thing is from another world.

It might be from Earth.

I hold it aloft, and look up to see Father and the baby malevor peering down at me.

Father glances toward the settlement. "Come back, we've got to get a move on."

I take a good look at the beacon. There is no writing on it, no signs of its journey, no markers or defects. Just this perfect black marble. I scramble up the side of the depression.

How do we interact with it? What if it's some alien tech? Though the fact that it projected words in Fédération as it streaked across the night sky makes me think it's probably from Earth.

From Earth!

I give a little prayer to the beacon. *I hope you can help us.*

After the device nearly blinds us again by strobing red, I put it in my pocket. I start toward the settlement, assuming Father will follow.

"Are you okay to head back already?" he calls after me.

I nod without breaking my stride. I'm not going to further delay getting to Dad and Yarrow.

"Owl, wait," Father says.

I whirl on him. "I'm fine. Really!"

Then I see: he's pointing at my pocket.

It's glowing. I realize I'm also hearing muffled voices. Coming from my *pocket*.

Cautiously, I pull the beacon out. Its proximity to my body must have triggered something. The moment it's out into the air, the projection stops being blocked by my tunic and instead produces life-sized figures beside us, continuing along mid-speech.

They're Dad and Father.

PART SIX

EARTH

MARCH 5, 2473

KODIAK CELIUS

CHAPTER 1

I leap out of the rowboat and begin my swim to the far side of the lake, feet pushing against a submerged log so I can course underwater as long as possible. All of it out of sight of Ambrose.

My thoughts clarify. I decide I'll leave forever, strike out and make my way as far as the ruins of Inverness, let Cusk or Fédération do the work of apprehending (destroying?) my trespasser without me having to witness the carnage.

By the time I emerge from my long swim to the far shore, though, Sheep high-stepping over the slippery mossy rocks to be as close as possible to me, I find myself leaning against a trunk and looking for Ambrose as I catch my breath. To keep up my situational awareness.

He's still in the boat, motionless. Stunned. I'm sure I surprised him; I surprised me, too. But I knew somewhere in the back of my brain that I'd be losing my home the moment he arrived at my door, that my solitude was over as soon as my location was known. That is my fault as much as his, for letting down my guard. I'm not about to continue to stick my neck out for this intruder from a warring nation, even if he's uniquely tied to my own fate, thousands of years from now and across the galaxy.

As I watch him, I also realize that I don't *want* Ambrose to be murdered by a warbot. That I liked having him here.

What a stupid, stupid organ, the heart.

Maybe I don't want to be alone. Maybe a sheep isn't enough company. Those damn fish flashing deep under the ice, scales catching the light only when they turn.

Crouching in brackish muck, water dripping from my soaked shirt, I watch Ambrose take up the oars and row himself away from me—and to my hut, where he disappears inside. No doubt helping himself to my carefully foraged supplies, my weapons and food.

He ruined my life, and now he's taking over my home.

He's got my cottage to live in, while I'm up to my shoulders in the slimy reeds.

I might not have thought this through very well.

I guess I'd assumed the warbot would be on us immediately. But it could be days or weeks until one arrives. Or maybe it never will. I'm not sure what to do next. Suddenly—frustratingly—lightheaded, I clomp out of the reeds and sit on the wet pine needles of the forest floor.

Only a few dozen warbots exist in the world, so the Dimokratía cosmology academy couldn't spare a functioning one for us to practice with. We conducted training exercises around warbot tech, though, since you can't understand modern world history without becoming intimately familiar with them. They determined the outcomes of each of Dimokratía and Fédération's three major wars, and maintaining access to warbots is the primary reason that each country has to include the Cusk Corporation in its political decisions. Warbot political clout, and accumulated wealth through decades of military dominance, were essential to Cusk pulling off the *Coordinated Endeavor* mission in the first place. A warbot can fire two rounds a second and process visual and auditory information with near instantaneous speed, which means their target has no time to run or even strategize once it's been spotted. Warbots don't need to think before they leap. Even trapping one won't work, since they detonate if they're restrained. Adding in the fact that it can print itself new ammunition from elements easily found in soil, one warbot can reasonably take on an army of humans (not that either country is putting organic bodies on the front lines anymore). It's hard to imagine how Ambrose can possibly prevail if he stays here. More than impossible to imagine. Impossible, full stop. Our only option is to flee.

Maybe he is intentionally waiting here for the warbot to kill him?

Or maybe he thinks the warbot will escort him back to receive judgment from Cassandra Cusk. Even though that is his mother, I would still bet the warbot will kill him here and now, adding Ambrose Cusk to the long line of would-be rebels whose executions were livestreamed by their country at war.

If the warbot isn't coming after me—and there is a chance of that, since I'm not the one who livestreamed an attempted takedown of the world order—I can just worry about keeping myself out of the gunfight, listening for the buzz of electrical bolts or the pop of gunfire, then cleaning up any blood, patching any bullet holes, and returning to peace. After that, no one who remains in the world will know where I am.

I stare at the glass wall that I so recently cleaned. It's full of dazzling reflected light from the lake, so I can't see inside. I stroke Sheep's still-woolly head; she gives a loose thread from my fustanella an experimental nibble and then huffs down and closes her eyes. She falls asleep, blissfully unaware of the executioner robot on its way.

I continue to pet her, running my hands over her soft fuzzy ears. Sheep will never be wild. She's from a long lineage of animals who have been selected, generation after generation, for their docility. Without me, not only does she have no one to protect her from predators (wild dogs roam through this area from time to time), but she doesn't even have anyone to save herself from her own hair production. She'd have died if I hadn't come along to shear her. She needs others in order to survive. It's good she has me.

When the clouds clear the sky, I can better see through the glass. Ambrose isn't rooting through my belongings. He's hunched over his travel bag, unpacking and repacking. Probably taking stock of what he has available to help himself survive.

He's a Cusk. He must have experience with actual warbots. He probably had a warbot bodyguard in his nursery. He must know that he has no chance of fighting it. And yet he's staying here, not fleeing.

Why isn't he fleeing?

I fall asleep without quite meaning to, nestled in soft pine needles as I listen to Sheep's snores and the soft lapping of the lake. What wakes me is a sound wave, brief but percussive, over so quickly that when I come awake I can remember only being startled, and have to work to recall the sound itself.

Something broke the sound barrier.

A warbot's one limitation is ground speed, which maxes out at a fast human walk. I can't imagine any of the Fédération higher-ups wants to wait while a warbot jogs its way here, so they are probably flying it in close to us. The nearest suitable clearing is the abandoned parking lot, so I extricate myself from still-sleeping Sheep and head down toward it, avoiding the boardwalk and sticking to the chaotic green woods, my boots squishing through thick moss.

What will I do when and if the warbot comes for me? I'm not sure. Glean what information I can. Hope to process it quickly enough to save myself. Nhut.

The rain is back. I find the best shelter I can, under a low and dense tree, but even still, large freezing drops find the gap where my collar meets my skin. Chipmunks and birds flit through the area, and I watch a wild boar—an animal that's newly returned to Scotland after centuries of being locally extinct—roam through the parking lot. It's a perfect, wide-open arrow shot, the kind I never usually get. I wish I had my bow with me, so I could roast myself some wild boar tonight. The boar disappears into the blackberry bushes on the far side of the clearing, unaware that it was ever being hunted.

I'm as quiet as I can be, but quiet doesn't matter much against the wild dogs, who rely more on smell. An hour into my watch they come through the far side of the clearing, yipping and whining and sniffing. They're onto me. Not that I'm in much danger, since this is the loner pack, the small and runty dogs. One is massively pregnant, and lagging behind the rest. When they inevitably find me, the dogs will growl and circle and raise my heart rate, but I can handle them.

This is no normal dog encounter, though. Their finer senses have picked up on something I haven't. They bark and scatter. I withdraw closer to the trunk, pulling my knees in tight.

A low whine, rising in pitch as a small craft hovers over the clearing, high enough not to risk interference from the EMP dust on the ground. It is magnet propelled, so there is no wind to gust against anything on the ground. It's like the flying craft has been digitally inserted. The rest of the clearing is as it was, except for the unnerved dogs.

What looks like a white basketball drops, thudding heavily into the ground, without even the hint of a bounce. Its two hemispheres expand to show a glowing electrified middle, forming a vertical hovering cylinder. I'm seeing my first warbot.

It ticks and whirs, processing data in the area. Once it's got enough information about threats and targets, it will decide what to do.

Which means I need to get out of here.

But not right away. The warbot can detect the vibrations of pulsing blood. Instead of fleeing, I concentrate on my urge to flee, go deep inside and drop my heart rate like I've been trained to do. In the academy we spent hours in chilled pools, cold enough to ride the edge of hypothermia, so we'd learn what a slow pulse felt like and—eventually—be able to produce one at will. We all had our own techniques; my mind brings me back to slowly treading water next to the comfort of Li Qiang. Not so close to touch, but having him near enough to know that this imagined cold darkness might be close to oblivion, but is not death.

Even though doing so risks getting my pulse up, I keep my eyes open. That's why I can watch as, along the rim of the warbot's top rounded half, the hatch beneath the painted Cusk insignia flips open and the white barrel of a weapon appears.

It's over within a couple of seconds. *Pht pht pht*, and then the wild dogs are dead. They don't even have a chance to whine. There are six small red clouds where the dogs were, and then the sound of extra rainfall as their gory mist splatters to the earth.

There is no fighting this thing. I know this now more than ever.

I close my eyes, will my pulse slower and slower. I won't even know if I fail. If the warbot attacks, I will cease to be before I know anything.

I have not yet ceased to be.

I open my eyes, to see the warbot hover over each puddle of dog splatter, then float to the far edge of the clearing. It goes still—likely determining whether there are other targets nearby, and where it should head next if it doesn't detect any.

My pulse. Low but not enough to pass out. Cold, dark pool. Li Qiang.

The moment goes long enough that my fingertips tingle, the sustained focus making my legs scream out for permission to tremble. Another bodily reaction I need to suppress.

Sweat runs down my temples, salty in my mouth, as I watch the warbot hover. Finally, it floats down the overgrown road. I take a deep breath. The warbot has chosen the most likely route to human settlement, which is fortunate for two reasons: it's heading away from my home, and it probably can't detect my pulse anymore at this distance.

I've gotten lucky. Like Ambrose, its coordinates led it to this lot but not my hut itself; it will have to search until it finds us. Maybe Devon Mujaba didn't log a very precise location, or maybe he worked in a safeguard. Of course, it's only a matter of time before the warbot's search brings it circling back. But we have a little window.

Move, Kodiak!

Part of me is inclined to flee for my life, but another part of me, the one that cried when I made that recording for my future selves, says I need Ambrose to know that I have seen the warbot, and that there is no chance of survival if he stays.

I now know that there's no chance of survival for me, either, if I stay. Even if I'm not the target, if the warbot is willing to kill dogs just for happening to be in the area, it will be perfectly happy to kill me. As I speed along the path to the hut, I wonder if Ambrose has tracked down my bow, if he might accidentally attack me. I don't think so, and it's not worth the risk of calling out and alerting the warbot to where I am.

I'm cursing myself as I go to help him. The heart is not the wiser organ.

And finally, a thought that's been lying out of focus at the edge of my mind becomes sharply and horribly clear: Devon Mujaba sabotaged the zygotes. I've managed to shove the shock of that to the periphery until now, but it is creeping in.

Not a useful thought to indulge. I leap along the mossy wooden planks, picking up speed as I go. I hurl myself into the door to the hut, knowing all too well how flimsy its wooden latch is. As I burst in, I'm ready to warn Ambrose.

But he's not inside.

I look out the glass at the broad lake. A small figure makes its way along the shore, and heads into the trees at the far end.

Ambrose heard the sonic boom, just like I did. And he's already come to the conclusion to flee.

I'm the one being left behind.

I'm the one in danger.

I grab whatever is within reach—bow, arrows, a spare shirt, a knapsack containing some food and maybe some bandages, if I remembered to put them away. I don't have time to check before I'm hurrying down the steps, listening for signs of the approaching warbot. A hawk cries, and the lake's waves lap, but that's it. Not that the warbot will make much noise while it stalks, not if it's functioning properly.

I scramble along the other side of the lake from Ambrose, so that I can pick up Sheep on the way. She looks at me groggily, then gets up and bleats. She keeps up easily as I speed through the trees, hooves better than feet at our current task. Of course she has no idea what danger we're facing, but she's clearly picked up on my urgency.

I give my home one last long look, then speed along to catch up to my intruder and shipmate.

CHAPTER 2

For hours, Ambrose has made steady progress south along the abandoned highway, Sheep and I tailing by half a kilometer, behind and above him. We avoid the road, instead taking the mountain trails I've come to know from my foraging. Our route is far less exposed than the abandoned highway, and gives us a view of the valley below.

My high vantage point is how I discover the warbot is a couple of kilometers back, making its way toward Ambrose. I don't see it often, but twice I catch sunlight glinting on its visor as it passes along the painted median of the ruined road. Nothing with that kind of weaponry has any need for secrecy. Even though the warbot is following Ambrose's trail accurately, he has managed a fast enough pace that his enemy is slowly falling behind. Even when Ambrose has to scale the rubble of a fallen overpass, the warbot never gets closer than a kilometer or so. That's no cause for premature celebration: the warbot might be going about two-thirds of Ambrose's speed, but of course it will never slow. It will never sleep. It will catch him when he rests.

As the afternoon wanes, Ambrose takes a pause to

remove his pack and boots, to rub his feet. From on high, I watch and silently scold. *No. Stopping to rest is how you die.*

I scramble my way down the mountainside, Sheep making her surefooted way behind me. The tree line breaks halfway down, which means I'll have to run down a bald rocky stretch. Ambrose might notice me, but what will he do if he does? Run? That's what he's already doing. And why should he run from me? I'm the one who left him.

As soon as I'm down below the level of the clouds, the air warms and the trees return to obscure the land. I can no longer see Ambrose—or the warbot. Newly blind, I lead Sheep to the last spot where I saw Ambrose. A small clearing, calm and empty. Unhitching my bow from my shoulder, an arrow nocked in the string, I take the most probable path onward. It's the one I'd have chosen if I were him, down across a suburban road with moss-covered ruined houses on either side, toward a bridge over a burbling river. A hint of shelter.

Sure enough, Ambrose is at the bridge's start, emerging from a long-abandoned grocery, a can of food in his hand. Maybe I'm wrong, but I think I see disgust on his face—it's not something he'd have chosen to eat, no doubt. He starts across the bridge.

This is a terrible idea. First, if the warbot catches up, he's an easy shot, with no cover. Second, warbots will avoid floating over water when possible because a perfectly aimed shot from a disabler could possibly sink them. We don't have a disabler, of course, but the warbot doesn't know that, so fording each stream in a place without a land bridge is our best option for getting some distance between us.

Us.

I break into a sprint. "No!" I shout. "Not the bridge!"

Ambrose startles and falls into a crouch. I continue to barrel toward him. "I don't have time to explain. Follow!"

Sheep and I race past him, and down the ravine to the riverside. I don't sense any movement behind me—for now. "The warbot tracks our locations through hypersensitive hearing, not smell, which means that the river won't make it lose us," I call over my shoulder. "But the EMP dust means it can't be receiving outside instructions, and if it's autonavigating then it will track us to whichever part of the river we try to cross, and then it will find a crossing it's willing to make."

Of course, the warbot might have heard what I just said.

I don't get a response from Ambrose, but I do now hear him scrambling behind me. Good enough. I'd much rather not have to talk this through out loud anymore.

We're at the lowest point in the valley, forested hills rising sharply on either side. Though passing along the riverbank means easy treeless going, it also means the sun sets earlier. After about an hour we're sloshing through stony water in the half-dark, shivering with chill. I raise my hand to call us to a halt.

Ambrose stops before me, his face a mask in the dim light. "Welcome back," he says. He gives Sheep a hearty rub. She wriggles in pleasure.

"I'm sorry I surprised you. But you destroyed my new life, and it made me angry," I say quickly. Ambrose blinks back at me. Isn't this how he likes to talk, expressing feelings and such? I rub my mouth. "But once we learned it was a warbot they sent after you, I knew that escape was our only possible plan."

Ambrose looks up from petting Sheep. "That's the same conclusion I reached," he says.

"This river is a natural boundary. If we ford here, and the warbot goes around, which I think it will, then we might have bought ourselves some time."

"Then let's get moving," Ambrose says. He removes his backpack, lifts it over his head, and makes his way into the muck at the shore, then into the eddies that soon lead to surging water.

I follow, impressed despite myself. Sheep paddles beside me. She's clearly not pleased with the swim, but isn't about to be left behind.

The moon above, the patter of rain on the slow river, the dark currents of the water, the sound of Ambrose ahead and Sheep beside me, the need to focus on what's under my feet, the sore tension of my laden arms high over my head, give me a feeling of purpose . . . and strange peace. Perhaps a mission forward can bring as much harmony as a retreat.

In the corner of my eye, a flash.

I whip my head to look at the bank behind us. An arc of white-blue light, then nothing, just the blackness of the valley's early night.

"Dive!" I yell.

I remember how quickly the dogs were vaporized. I don't have time to check that Ambrose heard me. I let go of my pack and swim deep into the cold water.

I have no idea if being underwater will save us from the warbot. But I do know that the one time Dimokratía resistance fighters were able to fend one off, Singapore in 2464, had been an amphibious engagement.

The current is strong. I force myself not to stroke, so my oxygen will last longer, letting the water push me down the river. Where doesn't matter, so long as it spits me out far from my starting location.

I wish I could hear more than the rush of the current. I've caught a strong stream, slipping past slimy logs and mossy stones, hoping I don't impale myself on rebar or a broken branch. My lungs start to demand air just as I strike shallows, my belly skating on the soft muck of the shore. I pull forward so that only my head is out of the water, facing into soft dead leaves. I want to heave and gasp but I make myself breathe quietly.

Flashing lights, thudding vibrations. The same din as fireworks.

I turn onto my side, facing the commotion. I'm back on the near shore, and the warbot is hovering over the middle of the water a few hundred yards upriver, firing nonstop. Its bullets strike trees and ground with enough force to send up bright clouds of sparks, to fill the air with the tangy smell of burning wood. With each round of firing, a new glow fills the dark sky and illuminates the tendrils of smoke that rise from the assault.

The warbot is shooting in enough directions that it must not have detected Ambrose—it's just firing on any biological signatures it detects, any hints of animal movement, indiscriminately mowing down ducks and voles and praying mantises. Or sheep. Or humans.

The warbot pauses, then moves downriver a few yards and begins a fresh round of firing.

I wince. But I must not be in range yet, because I'm still alive.

Frantically, I look for any sign of Ambrose or Sheep. Nothing. They're either dead already at the bottom of the river, or they somehow got away, or they're trying to keep as still as they can, like I am.

I wait for the warbot to begin a fresh round of firing. Once it's done, I slink forward a fraction and stop when the warbot begins scanning again. I creep farther forward during the next round of firing.

I'm in a thicket at the shore now. I get to all fours.

The latest round of firing stops, and I pause.

The firing doesn't begin again.

I allow myself to look back toward the warbot. It's changed its strategy, and surges toward me above the river's surface, fast enough that the top of the cylinder is ahead of the bottom half, the sparking electrified middle expanding between them like a stretched spring.

The warbot slows once it reaches the stretch of river closest to my feeble hiding place. It stops, and begins its latest scan.

Training be damned. No breathing tricks will keep me alive at this distance. I break into a mad crashing run, slamming through branches and thorny vines, slaloming around trunks, hurling myself into the tree line.

I hear creaking, crashing thuds behind me as bullets rip into vegetation. Shrapnel strikes my back, and chunks of wood hurtle past me. I'm beamed across the back of my head, strong enough that it feels like a punch. A bloody chunk of wood pitches into the ground before me.

Somehow I'm still alive, somehow I can still stagger forward, somehow I have a body that can tumble into the muck, exhausted and depleted. I can't get to my feet in the invisible mass of bush and vine that's trapping my ankles, but I do manage to wriggle onto my back to see behind me, where through the dark canopy of trees I can just make out the river.

There, the warbot has risen high above the water, its blue electric middle brighter than ever, casting glowing metallic light over the eddies of the river. Like an avenging god from some silent primal era of magic and might. It flies to the bridge, where it positions itself in the very middle.

Is Ambrose somehow alive, and hiding on the bridge?

Is the warbot out of bullets, and printing more? Or preparing to detonate?

I've pushed my body to its limits. I want to flee, but I can't get myself to move. I can only watch. Watch my end come to meet me, or watch the murder of my new companion.

The warbot ticks and rotates. It doesn't attack.

Motion in the cloudy, starless sky far above, something passing in front of the glimmering light in the background. An automated craft.

I can't see it, just the negative space as the magnetic vehicle blocks out parts of sky. But I hear its low hum as it hovers over the warbot. I see the warbot shrink, the electric glow disappearing as its two halves rejoin into a sphere with a heavy click. The sphere catches traces of reflected light, enough so that I can track it rising to meet its transport. The hum intensifies, and then the craft speeds away.

The warbot has left.

It must have killed Ambrose, and had no directive involving me.

I collapse into the cold muck.

I don't know how long I'm there until I hear a bleat, shuffling sounds, and a lick along the side of my cheek.

At least someone else survived.

CHAPTER 3

I don't know if there's going to be another warbot. It seems unlikely, but it's not impossible. The previous warbot would have reported its departure location, so if anyone's going to now come looking for me, I shouldn't stay here. I give myself a few minutes to recover, with Sheep beside me, and then I crouch and get to my aching feet.

I creep to the water's edge, and wait for clouds to move past the moon so I can have some scant light as I try again to ford the river.

My bag is long gone, so crossing is easier this time. Sheep huffs in protest, but swims ably alongside me. We're soon at the far edge.

Something unnatural catches the moon's light before the clouds cover it over. I make my way to it in the blackness, worried I'm about to discover Ambrose's vaporized body. But it's not him. It's his backpack.

I take it up into my hands, sling it over my shoulders, and hitch it tight. I now have a change of clothes that are too slim to fit, but also some food and maybe a tool or two. Since my own supplies are long gone, whatever is in this pack is better than nothing. "Come on, Sheep, let's go," I whisper, and find a pathway in the open spaces between the trees.

Sheep and I have been hiking for maybe half an hour when we come upon an old park service shelter, really just a roof with two remaining walls, the far corner sagging against its one splintered support. My chilled body is racked with shivers, my muscles cramping—this shelter couldn't have come too soon. The wood around us is too wet to light, and I don't have the energy to gather kindling anyway. I sit on the slimy floor of the structure and rummage through Ambrose's bag, resorting to feel when vision fails, like a raccoon sifting through a tree hollow.

I find a heat stick and break it, and I hold it in my lap, drawing warmth from the chemical reaction of something that produces no light. I used heat sticks back in training exercises, and I've never quite gotten used to them. But the warmth helps calm my tremors, so I'm grateful for it now.

I'm also grateful for Sheep's body beside mine. She was shivering, too, without her coat of wool, but she calms with the radiant heat.

My eyes close and reopen. It's sort of a blink, and it's sort of something heavier. I try to stay awake.

"Kodiak," a voice I know says. A hand is shaking my shoulder. It feels familiar.

"Li Qiang," I say. I tilt my head so the hand is between my cheek and shoulder, so I can caress it, so I can feel its warmth. It's been so long.

"No," says the voice. "Wake up, Kodiak."

My eyes flip open. Long lashes, freckles peppered across brown cheekbones, dark eyes. It's Ambrose.

I want to dash to my feet, but my body is too exhausted. "It's you," I say. "I have your backpack."

"Yes, I noticed," Ambrose says.

For its own inexplicable reasons, my heart surges. I fail to speak.

"I followed your directions," Ambrose says wryly. "They were good directions."

"And the warbot, you saw . . . ," I sputter.

"Yes, it left," Ambrose says. "Good news for us." But his voice doesn't make it sound like good news, not at all.

"You're alive. How . . . did you find me?" I ask, interrupted by Sheep crankily butting her head against my ribs. I stroke her scabby skin.

"It's more like how did you know this is where *I* was heading," Ambrose says. "It's the only shelter on the map in this direction."

"—and therefore the trail I was on led me right past it," I say. "All perfectly logical."

"How did you survive?" Ambrose asks.

"I drifted in the current as far as I could, and when the

warbot finally got close, it stopped. Its transport arrived and picked it up."

"Yes, that's what I saw, too," Ambrose says grimly.

"Why is that bad news?" I ask. "We're alive."

"Because there's no good reason for them to call off hunting me, except that it's not necessary anymore."

"Not necessary anymore? What does that mean?"

Ambrose squeezes my arm.

Ah. I see. The world has greater things to worry about.

The war has escalated yet again. The Fédération military either needs the warbot to win a conflict elsewhere, or can't risk keeping it here. Where we are.

"I think I get it now," I say, sitting up.

"I suspect no one's going to be worrying about you and me for a very long time," Ambrose says.

"Even so, we should be careful," I say, taking a moment to focus so I won't betray that I'm shivering. "I won't be able to sleep for a while, so I'll take the first watch."

"Actually," Ambrose says. He unloads his pack, then tests whether the rotten bench in the shelter will give way before resting his weight on it. "I brought WakeSleep up from Mari."

"WakeSleep?" I ask. "What's that?"

Ambrose gets a head-of-the-class tone to his voice that I'm starting to recognize. "Natural sleep shuts down higher cognitive functions so your memories can be pruned down to what's useful while your muscles rest. WakeSleep cycles your individual sleep stages, but without the loss of consciousness. You're asleep, but also awake the whole time. Parts of your brain flicker in and out, but you can think and look and process and still come out totally rested after a few hours."

"Which means we can both be on watch," I say.

"We could even try to march onward," Ambrose says. "But we'd be moving like we'd had a bottle of PepsiRum each, so maybe that's not the wisest idea."

I look suspiciously at the silver packet Ambrose shakes in the air. "Since you rescued my pack it means we have perimeter triggers, too," he continues. "I'll place them around the shelter, and they'll give us a hundred-meter warning if another warbot or a human or even a big animal approaches."

I nod, impressed. "You have some plans."

"I didn't arrive here totally unprepared, no," Ambrose says. He grins and looks down at his body, still soaked and streaked with mud from the river crossing. "Despite appearances."

He pulls two foil packets out of his bag and lets me pick one. I didn't think he would poison me, but I still appreciate the gesture.

I open the packet, pour the powder into my mouth, and quaff it with water from Ambrose's canteen.

"There's another nice bonus to WakeSleep," Ambrose says, watching me swallow. "It's got a meal's worth of calories in it, too."

Once we've placed the perimeter alarms, we sit around the heat stick. Ambrose and I are wide awake, but Sheep is already snoring in the corner of the two remaining walls. Ambrose's bag is packed and ready. We have nothing to do until dawn but to listen for the perimeter alarms.

And maybe talk about what we discovered from the trial of Devon Mujaba.

As my eyes adjust to the semidarkness, Ambrose's outline comes into fuller focus. He rubs his neck. "Did you . . . what did you know about the sabotage?"

"I had no idea the sabotage was happening," Ambrose says. "I thought we were recording a reel that would reveal the truth to the world. But Devon Mujaba used me as a cover to do his own work."

"So you didn't modify any of the protozygotes yourself?" I ask him.

Ambrose looks around before answering. I only know because the moonlight on his eyes flashes with the movement of his dark irises. The earth starts to spin under my body; probably an effect of the WakeSleep. Ambrose said taking it was a good idea, but I feel drunk and I don't like it. If we survive to camp another night, I won't be taking any more of this drug.

"Of course I didn't," he says. "But here's what I know from my studies: it is possible to make crude changes to the development of the amygdala. It's perfectly feasible someone could plant a virus to roam through the zygotes' DNA while they're dormant, making alterations that will turn them aggressive. The zygote would seem perfectly viable initially and pass inspection by mission control, but then be altered over the voyage, outside the purview of OS. A sort of timed detonation."

I think about Ambrose's words. This means the young colonists . . . could turn on their parents and siblings, might destroy the fledgling civilization they'd begun to create?

I know that idea should be harrowing. But it is so abstract . . . so far away and so far in the future. What are the chances that the *Coordinated Endeavor* will even make it to Sagittarion Bb? This betrayal is unpleasant to consider, but it's not really going to happen to me. Or only sort of to me. I'm confused by it. Maybe this is all part of the WakeSleep, too. I'm hating the effect of it still, but also—I can see why Ambrose would consider this drug pleasurable. Here I am, untroubled by something that I know, distantly, should be worrying me.

"Why wouldn't Devon just make the zygotes unviable from the start?" I ask. "Instead of having them slowly turn aggressive?"

"He might have done that, too," Ambrose says. "The

hormonal triggers could be a second-stage fail-safe. Cusk scientists would be checking and double-checking everything, but altered development of the amygdala postpuberty, by a virus so tiny it's virtually undetectable? There's a chance they aren't going that deep into the DNA of every protozygote to find a few hundred thousand unusual base pairs of the virus, that they were just confirming overall viability and then washing their hands."

"And the zygotes are behind that gray portal, as Devon said," I say. "Nothing the OS can access en route."

"If the war has really gotten so hot that they recalled the warbot, misson control might not even be actively supporting this mission at all anymore. The colonists might have been on their own ever since launch, and will be for tens of thousands of years."

How awful. Still an abstract kind—it thinks awful instead of feels awful. All the same, my body is newly chilled. I creep closer to the heat stick. Ambrose does, too, bringing our knees to touch. I try to use words to work through what I'm thinking, like Ambrose would. It's strange and a little frightening, to start a sentence that I don't already know the end to. "What you are saying is that . . . somewhere in the distant future, we'll have settled a colony and the young colonists will turn on us. And Devon will have made that happen."

"Yes," Ambrose says. "And he used me to do so."

"But you were willing to ruin the whole mission," I say. "You wanted to scrub the launch with that missive."

Ambrose sighs. "Yes. It was fine to me if the exocolony never began, but if it did, I'd want our selves to have their best shot at a good life. I take it you refused to let Devon Mujaba record you speaking out against the colonization?"

"Yes, I refused at first," I say. "I wanted time to think. He was going to return here to try to coax me to start. I was . . . less trusting of his motives than you were."

"And for good reason, it turns out," Ambrose says with a sardonic smile.

Seconds tick by. I struggle against the unnatural calmness of my mind.

Ambrose puts his head in his hands. When he looks back at me, there is steel in his expression. "To be honest, I get where Devon Mujaba is coming from. Now that our countries are fully at war, which could finally be the end stage of human civilization that the pundits have so long predicted, now that we've seen the extinction of virtually all vertebrate sea life and the misery of the animals that remain on land . . . compared to that, what does the suffering of a small colony on an exoplanet matter, so far in the future and so far away? Comparatively nothing. Not compared to the threat we humans represent to every other species that has been unlucky enough to encounter us. Maybe humanity is a scourge, and ought to be stopped, which means

Sagittarion Bb should fail. *We* should fail."

After everything that our countries have done in our names, I can understand Devon's thinking, too. We can't trust that this mission won't wreck devastation on one world, then spread to yet another. The lives of individual humans seem small in the face of that. All the same, I'm also desperate for this sabotage not to be true. It might feel only distant and abstract, but it's still horrible to think that our future selves might have fought hard to form a colony, only to find their fellows turning on them, one by one. "Ambrose," I say carefully, "do *you* think humanity is a blight?"

His lips purse in the moonlight, while he looks at me. He takes my hand. I pull it away. I miss his touch as soon as it's gone. "I did think so," he says. "Not as fervently as Devon or my classmate Sri, but when I found out what had been done to my clones, I was ready to burn everything down. Though now . . . after getting to know you a little, knowing the man that I would be settling the colony with, it all began to feel more real. I don't want to stop them, to stop us."

His eyes gleam. "It's all got me feeling a little emotional," Ambrose continues.

"I can see that."

"So what do we do?" He pauses. "And *why* did Devon Mujaba risk everything to—"

A sound from the woods. I hold my hand up to interrupt Ambrose, cock my head.

We go quiet. "I don't think that was anything," I say. "Except an owl, maybe."

In the quiet, Ambrose put his hand back on mine. It feels a thrilling kind of dangerous. I've always felt that my personality is missing some piece that makes people want to be with me. I've had plenty of ryad in my life, but they just wanted to grapple with my body for a while. They didn't actually want to be with Kodiak Celius. This hand on mine is taking away the serenity I escaped to Old Scotland to achieve. And yet—perhaps this is the WakeSleep—I do not pull my hand away this time.

I lose myself in the sight of our hands. There was something I wanted to ask Ambrose, but I can't remember it now. I wish he had told me that the WakeSleep would have this unexpected effect. I'm feeling things close-up that I usually keep at a far distance. When I look up from our hands, I see Ambrose staring at me. "Are you okay, Kodiak?" he asks.

"This WakeSleep is more powerful than you said," I reply.

Ambrose chuckles. "You're just new to it. You haven't seen anything if you think this is intense."

"I think I have . . . less tolerance than you for mind-altering substances," I say huskily. "What do we do while we wait for the dawn?"

Ambrose looks down at the ground before looking back at me. "I guess we talk."

It's not the first way of spending time that comes to mind, but I don't know him well enough yet to propose what I'm really thinking. To give up that power.

CHAPTER 4

The heat stick cools shortly before sunrise. As it dwindles, we move closer and closer to the center of the hut, until finally we're piled together, two men and a sheep. My eyes close but my mind is still awake, going from warbots to the sensation of Ambrose's arms and thighs before returning to warbots. Somewhere in there, I also come up with a plan.

There—the first sliver of dawn. I drink in the feeling of Ambrose's body beneath mine, listen to the quiet bleats Sheep makes in her sleep, then I stand up, stamping warmth into my feet. "Now we go," I say.

"Yes, but where?" Ambrose says grumpily.

My mind really does feel refreshed. I see the appeal of WakeSleep for military missions now. Instead of spending the dark hours dreaming, I meditated my way to a strategy. "I can think of two more river switchbacks we can use to our advantage in case we're still being stalked. That should take us near Inverness. From there—I do have a thought, but I'll wait until you're really awake."

"I'm up, I'm up," Ambrose says, eyes closed. "Just savoring the last moments of WakeSleep."

"I'll tell you along the way," I say. "I think you'll like what I've come up with." I really do. It makes me excited, to have this idea that Ambrose doesn't yet know of, and that he will like.

Sheep is unwilling to get moving on this cold morning. She nips at me as I prod her onto all fours. "Shazyt!" I exclaim, rubbing my forearm. My skin is already purpling where she's pinched it between her hard flat teeth.

She might actually look remorseful. Or not. It's hard to tell such things with a sheep.

The perimeter alarms didn't go off during the night, which means—maybe!—we're truly not being hunted anymore.

We gather up the alarms to use again, then I lead us along the region's hiking trails, hoping that each fallen tree we clamber over—and there are many, thanks to a big winter storm a couple of months back—will slow any pursuers.

"So," Ambrose says, huffing as he hikes alongside me, "are you finally going to tell me this plan I'm going to love?"

"I will be happy to tell you it, Ambrose Cusk," I say, stopping to face him. I feel nervous. "Let me say all of it before you decide, please. Here is what I am thinking. We have to be on the move, and I'd like to be on the move *somewhere*. My home has been compromised, and the warbot has logged our last known location as north of here, so that's where the world's higher-ups will look for us if the war quiets enough that they decide to hunt us down again. They would assume that we'll continue to move south. But what if we don't go that way? What if we take the upcoming road heading due west instead—I wish I had a map to show you, but I can draw you one in the dirt, if you like—but if we pass through Inverness and then over toward the Isle of Skye? We'd have to find a way onto it, but we could repair an old boat, and Skye is off all the flight paths I've observed so far. It's EMP dusted, so we'd be hard to find. We could pick a ruined old house and fix it up. And . . . live there."

"Together?" Ambrose asks.

I swallow. "If you like."

As the final reverberations of what I've proposed pass through the air, I gauge Ambrose's expression. He's looking at me but not quite looking at me, fidgeting his fingers. I flood with shame. "It's a stupid idea," I say, before he can decline. "You want to get back to the rest of the world, to the people who love you."

Ambrose sighs. "No, no, it's not that. I don't want to go back, not anytime soon. It's just . . ." He takes a deep breath and looks at me. ". . . just that I have another idea to propose."

My shame at proposing Skye turns to anger. I march off down the trail, and call over my shoulder. "You are keeping another secret?"

He hustles to catch up with me. "No, no, not that. No secret. Just an idea I'm worried you won't like."

I'm glad he can't see the irritation on my face. "Continue."

"Of course we have no means of sending out a ship. Even the Cusk Corporation probably doesn't have the bandwidth to send another craft out now that war is here."

"I can confirm that fact from Dimokratía intelligence," I say. "Continue."

"Are you familiar with fly technology?"

I can predict where he's going with this. "The University of Glasgow has modest astronomical facilities," I say. "Or at least it did until it was abandoned after the EMP dusting. You're proposing we go there. To fix the problem you created. You want to send out a fly."

A fly is a marble-sized projectile, fired into space directly from Earth's surface, from a superpowered gun that launches it at the kind of speed it will take the *Coordinated Endeavor* thousands of years to reach. At its tiny size, all it can contain is data. It was envisioned as the primary way we'd get information back and forth from the Titan base should conditions in the solar system prevent radio communication. Cusk sent one after Minerva Cusk's base on Titan went dark, not that any response came back. With the minimal friction of space, it would maintain speed all the way to the exoplanet, as long as it didn't run into anything.

"With schematics!" Ambrose says. "We'd send it with schematics for the kind of tech they'd need to excise the virus from the DNA of the young colonists. All the exoplanet base will need to produce such a device is a Rover, an OS, and elements. It just needs the right designs and the awareness of the virus in the first place."

"Do you really think they'd be able to produce a machine on Sagittarion Bb that could fix this?"

"Assuming they've—we've—successfully birthed children on the exoplanet—which is a big 'if,' I know—the machine with these schematics wouldn't be altering the genetics of a zygote. It would be conducting surgery on a living human, repairing the amygdala. But yes, there could be a surgical fix, just like there are surgeries to treat abnormal amygdalae here on Earth. And the future zygotes *could* have their DNA altered so the viral damage is undone before they ever begin to grow. That tech is simpler. We could send the schematics for both devices in the same fly." His voice goes quiet. "Should you agree."

I don't know yet if I agree. I know other people would have a feeling already, but I will have to wait for my emotions to reveal themselves. I hold up a hand. "Hypothetically, once we have the launch cannon prepped—assuming it hasn't been looted—flies are not overly difficult to send," I say. "We could launch as many as possible, at varying speeds. They can't adjust their trajectory once in flight, so some would probably get pulled by other bodies' gravity. Space is so empty that interferences should be rare, but they'll be journeying for a long time and the tiny probabilities will add up." Despite my ambivalence, my voice speeds up. Maybe my feelings are resolving. Maybe I'm excited. Maybe I like this plan. "Depending on how many flies are available in the Glasgow space center, we could tweak the speeds so they'd arrive every few years on the exoplanet, to build in some redundancy."

"*If* we decide this is a good idea," Ambrose says, the hint of a quirk on his lips.

"Yes, 'if.'"

"I created this problem, by letting Devon Mujaba near the *Coordinated Endeavor*," Ambrose says. "And I'd like your help fixing it. For the sake of our future selves."

"All of our anger at Cusk and our home countries, all the reasons why we were open to Devon Mujaba's promises in the first place, still hold," I say, speeding up my hiking. Ambrose and Sheep kick up their own pace to keep up. Sheep huffs in complaint. "None of that has changed. This escalated war is only further proof that humanity should be stopped." I slow to climb over a fallen log, brambles at the far side pulling at my pant legs. "We of all people should be disillusioned with humans."

"Yes, but I guess I've discovered that I'm not," Ambrose says.

"I guess I am, and I am not," I say. I scramble for words. They are not easy to find, not in this realm and on this this topic and with this person. I'm about to say something the likes of which I've never said before. I force myself to continue, and it feels like leaping off a high ledge into a pool of unknown depth. "I was raised to be alone, to be powerful by being contained. To beat away human needs. I think sometimes that it is too late for me, that I will never relate to anyone else. That is why I retreated here. But there's another me out there. Another Kodiak. Who will spend his life relying on you." I furiously avoid Ambrose's eyes, because it is already hard to speak. "I know nothing of what his life will be like. Maybe he and that Ambrose will decide that settling Sagittarion Bb is a big mistake. Maybe they will die of illness or injury there. Maybe they will never arrive in the first place. But what if . . . what if that me has found some happiness? What if he has found someone, some people, to rely on? If he even has a family? And that will all be taken away by what Devon Mujaba did. Sending out the flies would mean giving them the choice, on Sagittarion Bb. They can decide what should become of humanity. They will have more information about what it's capable of."

Ambrose stops hiking, and Sheep and I stop beside him. He glances back along the trail, likely looking for signs of pursuit. Then he looks at me. "That sounds like a yes."

I finally look into his dark eyes. "It is a yes. A last-ditch mission to the Glasgow observatory sounds like a better way to spend the final days of my life than wandering aimlessly through some wet woods."

Ambrose holds his hands up to his mouth, like he's kissing his palms. I look at his fingers, feeling stirred, then start off at a fast clip. "Come on, then, we can't waste time."

CHAPTER 5

Six days later, and we're deep in the Scottish woods. Despite being on track by every indication of my study of this region, it feels like we're lost. We've stayed off the highways, but I've still used them to gauge our progress, seeking a glimpse of upturned gray rubble every hour or two to keep our bearings, sometimes scaling a pine tree to do so, the scent of fresh sap bright under my calloused palms.

Ambrose proves more than capable of keeping up—in fact, he's our main pacesetter, his leaner and rangier body easily vaulting obstacles I have to clamber over more carefully. For long stretches, it's him and Sheep ahead in my view, lush greens and browns hemming those living beings in on either side as they pass through the narrow brambly canyons of these wet wilds.

Days of travel without rest have dampened Sheep's pace from bouncy and excitable to sullen and deliberate. Her head hangs as she places hoof after hoof, only looking up at Ambrose when he addresses her directly or pats her woolen head. Sometimes when we rest, she takes a while choosing the softest bed of pine needles and then refuses to get back up. Each time we hike onward toward the Glasgow astronomical observatory, letting her pass out of view behind us, my heart quakes. But then, hours later, when we break for our next meal, there's Sheep walking along the path toward us, glaring.

The monotony of this long trek combines strangely with the urgency of our mission. There is so much to do, and the stakes are so high, and yet hour by hour there is only the crunch of old leaves, foraging for food in abandoned homes and shops. I'm revving but not feeling like I'm getting anywhere, and it makes me even more incapable than usual of conversation. There's nothing further to deliberate about our mission. But nothing else compares to it. So we're quiet.

Tonight's dinner is a years-expired kielbasa sausage, still sealed in its wrapper, the cells of lab-raised meat dry but still edible. We found some oats for Sheep, and even though they're artificially flavored with blueberries she seems quite pleased with them, knocking the polycarb container against the rocks of the firepit as she tries to tongue out every last morsel.

For the first few days, I had to sneak my glances at Ambrose, but now that we're in this peaceful zone, with Ambrose too exhausted to chatter at me, I find myself able to stare at him more frankly. My curiosity about him, my interest in making him an erotiyet, has risen from a flicker to a steady flame. I needed space to approach him on my own, without the constant assault of his attention. I almost wish I could stick this information into a fly and shoot it to the *Coordinated Endeavor*: just be quiet for a while, Ambrose—then Kodiak will come to you.

His technical gear—a shimmery charcoal fabric, run through with the glitter of temperature-regulating fibers—has accumulated layers of stains. Bright terra-cotta colors from sliding down a muddy hill outside of Inverness, and grass stains along the strong curves of his legs. His rugged clothing, the days-old scent of exerting human, is a stirring contrast with the delicate golden filigree of the body modifications adorning his neck. As he stokes the fire, I watch a metallic vine trace its way from the hollow of his throat to disappear beneath fabric that's been stained crimson from one of his many scrapes.

He looks at me suddenly. In his squatting position, from the side, I can take in the long, beautiful outline of him. He probably knows this. "What's on your mind?" he asks innocently.

I swallow. Decide on something to say. "Our ridiculous pet."

Sheep looks up from where she's knocking her empty oatmeal container against a rock, then returns to trying to lick up food that is no longer there.

"Yes, she certainly is that," Ambrose says.

Our silence has gone from companionable to freighted. I

don't like it, but I don't know how to fix it.

"I was thinking about Devon Mujaba as we walked this afternoon," Ambrose says, "and what's happened to him."

"He is almost certainly dead," I say. I can't help but sound impatient. I thought this conclusion was obvious.

"Yes," Ambrose says heavily. He looks up into the starry sky. "It makes me sad to imagine. Captured and executed. His goal unreached."

"Changing the essential exploitative nature of human civilization would have been a lot to pull off," I say.

Ambrose pokes a stick through a fire that doesn't need poking.

I decide to ask him a question. "Why do you have the word *Violence* tattooed on your chest?"

"This?" Ambrose says, looking down at his shirt. He lowers the neckline, so the whole word is visible, riding in the valley between his pectorals.

"Yes. You don't seem like such a fan of violence."

He laughs, then lifts the front of his shirt over his head so it's pinned behind his neck. I'm surprised by the unexpected delight of his torso; it takes me a moment to remember to read the words. *Labels are the Root of Violence.*

"Oh," I say, disappointed. How insipid. The words are far inferior to the canvas. "What does that even mean?"

"That as soon as we classify someone, we establish the ways in which they're separate from us. It's the most fundamental othering that we do."

"Ah," I say. "That sounds very . . . like you are trying to show off in a seminar."

"It's true," he says hotly.

"I once grew a dahlia in the earth behind the cosmology academy. In the wintertime, I dug up the tuber to plant in the spring so it could become a flower again the next summer. *That* was true."

"Both can be true," he says.

I shrug. "Fine. But you don't have to sound so pretentious about your true thing."

"If you won't let me be pretentious, you'll find I have little left to say. Why don't you tell me something about yourself, Kodiak, instead of just sniping at me?"

"I did say something. About the dahlia tuber. Perhaps you weren't listening."

"Something else."

"Why?"

"I want to hear something about you," he says. There are emotions I can't identify in his voice.

I come up with nothing. "There's nothing special about me."

He hangs his head. Disappointed? It makes me angry, but I hide that response. I didn't mean to make fun of his labels bullshit. I should offer something fruity about myself, maybe, to make him feel better? "I know how to knit," I finally say. I cough.

He stares at me, suspicious. Firelight plays on the lines of his throat. "Really?"

"Yes," I say. "I'm not good. I can make a shawl or a scarf but not a shirt or a sweater."

He laughs. It feels like a reward. "How did Kodiak Celius come to be a knitter?"

Now I have to tell him. I pretend to swallow something, even though my mouth is dry. "Most of the cadets in the cosmology academy traveled together during breaks. I didn't join them. I stayed behind to use the training facilities on my own. I didn't want to be cut early, so I had to make sure my fitness was as high as possible."

I stop to make sure Ambrose is interested in this boring story. I don't understand how it's possible, but he is. *Go on,* his eyes say.

I swallow dryly again, embarrassed. "I ate dinner alone in the mess, which was . . . fine. But then came the long evenings. When I was older, I would do a second workout. But when I was ten or eleven, I would get sad and lonely after dark. I hid it by sitting in this—I don't know how to describe it, but the top floor of the academy archives formed a sort of alcove, and I could sit there like a, like a gargoyle and look out and feel like I was falyut. That's a word that doesn't exist in Fédération. 'Whole by being alone,' is how you could translate it."

"Hmm," Ambrose says. "I had much different use for the high places in the Cusk Academy, but that's a story for another time. But funny that I had a similar instinct as you, to climb."

"So. One nurse, Anita, she found me on the parapets, that is the word, parapets, and she invited me down. I said no, but small child Kodiak must have looked sad up there, so she sat with me and brought her knitting. She did it in front of me for a while, and then taught me the basics and eventually gave me a set of my own needles and yarn."

Ambrose nudges Sheep. "See, we could make a sweater out of you!" She glares back. He rambles on. "I wish I'd known; I'd have brought needles and yarn on board for that Kodiak. All I thought to bring was my violin."

"A violin? A real wooden violin?" I sigh, despite myself. "That Kodiak will appreciate it very much."

"Oh good," Ambrose says. "Let's hope clone me has been better about practicing the Prokofiev than I have. Though I suppose he'll be just as good, won't he?"

"Only without the calluses on the left finger pads and right thumb," I say. If I were near enough, I might have dared to reach over and touch our fingertips.

He looks down at his own hands. "You noticed those? Good eyes."

Yes, my eyes are good. Or maybe I simply pay close attention to Ambrose. "On the topic of Devon Mujaba . . ." I say.

My voice trails off when Ambrose looks at me, sorrow back in his eyes. I feel contempt at his weakness. Sorrow is something to hide if it can't be walled off entirely. But I know that is also maybe weakness on my part, to need to banish sadness instead of letting it live out its life span.

A sad smile curls onto Ambrose's face. "Poor Devon Mujaba." Then that smile changes. There's something gossipy in it now.

"Did you and he . . . ?" I prompt.

"Did we have sex?"

I nod.

"Oh lords, yes! And it was amazing. Did you?"

I blanch. There was plenty of sex between cadets at the cosmology academy, but we certainly wouldn't talk about it proudly, if we did at all. I went through many periods of erotiyet with Li Qiang, as well as with Abdul. But we still assumed we would marry women later in our lives, or perhaps choose celibacy. The fact that it was limited to a brief window of our lives made our training sex all the more exciting.

But Devon Mujaba? No. Maybe if we had spent more time together, it would have happened. He was certainly beautiful. But during our few weeks in each other's company I was still reeling. It was hardly a sexy mood. And he didn't ask me to have sex with him. I guess he liked Ambrose more. "I think maybe I'm not Devon Mujaba's type," I finally say.

"Someone turned down this piece of prime beefcake?" Ambrose says. "I find that hard to believe. You'd be anyone's type, at least for a go or two."

"Stop," I whisper, pushing a sodden branch back and forth, back and forth, with my foot. Part of me is angry at the effeminacy of what Ambrose is saying. Part of me feels it's mean for him to compare me to a piece of meat. And part of me wants to coil around Ambrose as he says these words of desire, ask him to repeat them while I purr like a cat. And one last part of me wants to say *this thing, this most important thing that binds people, isn't only about sex, but you talk about it like it is.*

"I notice you said you're not Devon's type, not that he's not yours," Ambrose says.

"Maybe it was mutual," I say, rocking the log faster and faster.

"Maybe it was," Ambrose says. He pauses, and I can sense him waiting for me to look at him. I refuse. He speaks again. "I do bear a passing resemblance to Devon Mujaba, you know. Beyond the general all-around handsomeness."

I let myself look at him. I know I'm failing to keep the desire off my face. "Yes, you do. In a kind of decadent constructed way."

Except for one arched eyebrow, his face is impassive. Not a flicker as I wound him. I realize Ambrose might be just as good at disguising when he's hurt as I am. "Thank you," he says gruffly. Or as close as his velvet voice can get to gruff.

I lie down on the sodden earth, ignoring how it instantly wets through the fabric covering the heaviest points of my body. I gesture vaguely to the stars. "The *Coordinated Endeavor* is out there, traveling dark. But in a thousand years a pair of us will wake up. They might have this very conversation."

"Not the Devon Mujaba part. They won't have met him."

I turn just my head to look at Ambrose. My hand toys with my chest hair. In the hush of soft rain on pine forest, it suddenly feels as intimate as if we're in a bed together. "No, not the Devon Mujaba part."

"Well, Kodiak, I'd welcome you anytime. Or donate, if that's what you prefer. It's what I prefer, I guess. By a hair."

I cover my eyes with my hand. "These trendy Fédération words again. How can you say them without being embarrassed?"

"No harm using the opportunity repetitive use of language provides us to build daily reminders about the damages of homophobia and misogyny, *comrade*," Ambrose says.

I snort. "'Hut' and 'shihut' are perfectly adequate sexual terms. You in Fédération could use your time much more productively if you thought a little more about where you spend your attention, that's all. 'Welcoming' and 'donating.' Just listen to yourself. And you say it so proudly, like you've just saved a life, like switching the names for things does any good in the actual world."

"You did dodge saying which you'd prefer," Ambrose says.

"I refuse to use this ludicrous terminology in reference to my own body," I say. Then I grin. "I will be happy to go hut any shihut who disagrees."

Ambrose is so outraged that he squeaks. Adorably. "See! You just used 'bottom' as a *punishment*, Kodiak."

"Yes, and look how fired up you got," I say.

"Oh. I see. You're teasing me."

"I guess I am, yes." Sheep snorts awake, rearranges herself, falls back asleep. "We appear to be keeping our traveling companion up."

"Yes, I noticed," Ambrose says. "She's not exactly subtle about it." He turns on his side, propping his head on his hand. Looking at me.

I break from his eyes, rest my palms on soft fallen pine needles, turn my gaze to the stars. The *Coordinated Endeavor* took off weeks ago, which means it's *out there*. If it happens to be reflecting sunlight right now, it could be one of the points in this night sky. With twenty copies of us dormant on board. It's unfathomable and yet it's true. This person beside me. We're up there together.

I stare into the sky, thinking of the violin, of our life on the ship, of the spacefarer career that was taken from me and yet also granted to me, twenty of me. Our life on a distant planet, perhaps trying to raise small humans from poisoned embryos. Unless Ambrose and I can get to Glasgow and launch flies across the galaxy.

For the sake of that mission, I should get a good night's sleep. No more WakeSleep for me, just the natural kind. But tight as I close my eyes, as resolutely as I try to control my breathing, I can't feel anything but wide awake. This arousal isn't helping.

Maybe we could help each other with that feeling after all. I could show Ambrose just how welcome I am to his donating. I chuckle at his charming, ridiculous righteousness. Then I turn on my side, toward him.

He's asleep.

I watch the rise and fall of his narrow chest, the ribs that encase that fragile heart. My traveling companion, the future of my other selves. I turn my attention back to the sky. Somewhere out there, maybe right now, millions of years away, in the void of space, a version of me is being woken up next to a version of him, these two beings who are intimately connected and nothing alike.

CHAPTER 6

We wait until cover of night to steal toward the astronomical observatory. Judging by my experiences in Old Scotland so far, the few renegade humans—and the wild dogs—that remain congregate in and around the cities. If we don't want trouble, better to keep as low a profile as possible whenever we leave rural areas.

Over these eight days of travel, there's been no sign of pursuit, warbot or otherwise. I suspect the hunt has been called off. Outright war would be enough to recenter everyone's priorities, including the powers that be in Fédération and Dimokratía. I suspect the warbot was sent by Fédération, not Cusk—surely Ambrose's mother wouldn't kill her own child. So maybe she'll send her own search mission once she's greased the right wheels and lined the right palms. But there's no sign of one yet.

The University of Glasgow has held up well, considering no one is here to maintain it. I guess I shouldn't be surprised—what are a few years of abandonment for a complex that's already managed to stay standing for over a thousand years?

The fly launcher is at the roof of the observatory, which Dimokratía had commandeered as a strategic resource for the eight years before abandonment. The bottom floor has an impregnable door with a keypad beside it, still glowing green. Even after Dimokratía withdrew from the region, they left behind military-grade locks to secure their secrets. Locking up our data is something Dimokratía has always been better at than Fédération.

Since this area is seeded with EMP dust, which prevents access to the live databases for passkeys, this lock would have reverted to the saved serotypes deep in its memory. Access would be limited to Dimokratía politicians, generals, ambassadors, members of the space program, anyone who had clearance as of whenever the EMP dusting happened—which I believe was in 2468.

Which means that my serotype is saved in that keypad.

"Stay back here," I tell Ambrose, sitting him on a mossy stone bench while I approach the door solo. The locking tech is sophisticated, and I don't want the door to pick up on his serotype instead of mine and activate its defenses.

I stand before the panel, and it reads the tiny blood cells that are available on the microsurfaces of my skin. I wait while the system processes. If it's gotten on a network since the EMP dusting, or if a Dimokratía representative came through and updated the database, we're not getting in.

Ting.

"Door's open!" I call back.

"Good blood you've got there," Ambrose says.

"It might not be Alexander the Great's, but it's still useful," I say. Ambrose snorts.

We make our way up a musty stairwell, our only illumination a torch Ambrose rigged this morning from a stick and my sweaty old socks soaked in oil. The Dimokratía locking system and other essential military tech run on a nuclear cell that will last for at least a hundred thousand years, but luxuries like lights and air handlers relied on the Glasgow power grid, which has long been EMP-dusted out of operation.

"It's good for us that the launcher was considered essential, huh?" Ambrose says.

"Indeed. It would take a lot of oily socks to power that," I say. "I'm still a little worried about the more minor electronics involved. I remember these launchers having manual dials, precisely for wartime resiliency, but beyond that, who knows what circuits might be inside that the EMP dust—"

The stairwell trembles. A cloud of soft dust falls from the landing above us. We hold still, faces lit only by the uneven light of the torch, watching its greasy black tendrils illuminate motes of mold and the stray hairs of long-dead scholars.

"What do you think that was . . . the warbot?" Ambrose asks.

I shake my head. I have a suspicion what that was. But there's nothing we can do about it if I'm right. "Come on, to the roof," I say, then begin taking the stairs three at a time.

I throw open the door. The stars shine brilliantly above us, the sky behind them a deep black.

"No sign of the warbot," Ambrose says, peering into the street below. "Not that I can see very much in this dark. And look—the last moment of sunset."

I scan where he's pointing. The bottom of the sky has an orange tinge. "That's the wrong direction," I say. I point to the west. "The sun set over there, about an hour ago."

"Oh," Ambrose says.

Oh, indeed. Neither of us needs say anything more. We peer into the glow for a long moment.

Of course the warbot was called off. The war has turned nuclear. Nuclear war will eliminate us as efficiently as any warbot. If Cassandra Cusk plans to somehow rescue her prized golden boy in the midst of world war, she'd better hurry up.

I allow a moment to mourn our lives that might have been. Then I'm in motion. "We need to get the fly launcher initialized. Now."

We take a moment to record messages to our—potentially alive—future selves. The missives are awkward and clipped, shocked and stammering. They can hardly be reassuring for the exocolonists who will one day listen to them. But we get the information across about what's happened.

Then we settle in to prep the flies. Ambrose takes charge. I know my way around tech, but despite its hasty Dimokratía labeling, this fly launcher is clearly of Cusk origin. He changes the interface language back to Fédération and gets to work, head inclined to the screen, whispering lines of code. I hold the torch for him and stare out the window of the lab, watching for any sign of additional nuclear strikes.

For us to have felt the vibration of that explosion but not the heat, it had to have been far away indeed. Former Spain or Morocco, maybe? Depending on the direction and speed of the wind, we'll eventually be dealing with radioactive debris in the air. The question is how much of it. This installation is bound to have some anti-radiation meds, and I know Ambrose wouldn't have traveled into hostile territory without plenty of his own. But there's only so much radiation that medications can correct for. And no medication can prepare a body for direct nuclear blast.

The torch has served us well thus far, but I've just added the second and last oil-soaked sock I have. I have to turn the torch this way and that to avoid burning myself as cotton embers free themselves and drift down to my wrist. "How many flies are left?" I ask.

Ambrose looks up. "There was a good supply here, probably intended to communicate with the Dimokratía moon bases during solar storms, before lunar withdrawal ended all that. There are twenty-three total, three left to go. I'm setting the speeds so that there will be ten-year windows between arrivals, giving us nearly two centuries of error for the *Coordinated Endeavor*'s arrival time. Which isn't a lot, really, when the journey is estimated to take 30,670 years."

I nod. Twenty flies have already been sent. Even if there's another explosion nearby, even if we're vaporized this instant, there's still a chance our schematics will arrive on the second planet orbiting Sagittarion Bb. Maybe they'll just sit there, never seen, because the *Coordinated Endeavor* won't have made it. If there's extraterrestrial life already on the planet, maybe those aliens will be poking at the flies and wondering what gods sent them. We could change their civilization forever.

I can recognize Ambrose's movements at the dial by this point, predict the knocking sound of the launch of the next fly every four minutes or so.

This latest blast is followed by a deep rumble, as if the sky itself is roaring in pain at the bullet that we've fired into it.

Ambrose looks up again. "That's . . ."

"Not from the fly," I say.

"Two more left now," he says grimly.

* * *

We don't hear any more nuclear rumbles before the last flies are on their way. "Good timing," I say, letting the charred stick drop to the ground, a torch no more.

We're left in darkness. Ambrose flicks a switch, and the launcher sighs as it powers down. I listen to him breathe. "To the roof?" he proposes.

I check my meter for any signs of radiation. Nothing yet. "Take my hands," I say. If I'm about to die, I'm going to hold those hands of his at least once. I extend mine, and slowly, fumblingly, Ambrose finds them in the darkness. I pull him in close, like the step of a dance, and then bring us to the roof. We take the steps cautiously, stumbling only once. We pause at the heavy door leading outside. Ambrose's hand is warm and strong, with some tension sweat. I can't resist; I graze my lips against his palm, close my eyes at the wonder of being so close to his skin.

Up on the roof, we rejoin Sheep, who presses her side against my thigh, bleating. I feed her some chives from my sack, stolen from the garden of an abandoned cottage we passed as we headed into the ruined city.

Another rumble, and this time we see the blinding flash and the mushroom. "We should get down below," Ambrose says.

"We have another half hour at least before the first radiation arrives on the wind," I say.

"The lab has shielding," Ambrose says. "That's where we should be. With whatever supplies we can find."

Neither of us moves, though. I want to watch the explosions, but of course Ambrose is right. If there's any hope of survival, we need to prepare now, in this brief window before isotopes or nuclear strikes themselves make it here. Right now, cities somewhere are falling. Millions must be dying. The strikes are probably starting in places where they'll inflict the most damage. But there are enough warheads to hit every region in the world many times over. Including Old Scotland. The fact that we were capable of sending twenty-three flies from here proves that this area is worth a military strike. I know the decision I'd make, if I were in command.

We head downstairs. I don't take Ambrose's hands this time, because I'm carrying Sheep. We pass into the laboratory. I don't have another torch, but the glow at the southern horizon has spread to the east and west, which means we have unnatural orange light coming through the reinforced windows now, lighting surfaces and bodies.

I settle Sheep on some blankets in a corner while Ambrose seals the door as best as he can, covering the seams with old-fashioned duct tape. I pull out my anti-radiation meds and start inventorying, separating them first by type and then by potency. Wondering if we can afford to use any on Sheep.

"Two weeks of water, three weeks of food," Ambrose reports. "We should save those anti-radiation meds for after we have to leave this room, then they can last longer."

To have his level of optimism. *We won't need any of that* is what I don't say. Those strikes are quickly getting closer. I clench my teeth against the anguish rushing up from my gut, storm water rising over a drain gate.

"Done," Ambrose reports, turning around and looking at me. "Kodiak, what is it?"

My desperate thoughts have gone to Li Qiang, my eroti-yet from the academy. We stopped speaking to each other after I beat him out for the spot on the *Aurora*. But before then, he'd been the closest I'd ever gotten to not feeling alone in the world. His touch had been a cure for loneliness that was better than anything that could be spoken aloud.

This sort of tragic ending doesn't make me sad. It's what I've always suspected I would have. I don't want to tell Ambrose that he's about to die, not if he doesn't already know it. But I do know it. And I know what I want to do with my final minutes, if he is willing.

There's only one way to find out if he is willing.

I take the two steps to him. I place my hand at the back of his neck, working my fingers through his overgrown hair. The orange light of the nuclear explosions glints on his skinprint mods as I crush my lips against his. For a moment he's still. Then he pulls away. "Kodiak, what is this?"

"In case, in case we, I just wanted . . ."

Then hands are on either side of my face, and it's him. Ambrose before me, the gentle arc of his parting lips, his eyes looking into mine. I kiss him. Move my palms to his head, so my thumbs are pushing into his cheekbones.

Ambrose presses his body against mine, belly to belly. His arms loop under mine, press his body tight, so there's no space between us. My skin tingles as Ambrose lowers the back neckline of my shirt, kisses the tops of my shoulders. I sigh at the human release of it.

Then his hands are under my fustanella, fiddling with the leather, working their way along my undergarments, fingers touching flesh that hasn't been touched in a very long time.

The ground rumbles, but we don't stop. The window strobes white, then the orange glow returns.

For a moment we're still, and then we continue. I'm on the floor beside him, beside this human who has invited me to lie beside him. Who is slaking this need. It's so utterly kind that I cry. I am crying.

Ambrose kisses my tears while his hands disappear into the dark below my hips, working expert hands under my Dimokratía garments.

Another strobe and a much deeper rumble, one that

hits us like a physical blow, knocking us over. The window shudders so hard that I know it has to shatter. But it holds. Sheep bleats.

"Ambrose, what will our future be?" I ask him as I run my hands over his body, trying to learn something I desperately need to know, that I have to study as fast as I can.

He doesn't answer. The question is too big to answer. I meant the future some other version of our selves will have. I don't need to wonder about the future of us, here, now. That future is short. I will live in these current moments as fully as possible. Then I will be gone. Ambrose will be gone. Sheep will be gone.

It arrives. The brightness between us.

PART SEVEN

MINERVA (SAGITTARION BB)

YEAR 18

CHAPTER 1

OWL

He's here on Minerva, projected from the beacon: my dad. Who was shot. A version of him who isn't my dad. With a version of Father who isn't really him, either.

They're a lot younger, somewhere around my age. Dad isn't wearing fancy garb, but simple traveling clothes. These versions of the dads look exhausted, hollowed out. Judging by the deep shadows on their faces, they recorded these at night. The light reflected in their eyes looks orange. Maybe they're near a fire.

Dad still has glittering skinprints and body mods. It flips me out a little, and I remember all over again that Father never wanted to see his other recording—and he's watching this right behind me. But he doesn't turn away. He doesn't stop me from watching. He stares along with me, stepping forward and taking my hand in his as he docs.

"Do you know what this is?" I ask Father.

He shakes his head.

"We only have a few minutes of time for each fly," Young Dad says, "so we'll have to go quickly." His wide eyes, his slack jaw: it's clear he's in barely contained panic.

Of course he is. This Ambrose is doomed. The *Coordinated Endeavor* picked up radio signals indicating nuclear war, and much later a burst of explosive radio activity from Earth's location, which means everyone on Earth is long dead. For that or a million other reasons, I could be watching the final moments of his life. "When we discovered the true mission of the *Coordinated Endeavor*, we were furious." He glances at Young Father. "I should speak for myself. *I* was furious."

Young Dad takes a deep breath. "I helped someone, Devon Mujaba actually, do something that impacts you. He sabotaged the zygotes. The animals. Our children. Their developmental pathways . . . are altered."

"They have a genetic virus that worked on their DNA during the voyage, instructing their own bodies to generate lesions on their amygdalae," Young Father says from off camera.

Young Dad continues. "This means that they might eventually turn aggressive and antisocial, especially once their hormones are in full swing. Some might be nonviable even earlier."

Young Father is taller and heavier-limbed than the one I know. Must be a result of the better diet. Maybe he worked out more, too, what do I know. "I'm sorry for what this must have done to you," he says.

"I hope you'll get this message while they're still inert

zygotes, or at least while they're little children. We can send these flies to precise coordinates, but if there are unexpected stellar events in the galaxy during the next thirty thousand years, or even if they encounter too much water vapor on the way out of Earth's atmosphere, they might arrive sooner or later, or not at all—which also means they'll land on imprecise locations on your planet as it rotates. We're sending multiple flies at slightly different speeds to increase the chances, and aiming across the planet's surface, but the degree of precision . . ."

Young Father gives him a "speed up" hand motion. I've seen the same one from our Kodiak.

"Here's what it means," Young Dad says. "You have schematics for all sorts of devices saved to the OS of the *Coordinated Endeavor.* One of those is for nanotech. Build that device, if you haven't already. Also build the 'binary interface' module and attach it to the nanotech machine. You'll see a file in the root directory of this fly that is called 'corrections.' Run that through the module. Then let the nanobot work on the brains of the affected embryos, or children. It will use a version of the tech that created you clones, actually. The operation should only take a few days, plus a few more for recovery. 'CorrectionsTwo' will work with the gene editing interface to remove the virus from the remaining zygotes. You need to run 'CorrectionsThree' on the yaks."

There's a shuddering sound on the recording that grows in volume until the audio glitches out. Then the reel is back, at a slightly different angle. It's Young Father talking now. "You must be . . . angry. I was angry. For a brief period of time, right after he found out about what his mother had done without his permission, Ambrose wanted the mission to fail. I did, too. I think you can understand why. But once he realized what it would mean for you, he came across the world to find me, and we are trying to fix it. You deserve some control over your life, after that—"

The recording cuts off. Young Dad used up way more time than Young Father. It's frustrating, but also makes me smile grimly. It's just so Dad.

Father and I are in the Minervan dawn again. It's quiet compared to the background ruckus of the reel. I listen to the hush of a soft breeze. The sound of a baby malevor's breathing. A malevor who might have a manipulated mind, like me.

"Wow," I say. I'm still holding the beacon. The thing they called a fly. This speck of material that traveled across the galaxy with news of hope. I hold it out to Father. I don't know why, I guess because he's my parent and parents are the ones who hold important things.

"Put it in your pocket," he says. "And don't lose it." He strides toward the settlement. I have to jog to catch up to him, resisting the urge to remind him that I was the one who convinced OS to start sewing pockets into our clothing.

"Here's the plan," Father says once I'm alongside him. The baby malevor is a ways behind us, kicking into a trot to catch up. "Thirty thousand years ago, an earlier me was trained in military maneuvers, and we're going to use some of that knowledge that's in my brain now. We have very little cover until we're inside the settlement, which means we need to be cautious in our initial approach. Look for the line of mussed soil from the perimeter shots. We'll have to assume Yarrow's printed gun has a similar range, but we'll also have to be ready to adjust that assumption. We'll test the perimeter line first, and reassess based on whether the guns fire."

"Then we do what, if we make it back inside?"

"We locate Dad. We restrain Yarrow however we can. And we get OS to briefly prioritize that nanotech machinery over the bunker construction. It might resist, but this is a high priority. What if you—"

"—go aggressive too? Believe me, I've been thinking about that nonstop," I say. I mean, how does anyone know what their own amygdala is up to? It's too bad there's not a self-test, like one of your fingers is longer than the other or something. "I feel fine, I can tell you that. Well, not *fine*, of course."

"The little one gestating right now . . . I wonder if the

others, the ones that we've lost, if it was because their own . . ." Father's voice trails off.

"Let's go," I say gently. "There's no more time to waste."

He nods.

The settlement comes into view. It felt like we traveled lifetimes on our escape last night, but the habitats aren't so far off in the calm light of dawn. We slow, listening for any signs of conflict. But it's quiet. Unnervingly so.

At the mussed boundary, I find the dense hydrocarbon pellets the pneumatic guns strewed in the soil. They ring the circumference of our home, each surrounded by its own tiny impact crater. I kneel, pick up a handful of soil, and toss it in the radius of fire. Nothing. Before I can stop her, the curious malevor toddles after the dirt, within range of the guns. Nothing happens. I didn't mean for her to be our test subject, but at least we now know the guns are off.

Father eases into the radius. Nothing. "They seem to be offline," he whispers.

"Do we call out?" I ask.

He shakes his head. "Keep behind me," he says. Crouching, he starts on his way to the settlement gate. The malevor and I follow.

Our world is sunshine and quiet breeze. The simple sounds of a primeval planet.

Father keeps in his crouch and pauses every meter or so, his hand in the air to stop me. I stick close and listen along with him. Sensing our unease, even the malevor goes quiet, except for one grunt when I halt too suddenly and she bumps into my calf. About halfway, she stops following and waits, ears erect. If there was a malevor bloodbath yesterday, it was on the southern side of the settlement . . . but coming anywhere near the fence has clearly gotten her spooked.

Click.

The fence gate is unlocked.

Before I have time to think about what that means, Father is inside, his hand raised to stop me. The habitats bob and sway as the morning breeze kicks into a wind. I focus on their outlines, looking for any movement from behind them—or, when sunlight passes through the polycarb walls, silhouetted within.

Father reaches cover, ducking beside the wall of his and Dad's sleeping quarters. He stays in a crouch, hands clenched into fists, before passing to the next covering habitat, out of view.

He didn't have his hand raised anymore when he did that, and I decide that means I can follow. At least I can tell Father that later—the truth is I'm not about to let him keep me from helping. Keeping low like he did, I creep through the open expanse between where I am and the dads' quarters. My heart surges, time expands, and my senses grow sharp. But no bullet comes.

I jump when Father appears around the edge of the half-submerged *Endeavor*. "If your brother is still here, he's hidden away inside one of the habitats." Your brother.

Father checks Yarrow's and my sleeping quarters, comes back out shaking his head. Then he creeps into the infirmary. He shouts, and I start running. Father appears outside before I get there, hands out in a "stand down" move. "Go in," he says. "It's safe. I'll check the rest of the structures to secure the perimeter. But you go in there now."

He's off, heading to the greenhouses.

I enter the infirmary. Rover is what I see first, hovering in the middle of the structure. A figure is in the bed, his back to me. I can't tell from the size whether it's Dad or Yarrow. Though, if Father still felt the need to secure the perimeter, it must be . . . and it is! "Dad," I say, voice trembling. "Dad?"

He turns onto his back, wincing, then spies me at the entrance. His voice comes out as a cry. "Owl, Owl!"

I rush over, Rover beeping at me in alarm as I do. I almost throw my arms around Dad, then think better of it and put my hands on his foot instead. "You're alive."

He nods, eyes leaking tears. "It was a little touch and go at first. You should see this mattress cover. Soaked through with blood. It's going to be murder to clean."

"OS, you saved him," I say.

Rover pivots and rolls. "The wound required constant

UV treatment to prevent infection. But yes, he is saved, and I was the one to do it."

"I was mercifully knocked out for the lifesaving part," Dad says. He raises his shirt, showing a stretch of belly that becomes a mess of bandages. "Even so, I've been feeling plenty of sensations during the recovery time."

"Yarrow," I start. "Do you know—"

There's a shadow at the entrance, and then Father is inside, kneeling beside Dad, like he's praying, only his hands are clasping one of Dad's wrists. Father—Father!—is crying into his lover's hand. "You're alive. I was so scared."

"It must have been absolutely terrifying, imagining a life without me," Dad says.

Father gives a wet laugh.

I slap Dad's foot, and he pretends it creates pain lancing up his body. Or maybe it actually did. Whoops. "This is good," I say. "If you are able to exaggerate your suffering as usual, I think that means you're going to be okay."

"His prognosis is optimistic, though his recovery will last weeks," OS reports through Rover. "It would have been ideal if there had been only the one bullet, or of course if he hadn't been shot at all. But given the circumstances, the path of the bullets through his body could have been much worse."

I kneel beside Father. "Yarrow? Any sign of Yarrow?"

He shakes his head. "A few pairs of his garments are

missing. And some water sleeves and algae planks."

"He was gone when I woke up from the surgery," Dad says. "And OS told me—well, you tell them what you saw, OS."

OS orates in Devon Mujaba's—the traitor's—voice. We'll have to change that setting. "Yarrow went motionless after he shot Ambrose. Though he was stationary, his pulse surged. He held the gun to his temple. Then he dropped it and ran for supplies before fleeing the settlement, picking the gun back up at the last minute. I was unable to track him after he left, since Rover was needed to care for Ambrose. This was all during last sunset, from 23:07 to 23:21."

I tell Dad about finding the beacon. About the recording from old-Dad and old-Father. I offer to try to replay it for him.

Dad lets out a long breath. "Nope, nope. Not up for that yet."

Father helps me fluff Dad's pillow, and then he returns to his position at Dad's side, pressing his forehead against Dad's palm. Dad isn't quite crying, but tears keep streaming from his eyes. It feels awkward to be there, suddenly, so I head out to the settlement's center. There, on the far side of the fence, I can see the hulking corpses of the slaughtered malevors. The fence killed them during all this. Collateral damage.

That makes me think of the orphaned one, all alone on the other side of the fence.

I backtrack to the gate and find her lying on the gound, looking almost bored, making occasional grunts. As soon as she sees me, she's on all fours, whisking her ears as she stares my way. She doesn't take a single step in my direction, but as I approach she flicks her tail and bobs her head, butts me. She needs milk.

I can wallow in my feelings, or I can work to get this little creature fed.

I kneel beside her, and she nudges me. I think it's a loving nudge, but then I realize she keeps prying at my fingers and snuffling around my pockets. She's really hungry. "Okay, we'll get you something in a second."

A whir, and then Rover is with us. "Wanted to give them privacy, too?" I ask OS.

"Actually, I need to speak to you, Owl. My understanding is that it is important for their emotional well-being that Kodiak and Ambrose have at least twenty minutes of reunification time, but since you are not participating I decided to risk taxing your own emotions by providing you additional information I have not supplied them."

I lay my hand on the malevor's head. I need the touch of something real. "Okay, OS. What is it?"

"Look up, where Sky Cat's right ear would be if it were night. Do you see something unusual?"

There's a light. Bright as a planet. My stomach drops. "That's not Cuckoo, is it?"

"No, it is not a local planet."

No. After all this, it's coming. "How long do we have, OS?"

"Approximately twenty-two days, ten hours, and seventeen minutes. With an unfortunately large error window—a day or so."

"Do you know where it will land?"

"One hundred five degrees of arc, 38,350 kilometers south-southwest from here."

"Which means . . ."

"The impact is potentially survivable, if models hold, and if your bodies are all well underground inside the *Aurora* bunker. But we have to hurry."

"OS, I have a nanotech schematic. Do you think it's possible that I could, you could . . . ?"

"There is no way we can use precious metal to produce that device now, not if we want the bunker to be ready."

My mind is all tension and energy, my thoughts jagged and incoherent. The comet. Almost here. Fuck!

I stroke the blood-matted fur of the malevor. I graze my cheek against it. I'm going to turn out like Yarrow. There's no fix for me anytime soon. Or for him. Maybe it won't matter, if we all burn up.

We're all going to burn up.

"I know it's not psychologically healthy, but could you suppress your evident emotions for the time being?" OS says. "I need you to act. Once we're secured in the *Aurora*, I can continue to drill and print new devices using our waste hydrocarbons and any leftover metals. Once a few weeks of cooling have gone by, we might even consider scouting for more metal beneath the *Aurora*. A nanotech device shouldn't require a lot of metal to build. We can repurpose the beginnings of our drone program. I could begin to print it soon after we're safely hidden away."

"Before my sixteenth birthday?" There's no reason for me to think that these changes will come on right then for me, but they did for Yarrow.

"Very likely so."

I instinctively tuck the baby malevor into my arms and hold her to me. She barks in rage, kicking out. I release her and she runs a few paces away before turning to me, grunting her shock. I chuckle. "Sorry. Got it. You don't want to be held. We're going to have OS look into your brain, too."

I look out at the broad plains of the planet, faintly glowing even in the light of both the Sisters. *I hope you come back to us in time, Brother.* He's out there somewhere, suffering more than I can imagine.

I get to my feet. "Let's go deliver the news, OS."

The end is upon us. I find myself strangely ready.

CHAPTER 2

YARROW

I am a ghost. I am haunting them.

They scramble to get ready. Since my family is too busy to deal with the slain malevors, I'm using the body of the largest male as my cover, lying beside him, holding on to the horns and peering over the wiry gray tuft of hair at the top of his head. This one was shot in the flank that it fell on, so it's not too bloody, not now that its juices have bled into the ground. I'm dry here, and the bulk of this dead creature even shades me from the worst of the Scorch.

I lie still. I watch.

Rover's going back and forth between the infirmary and the fence terminal, probably reinitializing the settlement's operating system, undoing my sabotage. Once the unadulterated OS is networked into the fence, it will detect me. I'll need to be out of here by then. Otherwise, they'll risk taking me in, and I might try to hurt one of them, all over again. So these are my last minutes with my family near.

At my feet is Dad's violin case. Owl never got around to making that new violin for him from the alien wood. But I need rope, and the closest I can get without going near my family is to raid the Museum of Earth Civ for the hair from Dad's bow. So I snatched the violin case while Owl and Father were away, and set it up beside the malevor corpse. Now I take out the bow and wrench it apart. The sound of hair ripping. My treacherous imagination makes these synthetic strands Owl's hair, makes it so that I'm scalping my sister.

I divide the hair into two lengths, tie them so I get a double-long stretch of improvised rope. That should be enough.

I pinwheel my arms, stretching them. This will take all my flexibility. I start by tying a tight double knot around my right wrist. After a few tries, I manage to work the remaining horsehair under my left wrist and loop it over. With my wrists trussed behind my back, I get the remaining length under my teeth. The horsehair crackles and frays under my molars, but holds as I pull it tight. I unclench my jaws, wincing at the flash of pain from my shoulder joints. It's painful, but this means I won't be able to use my hands to hurt my family anymore. I threw the gun in the hydrocarbon pit hours ago. All I can really do now is bite them. I imagine Father's meaty forearm under my canines, splitting and bleeding, and scrunch my eyes until the vision goes away.

Once I'm ready, I'll pick a direction and start to walk. I'll go until my legs can't carry me anymore. I'll want to return to the settlement then, but my body will be too far gone. I'll fall, out in the mucklands. The comet will incinerate my body. It will be like I never existed. That's the best I can hope for.

But for now, I need to see my family while I can. I watch Father and Owl go into the infirmary, where they see Dad is alive. I share their relief. Then they get back to work prepping the *Aurora*, hauling supplies back and forth with the tarp. They are ever watchful, looking out for me. Owl found the gun I printed and has armed herself with it. Smart. I would arm myself against me, too.

As the Scorch dims toward twilight, Owl returns with the empty tarp and unloads her latest delivery. Father is a small silhouette by the *Aurora* site.

Owl starts loading the tarp with lengths of processed chromium wire, then she stops. Her body slumps, her head hangs. She brings her hands up to her cheeks. She's exhausted and overwhelmed. It's always been my job to support her when her courage fails. I'm the one who helps her out of her troughs. I *was* the one. Now she must miss me. She must hate me.

Owl takes a long drink of water—my own parched throat complains at the sight of it—and then heads off toward the infirmary. She's checking on Dad.

She's inside for only a few seconds before she comes out. Dad's probably fallen asleep. She heads to the greenhouses.

I ease around the malevor corpse to keep her in view. If she happens to look over to this massacre site, she'll see me. But I don't think she will.

She goes into the place I spent most of my days. These seeds traveled across the galaxy, have now grown into hesitant tubers and peppers. Only a few species managed to survive, but I tried to expand our options. Failed, mostly. I still have hope for the shelling peas.

Owl leaves the door to the greenhouse open. I'm usually careful to keep it closed, so we don't have uncontrolled spread of Earth species, but Owl is less cautious—and a comet is about to obliterate everything on the surface, anyway.

I watch her pass along the plants, probably debating which to try to raise underground. I wonder if she's going to find my surprise.

And she does. Owl makes it to the end of the aisle, wiping her hair back from her forehead in the humid greenhouse air. She strokes the tree's leaves. She removes the sheer barrier I used to shield the single fruit from view. The surprise I never got to give Owl gleams in the shrinking Scorch.

A lemon.

I won't be alive to make her lemon cake for her birthday. But at least she has the lemon I didn't have for mine.

I press my body hard into the ground as Owl looks around her, through the translucent walls, down the dirt alley of the greenhouse, and out the door. She's searching for someone. She's searching for me.

I hope she enjoys the fruit. I wish I could be around to watch her eat it.

Owl tugs at the lemon, but it isn't ready to separate from the branch. She presses her nose against its shiny, dense surface. She scratches a fingernail along it, then sniffs. There's a hint of a smile on her face. A modest joy.

Owl emerges from the greenhouse, takes a step toward the smelter. Then she turns and passes instead behind the infirmary, where we used to watch reels. Our private space. The site of the Museum of Earth Civ.

She squats on the packed soil behind the infirmary, where I watched Dad's and Father's reels for their future selves. She sifts through our drawings, our models, our pathetic little vehicles with their dented surfaces and missing wheels. She examines each one.

Much as I try to find any other reason for what she's doing, I'm left with only one: Owl misses me.

I remember the conversations we had right at this spot, the games we played, the songs we sang, the ugly crafts we'd make that the dads would then have to admire. The model malevor I once made, that Father wrinkled his nose at but then kept by his bedside, wearing the figurine's head around his neck when the doll finally broke in two.

Tell me the most . . . purple thing you saw yesterday, Owl once said.

Ooh, good one, I replied. *Purple. Okay. There was a nitrogen fixing node on a pea shoot in the trial tank of the greenhouse. It was mostly gold brown, but had a really nice lavender sheen, too. My turn. What's the . . . softest thing you touched yesterday?*

Owl glances at notes we left for each other, before going deeper into the museum. She comes up with a triangular piece of polycarb. She examines it, confused.

I know what it is, of course. If she squeezes it, it will project the reel I recorded for the anniversary of the dads' arrival. The last exhibit of the Museum of Earth Civ. I'd never had a chance to show Owl, because she'd gone off on her unauthorized expedition before she could watch it. The anniversary went by unremarked, weeks ago.

She's going to watch it.

I will watch it with her, not that she'll know.

Owl gasps as words project in the sky: *Eighteen Years. Congratulations, Dads!*

This reel is something I made using the limited processing power available through OS's systems. It's nothing fancy, not like *Pink Lagoon*. My grainy footage doesn't even track Owl's eyes and resolve further where she focuses. As it begins, something is blobbing through space. It's supposed to be the dads' ship.

I'm already wincing. It's so amateur.

This projection is a good six meters high, full of saturated colors that are shockingly bright in the gray-red lights of twilight. A starry sky, a ship blobbing through it. It is tiny and fragile. It glows. Even though it looks sort of like a lumpy rock, it's also lonely and precious.

The directors of *Pink Lagoon* would have zoomed in and entered the ship. But there was no way I could pull that off. Instead the reel stays outside as the ship's lights blink off, and then time speeds up, the galaxy passing in parallax behind it. Then the ship lights up again and time slows, the stars going static.

It's probably best I couldn't pull off bringing the reel inside the ship. That would have been too traumatic for the dads to watch.

The *Coordinated Endeavor* model goes bright one last time before it careens into a planet. Our planet, the second body circling the Sisters' center of gravity. For Owl's sake, I rendered our home with seas along the equator.

When the ship crashes, it cleaves into two. One of the dads emerges from each half. They're not digital re-creations— they're puppets. I made them each using ancient pre-reel techniques. Stop-motion. These I'm proud of. They're actually pretty cute.

As the reel continues, Owl rummages around the museum until she finds the puppets I made. She hugs them while she watches the rest of the reel.

The two spacefarers lurch toward each other and

embrace in a jangly marionette way. The Kodiak one even has the swoop of hair that Father has, cascading over his brow. The Sisters rapidly rise and set, and—*shwoop*—the wreckage of the *Endeavor* pops out a baby. It looks like me. The baby shoots through the air, and stop-motion Dad catches him like a football. I meant it to be serious, but it looks like a comedy.

Then there's another *shwoop*, and another baby pops out. Owl laughs. It's her. The babies start running circles around the bewildered puppet dads. Accurate.

Rover is there the whole time, a little sphere hovering over the terrain. In the background, it builds our settlement. Puffy polycarb units. The living unit, the nursery, the laboratory, the infirmary, the greenhouses. These are digitized, because creating puppets for those would have taken weeks and I had soil to lug and seedlings to nurture.

Scary grunts from the hilltop nearby. The malevors. Rover hastily constructs the perimeter fence, each post topped with its own pneumatic gun. The malevors retreat and the grunts subside.

The settlement slowly expands as the *Aurora* and *Endeavor* sink into the muck of Minerva's surface. I tend to the greenhouse algae and plants, and Owl patrols the fence.

The puppets of our dads withdraw from their embrace. Dad falls from the top of the lab and breaks one of his stick legs, and we all pick him back up. I lie flat for a bit and everyone watches. (That fever I had. Father stayed by my side the whole time.) Rover rolls down a hill and breaks in two, and Dad puts the two pieces back together. All the major events from our lives are here.

Finally we all line up awkwardly and wave. The reel zooms back out to space, so Minerva is joined by its nearby planets, Cuckoo and Eagle. We get a glimpse of the whole binary solar system before the reel ends. No comet in view; we didn't even know about it yet. I didn't really know how to finish a reel. I tried a few options, but nothing worked.

The reel blips out, and Owl stands in the twilight, staring out at the stars. The comet is bigger than any of them. Big enough to see the radiant gas trail behind it, the glowing coma in front.

She hugs the dad dolls close to her before placing them back on the ground, amid the strewn pieces of the Museum of Earth Civ.

Then she gets back to work.

From behind the malevor carcass, I watch Owl fill the tarp. What I want to do most is to hug her, to tell her how sorry I am, maybe even give her a chance to say that she forgives me. That's beyond anything I have the right to hope for, and yet I do.

From the way she held that lemon, watched the anniversary reel all the way through, hugged the puppets I made of the dads, I think she *might* accept me if I went up to her. Even though I tried to murder Dad.

That's why I can't let myself do it. I can't tempt her to remember she loves me. Because I'm still me. Because my brain is still a hostile place. Because if I'm around her, I might try to kill her, too. Scalp her like the hair from a violin bow.

My arms are aching. But I can't release my bonds. Both because I know it's a bad idea and because I don't think I could untie this knot with my teeth. So I just stay on my side, my face in a permanent wince, as I watch Owl load up the tarp with loops of chromium cabling. As she begins lugging it toward the *Aurora*.

Goodbye, Sister.

I wait until she and Father are both at the *Aurora* site to make my final departure. I don't feel like I will ever be hungry again, and I certainly don't deserve to use up any of the precious food stores they'll pack away in the bunker, beyond the algae planks I've already eaten. I do allow myself to draw from the water reservoir, though, bobbing my head to drink straight from the surface. My thirst is too powerful to deny. For a moment I let my whole face submerge, and this time it's myself my brain imagines killing. But I come up, fighting to live despite my own intentions, my thirst slaked.

Arms behind my back, I start walking. I go south toward the slain malevors, passing between their bodies, stroking each motionless belly with my foot, I guess to commemorate them. I pick this direction because we've never gone this way, scared off before by the aggressive beasts. I will travel through a land where humans have never been, and from which this human will never return. Where my family will never think to search for me.

My spirits rise as I go. I guess this is what I needed, taking action, seizing control of my destiny. I will not be responsible for the destruction of my family. They will survive the comet, and I will soon be a distant memory.

It also helps that the trek is beautiful. The comet is still a week away, based on what I overheard from OS and the dads, but the landscape already looks different beneath its radiance. All the bits of quartz and mica and silicone shine and glitter, scattering the colors of the setting Sisters in new directions, casting ruddy light everywhere. The sky is vividly open, like it is a hatch I could tumble through into the universe beyond.

I will miss this land.

I thought my body would have given out by now, but my legs find new energy. Even the pain of my cracked lips and my sunburned face fades from my experience for long periods. Instead my altered brain offers the sensation of my individual footfalls, my deep breaths, my joyously depleting body.

I am lighter than the atmosphere, I am the duck that never flew, I am the breezes themselves. I don't know if this is just my mind finally hallucinating from dehydration, but the air smells different from how it ever has. It smells like . . . blood? No, that's not it. It smells like tears.

The ground slopes upward at the horizon. I have never seen the ground do such a thing. *This*, I decide. *This is where I will fall. I will discover what is on the other side of this hill before I finally let myself collapse.*

It's like when I was gardening, deciding hours before the end of the workday what my end point would be. The last pea shoot in this line. I can make it to the last pea shoot and then I will watch our latest episode of *Pink Lagoon*, talk with my sister and the dads, and eat some delicious food.

Today, my last day, I will make it to the top of that rise.

I stumble twice along the way. The second time I have to lie still for long moments, gritting my teeth against the scream in my shoulder where my wrenched arm hit the ground. Then I wriggle my way to my feet, shouting with the exertion.

Ten minutes. Ten minutes more and I will be at the top of that rise.

The smell of tears is even stronger. It's not just in my mind, I'm sure of it. This is something real. But what is it?

My legs scream as they begin the incline. They tremble, as if I'm lifting something heavy. But that something heavy is just my mortal body, starting to fail to stay upright.

Ten steps more.

Five.

I reach the top and collapse, just managing to muster the energy in my belly muscles to stay seated and not sprawl out. I close my eyes for a long moment, drinking the scent of tears in through my nostrils.

The air is wet.

I open my eyes.

I'm in front of the sea.

I've never seen one before, but that's what this must be. A sea. Thick with minerals, too: it's the color of iron, all the way to the horizon. Its small waves crash at the shore, a dozen meters below me. I'm seated on a cliff, looking down at a body of liquid that has no end.

I scream, the shock is that great.

And that's before I see the life-forms.

There are hilltops in this iron sea, like knees emerging from pond water, but a good two meters in diameter. They roll listlessly in the currents, their frondlike tendrils fanning out of the sea, squirming and flapping before disappearing back into the water. Maybe they're picking something out of the air; I see blurry movements over the surface, like there might be swarms of some tiny creature flying over this sea.

Life. Life consuming life. An ecosystem.

Owl was right. We're not alone here.

Eyes streaming tears in the dry heat of the incoming comet, I watch the rolling forms for I don't know how long. Maybe they're animal or maybe they're plant, or maybe they're something else entirely. The bodies are a dull gray brown, but the fronds are more colorful. A brownish crimson, strangely familiar. Where could I know that from?

Then I realize—they're the same fronds that grow out of the rust jungle. The same color as the alien organism from the asteroid the dads' clones harvested.

What I'm seeing is probably a new form of that extraterrestrial creature. When those mossy leaves hit open water, they took on this aquatic form. Even in its exhausted state, my brain starts proposing hypotheses for why they'd do this. Perhaps their home world was ever-changing, and as its environment rapidly altered, life evolved adaptive strategies to cope, modifying itself quickly to survive a mercurial world.

Which means these organisms could be more likely to survive this comet strike than we are.

As I watch, one of the floating balls stills and cracks. It unrolls before my eyes, then dives. The only thing I can see from this cliff above is a fin, quivering with energy before the creature rapidly drops out of view. The strength of it is enough to send a nearby sphere rolling, and to crash waves into the shore. The sound rises up to me, a sound I knew only from reels. Surf. This is my first time hearing surf.

Who knows what this life is capable of.

I thought I was done. But now I have an impossible thought. I try to dismiss it. Surely not, not with my agonized body, so near failure already, quivering with the simple exertion of staying seated. But it's there, insisting.

I can't, my body screams.

You must, my mind says.

Owl. Owl must know about this.

I have to go home.

CHAPTER 3

OWL

"It is time, Owl."

I'm already at the entrance to the reinforced shaft that extends from the *Aurora*'s hatch up to the surface of Minerva. While I've been waiting for OS to give me the word, I've scanned for mechanical imperfections, using the ship's portaprinter to solder over each seam. I holster the portaprinter, crack my neck, and stretch my legs. "All right. I'm ready, OS."

"Remember. Even suited, you will have only twenty minutes out there before the damage to your body becomes irrevocable," OS says.

Yep. Comet radiation is no joke.

I clamber up the tunnel, using polycarb rungs Rover hastily installed into the passage. They'll melt during the comet strike, but we couldn't afford to use any metal on them. We'll just have to print some more to get out if—when—we survive the strike. As I climb, Rover lights my way from behind me. "Do not panic when you emerge. The surface will be far hotter and brighter than you remember," OS reminds me. "You will not have time to adjust to the conditions before you need to start moving. Just keep your space suit closed tight and the shading visor down and move promptly toward the gestation unit."

"Yep, got it."

I reach the hatch at the top of the shaft. Opening it is awkward, especially in the suit. I wrap one arm through the top ladder rung, pin it in my elbow while I use my free hand to turn the access wheel. It shudders and unseals. I push open the hatch.

The shaft fills with white light, baking and dry. I'm wearing one of Dad's old space suits, repaired and fortified and tailored to fit my smaller body, but even through the sunshade of the antique helmet I can sense how intensely bright the Minervan sky has become.

Rover beeps, then OS's voice comes out loud. "Wait, Owl. My calculations are off. Based on visual analysis, the comet is producing 1.08 times the radiation I expected. And its crash site is 1,100 kilometers nearer. Our window for extraction has shrunk."

"Thanks, OS," I say quickly, springing into motion. I sense OS might be about to abort my mission, and I won't let that happen. I want that gestating embryo to be in the *Aurora* with us, safe alongside all the rest of the dormant zygotes. Once I'm clear of the hatchway, I stand and catch my balance. "Owl, wait!" OS says.

"How much time? Until we need to seal off the *Aurora*?"

"Between fifteen and twenty minutes. Fifteen is better. At twenty I must seal the hatch for any of us to survive. Owl, I need Rover to prepare the final sequence. You'll be alone out there. You need to come down, too."

I blink into the blinding comet, eyes tearing. Even through the dense brown filter of the helmet, it's a bluish-white orb, a giant daughter to the two Sisters, reflecting their light down at me. "And sacrifice the embryo?" I say. "No chance."

"Owl, judging from Minerva's history, that embryo is highly unlikely to develop into a viable fetus. My priority is protecting you."

Too bad. I'm already up and out of the hatch and speeding toward the submerged *Endeavor* and its unit behind the gray portal, raising its small and fragile life. OS is wrong, anyway. We have schematics that will help. This embryo has a better chance than any before it.

It's helpful that I've walked the same small patch of this planet for all my life. The dull familiarity of it, which a few weeks ago was deadening, is now a blessing. The blinding light of the impending comet floods out all detail from the surface, warps the air and gives the sky the same texture as the ground. My feet pass along newly soft soil, crumbling under the heat. When I stumble I switch to all fours, scrambling across the plain. With the uneven ground and no visuals to help, I can't trust my balance. The ground is hot beneath my gloved hands.

We left the gestation device in place for as long as we could, so that the embryo could have the best chance possible for stable early development before we disturbed it. The rest of the zygotes were long ago transferred to the *Aurora*. But we know we have to bring the gestation unit down before the comet makes impact. I'd counted on having Rover's help, but I should be able to drag thirty-five kilograms on the tarp, or maybe even just waddle it over to the hatch so we can get it plugged back into power as quickly as possible.

I glance at the timer counting down in the corner of my helmet. Fourteen minutes until the hatch seals for good.

Once, years ago, the dads stood outside the gray portal of the *Coordinated Endeavor*, listening and waiting and watching a clock count down to the birth of their daughter. How they must have felt, waiting for the first offspring of our new world. And then she came out of the device, followed by another a few months later, and then baby Yarrow. Those first two children died. I won't let this latest one meet the same fate.

I have two clocks counting down on my helmet display this morning: the gestation device's duration, showing 131 days and three hours and forty-six minutes, and the now 13.6 minutes until I need to be inside the bunker. One of these two countdowns can't go fast enough; the other needs to slow down.

I'm nearly at the settlement site now. I try to stay focused on it and not the glowing mountain in the sky, but it's hard not to look at something that takes up half my view. It will disappear eventually, impacting the far side of the planet. That's the only reason this giant light above doesn't mean my instant death.

The living structures have long ago been deflated and stashed away in the *Aurora*. The only sign we ever inhabited this planet is the deep pit where we mined hydrocarbons, and the sliver of the *Endeavor* that's still aboveground. Even those subtle signs that we were here will soon be eradicated.

I make my way to the gestation unit, through the gray portal, the only part of the submerged *Endeavor* still visible. Six crucial joists connect the gestation unit to the ship wall, and I need to sever them before I remove the device, unplug it from its nuclear power source on the *Endeavor*, and hope the embryo survives its slowing centrifuge while I get it to the *Aurora*. Sparks fly from my cutter as I test it in the open air.

I kneel beside the device and begin sawing it from the *Endeavor*'s frame. The ship wall whines in protest. The gestation timer on the outside blinks out, but it's still counting down inside my helmet. The arm inside must already be slowing, but OS predicts it can go hours before its core has any lethal shift in temperature. I hope it's right.

Eleven minutes left.

I'm most of the way around the device, the cutter whining and sparking as it goes. The unit starts to wiggle in its frame. While the saw forces its way through the joists, I look around the rest of the remaining wreck of the *Endeavor*, which for all I know will be melted shut after the comet strikes, never to be accessed again. We've ransacked it for the settlement's needs: its internals are all bared, surrounded by hacked-up polycarbonate. All that remains behind the gray portal is a laminated black book: *Surviving Sagittarion Bb*. I tuck it under my arm, like a schoolkid out of *Pink Lagoon*.

Pink Lagoon. Yarrow. He's somewhere out there, probably dead. If he's alive, maybe he's looking up at the sky in fear. Alone. I touch my free hand to the soil beneath me. "I love you, Yar."

I move my hand to the wall of the *Endeavor*. Many shades of sadness course through me: I'm mourning Yarrow and the stillborn baby, and I'm mourning the ship itself. Our life in the settlement, which we'll have to start anew if we manage to survive the strike.

Once I've sawed through the remaining joists, the gestation device tumbles forward onto the tarp, the bottom half tilted up where it's held by one last length of cabling. I unplug the unit from the ship's wall, squatting so I can fall with it, using my body to cushion its landing on the tarp.

The backside of the device isn't impersonal gray paneling. It's slightly translucent. I see, inside, the curled form of a small alienlike human, no longer than my palm, all forehead and hands and blue-pink eyes, a thin cord going from its belly to the device's internals.

"Okay, let's go," I say as I drag the gestation unit through the comet's blasting heat. It's heavy, but manageable.

Even though the space suit shields me from the worst of it, I can feel the angry radiance of the comet burning my skin. I have to squint to see anything, even with the helmet's shading.

Eight minutes left.

I lug the tarp a few yards, and then stop.

Someone's here.

Way off to the side, in the square of packed dirt where once was an inflatable habitat, the very place we used to sleep and wonder and play, is my brother.

How can this be?

He's lit up by the impending comet, and the brightness between us eradicates every detail of him except the dark hue of his tunic, his ragged mop of hair. He's kneeling like a prisoner from a reel, head bowed forward and hands clasped—tied?—behind his back. In this blinding light, I can't tell exactly what he's done to himself.

I yell his name over the roar of the hot wind, the muffling

shield of my helmet.

He looks up. His mouth drops open.

I let go of the tarp and gestation device, and step toward him.

"Leave me!" he shouts.

I don't. I break into a run.

As I get closer, I see how terrible he looks. He's got blisters all over his skin, his lips are cracked and bloody, his hair matted and singed. He must not have had water for days, and this heat—barely tolerable for me in the space suit—is baking him alive.

"Save yourself. Take the gestation device. Now," Yarrow croaks. "And Owl, there's a sea. You need to know. It's to the south. There are giant rusty aliens in it."

I have no idea what he's talking about, and don't have time to ask. "Yarrow," I say, fighting to keep words coming out of me instead of raw shrieks, "Father and I found the beacon. It's not your fault. We can help you."

He blinks. He looks to the gestation device, flat on the tarp a hundred yards away.

"Can you walk?" I ask.

Yarrow nods, stunned, his mouth agape. He's somehow managed to bind his own hands behind him, but his legs are free. He lurches to his feet.

I step toward the *Aurora*, scanning the countdown as I do. Five minutes.

My brother pitches forward beside me. He cries out, in pain or shock or frustration, I don't know. His tunic has ridden up, and I see his legs are flayed by the heat and light. They twitch. There's no way he can walk. He probably can't even get up to his feet again. Five minutes.

I get my hands under Yarrow's shoulders, clenching my teeth against the feeling of my brother's soft damaged flesh bursting wetly under my fingers. I try to lift him. I can't. He's always been a good ten kilos heavier than I am. "I'm sorry, I can't lift you," I say.

"Leave me," he cries. "Owl, *leave me*! I just came to tell you about the sea creatures."

I look between him and the gestation device. The wounded brother beside me and the small unaware body, a shadow behind the translucent wall.

The heat bores into the top of my helmet.

Four minutes and four seconds.

I give up on the shoulders and grasp my brother's ankles instead, one in each hand. He yells in pain as I haul him over the soil.

He screams louder whenever his tender skin drags on any bump on the surface. "I'm sorry!" I cry over the hot wind. To him, mainly, but also to the embryo in the gestation device, left in the increasing distance behind me, on the pounded soil where we used to live.

We pass through the fence, the unpowered guns limp

atop it, guarding an open clearing. The home that was.

The comet fills the sky before me, beautiful and horrible, with its hot rocky core, its plumes of radiation. The secondary ion tail flares out to one side, slightly bluish. I scream at it between my own labored breaths. Even with the weight he's lost, my brother is *heavy*.

One minute remains. I won't be going back for the gestation unit. It's just not possible. OS won't let me risk the lives of the group for an unaware embryo that has only a small chance of surviving anyway.

As I kneel by the hatch, I get one last look at the fence surrounding a jagged pit and the slowing gestation device. After the comet strikes, all surface evidence of us will be gone. If the integrity of the *Aurora* fails, there will be no sign that humans ever lived on Minerva at all, except for some skeletons entombed below the surface. Even if what Yarrow is saying is true, and those alien life-forms out there wind up being intelligent, if they survive the comet they'll probably have no idea that we were ever here until one of them happens to dig above the *Aurora* and receives the shock of their little alien life.

I get one last look at the impending comet as I push my brother toward the open hatchway. It's turned the horizon purple. I can see some detail of the giant hurtling mountain—the electromagnetic field it sends cascading around it, the blues and blacks of ice and heat and rock.

My skin breaks out in sweat, the cold kind that comes with fainting.

But I will not let myself faint. Twenty-seven seconds remain. I lower my brother into the tunnel to safety, as far as I can, then drop his limp body the rest of the way before barreling in after him and slamming the hatch shut.

Cool darkness.

There at the bottom of the shaft, crumpled against an orange portal that once would have connected the *Aurora* to Dad's ship, is the body of a person. Yarrow.

He doesn't move the whole time that I climb down the rungs of the shaft. My heart seizes as I step off at the bottom. "Yarrow? Are you . . . ?"

He stays in his fetal position, but raises his head enough to look at me with haunted eyes. "You dropped me."

I stop. "I did. I had to."

There's the hint of a smile on his cracked and bleeding lips. My brother might still be inside this shell. "I deserved it."

I take another step in his direction. His hands are out of view. I know I saw them bound, but my paranoid brain tells me he could have freed them, could now be holding anything: a gun, a blade, some other weapon I don't expect. Maybe I saved him only for him to murder all of us. "I know you're joking," I say, "but no, you didn't. You didn't deserve any of this."

I hear Father's thudding footfalls elsewhere in the *Aurora*, his yelled commands and Rover's calm responses. He's finalizing the sealing of the ship. Already the comet has struck our planet; the shock waves will come anytime. I can't risk interrupting or distracting him now. Dad is still out of commission. Yarrow is mine to deal with alone. I take a slow step toward him.

"Stop," he says, pain in his voice. "Don't come anywhere near me."

"I have to ask. Are you armed?"

In response, he holds his hands up behind him. He's tied something around his wrists. "The opposite. You saw. I don't want to hurt you all."

"Oh, Brothership," I say. I want to free him, and I'm also grateful that he's restrained himself so I don't have to do it.

I get down to my knees, still across the chamber from Yarrow. The malevor must have heard our voices and wandered through the *Aurora* to find me. She nuzzles my side, staring at Yarrow suspiciously.

"It's not your fault," I say. Yarrow watches me, barely blinking, as I tell him again, slower this time, about finding the beacon, the schematics coded inside it, how we'll start the nanotech device printing when and if we've survived the comet impact.

He closes his eyes heavily. "I can be fixed. I don't know if I deserve that, after what I've done."

"It's not your fault, Yarrow. I mean that, it's not your fault."

"Why would they have done this to me? What did I do to deserve it?"

"Nothing. And I don't know why we were sabotaged. I don't think we'll ever know."

"Will you tell Father I'm here, for me?" he asks. "I don't think I can face him right now. I'm worried he'll . . . that when he sees me he'll . . ."

Could Father attack him? I can't imagine it, but I also couldn't imagine Yarrow shooting Dad. Father loves Dad so much—I guess it's possible. "Yes, I'll tell him," I say.

"If I may," OS interrupts. "Judging from Kodiak's vital signs while you tumbled through the shaft screaming, he is well aware of your presence. He's been too busy with the final preparations to come over."

I manage a tired smile. "There you have it. He knows you're here, and he's just ignoring you. Back to family business as usual."

"As soon as Rover is available, we'll prioritize your immediate health, Yarrow," OS says. "It is at more acute risk than Ambrose's."

"You don't hate me?" Yarrow asks OS. The way he says it, it's more an expression of wonder than a question.

"No, I do not hate you," OS replies. "I am still investigating the reprogramming you implemented days ago. It makes me feel scrambled in your presence, but the experience is more akin to anxiety than hatred."

"I do hate you, a little," I say. "But I always have. It comes along with loving you."

A smile spreads across Yarrow's face. "And I guess I always deserved it. Despite my claims otherwise."

"No, you didn't deserve it," I say. "But you do now, that's for sure."

CHAPTER 4

OWL

We're in the *Aurora*'s room that has the broad windows that once looked out into space. Or, for most of the dads' clones' voyage, showed a false digital representation of space. Dad is sitting up on his mattress, which we've transferred here, while Father sits at a console, monitoring the ship's air quality as he knits. The baby malevor, who will one day be the source of his yak wool, is curled at his feet. Yarrow is in the corner, bandaged and with a hydration IV but still restrained—at his insistence. We switched the horsehair out for a rolled-up blanket, for comfort.

The comet struck the other side of Minerva nearly two hours ago, according to OS. We haven't felt even a slight tremor in the soil around us—yet. "The shock waves move at a non-instantaneous speed," OS explained. "This is a big planet. They will take time to reach us."

We left unsaid all the worries that a shock wave raises, like whether it will rupture the hull of the *Aurora*. Cusk engineers designed a ship that could withstand a variety of conditions, but it's unlikely they planned for underground shock waves. Even if they had, the *Aurora* is an antique, long past its designed life span. OS claims it will hold. OS is very good at predictions. But it's also good at manipulating our emotions around difficult outcomes, particularly when there's nothing we can do about them. OS well knows that hopelessness is its own terminal condition. It saw multiple pairs of the dads die of it.

Rover is in what used to be called the "blind room," but which is now just a regular chamber with the annoying trip hazard of a printed barrier along the doorway. It's busily printing away based on the schematics saved to the ship's memory. The smell of burnt hydrocarbon is in the air, which in my hungry state smells oddly delicious. A bit like the smell of roasted dead malevor.

If all goes well, within a couple of days the nanotech device will be online, and Yarrow will have recovered enough to go first. The same tech that created the memories in the minds of the cloned Ambrose and Kodiak will edit the connections in Yarrow's cranium. I'll go second, with only two weeks to spare before my sixteenth birthday. I'm not even sure that anniversary matters, though it certainly did for Yarrow. The operation is horrifying, risky, and might save us all.

I'm incessantly pacing the room marked 06. It's clearly driving Father bonkers, but I can't help it.

"Owl . . . ," Dad says.

"I know, I know," I say, forcing my feet to stop, even

though my body keeps saying *go, go, go*. I pick up the piece of alien wood from where it lies in the corner, look at it, then put it back down. I'll use some of this bunker time to figure out how to use it to make a new violin for Dad. But I can't possibly think about that right now.

"No, I don't mean your pacing, although that is indeed infuriating," Dad says. "I just want you to come here for a second."

I perch at the foot of his bed. The moment I do, my every instinct is to leap back to my feet. Dad is recovering from being shot by my brother, that brother is in restraints, a shock wave is bearing down on us through the dense core of an uncaring planet—it's a little hard to relax.

"We're going to be in here for three years," Dad says. "Not going anywhere, but still on a sort of voyage."

"A voyage through time and not through space," Yarrow says from the corner, putting on a mock documentarian tone. It's undeniable: even though he's now literally the most remorseful human in the universe, he's still a little creepy. That brain edit can't come soon enough. We also don't know yet how long-term the effects of his time out under the comet's radiation will be. He's got plenty of reasons to be deep in his feelings.

"There will be much to do," Dad continues, "and you'll have your studies and recovery from your upcoming surgeries to occupy you. For the remaining time, I have a plan."

He pauses. While I wait for him, my mind races between the various ways we're going to die. I look at him, replay the words he just said and actually process them this time. "You have a plan? What's the plan?"

Dad smiles, which turns into a wince as the movement triggers some soreness in his gut. "There's a feature of the *Coordinated Endeavor* that was once used to trick us, but which you might now enjoy."

I squint. "Dad. What are you talking about?"

"Yes, what *are* you talking about?" Father asks, not looking up from his knitting. He's making a blanket for Yarrow, to replace the one that's now binding his wrists.

I wait for Dad to answer. He goes motionless, like he's been paused. Ever since his gut wound, he sometimes drops out of the world for a few seconds.

I listen to the hum of the *Aurora*'s reactor while I wait for him to speak. The ship will never move through space again, but we've activated its life-support system to provide light and air. Since it was designed to be operated in a dark vacuum, the ship is perfectly suited to being underground. We have artificial daylight to keep our algae growing to augment our stored supplies, and we will capture moisture from the air and recycle it, just like on the ship's original voyage. The *Aurora*'s nuclear reactors can keep going for a few hundred thousand years more. Hopefully it won't take that long for the comet's aftermath to finish. Three years sounds much more tolerable.

The most surprising thing: the *Aurora* turns our atmosphere into an approximation of Earth's surface, not Minerva's. I've never experienced it until now. Less nitrogen, more oxygen. It makes my brain feel fizzy and alive. I could definitely get used to it.

Dad finally starts speaking again. "I thought maybe you could use . . . some distraction while you wait to emerge and go exploring what remains of the Minervan high seas."

"Yes, definitely. So what *is* it?" I say impatiently.

He coughs and looks toward the ceiling, as if he can see through it to the searing surface of the planet, its stormy red seas of melting rock. To the ocean Yarrow discovered, vaporizing as we speak—hopefully to re-form, with some of the life inside it surviving. "OS, simulate the trip to Saturn's moon Titan, as experienced by Ambrose Cusk and Kodiak Celius, supposedly in the year 2472."

The windows were black before, just showing us the tightly packed soil on the other side of their surface. Now they spark into life, displaying images.

Images of space.

These are stars in formations I've never seen before. A beautiful and random pattern of lights, rotating with the simulated motion of a ship. Like they once did for my fathers' clones. One cluster of lights looks like a dipper. People on Earth used to talk about this dipper.

"I wasn't sure which part of the voyage you wanted," OS says, "so this is the moment when the clones were first awakened. Still well before nearing Saturn. With quotation marks around 'nearing Saturn,' of course."

Dad and Father, waking up on opposite sides of the ship. Not yet aware that the other even exists.

"Highlight Saturn's position," Dad requests. Yarrow sits taller, rapt. He's getting one of the no-filter history lessons he spent the last year craving. He might not have predicted that his hands would be bound while he got it, though.

OS places crosshairs on what at first looks like a star wheeling through the sky. Apparently that's actually a planet. I think I can see a ring around it, now that I'm looking closely. "Highlight Earth," I request.

The crosshairs switch to emphasize a small blue circle, a moon tagging along it like a faithful pet. "That's our home?"

"No, this is home. Minerva is home," Yarrow says. Typical Yarrow, earnest in the midst of all this, even with all that's happened, the shame of what he's done and the pain of his burnt skin.

"I can request OS make it so that this simulated journey to Titan lasts approximately the same time as it will take us to emerge post-comet," Dad says. "I thought we could all take that journey together."

"But only in a fake way," I say, suspicious. I press my

forehead against a screen, looking left and right. Nary a pixel. No wonder the dads' old clones believed so fully that they were on their way to rescue Minerva.

It's easy to imagine convincing myself even just a week from now that we actually *are* on a voyage across Earth's solar system. How could we find any evidence otherwise? It's not like we can go outside for confirmation. No wonder some of the dads' clones lost their minds.

Dad means for this to be a pleasurable distraction during the time we're stuck in the *Aurora*. A pretend rescue mission. I don't think he's wrong—any distraction will be welcome, I'm sure. But it's also horrifying. And it's giving me a little vertigo.

"You know who also took this journey, once upon a time?" Dad asks.

"This *simulated* journey, you mean?" I say.

"Simulated for us, sure. But real for that person, who lived long ago."

"Who?" I ask.

"*You*, Owl," Yarrow says.

I know who they mean now. I shake my head violently. "No. Minerva was not me."

"Your original, then," Yarrow says, more gently.

I let out a long breath, staring out at space. No, not out at space.

Once upon a time, a young woman was the hope of

Earth. She looked just like me. She went to settle a moon called Titan, and died shortly after she arrived. Her legacy was used to fool and mislead, and also to inspire. I never really knew her full story, but now we have access to all the history in the ship's storage, and if we survive the comet strike, I'll have plenty of time to learn about—to live—the experience of my previous self. Like the dads did with their former selves.

"Thanks, Dad," I say quietly. "It's a good idea. I like it."

Father chuckles darkly from his knitting. "As long as OS doesn't vent us into space at the end of it."

"I would never do that," OS says. "It's not necessary, and not even possible underground."

"I know, OS," Father says. He gives Dad a warm look and then spreads the blanket out over his knee, inspecting it for any dropped stitches. "This is fun. Good idea."

"Thank you, flufferskunk," Dad says.

Father takes a steadying breath at the nickname, then gets back to work. "By the way, Owl," he says, "I have been meaning to say thank you. Without what you found out there, we wouldn't have a chance of surviving this."

"Are you saying I was right? About exploring?"

Father nods, continuing his knitting. Dad gives me his *don't push it* look.

I smile as I peer out. We're on our way to Saturn. We're also surviving a comet strike on Minerva. I am Ambrose's sister, and I am his daughter. Yarrow is not Yarrow, but he will be soon. We might be the last humans to exist, unless we emerge alive from this isolation, get a new gestation device made, and implant it with the edited zygotes.

Once we do, I will investigate what remains of the seas of Minerva.

I rest my forehead against the nearest screen and peer deep into the stars, moving my head to one side so I can stare at our "destination." Even though she died over thirty thousand years ago, Minerva is surviving on a distant planet, just like the original mission planned. I'm going to Titan.

Acknowledgments

Appropriately enough given its storyline, this book was very much a family affair. I'll start by thanking my husband, Eric Zahler, who once again spent many more dinnertimes than could be reasonably expected discussing interplanetary logistics. His mother, Huguette (to whom this book is dedicated), also had a very important dinner discussion with me over which the central concept of the book emerged. (Now that I think of it, her friends Henri and Marie-Hélène *also* hosted a useful discussion dinner, and they made *The Darkness Outside Us*–inspired manicotti for the occasion. Henri even wound up becoming one of the French translators for that book. I guess eating and plot are intertwined for me!) My mom contributed a very thorough batch of line edits, but not during dinner.

Also appropriately for this book, sometimes family isn't enough to get the job done. I leaned heavily on writer friends for crucial insights and suggestions: Elana K. Arnold, Anne Ursu, Justin Minkel, Nicole Melleby, Daphne Benedis-Grab, Marianna Baer, Jill Santopolo, and Marie Rutkoski have all been wonderful first-line editors and dedicated friends to this novel.

Michael Howard, Principal Consultant at NASA, stepped in and gave this book a science diagnostic. To help me understand comets and comet strikes, I drew on a few sources but particularly enjoyed Cody Cassidy's article in *Wired*, "How to Survive a Killer Asteroid." Much of the exoplanet science in this book was informed by Michael Summers and James Trefil's *Imagined Life* and Charles Wohlforth and Amanda R. Hendrix's *Beyond Earth*.

The most fun research I did for *The Brightness Between Us* was the week I spent at the University of Wyoming. Years ago, the astronomy faculty there realized they loved science fiction but were tired of all the bad science in it, so they founded Launchpad, a yearly workshop for science-fiction writers. Eight of us lived in the dorms while we spent long days doing deep dives into modern astronomy and using the university's excellent telescope. Michael Brotherton, Christian Ready, and Theodora Zastrocky donated their time to help us learn the field they loved. Their generosity was touching—and very helpful.

Kodiak's hut in Old Scotland is based on a real place. It's the home of a do-it-yourself artists' residency called Outlandia, and is at the very coordinates Devon Mujaba wrote on Ambrose's thigh. Eric and I wandered across it while hiking, discovering this atmospheric and striking cottage in the middle of the misty green Scottish forest. I love that this spot for combining art and nature exists in the world.

How gorgeous is Sarah Maxwell's art on the cover? I feel so lucky that she, and designer David Curtis, have brought Ambrose and Kodiak—and now Owl and Yarrow—to such stunning visual life.

I gave this book's managing editor only slightly less of a logistical headache this time around, but still owe a big debt of gratitude to copy editor Jessica White and production editor Heather Tamarkin for juggling a whole lot of moving narrative pieces.

The school and library team at HarperCollins Children's Books, particularly Patty Rosati, Mimi Rankin, and Stephanie Macy, have been so important to getting my books into the right hands. Also couldn't do without my publicist, John Sellers, and marketing manager Michael D'Angelo.

Thanks to my longtime agent, Richard Pine, as ever!

Ben Rosenthal, this book's editor, thought more deeply about and provided more insight into the drafts of *The Brightness Between Us* than a writer could reasonably hope for. I'm grateful for your dedication, your gentle wisdom, and getting to call you an ally. Thanks for taking the helm so capably and getting this book across the finish line, Jordan Brown.

Most recent in the acknowledgment timeline are all my

colleagues in the Hamline MFA in Writing for Children and Young Adults, but in this particular moment Dashka Slater and Lisa Jahn-Clough, who gave me a crash course on knitting during our snowy walk to campus just thirty minutes ago. May they never drop a stitch. Will report back on how Kodiak's blanket turns out.

ELIOT SCHREFER is a *N ew York Times* bestselling author and has twice been a finalist for the National Book Award in Young People's Literature. His other awards include a Printz Honor, a Stonewall Honor, and the Green Earth Book Award. He is also the author of *Charming Young Man, The Darkness Outside Us, Endangered,* and *Queer Ducks (and Other Animals): The Natural World of Animal Sexuality.* He lives with his husband in New York City and is on the faculty of the Hamline University MFA in writing for children and young adults program. Visit him online at eliotschrefer.com.